CW00470376

Seoul Searching

Samantha Ann

Edited by Aleda Stam & Proof Positive

Cover by Kim Cavrak

Formatted by Garnet Christie

Dedication

Dedicated to the man who is my real life MMC, my husband.

Hangul (한글) Cheat Sheet

Consonants:	Vowels:
ㄱ – g,k	ㅏ – ah
ㄴ – n	ㅐ – ay
ㄷ – d	ㅑ – ya
ㄹ – r,l (say "real" but with an l in the beginning "leal")	ㅒ – yae
ㅁ – m	ㅓ – eo
ㅂ – b	ㅔ – eh
ㅅ – s	ㅕ –yeo
ㅇ – no sound if it starts the word, 'ng' sound if it finishes	ㅗ – o
ㅈ – j	ㅘ –wa
ㅊ – ch	ㅙ –wae
ㅋ – k	ㅚ – oe
ㅌ – t	ㅛ – yo
ㅍ – p	ㅜ – u
ㅎ – h	ㅝ – whoa
ㄲ – gg	ㅞ – we
ㄸ – dd	ㅟ –wi
ㅃ – bb	ㅠ – yu
ㅉ – jj	ㅡ – oo
ㅆ – ss	ㅢ -ui
	ㅣ - ee
	ㅖ -ye

Seoul Searching OST

LET'S NOT FALL IN LOVE – BIGBANG
Toy – Block B
Do U Like – KIM WOO SEOK
Bean pod (Feat. Gonhills) – MAZ.B, Gonhills
Just Like The Rain – GRAY
Memories – KIM WOO SEOK, Lee Eun Song
Eternal Flame – PENTAGON
Daydream – THEY BOYZ
STAY – BLACKPINK
Beautiful – KIM WOO SEOK
Waterfall (EUNHO solo) – UNVS
Bad Habits – SHAUN
Don't Say No (Feat. Jay Park) – SURL, Jay Park
예뻤어 You Were Beautiful – DAY6
I Loved You – DAY6
Home – SEVENTEEN
Snow – SURL
Remember – WINNER
Give You Up – UNVS

Bump Bump – WOODZ
HOLO – LeeHi
nostalgic night – VICTON
My Flower – JBJ
Tulips – SNUPER
TMI – NeD
We Need To Be Careful To Love – Poetic Narrator

Chapter 1 (하나)

"You're what?" Maria jumped up in bed during her usual late night "chic chat" with her best friend Valerie.

"I'm getting married!" Val shouted, flaunting the large diamond on her left ring finger over FaceTime, causing Maria to lift the phone closer to get a better look.

Maria's best friend since diapers was getting married. *This is the beginning of the end,* she thought. Once one friend got engaged, the rest were sure to follow. And then there she was—Maria, the perpetually single friend who could never hold a relationship for more than a month. Mostly because all the men she dated ended up cheating on her, but also because "committed" was never a word that people would use to describe her behavior.

She had changed majors four times throughout her college career, and once she graduated she'd had a series of jobs that never kept her attention for longer than six months. The only constants she had were her mother and her best friend Val. Now Val was getting married, and lately all Maria's mother could think of was getting her only daughter down the aisle. It was almost to the point where she could have her own reality dating show.

Most people wouldn't believe that there were mothers like Maria's still around. Ones who showed off their daughter's picture to random men she would see while standing in line to get coffee at the local shop. The kind of mom who made fake dating profiles, essentially catfishing men, and then made plans that were just as fake with her daughter so she would walk into a blind date with said man who thought he'd been talking to her for a month.

A mom who, every single time a family friend announced their child was getting married, spiraled into a depression so deep, the only way to pull her out was for Maria to go on a few dates with men she had absolutely no interest in. Yeah, that kind of mom.

Val had always been there to help Maria get past all the skeevy men, the mom harassment, and everything else they ever got themselves into. Then Val had gotten her dream job as an interior designer to the rich and moved across the country. Maria knew things would never be the same, but it didn't end the bond they shared. They talked regularly and Maria would visit when she had free time between jobs. Now Val was about to lose her "constant" status. Marriage was a whole new beast, and Maria wasn't sure she could compete with a husband.

"I couldn't believe it!" Val said with a squeal. "We were out to dinner, and he was talking about taking me to go and meet his parents, and how he wanted a family of his own and then BAM! He was down on one knee," Val gushed and fell with a soft thud onto her bed.

"You've never met his family? Shouldn't that come before the wedding? Ya know, to see what you're about to get yourself into?" Maria fell back onto her own bed, twirling her long brown hair between her fingers.

"Well his family is all in Korea," Val explained as she snuggled into her comforter.

"Korea? Good or bad half? Are you sure he isn't a spy? Are you sure you're not about to be kidnapped? I watch the news!" Maria was both joking and fairly serious.

"You've met the boy. Does he seem like a spy?" Val said, rolling her eyes.

"That's what he *wants* us to think," Maria joked, putting on her best interrogation voice.

"They're from South Korea. The family lives in Seoul, in some well-to-do area. Apparently they are fairly wealthy on their own." The smile on Val's face couldn't be wiped off, and Maria could see her excitement radiating through the phone camera.

"Look at you, marrying for love and finding out he's also loaded as hell. Good things truly come to good people."

"You know I don't care about the money," Val said with a shrug.

Maria looked off to the side and scrunched her nose, trying everything not to roll her eyes at her friend, who wasn't quick to catch her sarcasm.

"I know that, Val. It's my way of saying congrats."

"I called for another reason," Val said and instantly exchanged her light laughter for a serious tone.

"Is this a shotgun wedding? Should I be buying you diapers and a cradle instead of a set of plates?" Maria said as she grabbed her computer to begin the quest for baby gifts.

"Oh my God, Mari! No, no. Nothing crazy like that. I wanted to know if you'd like to be my maid of honor?"

That halted all Maria's movements. *Maid of honor?*

Maria's heart flew through the roof with happiness but also with the realization that it could be as bad as a death sentence. Her mother, the woman set on trying to have Maria married by the end of, well, every year since she graduated high school, would more than likely hear about this and start the quest of finding Maria a date for the wedding and more.

"Are you kidding me?" Maria couldn't believe her bestie even had to ask.

"I've never been more serious. Except for maybe when I said yes to Jung-hyun," Val giggled.

"Yes! I would love to! OMG, I need to start planning a bridal shower and a bachelorette party—"

"Well Korean weddings are a little different," Val said, cutting off Maria's planning excitement.

"But you're not Korean."

"Since I never followed any religion and don't really know my cultural background, *one of the negatives of being adopted*, and Jung-hyun's family is steeped in tradition, I decided I'd follow suit."

"Ah," was all Maria could say as her mind was still processing her friend's decision.

"I mean, I guess we can still do the Western thing of a bachelorette party. You know I want to wear a crown."

"Western? You make it sound so foreign." Maria was starting not to recognize her friend, and concern grew with every passing second they stayed on the phone.

"It is...or it will be," Val said, clearly avoiding something.

"If you don't spit it out in the next sentence, I'm going to fly over there just to slap you," Maria half-kidded, her impatience growing.

"The wedding is going to be in Seoul...South Korea."

Chapter 2 (둘)

인 천공항. She stared at the screen on the headrest in front of her. The little plane hovered over a map of Korea, telling her she had arrived at Incheon International Airport. After sitting in a cramped seat for close to twenty-four hours, she was happy to let her legs get a nice walk. She didn't expect the walk to be almost a mile of twists and turns through customs and finally baggage claim to head to the concourse to find Val.

She was exhausted. Picturing a nice shower to alleviate her aching muscles and a firm bed and fluffy comforter for a well-deserved nap, Maria walked a little faster toward the exit. As she walked past the large airport welcome sign that read 한국에 오신걸 환영합니다, she felt relieved to see that although it was in what looked like similar hieroglyphics to those on the plane, the sign also had English underneath that said "Welcome to Korea".

Before she had time to look around, she felt a faint vibration in her pocket. Pulling her phone from her pocket, she saw the name and dreaded swiping to answer.

"Mom, I literally just landed. I haven't even found Val yet," she said, rolling her eyes and clutching the handle of her rollaway luggage tightly.

"Did you sit next to anyone nice on the flight? It was a long journey," her mom probed.

"Are you seriously asking if I met someone on the flight?" Maria hissed. Her mom was beyond unbelievable.

"You never know. And with a flight that long—"

Maria couldn't let her mom finish the ridiculous line of questioning and quickly cut her off. "I met a lovely mother and her baby daughter, who shockingly didn't cry for the whole flight, and the second flight was a sixty-year-old man who was going to visit his son, whose wife just gave birth to his first grandson."

"Really? Such a shame," the disappointment in her mother's voice wasn't surprising.

"By the way, I landed safely and none of my luggage was lost," she said with a heavy sigh as she was being passed by thousands of other travelers.

Geez, there are a lot of people here.

"Of course, of course. I'm glad you're safe. Give Val a hug and kiss for me. And maybe ask her fiancé if he has any nice single—"

"Gotta go," Maria said and hung up before her mother finished. Not only because she didn't want to hear the end of the statement, but also because she had walked into what looked like a city square in the middle of the airport. It was filled with thousands of people, both travelers and loved ones, offering their hugs of either hello or goodbye.

Hundreds of stores, some familiar, most unrecognizable, lined the raised walkways surrounding the square. A few had brightly colored dancing furries outside, while others had attractive women handing out samples of products enticing people to come in. Several of the clothing stores caught Maria's eye, with their mannequins wearing trendy outfits, but she was on a mission to find Val. A feat that was starting to look like a mission impossible as she made her way to one of the several escalators going down toward the exit.

Looking out among the sea of people and things, Maria also caught walkways that looked as if they were encapsulated in pristine glass. Colorful LED screens hung above her, with more of the Korean letters displaying products she had never heard of. She felt as if she had entered something out of a sci-fi future fantasy world and wondered if she would ever find her best friend among the masses.

Maria looked around, searching for the large pile of curly black hair atop tanned skin, when suddenly a loud squeal came from across the concourse. She spotted her best friend waving frantically, jumping up and down. Bolting past a mound of luggage, Val ran to wrap Maria in a huge hug.

"Mari!" Val squealed as she jumped up and down with Maria in her arms. Her face was buried in the lavender scent of Val's hair. Maria had forgotten how strong her bestie was. Interior design included a lot of moving heavy art and furniture around. And working for the rich and famous of San Francisco was proving great for Val's muscles.

"Val!" Maria squealed back, and they giggled their way through all the excitement. Having her best friend back in her arms felt like all was right with the world again.

"It's been way too long!" Maria was so happy to actually be able to hug her friend. "First you move across the country, and now we're more than halfway around the world for your wedding! P.S. Are we still in an airport?"

"I know, right?" Val chuckled. "When I landed I said the same thing. Jung-hyun gave me a tour of the place and, I kid you not, we spent half the day here. If you think this is impressive, Seoul is a twenty-four-hour city. New York is a total noob when it comes to all-night festivities. Seoul is the true city that never sleeps. You're going to love the food, the culture, the drinks, the people, the men." Val couldn't stop gushing about the place, and so far Maria had to agree the place was going to be some kind of sight.

"Did my mom already call you too?" Maria scolded her bestie. "I'm not interested in the men. I'm here to celebrate my best friend in the entire world getting married! But I'll admit I can't wait to see your Jung-hyun again. I only met him once when I came to visit, and we've maybe said a few words to each other during FaceTime. I'm glad I'm getting the time to know him better. Make sure he is one hundred percent right for my girl."

"Isn't it kind of late for you to tell me whether he's a good one or not?" Val laughed as she grabbed the handle of Maria's luggage to get them out of the prying eyes that seemed to be on the two of them. "He's staying with his family, but you'll get to see him again and meet his best friend tonight when we go for drinks."

"What do you mean *he's* staying with family? Where are *you* staying?" Maria had started to get weird vibes about this wedding since the day Val announced it was even a thing. There were too many variables that didn't leave Maria with the feeling she was going to be happy for her friend's marriage.

"His family put you and me up in an amazing penthouse a little way from their place. Traditionally, couples don't stay overnight, or even live together, unless they're married. It's changed a little bit over the years, but his family is old school so..."

"You're serious? You're actually living separately this whole month?" Maria grabbed her friend's wrist to stop her from avoiding more eye contact. When Val looked back to Maria, her deep brown eyes were swimming with emotion. Maria knew that look. She had seen it hundreds of times. Val wasn't happy with the situation, but she couldn't change it and was doing her best to keep a brave face until the problem would pass.

"Jung-hyun and I may not go home together, but we spend a lot of time with each other. To be honest, even when we lived together that week because of my apartment flood, we never actually spent the whole night together; well, not on purpose. I usually slept in his guest room," she explained calmly, her voice not wavering. Maria always had to praise Val's strength through adversity. While Maria would've found Jung-hyun's family and told them to shove it, Val kept it classy, and in the end would win exactly what she wanted.

"But when do you get to..." Maria trailed off waiting for Val to finish the sentence. What shocked Maria was the bright shade of red Val was turning. "You haven't...never...what the hell? Really?"

"진짜," Val responded nervously.

"Jin— Huh?" Maria knew whatever was said was not English.

"진짜," Val said, correcting her pronunciation. Then she quickly said, "미안해...which is Korean for sorry."

"*Mi...an...hae*," Mari repeated, thinking she'd be using that word a lot in the next month "Seriously?" she added, wondering if her friend was for real about learning Korean.

"진짜. Seriously. English isn't totally common here yet. I've been learning since Jung-hyun and I started dating, and it's getting more comfortable for me to speak it. Especially here."

"Could've given me *that* small heads-up." Maria could feel the anxiety creeping up on her as she realized how much of an outsider she was. Looking around to find the few English signs around, she noticed some people were staring and pointing at them but Val didn't seem to care.

"Just ignore it, Mari. But if you want to know, all of them are giving you some high compliments. The men think you're a hottie," Val said and laughed as she wheeled Maria's bag out of the airport.

The scent of the city hit Maria's nostrils and comfort filled her. She might not know Seoul, but city life was a happy place for her. When Val and Maria were kids, they had always talked about getting a small apartment in New York City together, living their dream lives in their dream city. But while Val had a life plan, big dreams, and a smart head on her shoulders, Maria had always lacked direction. While intelligent, she didn't know where to funnel her knowledge, and she hoped that one day she'd figure out what to do.

At the curb a man standing by a large luxury sedan noticed them approaching even though the place was packed full of cars, vans, buses, and people. He opened the car door as he executed a deep bow.

"This is yours?" Maria asked, opening her eyes wide with surprise.

"Jung-hyun's family prefers using a car instead of public transportation."

"These people seem to have a lot of say in what you do and don't do." Maria couldn't hide her concern about the situation any longer.

"Maria..." Her friend seemed to know where the conversation was headed and also that it was not the time or the place to be having the discussion.

"You can't live with him, you haven't slept with him, they won't let you choose how to get around. Next you're going to tell me they tell you what to eat, how to dress, and when you can use the restroom," she said as they climbed into the car.

Although Maria wasn't happy, she also felt impressed with the car service Val's fiancé's family had provided. The expensive vehicle was packed with high-end creature comforts. Leather heated seats, video monitors on the back of the front headrests, arm rests with charger ports, and cold water bottles in the cup holders were all peak luxury.

"It's a cultural thing. Be happy they accepted me at all. A lot of Korean parents have people already set up for their children, and even if they're in love with someone else, they marry who their parents choose. Don't even get me started on the whole interracial thing," Val explained, grabbing a water bottle and taking large swigs, clearly uncomfortable with Maria's slightly accusatory tone.

"You're joking, right? What century are we in? Did my plane time travel?" Maria hadn't expected to start this journey with a fight, but the worry about people she had never met was causing her to take it out on her best friend.

"Please, Mari," Val begged.

"I'm sorry, but the things you're telling me sound ridiculous and archaic. And I can't believe that you're going along with it so calmly."

"Because I love Jung-hyun. I would do just about anything for him. It's not like he hasn't fought for my side on some of these things.

He's a great man, and we are fine with this setup for now. It's only for the next month or so."

"*Or so?*" Maria's neck snapped as she whipped her head around to face her friend.

"Well, after the ceremony—"

"You're going back to your dream job in California, designing homes for the rich and famous, right?" Maria's nails dug into the leather as she fought to control her anger.

"I really like it here, Maria. This city is massive, and I could easily get the same job. Probably work a lot more and make way more connections..."

"*Valerie!*" Maria never used her friend's full name unless absolutely necessary, and this was definitely time for it. "Who are you? Have they brainwashed you? Are you joining some sort of cult? You've never jumped into something like this so quickly! Even the move to California was a two-month back and forth, and that was for your dream job. All of a sudden you're happy with just packing up and moving to a different country to make this dude's family happy?"

"It's not like that. I haven't even mentioned it to Jung-hyun yet. It's just that...I see how happy he's been with his family around, and I want to see him that happy all the time," Val said.

Her friend appeared to have entered her own world where dopey grins and glazed-over eyes seemed to be her new standard look. But Maria couldn't let it go. "You could make him that happy with just the two of you. Alone. Home. In California."

"It's a different kind of happy. Maria, I know you're worried and I understand. But please, for my sake, stop and wait until you spend more time with Jung-hyun. During all the times you've spoken with him, even when you met him, did he ever seem like some evil guy set on ruining my life and making me a stay-at-home wife, whose only job is to cook and clean?"

Val had a point. The several times Maria had spoken to Jung-hyun, he seemed like a great guy. Downright romantic, even.

With a huff of defeat, Maria nodded. "Fine. I will stop, for now.

But I'm gonna have words with him at some point. For today I will be the best friend who's super excited that her best friend is getting married."

"Thank you, Mari, honestly." Val's voice held desperation and Maria hated that she was the one to cause strain, but she wasn't someone who held back. It's probably why she was perpetually single and had very few good friends. Except Val. Maria would do whatever she could to see her friend happy.

As Maria sat back in the comfortable leather seat, she looked out the window to view the bustling city she was about to call home for the next four weeks. *Only four weeks*, she thought, and hoped her friend's wedding would go off without Maria accidently causing an international incident.

Korean Vocabulary:

인천공항 – Incheon konghang – Incheon Airport

한국에 오신걸 환영합니다- hangukae oshinkeol hwanyeong ham ni da – Welcome to Korea

진짜 – jinjja - seriously

미안해- mianhae – sorry

Chapter 3 (셋)

"형!" Hwan Soo shouted at the man who was truly more like a brother than a friend to him.

Jung-hyun, his best friend, flashed a million-watt smile. It was good to see his friend's face after so long. Four years. Four long years since he'd actually seen Jung-hyun in the flesh.

"Hwan Soo-a! 오랜만이다," Jung-hyun said, walking over to Hwan Soo and giving him a big brotherly hug.

"For sure. Too long if you ask me. You look great, 형," Hwan Soo said, repeating his earlier greeting.

"나?" Jung-hyun gave himself a quick once-over before glancing back at Hwan Soo. "Look at you! Clearly acting is treating you well." Jung-hyun strolled to the counter to order coffee. While tea might've been the lifeblood of most Koreans at one time, coffee had taken over top spot in recent years. Not only for the taste or trend, but because of the artwork and colors some baristas had created for their customers.

Hwan Soo loved this particular café because of its quiet atmosphere. Most people were there to get work done, keeping their heads down in a book or tapping away at a computer. It was the perfect place to stay anonymous. If no one looked, no one would recognize him. Not that many would as he had yet to make it big.

The café had stark white walls which let in light from the large floor-to-ceiling front windows, brightening the whole place even though it was tucked into a narrow alleyway.

Continuing the café's clean aesthetic, several small yet ornate flower arrangements lined the middle of the long obsidian bar counter, while shorter black-and-white tiled circular tables were scattered through the café.

The smell of the different coffees brewing blended and instantly woke any sleepy soul. Pastries, which looked more like works of art than something that should be eaten, lined the small glass shelves near the stark black counter.

As they approached the counter, the young man at the register bowed and said, "안녕하세요."

Hwan Soo reciprocated the kind hello and added his order. "커피이 인분 주세요."

"네," the server confirmed, and at Hwan Soo's nod, quickly got to work on making the coffees for them.

"How is my famous best man doing?" Jung-hyun said, resuming their conversation once the barista handed them their order.

"야, no one knows me," Hwan Soo said, downtrodden. "I'm still only a small-time actor, second lead material. No one wants to hire me for a lead. Not that being second lead is the worst thing. He just never gets the girl."

"I remember when you thought no one would hire you at all, but look at how far you've gotten," Jung-hyun reassured. "I've seen your name pop up more and more on the fan sites lately. I'm sure you'll hit it big soon. Have you auditioned for anything new recently?"

"Yeah, it's a lead role and casting calls end today. But as much as I want it, I haven't heard anything yet. If I were to get it, filming would start this month, and I know this is an important time for you. I want to be here to support my biggest fan for his wedding," Hwan Soo explained as they made their way to one of the small tables in the corner that looked out to an almost empty, hidden alleyway. Unlike in other countries, in Korea one could usually stumble on some of the best food, bars, and even cafés on the side streets. That's how Hwan Soo had found this go-to coffee shop, a bookstore, and a bar.

"Thanks. I appreciate you being there for me," Jung-hyun said, clapping him on the back.

"More importantly, where is the unlucky lady who agreed to marry you? I still can't believe you, the man who swore women were nothing more than a distraction from success, will soon be tied down. And that you were the one to suggest it," Hwan Soo joked.

"You'll officially meet her tonight. She's picking up her maid of honor, Maria, at the airport right now," Jung-hyun said as he sipped his coffee and let out a small moan of appreciation.

"I'm sure they are going to have a lot of stuff to catch up on before the wedding, so they're going to enjoy their time together. Just like us," Hwan Soo said and smiled.

"About that…" Jung-hyun's face contorted as he struggled to form words, obviously nervous to break whatever news it was to his friend.

"Spit it out, 형," Hwan Soo said impatiently.

"Maria doesn't really understand how Val and I started dating, and we don't want her to know just yet. Val wants to tell her at some point on this trip, but she isn't ready. So you need to keep our secret."

Hwan Soo knew the way that his friend's relationship had started had been unorthodox, but nothing that was unheard of. Having read enough drama scripts, he recognized that his friends had fallen in love in a fairly cliché trope. Wealthy man borrows not-so-wealthy woman to help him out of a jam and suddenly they fall in love. If Hwan Soo could pitch it to one of his director buddies, they'd eat it up.

"Why is it that she doesn't know? I mean if they're best friends…"

"As Val put it, Maria is the type who wouldn't be thrilled that her best friend was 'used to further a man's place in the world'," Jung-hyun said.

"That's a very negative view of what actually happened. It wasn't really like that," Hwan Soo argued. Was Val's friend really that stubborn that she wouldn't try to understand how her best friend had fallen in love? How could this person claim to be her friend at all?

"Unfortunately Maria has a skewed view of romance and falling in love."

"What woman doesn't?" Hwan Soo joked, thinking it was true though. Except for his last ex, the women he dated had mapped out their entire future from day one. Most of the women were blind dates his mom had set him up on for the sole purpose of becoming his wife.

His ex, however, was the one woman who'd broken his heart by not wanting more, and his heart was still on its road to repair. She had been the one woman he had wished to plan a future life with and when she left, he no longer had any interest in that kind of future. Bachelorhood was his best bet at enjoying life.

"Just please, keep it a secret for now," Jung-hyun begged.

"Fine," Hwan Soo reluctantly agreed for the benefit of his friend. But when he looked over at Jung-hyun, who was sipping his coffee slowly, thoughtfully, Hwan Soo knew there was something else he needed to say.

"I know there's more, so please spit it out," Hwan Soo demanded.

"How did you..." Jung-hyun started to say but didn't need to finish the question. Having been friends since they were four years old made it easy to read each other. "I need your help with Maria."

"Help how?"

"Since she doesn't speak or read Korean, you'll need to help her get around when Val and I are expected to do wedding planning. You're essentially going to have to be her lifeline."

"Lifeline? Isn't that just another name for a babysitter?" Hwan Soo sipped the bitter coffee, which left both a literal and figurative bad taste in his mouth. "How often are you going to be dealing with all this wedding stuff?"

"It's gonna be pretty packed with all the things Val needs to learn herself, and I don't want her having to go it alone. Even though my parents have accepted the marriage, I don't trust them not to try something to get her to run away. Not that she would, but I don't want them to give her a reason to do it," Jung-hyun explained.

Hwan Soo knew Jung-hyun's family was very traditional. Hwan Soo's family was pretty similar, but he'd never broken the rules by dating a non-Korean girl because from what he had seen, foreigners were loud, obnoxious, had few manners, and didn't dress all that well. Fashion was as important to Korean life as being well off and respecting elders.

After four years apart from the man who was like a brother, Hwan Soo had been sure that he was going to have time to catch up with his friend, reminisce, and make some new memories. Now that was being totally thrown away and replaced by having to hang around with an American girl.

But for Jung-hyun, Hwan Soo would use every acting skill in his arsenal to seem happy as he did what his friend asked. "I'm sure that if she's as great as Val, it'll be just fine."

His one hope was that Val's friend wouldn't turn out to be like the typical tourists that caused his skin to crawl.

～

When Maria and Val entered the bar where they were meeting Jung-hyun, all Maria could think was, "*Damn.*" It wasn't like any bar she had ever been to back home. The ceiling was covered, literally every square inch, in empty liquor bottles that had been repurposed with twinkling lights. The tables and chairs were all mismatched, and the bar itself looked like it couldn't make up its mind between bougie, noir, or hipster.

On the wall behind the counter, the liquor was stacked high on shelves with a library ladder the bartenders used to climb for the literal top shelf liquor. Above the bar was an insanely ornate chandelier that was easily six feet tall.

Unlike the mismatched furniture, the bartenders wore matching vests, striped shirts, and bow ties. The waitresses were all gorgeous, thin, and model-esque, swaying their hips in tiny black dresses that hid none of their curves.

When Maria finally took her eyes off the decor and staff, she noticed a handsome man waving at them who she immediately recognized as Jung-hyun. He was always well dressed, even when casual. Even though he looked like he'd just thrown on his oversized, large knit, electric-blue sweater, pale-blue ripped jeans, and Timberlands, she knew his outfit was carefully planned. His hair, black as the night sky and slightly wavy, hung just above his brow in a bowl-like fashion, clearly styled that way. Tall and lean, he had a sharply chiseled face accented by high cheekbones and a square jaw. Small black studs dotted his lobes and gleamed in the dim light in the bar. Looking around at the other men in the bar, Maria realized that men in the U.S. seemed to lack something Korean men had down to a science. Confidence in style.

Val's face lit up when she caught her soon-to-be husband's eye. His face brightened just the same as she ran over to gently peck him on the cheek as he wrapped an arm around her shoulder.

"Maria, I know you've met once before, but now I'd like you to formally introduce you to my *fiancé*, Park Jung-hyun." Val's smile spread nearly ear to ear. The excitement was evident in her voice. Seeing her friend this happy was really all Maria wanted.

She walked over to him with her arms wide and was about to give him a big congratulatory hug when there was a harsh tug on the collar of her shirt.

"What the—" She choked and spun around to see who the asshole was that had caused her to stop dead.

The young Korean man was handsome, easily over six foot tall, with a chiseled jawline and plump heart-shaped lips. He was dressed in an ornately embroidered denim jacket, white t-shirt, black jeans that hugged his toned thighs, and white sneakers. Even though he was a jerk, he was a handsome jerk with nice style.

"누구세요?" unknown rude guy said.

What the hell? she thought and wondered what the handsome jerk had said.

"아 친구야, 괜찮아, she is new to this," Jung-hyun said and clapped the man on his shoulder. "Maria, 미안해요, here PDA, like hugs, are not commonly seen or done. Couples will maybe hold hands and peck each other on the cheek, but larger gestures are just not acceptable in public. He didn't mean to tug so hard. He was just saving you from embarrassment."

Maria looked back over to Jung-hyun. "You know this guy?"

"Maria," Val jumped in. "That's Jung-hyun's best friend and also his best man."

"I don't care who he is, you don't go pulling people by the collar. And what the hell did he call me?"

"He asked who you were," Val said, translating what the man had said.

"친구, this is Val's best friend and maid of honor, and your new partner in crime for the next four weeks," Jung-hyun explained to the man.

"뭐라고?" he asked.

"Say what now?" Maria said.

They said the words simultaneously, and while Maria might not have known the language, it was obvious his reaction was the same as hers.

"I told you at the coffee shop that Maria is going to need to learn some Korean to give her speech at the wedding," Jung-hyun said.

"No one said anything about me giving a speech in Korean." Maria's jaw dropped open as her heart started to beat alarmingly fast. She sputtered trying to find the right words, but she was stunned. How could Val not mention something that pretty freakin' important?

Gathering all her composure and trying to act like the bomb they dropped wasn't the size of a meteor, she added, "If anything, Val can help me."

"But I'm going to be busy with all the wedding stuff. Jung-hyun-a and his family have me taking classes on the different ceremonies that are done as part of a Korean wedding."

"Shouldn't I be accompanying you to those classes? I'm part of the wedding too," Maria said.

"Yes, shouldn't she?" The deep voice of the man she thought couldn't speak English reached her ears. In surprise, her body warmed as she continued listening to his alluring voice. A shiver went down her spine.

"Yeah! Wait. You speak English?" she said, eyeing the man suspiciously.

He glanced at her, rolled his eyes, and didn't bother to answer her question, which, she admitted, was pretty dumb considering she had heard him speak in almost perfect English.

Jung-hyun reached out to pat his friend's shoulder. "친구야, you know just like I do that your jobs in the bridal party are just a Western thing. Maid of honor and best man are not a thing here in Korea. You won't do much of anything until the reception," Jung-hyun explained to Maria.

"But she's..." the man began, then stopped.

"I'm what?" Maria crossed her arms, dropped a hip, and looked over at him. His side profile was even more interesting than staring at him dead-on. The man was totally attractive, and if his gorgeous lips would've stayed shut, or if he'd kept his long, soft-fingered hands off her collar, she would have thought he was a total hottie.

His captivating deep brown eyes swung to Maria, raking over her with a smirk. "You don't want me to finish the sentence."

That smirk mixed with those full lips almost made her forget he was being a complete ass. The longer she looked at his lips, however, the more she lost her angry train of thought as her mind started picturing those lips moving down her neck and leaving little love marks along her skin. His voice alone was causing sensations through her body that not even her ex had caused when he'd physically touched her.

Somehow she fought back those thoughts and remembered that he was about to insult her. Her mind crashed back to reality.

"Oh please, I'd love to hear you finish," she said with as much bravado as she could muster. "What's your name? *Chingu?*" she said, repeating the name she'd heard Jung-hyun call him earlier. She gave Chingu an abrupt once-over, ready to pounce at whatever he had to say. She was also getting angry at how attractive she found him in his way too stylish outfit, obviously custom made for him, and how it was causing her body to react when her brain was screaming for her to ignore the jerk.

The two men of the group hunched over laughing while Val tried to nudge her fiancé to stop his near-tears chuckle.

"Where did you find this girl? This is a joke, right?" the still unnamed best man choked out through his laughter.

"I'm no joke, you little—"

"His name isn't 친구," Val cut in, trying to hold in her own little chuckle. Val looked at her fiancé for help—which he was unable to give—to stop Maria from saying anything potentially life ruining. "친구 means friend. It's a term of endearment between friends. His name," Val said, pointing at the handsome jerk, "is Lee Hwan Soo."

"Lee Hwan Soo?" Maria repeated, making sure she got the name correct.

Val nodded happily and Maria turned back to him to give him a piece of her mind. "Listen here, Lee. I don't-"

"Lee is my surname," he corrected.

"Last names come first? Where am I?" Her head pounded with anger and frustration and even worse, she hadn't even had a sip of alcohol yet. She was feeling more out of place by the second.

"You're in Seoul, South Korea, where English isn't the first language, and we have different customs. Start getting used to it. You're here for a month," Hwan Soo responded with curtness. His gaze held no mockery, only total distaste for her. His lips were pursed since he was clearly holding back even more things he wanted to say.

It seemed her comment had gotten under his skin. While she

wasn't sure what she had said that warranted such a heated response, she also felt compelled to defend herself. "This wasn't exactly a well-planned trip for me. I was told two weeks ago that my best friend was engaged and then was asked to fly out here for a month to help plan the wedding. So excuse me, Mr. High and Mighty, for not grasping all of your culture and language in the..." She paused and looked at her phone for the time. "Ten hours I've been in your country."

Always the one to try to smooth out awkward situations, Val interjected, "Let's get some drinks." When she handed the drink menu across the table, Maria blinked several times. There were the same characters she had seen at the airport, but this time they didn't have the nice English translations below.

"Val, I can't read any of this." Heat rushed up to Maria's face as Lee Hwan Soo scoffed while standing next to her at the bar-top table.

"Oh geez, I'm sorry Mari, right...umm..."

"Just get her one of the fruity soju drinks," His Royal Annoyance said.

"No, it's okay. I've got a headache so I think I'll just go back to the apartment." Maria had felt uncomfortable all day, and the night so far had only solidified how out of place she was. She wanted to be there for Val, make things calm and easy for her best friend's big day, but Maria being there seemed to complicate everyone's life.

"Oh come on, Mari. Please don't leave," Val said and tried to stop her from going as Maria stepped away from their table.

She leaned close and in a low voice that only Val could hear, said, "I can't speak the language, I can't even read it, I'm unfamiliar with the traditions, I know nothing. I don't want to embarrass you. Plus, with all the traveling I did the last day and a half, this jet lag has taken its toll." Turning to the two men, she plastered on a bright smile and said, "Enjoy your night." She bowed her head as she had seen others do during the course of the day, hoping she was at least catching on to that custom.

"You managed to get that right," Douchey McDouche responded as he bowed his head.

She was trying out different names for him, but nothing seemed to encapsulate everything she was feeling about him.

Why was that Lee Hwan Soo guy such a hard-ass? It wasn't like she had a crash course in Korean language and culture. She wasn't opposed to learning new things, but he seemed to take everything she said about not understanding as an insult. She was frustrated and flustered so maybe she didn't properly convey what she wanted to say, but it didn't justify his sneer and judgment. While Val tried to calm the storm brewing between Maria and Lee Hwan Soo by whispering something to him and jerking her head at Jung-hyun to get involved, Maria knew that if she didn't walk away, the situation would simply continue to deteriorate. That international incident she was worried about seemed imminent.

Hurrying from the bar, she found a long line of taxis outside, watching, waiting, probably hoping to see drunks stumble out to their cab. She walked over to one cab and climbed in. When he began to speak in Korean, she realized she was screwed. She bowed her head and was about to climb back out of the cab when her door quickly shut and someone rapped on the front driver window.

She was about to protest when the taxi driver rolled his window down and a too familiar and arrogant voice drifted in. Lee Hwan Soo pushed a piece of paper and a large wad of cash toward the man, whose face lit up like he had just received the biggest gift of his life. With a quick bow at Lee Hwan Soo, the driver immediately started his cab and pulled out onto the busy streets of Seoul.

She looked out her window as they began driving away. Douche Canoe stood in front of the bar and bowed several times with a cocky smirk on his face. His gaze met hers for a few seconds before he shook his head, scratched the back of his immaculately cut and styled black hair as if in puzzlement, and then he was gone from sight as the cab quickly shot around the corner.

This month is going to be an absolute bitch, she thought.

Korean Vocabulary:

형-Hyung – older brother (both literal and friend)

오랜만이다- oraenmanida – long time no see

나 – na - me

안녕하세요- anyeonghasaeyo - hello

커피 이 인분 주세요- kopee ee-een bon jusaeyo – two coffees please

네- nae - yes

야- ya – hey!

누구세요- nugusaeyo – who are you?

아친구야, *아 친구야*, 괜찮아- *ah chinguya, qwaenchanha – ah buddy, it's okay.*

뭐라고- mworago – what did you say?

Chapter 4 (넷)

A s the cab pulled away, Hwan Soo shook his head, realizing the trouble that girl was going to get him into.

She was gorgeous. He had noticed her about two seconds after she walked into the bar. Before he even saw her face, he appreciated the contours of her body. A slender waist leading to a round bottom he couldn't take his eyes off of as she strutted with confidence around the tables. Waves of shoulder-length brown hair swayed with every step. If he played his cards right, he'd love to pull her against him to make some serious not-drama-actor-contract-approved moves on her. While he loved his job, the rules he had to follow could be a bit dramatic. Dating was frowned upon when one started off. And even after one was allowed to date, it had to be "confirmed" by the agencies, producers and others. After a few years and some serious acting roles, fans started to hope the actors wouldn't date.

When he had realized she was with his best friend's fiancé, his excitement grew, knowing he would be spending so much time with her, being her lifeline. Being the one she would have to constantly turn to when she needed help to navigate the big city. He had thanked his best friend silently.

That was until she went to go hug a man who wasn't on the market, and in fact was her best friend's fiancé. Abruptly all of his daydreaming was thrown to the wayside as he jerked her away from Jung-hyun. Her lack of knowledge about Korean culture and the strict rules he had to follow for his career were bound to cause serious problems for him.

But seeing her face, even with its sour expression as she'd realized how out of place she was, still had struck him dumb. His gaze wandered over her full pink lips, wide hazel doe eyes, and rosy cheeks. She had a slender neck he wanted to bury his face into and taste, and it reignited his initial interest in the woman despite the almost major faux pas of hugging an engaged man.

It wasn't just her beauty that drew him in. With every word that left her mouth, her feisty attitude was a breath of fresh air from the usually subdued Korean women he was around. It was arousing until he realized how naïve, and maybe even condemning, she was being about his culture.

He had watched Val's face fill with guilt as her best friend left the bar, and he knew that since he had played a rather large part in Maria's storming out, he had to make things maybe not totally right, but better.

He had raced out of the bar in time to see her about to get back out of the cab and knew she wasn't going to go back into the bar. She probably couldn't tell the driver where she needed to go, and he was sure she'd never find her way back by walking. She probably had been upset by his paying off and directing the cabbie and his very determined bows. But with his final glance at her as the cab pulled away, he had seen her unsettled expression, which only made her desirable lips form a sexy and oddly more alluring pout.

Walking back into the bar and seeing his best friend all loved up caused him to feel seriously out of place. Hwan Soo had never see his friend's eyes glaze over with adoration as he fawned over the woman stood beside him. And when he caught the blush on Jung-hyun's cheeks as he pinched his fiancé's cheeks, there was no way Hwan Soo would go back over there to be a third wheel to their cringe. He chose to instead make a silent exit.

As he turned away, he couldn't help but imagine what it might be like to be all loved up with a woman who loved him just as much. A notion he hadn't thought in months popped into his head so easily. What surprised him was that he imagined Maria playing the doting female lead to his lovestruck fool.

Maria woke up the next morning with a jolt. She had forgotten she wasn't in her own bed, but in a lap-of-luxury bed in the most amazing penthouse apartment like the kind she'd only seen in movies. The bed she sat up in was nearly the size of her tiny studio apartment, not to mention the mattress was bouncy but also firm while the pillow felt like her head was being cradled by a cloud. And the windows behind her headboard were floor-to-ceiling, leading out to a small balcony with a large sectional outdoor couch.

She might've been frustrated with the way Jung-hyun's family handled the whole living separately thing, but she would admit the place where they isolated Val was no shack. While it was modern and devoid of any personal touches, the place had three bedrooms, an office space, and a large open living room-kitchen area. If Val was able to get her interior designer hands on the place, she could make a modern chic mix with cottage core, which would be a perfect mashup of Val's personality.

Speaking of Val, Maria looked to her friend's side of the bed and found Val wasn't there. While there were plenty of bedrooms to have her own space, Maria and Val had chosen to live out their old sleep-over days. They wanted to spend whatever time they could together, even when sleeping.

Maria was sure she had heard her friend try to sneak in stealthily at around three or four a.m. and slip into the huge bed beside her. The smell of alcohol was pretty strong and before she could ask if Val was ok, she heard the soft snores coming from her side of the bed.

So when she woke up and didn't have Val beside her she worried that Val's absence might mean she was super hungover and potentially could be puking this morning, Maria pushed off the covers and made her way to the on suite bathroom, only to hear loud noises from beyond the bedroom door.

When her morning brain came out if its fog she inhaled deeply to take in delicious smells that married with the sounds. *Val must be in the kitchen.* That meant a delicious breakfast was about to greet Maria's mouth and stomach. Maria charged out of the bedroom, not questioning that she should possibly change out of her booty shorts and oversized college tee.

The smell of frying eggs led Maria to the kitchen, but in her hunger-induced haze, she failed to realize they had guests. Jung-hyun and Snobby Pants (seriously, she needed to come up with a catchy name for him) sat at the counter, dressed to the nines, while Val was cooking up a storm equally well dressed. They were all smiling and laughing, making her feel as alone and grumpy as she had the night before at the bar.

Maria tried to back away slowly so as to not disturb the happiness with her cranky morning attitude.

"좋은 아침," the man she dreaded said, with a hint of amusement in his voice, obviously aware of the fact that she would have no clue what he had said. He wasn't even looking her way. She wondered how he'd known she was there but suddenly saw her reflection in the wall oven glass. His gaze met hers on the polished surface before Val and Jung-hyun turned to look at her.

"Good morning, Maria." Jung-hyun smiled, looking at Lee Hwan Soo with eyes saying "you know she doesn't understand".

"Ah, you're awake," Val said and smiled, while Maria took in the fact that Val was dressed immaculately and already had makeup on.

All Maria could think to do was bow. It was the one Korean thing she had picked up on the previous day. Val's smile got even wider as she bowed back. Lee Hwan Soo rose from his stool at the counter, finally faced her, and bowed with a small snicker. He gave her body a once-over, and she realized how poorly dressed she was compared to her counterparts.

She bowed once more and Lee Hwan Soo gestured to the barstool he had just been occupying as he rose and walked toward the front door.

"You can have my seat. 나 간다." He bowed his head again before making his way toward the large entryway where Maria learned everyone had to take off their shoes and put on house slippers before entering the home.

"Last day of shooting today, right, Hwan Soo-a?" Jung-hyun asked.

"Shooting?" Maria questioned and moved to take the now unoccupied seat.

"My good friend here is a pretty well-known actor and model in Korea," Jung-hyun boasted about his... 친구 *was it?* she remembered.

"Oh. Well, good luck," Maria said and smiled awkwardly.

"Don't forget you have to be here tomorrow morning to help Maria," Val reminded Hwan Soo as she placed a plate of food in front of Maria.

"Help me?" Maria wondered briefly as the sight of a rather different kind of breakfast made her stomach rumble with nervous anticipation.

"You couldn't even get home last night without my help," he hollered from the doorway as he put on his expensive-looking dress shoes. "Don't look so thrilled," Lee Hwan Soo added.

Maria hadn't realized that she had cringed. Fixing her face to what she hoped would be mild annoyance, she listened to what else he had to say.

"I already talked to my manager and arranged for my workload to be lighter this month, so Jung-hyun put me on 'Maria duty'." He pulled on his light overcoat, and while she really did find him a rather annoying thorn in her side, she admitted to herself that he pulled off a casual dress suit like the men she'd seen in high-end magazine spreads. It made sense he was a model.

There was no missing the grumble in his tone. At least she knew they could agree they weren't going to be pleasant company for one another.

"This pity party you guys have been throwing me is getting a little bothersome," Maria said. She hated that it wasn't even nine a.m. and she was already in a foul mood.

"What's really a pity is you knowing nothing about our traditions and getting angry when we're offering to help you learn them," Lee Hwan Soo said, crossing his arms.

Just thinking his name was starting to become a bigger insult than anything she could come up with on her own since everything about him annoyed her. The little voice in her head called her a liar, but she ignored it.

"Who do you think you are?" she said, her voice raised in displeasure even though there was some truth to his words.

"Your new instructor." He walked back toward the kitchen, reached into his bag, and tossed a book onto the countertop. A quick look at the cover told her it was educational as he continued. "See you tomorrow. Read and write all the exercises in the first chapter. I will test you on them tomorrow morning as well as your pronunciation. And maybe put some clothes on or something before I arrive." Without waiting for a reply, he bowed, hurried back to the front door, and left.

"How is that guy your best friend? He's impossible," she hissed. Maria finally looked more closely at the breakfast Val had put on the table. Soup, rice, some odd-looking red cabbage, and...was that fish? The only thing she was able to recognize as breakfast food was the fried egg, and so she started with that.

"He's just stressed at the moment. I promise you that he is one of the most reliable, smart, and kindest guys I know," Jung-hyun said in defense of his friend. "But then again, I'm sure Val would say the same thing about me, but we all know I can be a tough one. The difference is, I acknowledge it."

Jung-hyun placed a cup of coffee in front of Maria, and her mood was instantly lifted, appreciating the change in subject.

"What are your plans for the day, Val?" she asked.

"I'm going to meet Jung-hyun-오빠's ancestors." Val fumbled the dishes she was cleaning as she explained.

"Nervous?" Maria asked.

"Yes and no. Yes, because I have to introduce myself, no because, well..."

"They're dead," he laughed.

"Oh?" Maria choked on the hot coffee at the calm intonation of Jung-hyun's voice.

"It's tradition to introduce loved ones, serious girlfriends, boyfriends, and fiancés to everyone in the family. Literally everyone." He laughed again. *He probably knows that might sound bizarre to some people*, Maria thought. That's when she realized he was an understanding man, like Val had argued he was. She could see that he knew some of their traditions were outside the norm to a Westerner like herself, and he was clearly trying to make her feel comfortable with that fact.

"Wow, that's a new one. Sounds weirdly interesting." Maria felt bad for not eating a lot of the food on the table, but her nerves had gotten the best of her and so she began to pick up the plates to start cleaning up. "Most relationships I have never last long enough to even think of introducing them to the living relatives," she said and smiled, feeling a little bit more accepting of Jung-hyun. "I should probably hop in the shower and get on with my day."

"What were you planning to do?" Val asked, taking the dishes from Maria to clean them herself, a quirk of Val's that Maria was familiar with. She had to make sure the dishes were polished to perfection and placed aesthetically. Even in their college dorm Val's interior designer instincts came out to keep everything as if it was staged. Probably why the campus used any dorm room she lived in for the next four years as their showroom to prospective students. Val finally finished the dishes without breaking any despite her earlier fumbling.

"Well since the only person I know is leaving me alone for the day, and next to nothing in this country is in English, and your language looks like hieroglyphics at the moment, my plan to lounge on the couch sounds just about right," Maria said.

"Maybe have a look at that book Hwan Soo-a gave you," Val hinted.

"Yeah, maybe." Maria eyed the book on the shiny white marble countertop, noting how thick it was. Her stomach twisted recalling his statement about her not knowing anything about his culture.

"Seriously, you really should. Hwan Soo 형 doesn't joke," Jung-hyun said and pointed to the book as he stood to leave with Val. "He expects all that to get done. He's been like that since, well, since as long as I can remember. He once let me slice my finger trying to cut open a daikon radish because I didn't watch the video he sent me on the proper way to do the job."

Maria refrained from chuckling and rolling her eyes, rose and bowed as they left the apartment.

Lee Hwan Soo might be a tough nut, but so was she. It made her wonder which nut would crack first.

Korean Vocabulary:
좋은 아침- *Chohona Chim – good morning*
잘 잤어? Jal Jasseo? – Did you sleep well?/Good morning
나 간다 – na kanda – I'm leaving

Chapter 5 (다섯)

The whole TV thing was a bust being that most of it was in Korean. Hopping off the couch, Maria saw the book Lee Hwan Soo had tossed at her that morning.

There literally is nothing better to do, she thought and shrugged, grabbing the book and cracking it open to the first page. "Oh. My. God," she whispered.

Scanning through the book, she realized the first chapter was close to thirty pages long with every five pages being some kind of exercise where she would have to write out all the phrases over and over.

"Did I just re-enter college?" She scoffed, closed the book and pushed it away in frustration. "Why do I need to learn an entire new language for one month of use? This is so ridiculous!" she complained.

No way that Lee Hwan Soo could be so strict with his "lesson plan," but she also knew that she didn't want to sit in the apartment for the next four weeks doing nothing while her best friend was going out enjoying her final nights as a "single" lady. Looking out the window of the high-rise, she saw how beautiful and lively the city seemed. A place more crammed with people, places, and things to see than New York. She wanted to experience the city from outside the walls of the apartment, so maybe grasping at least the basics of Korean would be helpful.

Reaching for the book once again, she got comfortable on the couch, opened to the first page and dove into the symbols she had seen all over the streets of Seoul. The first thing she learned was the alphabet was called Hangul.

As she pored through the pages, she didn't realize how much time was passing until someone grabbed her shoulder. She screamed bloody murder until she saw it was Val, who was screaming equally as loud.

"Jesus, Val! Why would you sneak up on a person like that?!" She grabbed her chest to try to calm her heart, which seemed to be trying desperately to escape her body.

"I was talking to you for a solid thirty seconds with no response. You were sucked into that book." Val was likewise trying to calm her breathing as she sat on the edge of the couch.

"Really?" Maria looked at her phone. "Holy crap, it's almost nine! I haven't even had dinner yet."

"Perfect! Neither have I. I'll order us some 치맥, and we can watch a drama I'm obsessed with," Val said, jumping up to grab a takeout menu.

"I know that most of what you said was English, but still..."

"치맥. Chicken and 맥주. 맥주 is beer. It's literally fried chicken and beer, and it's amazing. And a drama is just a TV show. Same as any of ours, just somehow more interesting. You won't be able to understand most of it, but I'll translate what I can since subtitles won't be available until tomorrow anyway. Plus, you'll be tucking into wings and beer, so you'll be too preoccupied." Val smiled, grabbed her phone and expertly placed an order using only Korean.

Maria was impressed with her friend. The girl had picked up a whole new language and was able to use it regularly. Maria's high school Latin never seemed to crop up in a conversation.

When Val came back to the couch, Maria felt the need to ask, "How long have you been learning Korean?"

"Since Jung-hyun and I started dating. I knew some only because of my job—I worked with a lot of Korean customers. I mean, he speaks almost perfect English, but he would accidentally throw a Korean word or term into conversations, and I could see he would get embarrassed when I had to ask him what the words meant. So I asked him to start teaching me. He started with the Hangul, like you're learning, then from there he would teach me a word or phrase every day. By the time he proposed, I was able to hold pretty decent conversations."

"That's really great, Val," Maria said and smiled warmly at her best friend. Guilt was settling into her stomach over how much of a pain she had been about the whole situation. She needed to give the stuff a chance. Leaning back on the couch, she remembered what Val had been doing all day. "How was seeing and talking to dead people?"

Val chuckled, leaned back, and dropped her head onto Maria's shoulder. "Weird. Talking to someone who wasn't physically in the room, or even on the phone, was bizarre. Jung-hyun being there and being so comfortable made me feel a lot less worried."

"You really love him." Maria was listening to her friend's voice as it had a melody, a sweet happiness, that Maria had never heard before. It made her realize that this guy really had a strong effect on her bestie.

"I've never felt this way," Val said thoughtfully. "I always thought I knew what love was, but when Jung-hyun came into the picture, it was something so different. It was a shock to my system. It brought me to a whole new level with new experiences. I hope you'll find that love one day too."

"Oh jeez," Maria rolled her eyes. "My mom still has her grip on you, doesn't she? Did she call you and ask who *really* sat next to me on the flight? This convo *would* lead to the 'Why is Maria single?'

speech." She was ready to dial her mom and tell her to stop her meddling.

"That's not what I meant at all! I know she gives you enough of that," Val said and pinched Maria's side, lightening the mood.

"Oh! The drama's about to start. 가자!" Val jumped up and started futzing with the remote to get to the proper channel.

Maria might not have understood the Korean words, but she could grasp by the excitement what Val was trying to tell her. And so their night consisted of eating probably the most delicious fried chicken she'd ever had, watching a show and barely getting the gist of it, and drinking a lot of beer.

A. Lot. Which had her hoping that they both wouldn't be paying the price for it in the morning.

"She is one of the most unattractive sleepers I've ever seen," someone said.

Maria thought she was dreaming. But when she recognized that voice, it became more like a nightmare.

She heard another, much nicer person defend her. "Hush, 형. She and Val had a girls' night, and I think Maria might've had too much to drink.

"She knew I would be here this morning. Why would she inconvenience me like that? I could be doing a million other things."

She rolled her eyes behind closed lids, realizing it was not a nightmare and she was in fact awake.

Groaning, she finally said, "Then how about you go do those millions of other things instead of running your mouth and giving me a bigger headache than I already have. Ass hat." *Oh, I like that one.*

She could hear both Val and Jung-hyun snickering as Maria slowly opened her eyes.

"I'm sorry. She's not a morning person. Plus, with all the beer last night, she's *really* not a morning person." Val came to her defense as she placed a soothing hand on Maria's back and gently rubbed. "Mari, you gotta get up," Val said.

"Why?" Maria knew she sounded like a grumbling child, but she really didn't think she was of much use to anyone in her condition.

"Remember all that work and reading you did yesterday? Hwan Soo-ah is here to help you with it."

Maria flapped her arm in the direction of the kitchen. "Book is in there."

Well-dressed feet clacked toward the kitchen, indicating Lee Hwan Soo had left the room, giving Maria a little breathing space to try to get her nausea to subside.

"자기야, we gotta get going. If we're late my mom will kill me," Jung-hyun said.

"Seriously?!" a loud voice boomed from the kitchen.

Maria covered her ears and threw a pillow over her head wanting to rip that man's tongue out of that pretty, well-shaped-for-making-out mouth.

"You only got halfway through the first chapter!" Hwan Soo said and ripped the pillow off her head. "Get up."

His command sent an odd shiver down her spine. It wasn't totally unpleasant. But it wasn't enough for her to actually listen to him. She turned her head toward him and saw he was immaculately dressed in a well-tailored, uniquely pinstriped suit, with a white button-up shirt and simple black tie. His Oxford shoes were so shiny, she could see her reflection in them. When she looked to her friend, she saw all of them were dressed to impress.

"Seriously, what time do you people wake up to look *this* nice so early in the morning?" Maria complained.

"Why didn't you finish the first chapter? It's literally the simplest chapter," he said, ignoring her comment completely as he continued to yell at her.

"I didn't come here to learn a whole new language. I came here to see my best friend get married and ride into her little happily ever after. You should be impressed I got any of it done," she said and finally sat up. Her head was not happy about the movement, preferring to be cradled against the couch pillow once again, but she fought that desire.

"Are you two going to be okay?" Val asked.

"We'll be fine. If you don't leave now, you'll be late. And he isn't lying when he says his mom will kill him. 가," Lee Hwan Soo said and waved at the couple to leave.

They all bowed, and Maria was left alone with the handsome devil.

"Get up, get dressed—"

"Did you think I would just follow your orders the second they left?" she said, narrowing her eyes to examine him.

"Did you think your little bout of childish rebellion would stop me from enforcing what I instructed?" he said, walking back over to her and bending over. Before she knew what was happening, he threw her over his shoulder.

"What the hell?" she screeched as he carried her away from the couch. Her stomach churned and the possible onslaught of vomiting reared its ugly head as she lay over his shoulder.

Dropping her onto her feet, she realized they were in the bathroom. He turned the shower on and walked back over to her.

"Take a shower. You reek," he hissed and walked out of the bathroom.

Korean Vocabulary:
자기야 – jagiya – honey/sweetheart
가 – ka – go/leave
가자 - kaja – Let's go!

Chapter 6 (여섯)

M aybe throwing her over his shoulder wasn't the smartest idea. Feeling the curves he had observed gently swaying at the bar moving around in his hands and on his shoulder, a slight discomfort arose in his tailored trousers. If her shirt rode up any more, he would have felt her bare skin against his fingertips, which could cause a whole new string of thoughts that wouldn't help his issue below.

Even her beer-tinged breath didn't stop him from wanting to halt her screams for help with kisses.

What is wrong with me? This girl is rude and naïve. Nothing about her should be appealing. But that was a lie, and he knew it.

Her crassness, while rude, was enjoyable. Which was surprising. While every other foreigner's voice was like nails on a chalkboard, hers, having a bite, egged him on to pick a fight. A fight he desperately wanted to continue until blue in the face. The women he usually met, hand-picked by his wedding-hungry mother, would back down from a fight. Sure, they would come on strong at first, make one think they would be independent. But soon they'd give up, playing cute and asking him to do everything for them. It didn't help that when things didn't work out well, the women would go to his mother, who would then berate him about his behavior and tell him to do better on the next date. He didn't think Maria was that kind of girl, and he knew for a fact his mother had nothing to do with Maria.

His ex also was not the type to back down, one reason he was so sure he loved being with her. She took the initiative from day one. She never asked anything of him except, well, to be a great lay. She didn't want him to dote on her, because she never assumed that behind his starving artist exterior, his family was beyond loaded. And so she was the breadwinner. Whenever they argued, she was able to win him over. Most often by taking her top off. It was what he fell in love with.

As he thought about it, maybe it wasn't love after all. It was simply lust in disguise.

While Maria was definitely not asking for marriage, dating, or even sex from him, he did take notice of her strength and determination. She didn't back down. She also didn't need to take her top off to make a point stick. However, after dropping her in the shower, the water soaking her rather light-colored shirt, he wouldn't have minded seeing everything she had to offer.

정신 차려, he thought taking a deep breath to shake the dirty images from his mind before sitting down to read over her poor excuse at work.

Frankly, he was surprised she'd done any of it, but the fact that she couldn't even finish the second half of the chapter was cause for concern. Was she really not able to grasp the basics in one night? How was he supposed to have her ready to give an entire speech by the end of the month? While he read over her work, his phone buzzed in the back pocket of his pants. Pulling the phone out, he saw the screen light blaring his manager's name.

This could be the call that changed his life. It could make his career and launch his name and face into ultimate stardom. That was, if he landed the part. Taking a deep breath, he swiped to answer the call.

"여보세요?!" His voice cracked as it rose, totally failing to control his emotions. So much for being even a remotely decent actor.

"Hwan Soo-a! I have some news. They wrapped up the callbacks for the drama you auditioned for," his manager said, but as his voice trailed off, Hwan Soo's heart pounded even faster.

"And?" He couldn't wait any longer for the answer. His feet were tapping fast, he was rocking in his seat waiting for the answer.

"They really liked you..." Something his manager had always said before delivering the crushing blow, and all his excitement halted.

"Did I even get an option to audition for the second lead?" Hwan Soo slumped, falling back defeated in the chair. He knew he had no shot. What was he thinking even trying to be a lead? He never fit the role and never would.

"미안해. But they did choose to offer you something," his manager said brightly, clearly trying to lift Hwan Soo's spirits.

"Oh yeah? What? The lead's annoying brother?" Hwan Soo said sarcastically, somehow managing to cover his disappointment.

"No. They decided you were a perfect fit for the lead."

"Okay what time do I need to...wait...WHAT?!" He was sure he had heard his manager incorrectly.

"You're the lead. You got the part." Hwan Soo had never heard his manager's voice so jovial in the five years they'd known each other.

"I...I... You're not playing a horrible joke on me?" Hwan Soo needed confirmation it was real. Trying to take deep breaths, he wasn't sure he could breathe steadily.

"I'm pretty sure my whole trying to lead you into believing you didn't get the part was supposed to be the horrible joke. And for the record, I'm not kidding. You will be the lead in the next big romantic comedy drama of the year. They haven't mentioned who would be opposite you. I'm not sure they've reached a decision yet," his manager continued to explain, but Hwan Soo's mind was on the fact that his dream had been accomplished. He was about to be the star of a drama.

His excitement was cut short when heard the shower shut off and the light hum of Maria's voice in the other room.

"형, I need to go." He whispered in a rush, hovering his finger over the End button.

"Are you with someone? 야! You know you have a strict dating clause! I can't cover for you again!" His manager yelled loud enough for Hwan Soo to pull the phone away from his ear.

"No! I'm not with someone. Well, yes I am, but it's just my best friend's fiancée's maid of honor. I'm showing her around before the wedding," he explained. He had mentioned his friend's wedding to his manager, but while Hwan Soo had been blindsided by his babysitting gig, he forgot to mention that new detail to his manager. The man who would have to cover his ass if anyone were to see or post something of him and Maria out in public. Bad move on his part.

That's when another rather important thought hit him. The wedding. He promised Jung-hyun that he would keep his load light to be able to accommodate any needs. 젠장.

Korean Vocabulary:
정신 차려- jeongshin chreyo - Wake up (come to your senses)
여보세요- yobosaeyo - hello
젠장- jaen jang – damn

Chapter 7 (일곱)

W hen she walked out of the bedroom, dressed and drying her hair with a towel, her eyes landed on Lee Hwan Soo sitting on the couch reading over her work. She could've sworn she'd heard him shout and was nervous her work was really that bad.

"How'd I do, teach?" she said, sauntering over to him.

When he spun around, his expression was confusing. His eyes went wide as if surprised she was standing in front of him. His cheeks were growing red and his mouth was pursed as if he was trying to solve a difficult problem.

"You wrote the words over and over again, but do you know how to pronounce the Hangul?" He tossed the book loudly onto the glass-top coffee table with a loud thud that sounded like he had shattered it. He stood with a cocky confidence that she only ever saw on men in expensive suit ads. He radiated an unobtainable hotness, and she was sure had a sexy six-pack hidden behind his button-up and suit jacket. If only he could keep his luxuriously plump lips shut long enough not to constantly ruin the image of him ravaging her.

"Well I said them out loud once or twice, but I was alone, so how would I know? What does that matter? If I can read it, I can get myself around easy enough," she said as she continued to shake her hair out, letting it air dry.

"Oh really? So when the cab driver says, 어디가세요? What will you write? Can you read what I said? Do you even know what I said?" He walked toward her slowly, looking her up and down as one of the sexiest smirks she had ever seen in real life pulled at the corner of his lips. When he stood right in front of her, she swallowed hard, trying to moisten her mouth that had gone completely dry without her knowledge.

It infuriated her that he had to possess all these powerfully sexual characteristics. Why was he able to make her feel a tension in the pit of her stomach most men she dated couldn't even cause? And they had her naked in bed. Sure, Hwan Soo was handsome, like a freaking god, and his voice was that kind of low, slow, deep voice a girl would love to hear moan her name. And while all of that made her body ignite with passionate bliss, he also had to argue against every single point she made, and with a venom that caused her to question if he hated the fact she wasn't Korean, which easily extinguished that lust.

She tried desperately to look everywhere else but at his face. He placed one of his long, slender fingers under her chin, the smooth, slightly cool finger pulling her face up to look him in the eyes. Eyes one wasn't sure where the pupil met the iris as the iris color was nearly black; those eyes bore down into her own, sending a shiver through her whole body.

"You can't just write your speech. You have to actually speak." His breath fanned along her cheeks, making heat rise even further onto her cheeks, possibly even her ears.

"M-m-my speech has to be in Korean?" she stuttered, relieved she even had the ability to form words but pissed he caught the fact that his touch did something to her.

"Ninety percent. Most of the party will be Jung-hyun's family and friends," he said, moving away from her, causing her sexual fantasies to disappear immediately.

"What about Val's family and friends? Huh? What about us?" she spat out as she was slowly coming back to her senses following him back to the seating area of the living room.

"You're that other ten percent of the speech. Be happy you get that. If it were his family's choice, you wouldn't even be making a speech." He pulled the towel from her hand and tossed it on the couch. "Get dressed, we're going out. I'll show you why you need to know how to speak."

"I am dressed and what do you mean about his family?" She looked down at her loose-fitting sweater and yoga pants.

"His mother is very traditional. I am shocked she willingly let him marry Val. Something must've happened in San Francisco to make her be so open to this marriage," he explained as he chuckled, pointing to her outfit. "Is this all you packed?"

While she wanted to question further about what he meant concerning her friend's future husband and family, she felt embarrassed, not understanding what was so wrong with her outfit. It was casual and comfy. What else did she need? She wasn't there to impress anyone.

"Oh, you're in for the rudest awakening, 가요," he said.

"I know that phrase! Val said something similar last night. It means like 'come on' or 'let's go'." She was totally guessing, but from the context of Val's comment last night and now his, the meaning seemed to be along those lines.

His eyes went wide for a quick second, giving her the vibe that she was correct. He said nothing as he walked to the door and pulled his shoes on. Another one of the cultural things she picked up on was the fact that whenever entering a house, shoes came off. No matter what. There was even a hidden cubby in the wall next to the entrance that housed all the shoes. She followed suit and when she got to the door, she nudged him out of the way to reach the elevator.

"가요!" she shouted as she hopped onto the elevator and shot him a wide smile that had a heaping hint of "fuck you" mixed in.

He was silent as he joined her in the elevator and when it began its descent, she thought to try to start a conversation, feeling slightly satisfied she had been able to one-up him with the one word she could say properly.

"So Hwan Soo—"

"Lee Hwan Soo. Lee Hwan Soo-씨 to you. You don't drop honorifics with me. Not until we establish that we are comfortable together, which I have a feeling won't happen in a month. And when you meet Jung-hyun's parents, you never drop it. They are elders. Respect your elders. Always," he snapped.

"Jeez, okay. Lee Hwan Soo-씨, where are we going?" she asked.

"You need clothes."

"I have—" His neck snapped to her, causing her to cut herself off. She was intimidated by his clenched jaw and furrowed eyebrows, but she also admired how sharp that jaw of his really was.

"No, you don't. What you have are pajamas, at best. Here, we pride ourselves on how we look. Call it superficial all you want, but what's wrong with wanting to look your best? And are you going to turn everything into an argument? Can't you just be quiet and trust me?" he hissed.

Wow. No manners on this guy.

She wanted to fight back, but all that would do was prove his point. She took several deep breaths and chanted in her head, *Do this for Val.*

"All right. So where are we going shopping?" She plastered the fakest smile on her face in her attempt to be civil.

"Here's the place," he said and pointed to his phone where a map, covered in Hangul, lit up the screen. There was one name bolded with a large red dot to indicate that was the desired location: 명동

"Get us there." He tapped the bold name to make the area larger on his phone, but it did nothing to help her. Street names popped up, small shop icons, with some names that were in English but in no way helpful to her.

"What?" she asked in disbelief.

"You heard me," he said, a warning tone in his voice.

"I've literally only learned how to write this and now you want me to find this shopping area?" She tried to grab the phone away from him to simply hit the directions button but he pulled it away, locking his screen and tossing it into his pants pocket.

"You said that if you can read it, you can get around the city. So here's your chance to prove yourself correct. But if you had bothered to finish the chapter, you would've learned how to ask for directions, out loud." His smirk was so triumphant she wanted to slap his immaculate cheek so hard, it would wipe those kissable lips right off his face.

"But I didn't finish the chapter," she said, fuming, knowing he was trying to prove a point with his cocky grin and his little sway from the balls of his feet to his heels.

"That's not my problem. I'm not going to change my lesson plan and time schedule because you decided to drink and watch dramas last night." He crossed his arms and his smug smile grew at her flustered state. Jung-hyun warned her Hwan Soo was like this, but she believed him to just be rattling her to get her to study harder.

"I haven't seen my best friend is six months! You expect me to study when I finally have free time with her? Screw that. And screw you!" She didn't want to argue. She really tried not to, but when he tried to make her feel guilty about spending time with her friend, he not only pushed a button but flipped every damn fuse in the box.

"I haven't seen Jung-hyun-ah in four years and yet here I am, with you, instead of my best friend. I don't have an ounce of pity for you and your measly six months. So don't try and think you can guilt your way out of this," he bit. If she thought his jaw was clenched before, she was currently worried he might shatter his teeth just to clamp a little tighter. When she looked down his body, even his hands were balled into fists that had made his already pale skin impossibly whiter.

Four years?

"That's a long time," she whispered. Her guilt trip had suddenly spun a whole one hundred eighty degrees and now she was the one who had a small pang in her heart. How could friends be apart that long? Six months felt like four years to her and yet here were two people who legitimately hadn't seen each other in such a long span of time.

"Why so long? Doesn't he come to Seoul often? From what Val said he's here several times a year. Can't you go visit him in California?" She now had to find out what would keep such close friends apart for so long.

"He comes back every couple of months for work, but between modeling and dramas, I end up being the one who can never get off to see him. I tried to see him when I was out in L.A. for a photo shoot but we ended up missing each other. When he told me he was going to be in Seoul for a whole month because he was getting married, I was excited. He even asked me to be his best man. I couldn't turn that down. I made sure I could see him, even canceled some decent modeling jobs because it had been too long. And on the first day I do see him, he asks me to teach his fiancée's best friend Korean, since he's going to be too busy with the wedding planning," he said, kicking the wall behind them over and over again throughout his monologue.

She wasn't sure he had meant to reveal all of that, but when people need to vent, strangers were often the best people to talk to. She understood how he felt. Her heart even skipped a beat, feeling they were able to relate.

"Well since this ended up being a bust for both of us, why don't you just call your manager and book some jobs? I'll tell Val and Jung-hyun it was my idea. I will stay in the apartment for the month. Or for your pleasure, I'll go out, get lost, and never been seen or heard from again." She tried lightening the elevator's heavy mood, which actually received a deep chuckle from Hwan Soo. A baritone chuckle that made her thighs clamp shut to control her insides from pooling out all over the floor.

"As infuriating as you've been, I wouldn't want to hear you disappeared. Mainly because Jung-hyun-ah would hate me," he said and brushed his hand through his hair.

Jesus. Jung-hyun this. Jung-hyun that. Jung-hyun...wait!

"Are you in love with Jung-hyun? I mean that's totally cool, to each his own, but he's marrying my best friend so I feel I need to step in here to tell you to snap back to reality." She was all for every kind of love, minus the obvious illegal kinds, but if Hwan Soo really was in love with Jung-hyun, it was not smart or healthy for him to be the best man.

"뭐라고?" he nearly shrieked. His voice cracked to such a level, he sounded like a mouse screeching.

"Yeah, definitely don't know what that means. But...wait...you said that before. I remember. When we were told we were gonna have to be together for the remainder of this month." She closed her eyes and tried to run through how it was said in that scenario. "I say you're asking me something along the lines of 'excuse me?'!" she said, re-enacting his movements and facial expression trying to find the meaning. She shot her hands up in surrender, keeping her eyes closed waiting for him to come down on her with hellfire.

When she felt and heard nothing, she slowly peeled her eyes open to see more surprise etched on his face, and she again knew she had guessed correctly. For a supposed actor, his face couldn't hide his feelings well. When she brought her hands down and watched his face turn back to its angered look.

"I like women, okay? Love 'em. But Jung-hyun-ah and I have been best friends since we were kids. Our whole lives it was us against the world. We're really more like brothers."

"Hyungs? Is that a thing?" she questioned.

He laughed. A genuine, not mocking laugh, and she was surprised at how much she enjoyed it. His bright white teeth gleamed in the light of the elevator and his lips formed a sexy heart-shape as he tried to hide said smile. His eyes, which had scrunched almost closed, glistened with amusement, keeping her watching to see what they would tell her next. She wasn't surprised he was a model. If he kept from talking, she saw why people could fawn over him.

"Well he is older than me. Hence me calling him형and him calling me 친고. But if there were more than one friend, there isn't truly a plural. Most would say친고둘," he explained. "I'm glad you no longer think my name is친고though. Good job." It had to be out of total instinct but he reached out to pat the top of her head.

She laughed, trying to hide how tender the exchange was, feeling something had quickly changed between them, and got back to the subject at hand. "So you're not gay?"

With a roll of his eyes he responded, "Seriously?"

His happy, cheerful face was instantly replaced with annoyance as the same hand that was inciting enormous amounts of pleasure through her hair tugged strongly at a tendril.

Before she could gripe about the tug or even apologize, she was no longer staring at the numbers on the elevator panel decreasing, but instead she was face to face with Lee Hwan Soo. Staring into his deep, dark brown eyes, she understood even more his marketability as a model because those eyes could convince her to do...just about anything. Trying to avoid any more eye contact, she skimmed her gaze around his face and noticed everything else that was attractive about him. For instance, he had two little freckles on the long bridge of his nose, which led to lips that were created for sin, a sharp jawline that could cut glass, and a complexion smooth like marble.

She tried to move to the side to retreat from his enticing nature, which he stopped by slamming his hands on either side of her head. He dipped his head to get even closer, giving her an even better look at all those perfect features.

"Want me to prove it?"

Korean Vocabulary:

어디가세요- odigasaeyo - Where are you going?

가요- kajayo - let's go

씨- ssi (she) - Mr./Ms.

명동 - myeongdong (Same in English)

친구둘 - chingudul – friends

Chapter 8 (여덟)

He really liked putting himself in positions that were problematic for his manhood. Being that close to her, Hwan Soo was even surer of how attractive she was. Her skin was olive-toned, shockingly smooth, not a blemish. Women anywhere would be jealous, but women in Korea, who followed ten-to fifteen-step processes to make their faces that flawless, would kill for it. Her lips, which he had already noticed were slightly chapped—he hazarded a guess it was due to dehydration from her flight—were slightly thin but pouting in surprise by his actions. Her eyes, which were roaming all over his face, were almost golden-green, if that were even possible. His eyes meandered down to her neck. He enjoyed watching as she tensed up and tried to breathe calmly but couldn't, as her jaw muscles clenched and unclenched and her chest rose and fell quickly.

"I didn't ask you to prove anything. I was simply making an observation and then needed confirmation. Verbal confirmation would've been just fine," she said and smirked, clearly trying her best to hide the fact that he had gotten to her. He knew fully well he had, but damn, did she wear that grin well.

"Your observations are insanely wrong and that is my verbal confirmation," he bit back and moved away from her before his hormones caused him to do something he might regret. As if the elevator knew their conversation needed to come to an end, the doors opened and he made his way to the exit of the building.

Walking out the door of the apartment building, he was surprised to hear a loud thud behind him, followed by Maria's angry voice screaming, "What the hell?"

He turned to see her holding her nose as she was pushing the door open to catch up with him.

"What did you do?" he asked with concern as he walked over to make sure she was okay.

"What did *I* do? You could've at least held the door! I was right behind you," she complained as she rubbed her nose.

"If I did that, we would never be able to leave. I would've been holding the door for the rest of eternity. Look around. Not a single person is holding the door for the person behind them. People don't thank you for your consideration here. Just grab the door and keep walking. Decent lesson to learn your first day out. Now on to shopping," he said and walked ahead of her.

Suddenly realizing that would defeat her learning the consequences of not finishing her lesson, he took smaller steps for her to catch up and ultimately pass him, which felt like it took a millennium. She kept touching her nose, rubbing it and making odd "O" shapes with her mouth. And while very cute to watch, he also huffed at the fact that she was making such a big deal out of the littlest issue. *Kind of like most actresses I work with.*

Maybe she would fit in perfectly fine. Which caused him to laugh to himself.

When she stopped dead in her tracks and began to look around, he saw that button nose, which had almost gone bright red from all her rubbing, scrunch up as she squinted her eyes and looked all around. Puzzlement soon filled her features.

She's lost. Perfect.

The feeling of his small win overtook him as he made his way up to her.

"Give up?" he smirked.

"What gave you that idea? Did I say that?" she retorted and continued looking around. Something caught her eye and she bounded down the block like a woman on a mission. He followed behind her, watching both her navigation as well as her nice round bottom sway and bounce.

Arriving at a bus stop, he was pleasantly surprised she had located it. It was not a bus that would take her where they needed to go, but he would give her credit for finding it, although not to her face.

She stared at the map, clearly struggling to comprehend the information, and he watched as her lips tried to read the words aloud, unsure of themselves.

"You're seriously not going to help at all?" she finally said, refusing to even look at him.

Shaking his head and laughing, he said, "If you had finished the chapter, I wouldn't have to help you."

"That's bull. Even if I finished it, got everything perfect on paper, what does that mean when I couldn't actually practice with anyone? You say I should learn how to speak, yet I had no one to speak to. Your system is flawed," she said. He had to admit she made a fair point.

He hadn't thought of that. He huffed, not wanting to admit that she was right, and was about to help when a little old lady walked over to sit on the bench of the bus stop.

Maria's eyes lit up as she quickly walked over to the woman and bowed.

"English?" she asked.

The woman waved her hands violently. Maria pulled out a pen and paper wrote something speedily, and the woman's eyes went wide with recognition.

"Oh...Myeong-Dong," she said, pointing to the word on the

paper.

"Myeong-Dong?" Maria repeated as Hwan Soo's eyes went wide.

"내." The woman nodded over and over, a smile growing as Maria began bopping in excitement for getting someone to understand her.

Maria bowed several times to the woman and walked back over to Hwan Soo with the largest triumphant smile on her face. He stared in amazement. She had solved the problem of how to get around without being able to pronounce the words.

"So Myeong-Dong? What is that? A store or something?" she asked.

"No, it's a district here in Seoul," he said, annoyed that she had even made it that far.

"Cool! So this bus doesn't seem to take us there, but if we grab a cab I can just tell them that's where we want to go," she explained, more to herself than to him. But as if the gods had heard her call, several cabs suddenly drove past. Putting out her hand, one pulled right up at her signal.

What the hell? Lucky girl, he thought.

After they climbed in, the driver greeted them and asked where they were going. He looked over to Maria, who had a slight look of panic in her eyes, which gave Hwan Soo a sick kind of satisfaction.

"명동?" she said nervously.

"내," the driver responded and took off.

"뭐?!" Hwan Soo spat out. Why was everyone making it so easy for her? It wasn't like she gave a full address, but the driver just said yes to taking her to the general area.

The cab driver jumped a bit and made eye contact with Hwan Soo through the rearview mirror but continued his drive, only much more cautiously. Falling back into the seat, Hwan Soo let out a huff of annoyance.

"What are you? Four years old?" Maria said with a mocking laugh.

"They're taking it easy on you," he said, pulling his hair back in frustration. He wanted her to learn a lesson about not finishing what was asked of her in the proper amount of time, but so far everyone had been kind and understanding of her situation.

"Maybe they sympathize. Clearly I'm not from the area, so they know I am going to need help." She shrugged, appearing to either ignore his sourness or rub it in with a sick sweetness. She turned away from him, looking out the window at the sprawling metropolis as it passed by.

"It's because you're a pretty face. If you were just the least bit unattractive this would've been ten times harder," he scoffed...until he realized he had called her pretty. Out loud. To her face. Well, the back of her head.

As if not caring about what he had just revealed, she retorted, "Is that the excuse you use for your attitude? I'm attractive so people do as I say and treat me like a god among men?"

"Pretty sure that's not a new concept. It's how the world works everywhere," he said as he, too, turned his face to gaze out the window to a city he loved calling home. In the window's reflection, he saw she now faced him, her mouth ajar and her eyes as wide as saucers.

Chapter 9 (아홉)

The cab pulled off to the side of the road and the driver began speaking to her again. She knew he was telling her how much the ride cost, but when she went to grab her wallet, she realized she hadn't put any of her exchanged money inside.

"Lee Hwan Soo-씨...I...I don't have any money."

"You didn't get any money exchanged?" He spoke loudly, causing the driver to yet again jump nervously.

"I did, but I was sort of rushed out of the apartment and had no time to organize myself," she explained, trying very hard not to show how embarrassed she was knowing the driver was watching her through the rearview mirror. *He's probably wondering when he's going to get paid.*

Lee Hwan Soo pulled out his wallet, handing the man several bills, bowing his head and saying a word she had heard fairly often in the weird K-drama she watched with Val the night before: "감사합니다."

They climbed out of the car and she finally had a better perspective of the area. It was an attack on all her senses. Maria's emotions of excitement and nervousness coursed through her body. This is what she had hoped to feel when she looked down from the penthouse windows. Hundreds if not thousands of people roamed the streets, filling all the shops. Some shops looking similar to ones Maria had seen at home, while others were totally new and fascinating. They all had window displays that could lure anyone with a keen eye for fashion. And the makeup boutiques had people handing out what looked to be free samples of their products.

Mixed between all the fashions were cafés, small food stands, and multi-story high restaurants. As she passed menu boards, her mouth began watering at some of the fun and creative-looking food and drink items. Some places even had their employees hollering to get passersby to stop for a delicious meal.

While she wanted to stop and take in the magic of all the shops they passed, she realized she couldn't understand what the shops sales were or even what the salespeople were saying to customers who were walking in. Maybe Lee Hwan Soo was right. She was able to get to the location, but it wasn't because she had actually learned, it was because she mooched off the kindness of others.

She started pulling out her phone to snap a few pictures to send to her mother but was stopped when she saw Lee Hwan Soo had already walked into a store. She followed him inside.

"How do you expect me to buy anything when I don't have money?"

He turned to look at her and his mouth dropped open. His lips, when they weren't mocking her, were so sultry, they were all she could focus on. When she realized she had been staring, she shook away her R-rated thoughts and waited for his reply. What she wasn't expecting was to see he had a similar expression on his face.

Waving her hand in his face, he broke out of whatever thoughts had been playing in his mind.

"You okay?" she asked.

"I'm fine," he cleared his throat, "we just really need to get you some makeup."

Ugh. She definitely misinterpreted his face. He was looking at her with vain disinterest, not lust. *Didn't even know those two looks could be similar.*

He perused the makeup, picking up, smelling, and testing everything that he walked past. She noticed he was in his element. An element most straight American men would find annoying and kind of weird, but Lee Hwan Soo was thriving. She again had to bring up the fact that she didn't have money with her. "Lee Hwan Soo-씨-"

"됐어요. Buy what you like." He waved his hand at all the merchandise.

A young, dainty, and downright beautiful woman walked over to help them. When she got a look at Lee Hwan Soo, her eyes went wide with excitement. She covered her mouth with her hand and, turning bright red, she began talking to him excitedly. He bowed, nervously accepting the fact that he had been recognized as the young woman continued to hide her smile from Hwan Soo.

Wow, he really must be well known.

He continuously bowed to her with an awkward smile, clearly not comfortable in the position he had been thrown into. Maria made her way over to them and suddenly the girl's eyes turned to ice.

Lee Hwan Soo looked over and quickly tried explaining something Maria couldn't understand. The woman, after giving Maria a once-over, walked away.

"What did you say to her?" Maria asked.

"I just told her we were looking for some everyday makeup for you."

"She didn't seem too thrilled I was with you," Maria blurted out. "Are you that well known?"

"While Jung-hyun talked me up like I'm a big star, I'm not really. I was surprised she knew who I was. I've only gotten small roles or second leads."

"Second leads?"

"To put it bluntly, the guy who doesn't get the girl," he laughed deprecatingly.

"Hey, but you get roles. Look at it this way. You could be second lead, or you could be nothing. And while your tyrannical work ethic is ridiculous when it comes to me learning a whole language for all of a month, I can see it being beneficial in pushing yourself to getting that lead role one day."

"What's with the inspirational speech?" he questioned.

"Fine, I'll keep my mouth shut," she huffed and started to walk away.

"No, no. That's not...미안해요...that's not how I meant—" He was trying to apologize when the woman came back with a small basket full of makeup.

"What is all that?" She looked at the ridiculous amount of makeup, face washes, and even weird-looking cloths that supposedly were meant to sit on your face. The woman held out the large basket for Maria to grab. She wanted to mention that she was only in Korea for a month, not a year.

"It's what you'll need." He nodded to the woman, agreeing to take it all.

"That's ridiculous! And you shouldn't pay for all of that," she complained, walking up to the counter and looking at all the stuff being rung up. "I don't need all this."

The woman looked at her with wide eyes, clearly confused as to what Maria had said. *Shit.* Maria looked around and saw Lee Hwan Soo taking his time walking up to the counter.

"Can you tell her I don't need all of this?" Maria asked.

Korean Vocabulary:

얼마예요? – ulmayaeyo?- how much?

오만 원- ohman won- 50,000 won (roughly $50 US dollars)

감사합니다- kamsahabnida- thank you

됐어요- dwassoyo- forget it or don't worry about it

Chapter 10 (열)

When he'd first entered the story and turned to tell her not to worry about money, he was surprised by the way her bottom lip pouted and her cheeks flushed from the slight chill outside. She looked downright sexy and he couldn't take his eyes off her. And then she threw him for a loop with her positive outlook on his career. So when she asked him for his help, he almost gave in but remembered the whole point of the excursion was to show her she needed to know the language.

"I believe you should know how to say that." He bowed to be face-to-face with her.

"Come on, Lee Hwan Soo-씨. You can't be that serious about this," she grumbled, and like a child throwing a tantrum, lightly stomped her feet.

"Oh, but I am. What did you call it? 'Tyrannical work ethic'?" He smirked, crossing his arms over his chest.

"Fine. Then I'll take none of it." She grabbed the bin back from the lady and started to walk around the shop.

"What? You need that stuff." He grabbed her wrist and pulled her back from the cosmetics counter. He was stronger than even he anticipated and she ended up face-planting hard into his chest.

"OW!" When she pushed away from him, she stumbled, which made him reach out, wrapping his arm around her waist, pulling her back into him.

Time felt like it was moving in slow motion. He looked down to see her slowly looking up. She held her nose gently, but as they both looked at each other, he could feel that heartbeat in his chest that he thought could never be felt again. Just having her close to him, up against his chest, made him want to protect her, care for her, and even the scariest thought, love her.

Suddenly there was a hard push on his chest and time resumed its normal pace as they separated. Coming back to reality, he watched as she rubbed her nose. "At this point you're paying to get my nose fixed."

"Here in Korea that's a cheap fix," he laughed, grabbing the bin back from her and walking back to the cashier. "You're not putting any of this back."

"If you broke my nose—"

"I didn't, so calm down. Let me get this stuff for you and we can get out of here." He watched the woman quickly begin to ring up the items. Most likely so that Maria couldn't grab them again.

"You act like you're the boss of me." Maria crossed her arms, still throwing her fit.

"For the next month, I am." He reached out with his finger lifting her chin so they made eye contact. He knew he shouldn't have done it. When he had touched her before they left, his finger didn't want to leave that soft skin of hers. He knew the second he saw the look in her eyes he shouldn't have made the move again. It wasn't anger or annoyance in her eyes, it was guilt.

Did she feel bad for not learning? Or was it because he was buying her all the makeup? Maybe both?

He dropped his finger from her velvety soft skin and paid the cashier quickly.

His finger was slender and long and had traced along her chin, causing her mouth to go dry and in between her thighs to grow wet. She wasn't a fan of the fact that he was able to cause such a reaction. She was mad at herself for reacting at all.

When they finally wrapped up shopping she had four or five bags filled with makeup and clothes. And everywhere they went, he refused to help her with even the basic of words. She instead would just quickly pick things and put them on the counter, keeping her distance from any salesperson and avoiding all types of communication. At one point, she even pretended she was deaf. Not a highlight in her life.

Walking out of the last shop, Lee Hwan Soo looked at his watch.

"Perfect timing. Dinner with Val and Jung-hyun is in a half hour," he stated matter-of-factly.

"I didn't know about this." Maria was still feeling flustered after the last cashier kept trying to put extra things in her bags, repeating the word "service" like that would help Maria understand.

"Since you've been here, what exactly have you known?" he jabbed but with a smile, which she understood meant he wasn't trying to be malicious.

She couldn't even argue with him. From everything she experienced that day, she knew nothing. She was in a whole new world where she was the outcast, and not everyone was going to take it easy on her just because she was naïve. Lee Hwan Soo had been right not to help her. It was a wakeup call.

"잘했어요." He pulled her out of her thoughts with an unknown term, making it even more clear she needed to learn the language. She was about to admit defeat, call him a jerk and say she would study hard, and then he spoke again.

"You did well today," poured out of the magical mouth of the pain in the ass she was contemplating.

"What?"

He had done nothing but torture her and complain about her incompetence. Now he was giving her a compliment.

"I put you through hell. You hadn't learned all you should've. I'm big enough to admit that what you did today was mildly impressive. You were resourceful and made it through the day and to top it off, it was done without either one of us killing each other. 잘했어요."

"I'm shocked on that last point," she laughed, relieved. "But I don't think I deserve any credit." She felt so crappy for acting like such a bratty child. "I'm sorry I didn't finish the chapter. And I'm sorry I've been resistant. I think, like you, I expected to spend time with my best friend and it got taken away from me."

"That sounded sincere," he laughed.

"It was, you ass." She jokingly pushed him and suddenly they were laughing in unison as they walked down the street.

"Apology accepted." He smiled as he took several of the bags from her hands in a sign of peace and civility. "I hope you finish chapter one."

She was surprised by his kindness. It even caused her heart to do a weird kind of jump.

"I will have it done by tomorrow morning," she said, saluting.

"Great! Add chapter two and we will stay on track." He sped his walking pace up.

"WHAT?!"

Korean Vocabulary:

잘했어요 -jalhassoyo- good job, you did well

Chapter 11 (열하나)

They arrived at the restaurant and saw through the large front opening that Val and Jung-hyun were already sitting at a table. The place was both indoor and outdoor at the same time. While it had glass windows, they were pulled off to the side like large sliding doors so that the heat from what looked to be indoor grills mixed with the cooling night air. Whatever was cooking on those grills was making her mouth water. While her stomach growled, there was one glaringly obvious issue.

"I'm not the only one who finds eating with them odd, right?" She stared at the happy couple, Val play hitting Jung-hyun's shoulder as he whispered, most likely, sweet nothings. While it was romantic, Maria felt a pang of jealousy toward her happily coupled-up friend.

It wasn't like she had never been a third wheel. But when the only people she knew in the whole city were the people she would be eating every meal with for a whole month, the third wheel loneliness hit like a truck.

"뭐?" he asked, following her line of sight to their friends.

"Well, them all loved up, and us...well, insanely far from that."

She looked over to him as he continued to watch their friends with a smile of total happiness and even the same kind of envy she had for them.

"I didn't think about it," he shrugged pulling open the door for himself.

She rolled her eyes, following after him. Val and Jung-hyun waved the two over standing to bow before the four took seats around the circular grill top table.

"How was your day?" Val asked, but Maria could tell she was nervous asking. Being best friends, Val knew how Maria could be. Especially in the company of someone she was not a fan of.

"Fine. I had to pick up a few things I forgot and Lee Hwan Soo-씨 helped." Maria kept herself calm as she lied. But was it really a lie? He did help her realize that she needed to learn the language or she was going to be totally lost for the next month.

Jung-hyun's ears perked up at the sound of them actually getting along. "Really? 그 남자? Helped?"

She nodded as she opened the menu, trying to hide her reddening face. And once she saw the menu she felt the heat even more. Knowing the alphabet didn't help at all. Hoping she could piggyback off someone's order, she saw Val and Jung-hyun were back in their World Of Love and Lee Hwan Soo had already closed his menu.

"Do you know what you're getting?"

"Yes, I come here often. I always get the same thing." He crossed his arms

"Why?" It wasn't the question she meant to ask, but it was what came out.

"뭐?" He tilted his head to the side like a puppy.

"Why not try something different? Sure, I go to the same places, but I usually try to have different things. There are some things I like more than others but having the same thing over and over again is so boring." She cringed at the thought of being so consistent. As she continued looking at him, his eyes appeared to glaze over and his mouth hung open, similar to when they had walked into the cosmetics shop.

"What? I put some of the makeup on...did it smudge?" She touched her face, worried.

As she rummaged through her bag for a mirror, he finally responded, "Your makeup is fine." He cleared his throat and continued, "I will argue that having something you like and can enjoy over and over is not a bad thing. Change is all good and dandy, but consistency can also be rather comforting." He looked over at her with a crinkled face and a small smile as he said, "This has weirdly caused me to understand you."

"Huh?"

He didn't have time to answer as the waiter came over to take their order. After everyone else gave their orders, they looked to her and she shook her head, dipping it gently and handing him the menu.

"왜 안 먹어?" Val asked, worried why her friend hadn't ordered anything.

"Ummm...I had a really big lunch when we went out," Maria lied. Even though she wasn't sure of the question being asked, she could understand her friend's concern. When no one questioned her, she figured that her answer was correct.

Val nodded, clearly believing the lie, and continued her lovey stares at Jung-hyun.

A shadow moved swiftly toward her, covering her face with the drink menu, and that deep sensuous voice that made her clench her legs together whispered, "You were able to figure out what Maria said?"

"I just kind of figured she was asking about my lack of appetite." She shrugged.

"Close. I will give it to you. But you didn't eat lunch. I was with you all day. Why'd you lie?" he questioned.

How could such an annoyingly temperamental man's voice cause goosebumps and shivers down her spine?

"Because I didn't finish chapter one."

Korean Vocabulary:

그 남자– gu namja – this guy

왜 안 먹어? – wae an mogo? – Why aren't you eating?

Chapter 12 (열둘)

H er face spoke volumes more than her simple statement. Her eyes had lost their twinkle. The corners of her mouth dropped to a frown, and she swallowed hard, letting out a silent but very deep exhale of frustration. She wanted to cry, and he knew it was partially his fault.

When the bright red soups, still boiling in their black stone bowl came to the table and the meats were placed on the grill, he watched her eyes dance with intrigue. The small fire in the middle of the table reflected in her eyes. She was like a child seeing something for the first time and it even made him feel like a child again.

"밥먹자!" He clapped his hands together and began hungrily looking at what he would make first.

"형, did you—" When he looked over to see his best friend already feeding his fiancée, he came to the conclusion that Maria had been right. Being there was awkward. And when he looked at Maria to say something to her, she still seemed entranced by the food and he didn't want to ruin that joy for her.

She chose to eat nothing, not even when he offered her a neatly wrapped piece of meat in lettuce with 쌈장 sauce and garlic, but she politely declined, keeping up the ruse that she was full. Her constant licking of her lips, the wide eyes and clutching of her stomach were dead giveaways of her lie, but the couple who sat across from them were too into each other to notice or care.

-*-

When they all climbed out of the cab at Val and Maria's apartment building, Val and Jung-hyun continued to stay in their own world, and the awkwardness Maria mentioned was hitting him every time he looked over at the couple.

The two of them stood in silence waiting for the rest of their party to finally separate, when he looked to the side and saw a food cart selling one of his favorite snacks. Looking between Maria, who wasn't even looking at him, and the snack, he smirked and bolted off.

The woman running the stand greeted him and he quickly ordered, "붕어빵 주세요."

Her face lit up; clearly it had been a slow night for her, as she quickly packed up piping-hot fish-shaped breads, more than the one he excepted, into a bag.

"잘생겼어요. Just like on TV," she kindly gushed, staring at him. He almost expected little hearts to start popping out of her eyes. He rarely was recognized, and in that day alone he had been noticed twice.

He bowed politely, taking his change from the woman and making his way back over to the group. Maria seemed confused as to why he would come back. Did she honestly think he would just walk off? He lifted the bag to her face, where she examined it questioningly.

"붕어빵. Fish bread. Since you had such a big lunch," he said, playing off her lie, "this is the perfect late-night snack."

"Fish bread?" She visibly cringed.

"It's not actually fish." Rolling his eyes, he pulled one of the warm, doughy fish-shaped breads out of the bag, "See? It's just shaped like a fish. They have different fillings." He saw her about to argue over what they could possibly be filled with. "None of them fish."

He took a bite of the one he had grabbed, puffing out the hot steam from his mouth as the red bean flavor enveloped his mouth. He then handed the bag to her.

"감사합니다." She bowed, taking the bag from him.

"You...y-you," he stuttered in surprise. She had thanked him in perfect Korean.

"I heard you say it to the cab driver, the cashiers, and our waiter. And it was said fairly often in the show Val had me watch last night. I took a shot in the dark. Was I wrong?" Her eyes were losing their sparkle again and he had to stop that from happening. He didn't want to be the cause of her light diminishing.

He reached out and patted her on the head again, noting how amazingly silky her hair felt slipping between his fingers. "No. You were correct. It's a common form of thank you."

"Ready?" Val wove her arm through Maria's, causing him to quickly pull his hand away from her hair.

Maria's eyes never left his—they seemed to be asking him silently if he really was ready to part with her. He didn't have the answer. In fact, he was leaning toward never wanting to leave her side. He felt like he was being put on display more than any time he had stood in front of a camera.

"Oh, is that 붕어빵?!" Val dug out one of the fish shaped objects taking a large bite, completely oblivious to what was happening between Hwan Soo and Maria.

"Hey—" Maria was about to protest when Val shoved the second bite into Maria's mouth. Hwan Soo watched her face go from nervous that he could've been lying to her eyes widening in surprise that the flavor was actually sweet.

"감사합니다 친구야." Val smiled and pulled Maria away toward the apartment entrance.

Korean Vocabulary:
밥먹자- bap mokja – let's eat
붕어빵 주세요 – beong oh bang jusaeyo- fish bread please
잘생겼어요 – jalsaengkyeossohyo – Handsome

Chapter 13 (열셋)

"He bought so many. Guess he assumes I'll be up all night studying that stupid workbook." Maria laughed but behind it she was thankful for the thoughtfulness Hwan Soo had offered.

"Aw, so nice of him," Val gushed. "While you study, wanna watch that drama again? New episode's out tonight!"

"Didn't a new episode come out last night?" Maria asked, confused.

"Oh my dear, you have a lot to learn." Val rushed them into the apartment to explain that K-dramas came out twice a week versus the American schedule of once a week. As they sat on the couch to begin watching the show, Maria heard her phone ring in her purse.

Grabbing her phone, Maria saw her mom's name pop up. And Val instantly ran away knowing from previous experience that when Maria talked to her mom, pillows and other things not as soft might potentially be thrown around the room.

"Yeah, Mom?" Maria rolled her eyes, already dreading what her mother was calling her for. After spending twenty-four years with the woman, Maria knew exactly what her mother was calling to ask about.

"No 'Hi, mom! I miss you!'?" she responded sarcastically.

"Because I've known you my entire life, remember? I know you're calling me for a reason. A reason I can tell I'm not going to like." Maria trudged to the couch and plopped down loudly, getting ready for whatever her mother was going to say. Sitting was probably the best position for her to be in. Less room to pull back her arm if she chose to throw something.

"I'm calling to check up on my daughter in a foreign country. A foreign country that she's never been to, where the culture shock could be pretty hard to handle. That's it. How is it?" The genuine concern in her mother's voice settled the nerves that had built up in Maria, and she almost felt bad for her immediate assumption.

"It's great," she replied with a bitter tone, knowing her mother would get it instantly. "I can't speak the language, I can't write it, I can barely read it, and I've found out that I have to give my maid of honor speech in said language. So, so far the trip is going off without a hitch," she unloaded. She may complain about her mom's constant need to marry Maria off, but sometimes she was the best listener a girl could have.

"I'm sorry to hear that. But I'm sure Val is helping you, right? She wouldn't just throw you into this expecting you to know everything," her mother said, trying to offer a tiny bit of comfort. The best she could for being half a world away.

"She's busy with all the wedding planning. I've been assigned to Lee Hwan Soo-씨." And that's when Maria realized she had fallen into a perfectly laid "Mom is probing for a possible husband" trap.

"Lee Hwan Soo...씨? Who is that?" her mother asked with a lilt of excitement.

"No one, Mom," she huffed internally cursing herself for not seeing where her mother's line of questioning would be going.

"If this person is no one, why does Val trust them enough to 'assign' you to them?" The quizzical way in which she phrased her question caused Maria to sit straight up on the couch with a realization.

I don't think she knows if Lee Hwan Soo is a man or woman.

Maria was praising the gods above for her mother's lack of knowledge of Korea.

And with that in mind, Maria began the easiest fraud ever. "She's just a friend of both Val and Jung-hyun. She offered to help them out since they're stressed with all the wedding things. She's been pretty cool so far and has been giving me Korean lessons. We went shopping for makeup and some new clothes today."

It was a real struggle to keep her laugh from escaping as she pictured the real Lee Hwan Soo dressed as a girl, doing everything they actually did. The funny part was that in her mind, he still looked amazing as a woman. Covering her mouth to make sure she didn't give away the lie that would keep her sanity for the next month, she waited for her mom to start inquiring about the men she had met. Her usual husband-hunt.

"Well maybe she will be able to introduce you to some nice men while you're out with her on these 'lessons'." Her mother always found her way to get to her main objective, or what Maria had started to call her mom's "man objective".

"How?! How are you able to do that?! I'm not here to find a husband. And for the love of all that is holy, if I did in fact meet someone here, how would a relationship like that work? Huh?" She gripped the pillow in her lap tightly.

"I'm sure we could—"

"No! There is no 'we' in this. There has never been a 'we'. I'm not looking for a husband here!" Maria grabbed the heavily sequined throw pillow, which was about to fulfill its name across the room.

"So does that mean when you get home—"

"FINE! FINE!" Maria shouted. "When I get home you can set me up on a million more blind dates, with whomever you want, and I will pick one to marry. Okay?"

"Oh! You better be serious! I will start making plans right now."

Maria could actually hear her mother typing up her dating profile on the computer.

"Yes, I'm serious," Maria sighed, defeated. Val walked out of the bedroom, giving Maria the perfect excuse to cut the conversation short. "Mom, I gotta go, Val and I are about to watch some dramas."

"What's that?"

"Don't worry about it. I will talk to you some other time. Good night." She quickly hung up the phone and huffed.

"Did I hear you call Hwan Soo-ah a girl? 여자?"

"If I told my mom you had left me in the hands of a man, single or not, she would already be on a plane and you know it." As Val nodded in total agreement of said fact, Maria leaned back on the couch, worn out from the brief conversation, and watched the light dance on the wall around the large chandelier hanging from the high vaulted ceiling. Maria still couldn't wrap her head around the whole living separately thing, but the penthouse Jung-Hyun's family had set them up in was forever Instagram worthy.

Val laughed, grabbing the large remote for the TV. "So you ready to watch?"

"I have to study. I got royally screwed today. Lee Hwan Soo-씨 refused to help me at all since I didn't finish the chapter. I now need to finish chapter one and all of chapter two." Staring at the daunting book on the table was causing restlessness through her whole body.

"Jung-hyun told you he was like that," Val joked. "But at dinner you said—"

"I promised you I would be the loving friend, excited about your wedding. I didn't want to cause another scene like at the bar. And to be fair about what Jung-hyun said about Lee Hwan Soo-씨, I'm glad he didn't let me off the hook. I realized how far out of my comfort zone I really am here. And if I don't take the time to learn simple basics, I will probably feel that way this whole month, and I don't want to be that person." Maria grabbed the book, cracking it open on the coffee table with a loud thud.

She looked back to her friend, whose mouth hung open, her eyes staring dead at Maria, seeming to question whether maybe she wasn't the same Maria who had woken up that morning. Maria chose to ignore the incredulous look, nodding to the TV and said, "You can watch. Maybe it will somehow help me stick millions of words in my head."

Korean Vocabulary:

여자- Yoja- woman

Chapter 14 (열넷)

H wan Soo watched as his best friend stood outside the cab looking at the skyscraper apartment building the girls had just gone into. He knew why his buddy was waiting. He hoped his fiancée would come running back to beg him to stay. He may not have seen Jung-hyun a lot but they did talk, and he knew what his best friend wanted and needed. Plus, Jung-hyun always talked about how he would wait outside Val's apartment building. He said that even when they spent the few weeks together in his apartment he would look over at her sleeping, wondering about their relationship and when they would take it to the next level.

"You comin'?" Hwan Soo finally broke the silence.

"Yeah, yeah, just waiting to make sure she got in." He continued staring up at the building. Hwan Soo looked up—there were close to sixty floors and factoring in that one floor was a massive gym, another was a spa, and the top was a pool, he doubted the likelihood of Jung-hyun guessing which windows were his fiancée's.

"Or are you really waiting for her to come running back out that door to ask if you want to come up for some '라면'?" Hwan Soo joked, smirking mischievously. A line Hwan Soo would admit he had used himself to get women come back up to his place for some adult fun. Like in America, it's asking if the person wants coffee, or England if they want some tea. Koreans ask for hot noodles. And that meant sex will inevitably follow.

"You know we've never..." His friend's face was starting to turn a shade of red he had only seen in bowls of 떡볶이 in the street food stalls at night.

"It's why I made the joke. Come on, let's get you home. But one of these days, I'm betting before your wedding, you're going to give in to temptation and eat that 라면." Hwan Soo winked, wrapping his arm around his buddy's shoulder before waving down a new 택시 they could grab home.

"How about we go for another drink instead?" Jung-hyun suggested, his eyes lighting up with hope as he changed the subject to something they both could enjoy, and a childlike glee filled Hwan Soo.

As they climbed into the car, Hwan Soo starting jumping in his seat like a kid who finally got the gift he had been begging for for ages.

"술?술! 빨리 가자!" he exclaimed.

The cab was soon on its way to their old usual haunt when Hwan Soo's phone began buzzing in his pocket. Pulling the phone out, his manager's name lit up the screen, and suddenly the realization of what had happened that morning came flooding back.

He had nearly forgotten the most important news of his career because of a snarky, feisty woman who seemed to slowly consume his mind. But how was he supposed to tell his best friend he could no longer babysit Maria?

It wasn't all babysitting, at least not as much as he thought it would be. And he was surprised at the small phrases she had already been able to pick up.

"형..." Hwan Soo spoke as his manager was sent to voicemail.

"어?" Jung-hyun looked away from the window and to his best friend.

"My manager called me this morning," he started. Jung-hyun waited for his buddy to continue. "Remember I told you I auditioned for a lead role in a drama? And how I didn't think I would get the part because no one's ever given me a lead role before?"

"And I told you not to be so negative." Jung-hyun clapped his hand on his best friend's shoulder in an act of comradery.

"I got it."

"어?!" Jung-hyun shouted and soon his shock was overtaken by joy. "That's amazing! Congrats! 축하한다! When do you start filming?"

"Not sure but my manager just called and has now texted me to call back as soon as possible." He was turning his phone anxiously between his hands.

"Call him!" Jung-hyun was speaking with as much enthusiasm as Hwan Soo had when he first heard he got the part. His nervousness of telling his friend was replaced with the same initial excitement.

He dialed quickly and his manager answered in a worried tone. "Hwan Soo-a..."

That tone was not a good thing. "Did they revoke their offer?"

"No...worse," his manger said with apprehension.

"What could be worse?" Hwan Soo looked to Jung-hyun, who had the same confused expression.

"They announced who you would be working with." Hwan Soo was getting to the point where the suspense his manager constantly seemed to speak with was no longer appreciated.

"딱말해!" He didn't mean to shout but he was getting antsy.

"It's Kim Hae So." His manager spoke so quickly that Hwan Soo thought, actually prayed, he misspoke.

No. No. No. He lost all control of his motor skills and dropped the phone onto the seat. Not her. Of all people, why was it her?

"야! 너 괜찮아?!" Hwan Soo could hear his friend asking if he was okay, but he couldn't respond. His body had given up. Her? Her?! Jung-hyun picked up the phone to try to find out what had caused Hwan Soo to simply stare into the back of the driver's seat. "여보세요? 어...어...어...어?!?!"

Jung-hyun's expression was now very similar to Hwan Soo's. Mouths hung open, eyes unblinking, bodies unmoving. After hanging up the phone, they slowly just turned to each other and said nothing, but both were thinking the same thing.

Why her?

～

After they each downed about two bottles of soju, Hwan Soo finally felt able to talk.

Leaning back on the large deep-gray velvet couch, he looked to his friend and spoke low and slow. "Kim Hae So..."

They both looked around the fairly dead bar, scared she might pop out if he said it too loudly. Luckily the bar was like a speakeasy and they'd entered through what looked to be a small fruit stand that had a hidden door in one of the refrigerators. A short stairwell led up to the small bar, but the back wall was all windows looking out to a little garden, making the place look much more open and comfortable. They discovered the place through a celebrity friend of theirs who loved to go out but hated to be found. It soon became the place they chose to go together whenever they had the chance.

"Kim Hae So..." Jung-hyun repeated and added, "is your co-star."

"Kim Hae Shhoo is my co-shtar who I have to 'love'." Hwan Soo slurred and as he spoke the word "love", he felt his stomach churn. He needed more alcohol. And fast.

"저기요," he raised his hand to grab the bartender's attention, " 소주 더 주세요."

"네," the man behind the fine dark wood bar counter responded as he grabbed the items ordered.

"The same Kim Hae So who broke your heart seven months ago?" Jung Hyun said in a monotone voice as he stared out the window at the few large-leafed plants that were lit by small spotlights.

"The very shame." While he tried desperately not to slur, the word "shame" seemed to fit his ex very well. It was a shame she had ever been in his life outside of the capacity of co-stars.

"Was that ever released to the press? Did they do this as a huge publicity thing? How are you feeling right now? Because I feel like I'm about to lose my mind and I never even met her. Do you think you can handle working with her?" Jung-hyun started breathing quickly, followed by a quick shot of soju to try to calm himself down.

"I'm a professional." Hwan Soo slurred, cracking open the third bottle of soju. "This wash bound to happen. I didn't think it would it would happen sho shoon. I'm not sure how I feel." His words were jumbling together, and the shock was finally starting to wear off. "As for the pressh. They never knew we were dating. They didn't care, I'm a nobody. They won't be able to report a breakup or 'potential rekindling'." He squirmed at even the thought.

He hated her. There were few people in the world he hated, and she was one of them. There was no kind way to put it. And he didn't think he needed to be kind to the woman who left him because his star power wasn't growing fast enough for her, and so she slept with his lead co-star on another drama. She was vile, and having to feign love was going to be the real test of his acting skills.

SLAM! Jung-hyun slammed his third empty soju bottle down on the table, causing Hwan Soo to nearly fall off his stool. How did he drink that bottle so fast? When he looked to his friend, he saw a mischievous look he hadn't seen in years. A look he knew all too well was probably going to get Hwan Soo, or possibly both of them, in trouble.

"You're not going to like my idea..." Jung-hyun started.

"If it causes me to end up in jail, you're right." Hwan Soo poured himself a shot, thinking Jung-hyun had had enough.

"Maria could help," Jung-Hyun said quickly and moved away from the hand he presumed Hwan Soo was about to beat him with.

"You're right. I don't like the idea and yeah, I can see myself ending up in jail." He had sobered up instantly at the sound of Maria's name.

"Hear me out, okay? She can be bene-bene-beneficial to you." Jung-hyun waved one of the bright green bottles around like it was a magical wand.

"How?" Why Hwan Soo asked baffled even him.

"You're about to be taken way more seriously as an actor. You've finally got a lead role. People are going to be paying attention to see what you do, where you eat, what you're wearing, and who you associate with. If the world is focused on you and a mystery girl, they won't even question a relationship with...blegh...I can't say her name anymore. It may cause me to vomit." He burped, at least Hwan Soo hoped it was just a burp.

"Are you hearing yourself? You want me to use your future wife's best friend as a publicity stunt." Hwan Soo had passed sober midway through Jung-hyun's little plot. He was now clear and level-headed while his friend continued his insane thought process.

"I wouldn't say 'use'." Jung-hyun cringed, making Hwan Soo recognize this all-too-similar idea. It was how Val and Jung-hyun started their relationship.

"But it's what you're saying," Hwan Soo said truthfully. "I get that it miraculously worked out for you. I am truly happy for you, but this is Maria and me we are talking about. The woman hates me. If I started pretending to be nice to her, she would be suspicious. Hell, I would." Hwan Soo and Maria may have made a positive step to becoming civil toward each other that day, but it was most definitely not leading up to them becoming anything past friends. He may have found her attractive, but any man would.

"Didn't you just buy her 붕어빵? You're already playing the part. Think about it, Hwan Soo-a. Dress her up, smile, make it look like you're having a great time with her, and people won't wonder about that other woman. That will give you attention, which then gives your drama attention. In fact, you'll make people pay less attention to

Hae So by keeping more people focused on you and what you're doing." Jung-hyun's mischievous glimmering eyes telegraphed to the entire bar that he was loving his idea.

"It will put Maria in the public eye. She hasn't agreed to any of this." Why was he even arguing the logistics of Jung-hyun's insanity?

Maybe because weirdly, it wasn't a half bad idea. As crazy as it sounded, Maria could help Hwan Soo. Whether he wanted to admit it or not. And as much as they argued, they did seem to become more civil over the course of the day. They were even able to have a laugh or two together. So what's to say she wouldn't be a good pawn?

"Keep her face hidden. Hello, we are in a country that is filled with both germophobes and semi-toxic air days. You have an entire drawer in your walk-in closet filled with high-end masks. Give her one or two and make sure she wears them when you're out together." Jung-hyun was making sense like he was always able to do when he planned his schemes.

"You're serious about this?" Hwan Soo had to make sure that what he was hearing wasn't just a total drunken joke.

"I'll talk to Valerie about it, but I'm sure it will be no problem. Especially since you're a man, and from what I've heard about Maria's mom, apparently you might be helping her get a reprieve from the constant literal man hunt. Seriously, if you'd heard some of the stories Valerie has told me, you would be doing this for Maria's sake."

Maybe he was right and Maria could actually help him. His mind raced with thoughts of how poorly this plan could go, but then his mind stopped on Kim Hae So. That woman who tortured him. Ruined him. And like that, Hwan Soo made his decision.

"Fine. But you need to get the okay from Valerie and once you do, I will talk to Maria about—"

"Best keep this a secret from Maria."

"What? Why?"

"Valerie tells me she's not the best at keeping a secret...especially when she's been drinking. And since we tend to drink...every night...

loose lips concept, understood?" He put his finger to his overly puckered lips.

"형, as much as I'm not the biggest fan of the woman, I don't feel comfortable using her...even more so without her knowing. At least my few one-night stands knew I was using them for one thing and one thing only." Hwan Soo ran his hands through his hair several times, imagining what would happen if or when Maria found out what was going on.

"Again, we need to come up with a word other than 'use'. It'll be fine. When have my plans ever gone wrong?" Jung-hyun brushed it off, pulling out his phone to text Val the plan, which she was shockingly all for. She said Maria would most likely be oblivious to him "making moves" and that if Maria's mom were to see anything in the news, she would get quite the shock since Maria had just told her mother Hwan Soo was a woman just to keep her from having to answer more questions.

"Even if you guys think this is okay, I will throw you and your fiancée under the bus if anything goes wrong," Hwan Soo said as he decided to find a bit more solace from the new bottles of soju that had appeared on the table.

Korean Vocabulary:

라면- ramyun- ramen

떡볶이- ddeokboki – a spicy rice cake dish

탁시- takshi- taxi

어 – oh- the word that can mean so many different things. It can mean yes, sure, of course, what?!, etc.

술 – sul – alcohol

빨리 가자 – bailee kaja – let's hurry (literal: hurry go)

축하한다 – chukhanda – congrats

딱 말해 – dak malhae- just say it

너 괜찮아 – no gwenchana – you okay?

저기요 – chogiyo – excuse me

소주 더 주세요 – soju doh joosayyo – more soju please

Chapter 15 (열다섯)

M aria woke up to no sounds or smells coming from the kitchen. It was silent. Eerily so. She waited in bed for someone to come and wake her up. A certain annoyingly handsome someone who worked on a schedule so organized that even being behind by a minute would drive him up a wall.

But no one came. Deciding to climb out of bed to find out what was going on, she walked into the living room to see Val sitting on the couch, hair untamed, still in her pj's, digging into a massive bowl of cereal while watching what looked to be another one of the dramas she loved. That's the Val Maria grew up with.

"No bowl for me?" Maria joked and saw her friend jump a bit from the sudden extra voice in the room.

Val lifted up a second spoon for her friend. "I thought we could share."

Maria giggled, running over to the couch to dig in.

"So why am I getting the privilege of not only seeing you here at this hour, but seeing you not dressed to the nines and cooking a five-course breakfast?"

"I only do that when Jung-hyun is coming over. I watched the women in the dramas always wearing makeup and being dressed well even when they wake up. I started to want to be that well dressed and ready to go for the day. It really does get me excited for what they day will bring. But sometimes I like just being a lazy bum and just sitting on my couch all day. Plus, the boys went out last night after they left here and apparently drank a little more than they could handle. Jung-hyun sounded like he was on the verge of death when he called this morning," Val explained before shoveling another spoonful of cereal in her mouth.

"Oh, do you want to go and check on him?" Maria was happy to have the rare time with her old best friend, but she also knew that a hungover fiancé should probably be checked up on.

"Nah, he and Hwan Soo-a are headed to some meeting about something...he started to trail off. Best man stuff, maybe? I don't know, but guess who gets me all to herself today?" Val smiled, taking another huge mouthful of cereal.

"So they're too hungover for him to see you, but not too hungover to go to some meeting?" Maria's suspicions rose.

"걱정마, Maria. This is weirdly the everyday life of Seoul. I told you it's a twenty-four-hour kinda place. I'm assuming they're doing some groom-best man stuff. They haven't seen each other in—"

"Four years, yeah, I know." Maria was now the one to stuff her mouth full of cereal.

Val choked, coughing out, "Who told you that?!"

"Lee Hwan Soo-씨. I don't think he meant to, but one of the many times we've argued since I've been here for a solid two days now, I told him how I hadn't seen you in months and he pulled the four-year trump card."

Remembering that brought back the face of Lee Hwan Soo. He was hurt by the fact he wasn't able to see his friend as planned this trip. He didn't try to hide his disappointment to her but would always put on the happiest of smiles in front of Jung-hyun. He should be allowed to have their time together like she was about to have with Val.

"Well, they can enjoy their day and we can enjoy ours. What did you want to do?" Val smiled cheerfully.

Maria thought about it and for some reason the image of the woman at the cosmetics shop getting all giddy about Lee Hwan Soo flashed in her mind.

"Have you watched any of Lee Hwan Soo's dramas?"

Val spontaneously spit a mouth full of cereal back into the bowl, subsequently ending Maria's meal. "You want to watch a drama? Not only that, a drama with Hwan Soo in it?"

Maria shrugged. "While I'm lost for the most part on the drama you're currently watching, I want to see what people see in him that I'm clearly missing. And since you love dramas, and you will probably have to continue running around like a maniac soon, we can have a nice lazy day since we don't know the next time we will get the opportunity during this trip. Besides that, when am I ever gonna be able to say, 'Hey, I know him' again?"

Val continued staring blankly at Maria. It was a surprising suggestion, but she didn't think it was so shocking it left Val speechless.

"What? Why do people keep looking at me like that?" Maria leaned slightly away from Val, looking down at herself to see if something was wrong with her. Lee Hwan Soo had given her a similar look the night before when she had spoken Korean to him.

"Probably because you're surprising us." Val smiled lovingly at her bestie having the best intentions with her statement, although Maria didn't see it that way.

"Surprising?" Maria was offended, moving farther away from her friend.

"Don't take this the wrong way but, I was worried about having you here for the month. Like, you would hate coming here and having to be speed-taught everything. But I can see you trying and I definitely heard you use Korean last night. This place must be rubbing off on you...or is it your instructor who's doing the rubbing?"

Val wiggled her eyebrows suggestively while shimmying her shoulders.

"Don't make me vomit this early in the morning," Maria tossed her spoon into the bowl of cereal she had already given up eating, trying to swallow that last bite before it tried to come back up.

"You spent the whole day with him yesterday. By the time you got to dinner, you seemed to be at least civil, and by the end of the night I would even say friendly when he gave you the붕어빵. Who says you can't be rubbing each other?" Val smirked as she nudged Maria for her answer.

"Civil? Yes. Sexual? Hell freakin' no." She grabbed the bowl so she could make her way over to the kitchen to clean it off and get away from the ideas Val was currently dreaming up in her sex-starved mind. The only problem was she couldn't help admitting, only to herself, she had similar thoughts last night while she lay in bed.

"If me asking to see his drama is about to make us go into some weird conversation about whether I have feelings for a guy who I've known all of two days, we can watch a drama without him. I'll watch whichever one you wanna watch. I just think they will help me learn some more stuff about your future hubby's culture." She quickly cleaned the bowl and then dried it, waiting for the conversation to change before she went back to the couch for more Hwan Soo probing.

"No, no. Since you miss Hwan Soo-a so much, we will get you your fix." Val grabbed the remote and began searching for a show to watch. "Well since he's never had a lead role, you'll have to handle one where he isn't always in a scene."

All of Val's snide remarks were making Maria regret asking for a Lee Hwan Soo drama and clearly they weren't going to end anytime soon, so Maria plopped down on the couch resigned to listening to the jokes.

"Here's his most recent. You're in luck, it's completely subtitled." Val clicked Play and tossed the remote to the side, cuddling up with a pillow, appearing hyped to start a new show.

"No subtitles," Maria commanded.

She could practically hear Val's neck snap as she looked Maria's way. But she had a good reason for the request.

"I won't have subtitles in real life to help me."

Three-and-a-half episodes in and Maria was hooked. The binge was real and she didn't want it to end. She understood why people could be enthralled to the point of forgetting what time or even what day it was. She couldn't understand the language fluently, yet she couldn't look away. Besides all the drama, she loved the clothing, the sets, even the cinematography of the world around the characters was enough to make her never want to peel her eyes away from the TV, but it also made her crave walking out into Seoul to see what the actors were seeing.

"So you're telling me he doesn't get the girl? I'm sorry but that's bull. He's so much better than this other guy. This other guy is such a tool. He's been using her these entire four episodes!" She was pointing to the TV and getting heated about the character's plot lines.

"You're grasping that?" Val handed the bowl of popcorn she had just finished popping to Maria with the largest smile, clearly fangirling over the fact that she and her best friend now had another shared interest.

"I mean yeah. It's obvious. His mannerisms and his clothing really give away the fact that he's some rich tool, and he clearly is speaking down to her instead of seeing her as an equal. You're telling me the guy who's obviously been her friend since they were kids, who obviously had a crush on her since day one and has been nothing but kind is the dude who doesn't get the girl? Are all the dramas like this?" She jumped up and began pacing in front of the screen, still unable to peel her eyes away, needing to know what was going to happen next.

"No. There are all kinds of dramas. Murder, mystery, action, comedy and so on. They cover all the same bases as our TV shows do. But the one thing that is hugely different from us is that sex is almost always taboo. Some might imply the act happened, some may even push the envelope with the couple tumbling into bed, but a steamy kiss is about as far as most get," Val explained as she stretched, lying on the couch to continue watching.

"For real?"

"진짜." Val smiled, knowing Maria had heard the word several times and could pick up what she meant. "But I think that is the most fascinating part. After watching these shows for so long now, the sexual tension of a simple wrist grab, a tug to pull one to safety, a hug to comfort throughout the several episodes leading to a kiss sends shivers down your spine in anticipation. And when they finally kiss? Forget it!" Val let out a loud moan of pleasure.

"Jesus," Maria stopped her pacing to watch her friend, who was clearly having a moment.

"Trust me, Maria, you're already on your way to feeling this way too." Val smirked. "And now you'll have something to talk to Hwan Soo about."

Before Maria could answer, she heard the front door keypad being tapped.

"The fiancé must be here." Maria smiled as she plopped back down to watch the TV, making sure she didn't miss a moment.

Val sat straight up and looked at the clock. "Oh shit."

She tossed the bag of popcorn to Maria, throwing off the blanket she had snuggled into as she bolted to the bedroom.

"You know he's going to have to see you in all your basic glory one of these—"

"Have you seriously not changed out of your pajamas all day?" The judgmental voice of the boy she was rooting for in the drama spoke from behind her.

"Good afternoon, Maria." Jung-hyun bowed behind him, ignoring his friend's rude statement.

"안녕하세요," she said, ignoring Lee Hwan Soo's rude comment and focusing on greeting Jung-hyun. Both mouths dropped open with surprise and when she looked back to the one she chose to not greet and said, "Lee Hwan Soo-씨, why is it you never get the girls in your dramas? I mean, you're not being yourself, you're actually a nice dude, so why is it the characters you play never get their love?" She snorted at her own insult while tossing popcorn to her mouth and missing. It fell down her shirt and against her chest.

"무슨—" He stopped mid-sentence when he looked past her to the TV. He reached over the couch to grab the remote, shutting the drama off immediately.

"야!" she yelled, trying to get the remote back. His eyes went wide with surprise but he was still faster than her and pulled the large wand-like remote farther away from her. But that didn't stop her from trying to get it back. As they continued to play the cat-and-mouse game, she huffed loudly.

"너 미쳤어?!" she yelled as she continued to battle him for possession.

"네?" he said, stopping the light play fight, only to look at her with shock and awe.

Thinking she had said something wrong she said slowly, "너... 미...쳤어?"

"Holy crap." Val had come out of the bedroom dressed to perfection. Maria was shocked at how fast she had become at getting herself all gussied up.

"You're one fast learner, Maria." Jung-hyun applauded, looking her up and down, clearly impressed.

"What do you mean?" she asked him, not grasping why everyone had chosen to look at her with incredulous faces.

"Do you know what you said?" Val asked.

"From context of the show, I gauged that it meant something about being crazy. When Lee Hwan Soo-씨's character came to help out the girl from the advances of the main dude who grabbed her in the club, she yelled at you because she knew that the guy was her boss and you potentially ruined her job..." she explained. Everyone's eyes almost fell out of their sockets.

They all seemed frozen in time. Like what she was saying was not common knowledge. She was confused as to why they seemed so surprised she was learning what she was asked to learn. Had she gotten it wrong?

"You've grasped a lot in two days, Maria. That isn't super common," Val said, walking over to the group.

"Well then you should congratulate me...by giving me back the remote!" She turned it back to the situation at hand and latched onto Lee Hwan Soo's wrist. Unfortunately, she lost her balance on the couch and felt her body falling forward. She braced for a hard impact on the marble floor but it never came. When she opened her eyes she saw only black, and when she took a breath, a manly musk scent wafted into her nose. She knew she wasn't on the floor; she was on top of Lee Hwan Soo. Moving her head up a bit, her eyes met those she had expected to see. Maria felt her heart doing that weird hop thing she had felt after he had given her the fish bread.

Like in a drama, she felt everything was in slow motion. She was trying to assess the situation as his arm wrapped her up in a strong hold against his chest. Their eyes continued to just watch each other, wondering who would make the first move. But the world came back into focus when a throat cleared from behind the couch.

His arm that had been wrapped around her waist pushed her, causing her to roll off him as he quickly jumped to his feet and adjusted his clothing.

"You can watch when I'm not around," he said, placing the nearly forgotten remote on the coffee table above her and then fumbling with his sweater. From her angle on the ground she was able to see right up under said item of clothing and was not surprised to see the very well-defined chest she had felt under her only seconds before as it tensed to push her off him. But seeing it was a whole different beast.

"He doesn't like seeing himself." Jung-hyun interrupted her lust-filled gaze. "He gets nitpicky about how he could do better," Jung-hyun explained, but something in his face was curiously watching her and Lee Hwan Soo.

"But the drama was getting good! How can you ask me to pause my binge like that? That's cruel." Maria pouted like a child hoping that she would get her way.

"I've created a drama monster," Val laughed, grabbing her purse off one of the many hooks by the door.

"Where are you going?" Maria asked, popping up from the floor and skipping over to her bestie.

"We're having dinner with his mother tonight," Val explained.

"But…" Maria had been enjoying her time with the Val she grew up with. But there was a new part in her best friend's life Maria was realizing she needed to learn to accept. "Never mind. Have fun."

They all bowed and once again Maria was alone with Lee Hwan Soo. When she saw him standing by the couch looking between the TV and her, she already knew what he was going to say.

"Yeah, yeah, 'shower and get dressed', I know, I know." She waved her hand as she finally climbed up from the floor to make her way to the bathroom.

"Did you really learn what you said from watching the drama?" He didn't even acknowledge her mocking.

"I guess," she shrugged, "it's not like I would know it from anywhere else. The book you gave me is still on the basics of forming sentences." She ran over to the book and tossed it back at him. "I got as much as I could done. Since we went out to dinner late last night and today Val and I watched the drama, I didn't finish but—"

"It's fine," he said, cutting her off, which made her stop dead in her tracks.

"What?" She needed to make sure she heard him correctly. This couldn't be the same guy she had spent the whole day prior with who wouldn't let a single little mistake pass.

"I said it's fine." He closed the book, tossing it onto the couch.

"Are you the same Lee Hwan Soo-씨 from yesterday? Who

tortured me for not finishing my work? Do you have a super-under-standing twin who took your place for the day? Or maybe you're still drunk from last night? Val told me you had a pretty wild boy's night. I'm sure you enjoyed your time with your bestie." She walked over to him to quickly inspect his clothing and facial features. Whoever this person was, he looked and dressed just like the Lee Hwan Soo she had known the past couple of days.

He put his hand on her shoulder, pushing her away with an eye roll and a hot puff of minty air. Afraid she was about to lose her balance, she gripped his large knit sweater.

"I noticed something," he continued, ignoring her sarcasm as her hands fell away from his body. "You grasp things by context. This book won't help you as much as being put into situations. You learned 가자 from hearing it in context, same with 감사합니다. Even your bowing was all learned from just noticing what's going on around you. So that's how we're going to go about this from now on." He walked around the couch and fell onto the cushions with a loud plop.

"So..." She was hoping that she was following his train of thought.

"If dramas help you learn faster, we will watch a drama and then take you out into the world to practice."

Her eyes lit up as she jumped over the couch, landing next to him. She grabbed her blanket and pillow and wiggled to make a comfortable butt impression in the cushion. She was about to start up the show when he grabbed the remote from her.

"Just not mine." He turned the TV back on and began scanning through genres.

"But...I liked yours. You're a good actor. You had me rooting for you, and I know you." He ignored her comment yet again, raising one of those sexy eyebrows and waiting for her to concede.

"Fine, fine. I'll finish yours on my own time, so just pick whatever you want to watch." She huffed, leaning back onto the plush cushion like a pouting child.

"아이구." He lifted his hand to rub her head, but his fingers got caught in her hair, so he began slowly stroking her hair. Those goosebumps that prickled up when his breath whispered across her neck the night before made a reappearance. And since he wasn't paying much attention to what he was doing, she dipped her head closer to continue feeling the sensation a little bit longer.

"Ah, this is a good one." He smiled, pulling his hand away from her as the opening credits of a new show started playing.

"Hold up." She sat up, recognizing one of the actors.

"잠깐만요," he said calmly, clearly reiterating her sentiment in Korean.

"Yeah, sure." She waved her hand to stop him from making her lose her train of thought. "That guy...he's the one in your drama."

"맞아요." He reached over, patting her head once again. This was clearly his way of telling her that she was doing something correct. And every time his hand came in contact with her hair, she noticed his touches became slower, turning into what felt like small pets. His fingers once again tripped through the few strands of the hair falling out of her messy bun.

"He's a great actor—" he began.

"Extremely handsome. I wouldn't kick him out of bed." Suddenly her hair was being pulled. "Ow!"

"I'm sure many women would agree with you," he said coldly.

"Introduce me sometime." She nudged him jokingly.

"Shh, this is a great show. You should watch and learn," he hushed her abruptly. Was he jealous? She watched him as he leaned his arms on his legs, his palm holding his chin up as a finger traced his bottom lip. It was as if he was studying the other actor. Taking mental notes on how he may portray a similar character. She could see the ambition he held for his job, and she envied him. She had never felt that kind of drive in any of the countless jobs she'd held.

And while she continued to watch his attentiveness, her mouth went dry as she pictured those lips he had been rubbing on hers. Tracing down her throat, sucking gently on her collarbone. When she realized how insane her thoughts were, she shook her head to rid the thought and moved off to the corner of the couch as she started paying more attention to the show. She became super focused, using everything in her power, both mentally and physically, to ignore how alone she was with Lee Hwan Soo.

Korean Vocabulary:

걱정마 – gokjongma – Don't worry

무슨 – moo sun – it's kind of like "what are you-" it's a cut off question.

너 미쳤어 – no michosso – are you crazy?

아이고 – aigoo – kind of like sheesh. it can be used in both a judgmental way or a loving term of endearment.

잠깐만요 -jamkkanmanyo – wait

맞아요 – majayo – correct

Chapter 16 (열여섯)

He was right. The show was amazing. A totally different kind of story than the light fun and fluffy one Lee Hwan Soo was in. It was a powerful tale of family and friends, and how every choice can change all of the lives in the group. Four episodes in and she had tears running down her cheeks as one of the main characters had her heart totally crushed by one of the male leads who was her best friend. Maria was trying to hide her sniffles as much as possible, but because he always seemed to be aware of her actions, a handful of tissues was in her face.

"감사합니다," she choked out.

The credits rolled and a new preview started playing. Reaching up to stretch, her eyes landed on the time.

"어머! It's eleven o'clock! I've been watching dramas all day! I've learned nothing. How am I supposed to write this speech by the end of the month?" Her heart started racing as panic set in on the fact that she had done nothing productive all day.

"괜찮아요?" he asked randomly.

"Yeah. I'm fine. Just a bit panicked. What's with the random question?" She ran a hand over her hair.

"그럼, 누나—" He gently smacked his legs as if about to stand, but she cut him off angrily.

"누나? I'm not your누나! I thought you said we weren't close enough to be dropping honorifics. Want me to start calling you 오빠?" *Wait. How the hell did I know all that?* Her mind had processed everything before she even realized it.

"You wouldn't be able to call me오빠 if I call you 누나. They are terms of endearment said to those older than oneself. A male says 누나to an older woman. Whether he is interested romantically or she is simply an older friend. Or it's actually his older sister. 오빠, however, is what women use the phrase to refer to an older male. But you see how you picked some words up? I guess I was right about how you need context more than a textbook." He laughed, falling back onto the couch as he pushed up the sleeves of his sweater. With a genuine smile on his face, his eyes crinkled so that she could barely see them anymore, she saw how proud he was to have figured out a way to get her to learn. It was the most relaxed she'd seen him.

They hadn't spoken since the show started, and his voice was trying to find itself again, much like morning voice without the struggle of waking up—it was sexy. She smiled nervously at his compliment as she also fell back into the cushions of the couch.

"Val is gonna be back soon, and you probably need to get home," she said, trying to make herself feel less awkward about all the nice thoughts she had been having of the man she swore was a total ass.- Maybe it was just sexual frustration. She hadn't had sex in a year. So anyone would do at that point.

"They won't be home for hours. Have you not checked your texts?" He nudged her phone sitting blank-screened on the coffee table.

Pushing aside the snack bags and empty glasses from her raid of the kitchen several episodes ago, she grabbed her phone to see she did in fact have messages.

Two texts from Val read:

Mari! Jung-hyun surprised me with a romantic

after-dinner date. Won't be home until super late. No need to wait up. Ask Hwan Soo-a to order you guys some치맥.

Please don't kill each other. Blood is hard to get out of a white carpet. :*

"치맥...again..." Maria rolled her eyes and tossed the phone onto the couch. "You can go. I'll tell them you were here so Jung-hyun won't be mad, and we dined on the best 치맥 the city has to offer." She bowed and he followed suit. "가세요," she said, waving him to the door.

He hopped up and left with no hesitation. She thought that the sight of him leaving would fill her with instant relief but instead a sharp pain ran through her chest. Why was she so bummed to see him leave so fast? Did he really have that bad of a time with her? She would admit it wasn't an exciting day, simply binge-watching what he literally does for a job, but she thought they had gotten along a little bit better.

After cleaning up all the remnants of her binge snacks, she hopped in the shower to wash away the thoughts of Hwan Soo. Plus she had been in the same clothes since the previous night. And also if she showered at night, she would be able to wake up at the crack of dawn and dress properly for whatever she would face the following day.

As the hot water steamed up the shower and massaged her lazy bones, her mind wandered to Lee Hwan Soo and what he possibly looked like in the shower.

Korean Vocabulary:

어머- omo- OMG

그럼, 누나 – crom noona -well then Noona (we really don't have a term like this in English other than friend but it's a little closer than that so it's hard to define)

오빠 – oppa – similar issue to noona. Older brother but like friend and more than a friend

치맥- chimek – chicken and beer

가세요 – kasaeyo – go

Chapter 17 (열일곱)

H e was excited to be able to get out of the apartment earlier than he expected. Not because he wanted to be away from Maria, which surprised him a rather enormous amount, but after the late-night drinking, and then the contract signing, script pick-up, and his home read through for his drama, his body literally begged for him to sleep. He didn't want to leave. In fact, he wished he had made up an excuse to stay.

When the wind hit his face, he shivered, bundling his thin jacket closer to his frame as he made his way past several food stalls that had large clouds of white steam coming from their tents. Guilt consumed him for not having Maria eat a proper meal before he left. Heaving a large sigh, he stopped walking, looking around at the large orange tents with people sitting around, waiting for the food to warm not only their bodies but their souls, and he made up his mind.

"Crap." He quickly turned around and headed right back up to the apartment, phone to his ear to order food he knew Maria would never have had before.

❧

After receiving the ordered food from the delivery man, he plopped the large blue and yellow plastic container box on the kitchen counter, unpacking the plastic bowls and all the side dishes as he heard the shower shut off. He could make out some light fumbling as well as light humming coming from the bedroom, so he started unwrapping all the food knowing Maria would probably be excited to eat the second she came out. When he heard footsteps coming closer, he smirked, grabbing hold one of the many items of food, excited to see her reaction.

"Since you already had 치맥, I thought you would want to try other delicious delivery food Korea has to offer." When he looked to his side, a damp, chocolate brown haired, flushed, towel that left little to imagination wrapped, Maria, stood frozen. Those wide eyes that he wanted to stare into for hours on end as well as make flutter closed in fits of pleasure were as wide as doe eyes, and her chest was voluptuous, being tightly held to her by her hand's death grip on the towel. He was attracted to her. It was undeniable. And a major problem. He tried to look anywhere other than at her, but it was impossible.

Saying nothing, she turned and made a mad dash back to the bedroom. He couldn't even process what had happened fully before he heard the bedroom door slam. Hwan Soo couldn't get the image of her standing in the kitchen out of his mind. His mind went 18+, picturing her or even him ripping off the towel to reveal her dewy skin that was, in that moment, calling to him. And he couldn't ignore such a call. What straight man could?

She arrived back in the kitchen in a clean pair of bright blue leggings and a white oversized crew neck sweater, taking a seat next to him as they both cleared their throats.

"미안내요." He dipped his head slowly, begging for forgiveness, but even looking at her fully clothed, the image of her nearly naked was unforgettable. It tortured him unforgivingly, and the lack of room he had in his choice of pants.

"Let's just not talk about it. It never happened. But how the hell did you get back in?" She couldn't look at him either as she asked.

"Jung-hyun 형 gave me the key code in case of an emergency. While this wasn't an actual emergency, I felt bad you didn't have anything to eat and if you ratted me out to our friends, I would be in deep shit. I took the risk of letting myself in to bring you some food," he explained, putting down the bowl full of noodles in front of her.

While she said nothing, he saw the quirk of a smile grow on her lips, and a brighter flush rising on her cheeks as she looked at the bowl in front of her. With a raised eyebrow she asked, "What is this exactly?"

"짜장면." He handed her a set of chopsticks which she nervously grabbed, breaking them apart, still unsure of what she was looking at.

"Yeah...that doesn't help me." She began inspecting the noodles.

"You saw them eat it in the drama. It's better you don't know what's exactly in it, but know that it's delicious. Like any takeout or fast food. We even eat it for certain occasions, like a first night in a new apartment or on Black Day," he said as he looked over to see she had lifted up the entire bunch of compacted noodles on her chopsticks.

Rolling his eyes, he instinctively took her plate back and began to pull apart the noodles, letting the blackish brown sauce mix through with the veggies and bits of meat.

"Black Day?" she asked as she watched his hands while he broke apart the noodles.

"So we have Black and White Day. 화이트데이being like your Westerners' Valentine's Day. Filled with all those gross loved-up couples doing gross lovey dove-y things. But while it is a couple's day, it's usually the woman who is buying the chocolates for the guy she likes. Taking charge of her feelings. 블랙데이 is the same day only the month after. When single people, either together or alone, 'celebrate' being single. And짜장면is like the go-to meal since its sauce looks black."

The sloshing of the noodles let him know they were getting coated evenly as he explained his culture.

"That sounds kinda depressing," she grumbled.

"It's actually a lot of fun. My friends and I get together, drink, eat, sometimes hit up a 노래방, and have a laugh." He chuckled, reminiscing about the last time he went out with Jung-hyun on a Black Day singles event. They got so drunk they woke up spooning each other.

"노...래...방?" She squinted trying to figure out what that was but couldn't come up with even the slightest hint about what he was trying to say.

"노래 means song, and 방 means room," he explained.

"Song Room? Do you mean like karaoke?" she questioned

"맞아요." He smiled, handing her back the bowl of perfectly mixed noodles.

"So instead of going on a date with a significant other, you basically go on a large date with all your single friends." She was leaning on the counter, her chin resting in her palm as she learned about the culture.

He appreciated the fact that she had turned over a new leaf and wanted to learn about what his world had to offer.

"I guess." He shrugged, grabbing his bowl. "Are you going to eat or what? I haven't had this in ages and I'm dying to eat. My strict diet needs one cheat day, in my opinion. Just don't tell my manager about this." He smirked, rounding up a large amount of noodles on his chopsticks.

"My lips are sealed." She pursed her lips in exaggeration. Hwan Soo was surprised to see her lick her lips and dig her chopsticks in with childlike enthusiasm.

Slurping it into his mouth, the greasy, salty deliciousness caused him to let out a pleasurable moan. He hadn't had 짜장면 since his manager literally pulled the bowl out of his hands on set a few months prior. When he looked up to see what she thought of the food, he saw her eyes completely focused on him. Noodles held midair in the chopsticks, her mouth open wide, and a blank stare.

"Why are you looking at me like that?" he mumbled out with a mouth full of the fatty noodles.

"For such a handsome face, you are one vulgar eater." She cringed.

"야!" he yelled, sending bits of noodle flying out of his mouth.

She burst out laughing, her brilliant white teeth on display after being hidden behind her sulking lips for most of the time he had been around her. It was such a lighthearted laugh, it even made him smile.

"If only I was one of those people who sends videos to the paparazzi, I would have some amazing dirt on you. Lee Hwan Soo-씨 eats messily and loud." She flashed her hands like an old-timey news reporter talking about a brilliant headline.

She tossed him a napkin and wrapped a large amount of noodles on her chopsticks and brought them to her mouth. She stopped all movement the second the food touched her mouth, looking back down to the bowl with an excitement he had only seen when people really enjoyed what they had eaten. He felt a sense of pride that he made the right decision in coming back to feed her. A larger amount was soon wrapped on her chopsticks and brought to her mouth.

"Oh wow," she moaned with her mouth full of noodles, "this is so amazing!"

He found it endearing how excitedly she was eating, so he reached for his phone and began filming her eat. He could send it to Jung-hyun, showing they could shockingly get along. He was dazed to the point he hadn't realized she was looking at him.

"Hey! What are you doing?" She tried blocking his phone, but he simply found new angles.

"Just making sure you remember how much you enjoyed eating this. See why I ate it so fast?" He wanted to catch her agreement on camera so if she ever tried to argue about it in the future, he would have her words recorded for posterity.

"네, 네." She nodded, continuing to eat and gulping a large amount down.

"You're starting to speak Korean so easily. I didn't think you would be able to even pick up the basics. I underestimated you." He put his phone down, picking up his chopsticks and grabbing the bright yellow pickled radish, tossing it onto her noodles. Her eyes looked at him questioningly, but he nudged for her to eat it before she judged and went back to digging into his own bowl.

"I do have you to thank for most of that, but I also have this thing where I am able to pick things up rather quickly. I think it's why I can't stay at a job longer than a year. I get bored and want something new." She grabbed the yellow semicircle with some of the noodles and once it hit her lips, he saw her appreciation of the tart flavor and loud crunch mixing with the salty soft noodles. She stomped her feet happily against the stool and shimmied in her seat.

She looked behind them and motioned toward the couch. "How about we eat while watching a few more episodes?"

She jumped up from the stool, making her way back to the couch. He really did enjoy watching her walk away. Her hips had a natural sway that made his eyes instantly fall onto her butt as it gently bounced side to side. When she plopped down on the couch, he made his way over as well.

He sat down next to her, when his hand brushed along her thigh unintentionally. There was a tension building in his chest that had caused a sense of nervousness throughout the rest of him. She seemed totally unfazed by the touch and so he played it cool as they both continued to eat their food while enjoying the drama.

After another episode, he started to feel his eyes getting heavy. He knew he was exhausted. His body had been put through worse when he was filming, but sitting next to Maria was comfortable. More comfortable than he anticipated. After his previous night and busy day, eating a heavy and filling meal was getting the best of him. He was trying desperately to keep his eyes open.

His body, on the other hand, wouldn't listen to him, and started relaxing into the comforting pillows on the couch.

Korean Vocabulary:

짜장면 – jjajangmyun – a black bean paste noodle dish. Delicious if we say so ourselves.

화이트데이 – White Day- well Hwan Soo explained it better than we could lol

블랙데이- Black Day – same. Hwan Soo, thanks for explaining.

노래방 – norae bang- karaoke bar

맞아요 – majayo – correct

Chapter 18 (열여덟)

To say she had been mortified to find him in the apartment when she got out of the shower would be...well...a lie. She wasn't all that thrilled that he saw her nearly naked, until she saw how his eyes raked over her. She felt a heat pool below her stomach as she wondered when he had come back and if he heard her humming the theme song to the drama they were watching. The heat had then risen to her cheeks in total embarrassment.

When he handed her the bowl of weird black sauce-coated noodles and they sat on the couch to continue the show, she felt her embarrassment had dissipated and there was a calm between them that she hoped would continue the rest of her trip. But then his hand grazing her leg made her jump in her skin, sending that heat back to her stomach and lower. She tried to play it as cool as she could, not acknowledging that that small area on her thigh was making goose-bumps rise along her entire leg. He hadn't said anything and she went with the idea that it was nothing other than an accident.

After the sixth episode ended, she grabbed their empty food plates and followed Lee Hwan Soo's previous explanation of leaving the large bucket the food was delivered in outside the front door for the delivery man to pick up. No cleanup required on her part. Korea had some cool delivery perks!

Coming back to the living room, she was about to make a remark about how he hadn't cracked a joke about her possibly packing the large bin incorrectly. She noticed he hadn't moved in a bit and when she came around the couch, she saw he was fast asleep. She chuckled at how angelic, one hundred percent at peace he looked. She also admired the angles of his jawline, the slightly longer than average bridge of his nose, and that pale but not sickly complexion that didn't have a single flaw to it. He was handsome.

That was the second time that night she had thought of him in more than just a positive light. She didn't feel the need to wake him and instead grabbed one of the large blankets lying on the other couch.

She didn't care that he crashed on the sofa. She was feeling the effects of the food as well and was about to ask him to leave so she could go to sleep anyway. Walking back over to him, she gently placed the blanket on him, and he instinctively grabbed it, drawing it to him and engulf himself in its warmth. However, he pulled rather hard, throwing her off balance and pulling her along with it. She made as quick a recovery as she could, bracing her arms on either side of him as to not land on him. But her face was so close to his, she could feel his steady breaths fan across her cheeks.

Her breathing was nervously rapid, and while trying to calm herself down enough to push herself back up, he shifted his position, leaning up on the pillows, and those lips she had thought about being on hers were actually on hers.

She didn't move. Her eyes kept looking around his face trying to confirm what was happening was real. His lips stayed, unmoving, against hers. Soft and as plump as they looked, she prayed he simply would move a different direction so she could chalk the situation up to her clumsiness and his deep sleep.

She got that he was an actor, but did every interaction they had have to be like a drama? Why couldn't she move? Why did she just sit there and continue to let his lips touch hers? She decided it was time to finally get off him, but something changed. A slight pressure of his lips. He was kissing her!

His bottom lip had slipped in between hers, and she could taste the saltiness of the 짜장면 mixed with the scent of his cologne. His arm wrapped around her waist, languidly trying to tug her closer. As soon as she closed her eyes to enjoy the kiss, she quickly ripped her eyes back open.

This is Lee Hwan Soo! Don't enjoy this!

She finally tried to push herself off him but was stuck as his arm still held her waist. The force must have made him stir, because slowly and sleepily, he opened his eyes. When he saw how close she was, he pushed her away and jumped off the couch.

"What the hell, Maria?" he said in a higher octave.

"You're the one who fell asleep. I was trying to be nice by letting you crash on the couch and giving you a blanket, but then you pulled me and kissed me."

"Kissed you?!" He began wiping his lips, cringing as he continued to nearly scrub them off his face.

"Calm down, it isn't that bad." She stood from the couch, insulted by the way he had wiped his lips like she was a bad-tasting food and he wanted to rid the flavor from his mouth.

"I...kissed...you?" he said slowly, as if still processing it.

"Yes, you did. Bit salty, but let's blame that on the noodles," she joked, but deep down her heart was racing from how the light pressure of his lips still felt on hers in her imagination.

"거짓말하네," he said under his breath as he ran his hand through his thick black hair.

"I am not lying! Yes, I was shocked, but you were asleep, so we can, like the incident in the kitchen, forget it happened." She grabbed the blanket off the couch, folding it to try to calm her still racing and pounding heart, desperately forcing her mind to forget how scandalous his lips felt.

"Are you sure you don't actually already know Korean? Are you lying to get attention? There is no way someone can pick up phrases and words in the span of two and a half days." She knew he was trying to stir up a fight. It was a defense mechanism that had been used on her countless times by her exes.

"Since yesterday, I've heard more Korean than English. I binged dramas all day. Stuff sticks. I already told you, I've always been like that." She crossed her arms, dropping a hip and tapping her foot, annoyed at his accusation.

"Not possible," he bit back.

"That's your opinion. Anyway, since you're awake, maybe you should head home." She gestured toward the door.

"Right, well, I'll see you tomorrow. And as for the ki—"

"It never happened," she said, cutting him off. "And the incident in the ki—"

"I saw nothing," he said, quick to cut her off as well as he tossed his hands up in a surrendering manner.

They were both on the same page.

Lee Hwan Soo bowed and quickly left, leaving her alone with her thoughts. Which were now totally consumed by the feeling of his lips on hers and his soft but sturdy hold on her waist.

Hwan Soo bolted out of that apartment like it was on fire for the second time that night. No way he kissed her. 말도 안돼!

But why did his lips feel tingly? And why did his body feel like it had been through a pleasurable, almost sexual experience?

Maria wouldn't lie about something like that. What would she gain from it? She even told him she wasn't the kind of person to record him eating and send it off to the gossip rags. So why would he think her telling him they kissed would be a lie?

Disappointment set in. Why couldn't he have been awake? He had thoughts about how kissing her would feel, more often than he would care to admit in the limited time they had been together. But when he actually did it, he was asleep.

Falling against the wall of the elevator he heard his phone ding from his pocket. Assuming it was a text from Jung-hyun about how the night had ended, Hwan Soo quickly went to reply. But all the questionable pleasure he was feeling quickly drained from his body, replaced with a sinking gut.

김 해 소

Why he still had her number in his phone was beyond him. And since he kept it, why didn't he change the name to "Heinous Bitch" so he knew not to answer?

He didn't want to open the text. He knew whatever was to follow was sure to be filled with drama. And not for the show they were about to start working in together. He was about to ignore the text when his phone lit up again with a follow-up message.

Maybe it was about working together. Even with her horrible way of life, when it came to work, she was always professional and if he was going to have to work with her, the least he could do was also be professional.

Opening the text, he was shocked to see:

우리 만나자.

The follow-up text being an address and time.

What was she planning?

Korean Vocabulary:

거짓말하네 – kojitmal hanae- you're lying

말도 안돼 – maldu andway- no way

김 해 소 – kim hae so – you know who she is

우리 만나자 – uri manaja -let's meet up

Chapter 19 (열아홉)

V al was jumping up and down on the bed, waking Maria up from her light sleep. If she could even call it that. All she did the whole night was toss and turn, her fingers tracing her lips with the memory playing on repeat of Lee Hwan Soo's plump lips on hers. At the current moment she was thinking she was about to knock her bestie off the bed so she could try to get some semblance of rest.

"I get to try on dresses today!" Val continued jumping up and down.

"Yay you!" Maria wanted nothing more than to stay in bed, curl up under the sheets, and stay hidden in case the men came calling.

"You're coming with me! Come on!" Val pulled the covers off and began hitting Maria's butt repeatedly like bongos.

"Whoa! Just you and me?" Maria faked shock even though she was actually happy to have another day alone with her best friend.

"Oh hush. Your time spent with Hwan Soo-ah hasn't been all bad. You went shopping, binged watched a drama, and I saw those 짜 장면 bowls outside the door last night. You two clearly enjoy spending time together." Val nudged Maria, insinuating that she had feelings for Lee Hwan Soo. Maria thanked the Lord she hadn't told Val what happened the night before.

If she told Val how he saw her nearly naked, followed by a sleepy accidental kiss, Val would start plotting like her mother to get them together. Maria and Hwan Soo had also made a pact to forget it even happened. And like that, the image of Lee Hwan Soo was back in Maria's field of vision. Val poked at Maria's sides to finally make her jump out of bed.

"You at least get to call him Hwan Soo-ah. He still insists on my calling him Lee Hwan Soo-씨. I tried once to call him Hwan Soo and I swear his neck nearly broke when he spat that I will never be comfortable enough with him to be Hwan Soo-ah." Saying his name so much was causing her to continuously play the kiss over and over. It could never leave.

Like he could hear them talking about him, Val's phone rang, and Lee Hwan Soo's name lit up.

"여보세요?" Val answered. "어, 여기."

Val tossed the phone to Maria, who awkwardly answered, "H-hello?"

"It's Lee Hwan Soo," he spoke quickly. He actually sounded a bit nervous.

"Yeah I know, I saw your name pop up on Val's phone," she said, stating what she thought to be pretty obvious.

"Right. Listen, I'm not going to be able to come over today. I have some stuff I need to get done with my manager," he explained, but something was off. He sounded preoccupied and not in a good way. She may not have known him long, but she did know men. He was lying.

"That's fine. I'm actually going wedding dress shopping with Val," she responded, trying to ignore her gut feeling. But with every word he spoke, her gut wrenched more and more.

"Great!" he replied a little too enthusiastically, then went silent. She sat there awkwardly as Val stared, waiting to see where their conversation was going.

"Um...well..." His voice was faint as he tried to speak.

"Is there something else you want to say, Lee Hwan Soo-씨?" She felt the need to at least give him a chance to explain. Could it be he felt awkward talking to her because of what happened?

"Yeah, actually, I wanted to know if, after we have dinner with Jung-hyun and Val, you want to come over tonight and maybe watch some more of the drama we didn't finish last night?" Even though it was nervously asked, she could tell that wasn't what had been on his mind. Something was up and she was actually concerned. Her heart did a small jump, while her stomach seemed to be dancing the mambo.

"Come over? As in, to your place?"

"Where else?" He laughed nervously. "And to be honest, it's not the only reason I want you to come over."

Her heart was no longer doing small jumps, but gigantic ones off a cliff into her stomach, which was still dancing the mambo. Maybe the kiss had changed something in their relationship more than she thought. But because it was so uncouth in Korean society, he was going to let her down kindly.

She heard a melodic sound like a wind chime in the background, and he spoke more quickly. "I'll see you later. 나 간다."

Before she could respond, the line went dead. She handed the phone back to Val, who was watching Maria's so intently.

"He asked you to go to his place?" Val's eyebrows raised as a smile started to spread from ear to ear. Her reaction was much different than Maria's—she seemed to be just below her previous jumping-on-the-bed level of excitement. "This is a good thing, Maria!" Val said excitedly.

"Calm down there, sailor. He asked so we could study. Remember how you have me learning a whole new language and all?" Maria said, attempting to cover up that even her imagination was running wild with ideas of what he could want to talk to her about.

"I call bull! He's got a little crush on my bestie! No way would he invite you over if he didn't!" Val ran to a rather large door that hid what Maria had learned was a walk-in closet the size of her entire apartment. And then Maria was blinded by an item of clothing being flung at her face. And there was weight piling on top of her blindness. When she was finally able to move her head to get some air, she saw the clothing on her lap. Most of the items still had tags on them, and the prices had so many zeroes it made her head spin.

"미쳤어! He invited me over because we're going to study. And what on earth are you doing?" She pushed the never-ending mound of designer gear off her to stop her friend from pulling everything from the closet's racks.

"You need to look absolutely flawless. I don't have any really sexy lingerie here but maybe we can get some while we're shop—" Val was pulling apart some of the drawers filled with bras and underwear that looked more expensive than Maria could wrap her head around.

"VAL!" Maria shouted to halt Val's movements as well as her insane train of thought. "It's not like that, so put the dresses and the underwear down. I will wear a normal outfit for my normal day of normal learning. For now, we need to go and find you a wedding dress." Maria brought the subject back to what was most important that day.

"You're right! Oh my God! I'm getting a wedding dress!" Val dropped all the clothing in her hand and began her joyous jumps once again.

∾

Hwan Soo hung up the phone with Maria the second he saw her walk in the door. Never in a million years did he think he would receive a text from his ex, asking to meet up. And the kicker? She was still as stunning as ever.

But this time he wouldn't be fooled. She was a wolf in sheep's clothing. Those innocent large eyes, her blush-red lips, the pale complexion and rosy cheeks all tied into the naivety act. Even her tall, slender frame that walked farther into the shop with a calm, cool, and collected attitude was a front for the harlot she really was.

She pulled her sunglasses farther down the bridge of her nose as she looked around the café. Meanwhile, he was hoping to hide for as long as possible. But as there was no one in the café, she unfortunately caught sight of him immediately and gave a small wave, a big fake smile and strutted over to him.

"오랜만이야." Her lips curved into a devilish grin. Kim Hae So, the gorgeous Next Big Thing and his ex-girlfriend, greeted him like they were longtime friends calmly meeting for drinks. She stood waiting for him to greet her with a similar kindness.

"There are no cameras, no managers, and no customers here. Cut the crap." He stayed seated, arms crossed, trying very hard not to stare at her.

He had chosen that specific café for its privacy. It sat on the third floor above a chicken restaurant and a flower shop. It was tiny to the point that there were only six or seven small wooden tables with small vases of flowers that had clearly been picked from the flower shop downstairs, as well as a small lacquered-wood counter lined with milk, sugar, and more filling mason jars. The cash register area with the tiny selection of pastries and a chalk menu with all their coffee specials was in the far back. The small windows at the front of the building had views across the way into another small business office. It was much more rustic than the minimalist café Jung-hyun and he had visited. He would never take her to a place he frequented, but he was also bummed he would probably never be able to come to this café again.

She remained standing, giving him more time to look her over. She was an actress that one couldn't take their eyes off of. She had a presence. It was what caught his attention the first time he saw her on the set of his first major drama.

She was still a newly cast lead when they met. She was friendly to all the other smaller cast members and offered advice to them all, but she had taken more of a liking to Hwan Soo. With that came the sneaking around in her company van or meeting up late at night or early in the morning at her place. The things that made his pulse race, his heart soar, and his mind to go blank with pleasure. He was so sure it was love at the time.

Now, however, when he saw her, he could only see an ugly presence. Which had been solidified by her fake smile turning down to a frown, her eyes rolling, and her slump into the seat across from him.

"잘 진냈어?" she asked him informally.

"Are you seriously asking me how I am? Do you care? In all actuality?" he scoffed at her.

"Now that we will be working together in a much larger capacity than before, it's my job to know and, well, pretend to care." She shrugged as she gave him a once-over and then looking out the window, waved her hand for a waiter to come over. He laughed, knowing no one would come because he paid them all to leave the shop for an hour.

"Why did you want to meet?" he asked, trying to make her get to the point so he could get out of there as fast as possible. His blood was already boiling just having to be in such close proximity to the snake.

"You never told anyone about us being together, right?" she said, cutting to the chase as she continued to wave her hand in the air.

"Is that really the reason you had me come out to see you? This couldn't be done over the phone? Or even in a text so I didn't have to hear your voice?" He held onto the handle of his coffee mug with every bit of control he could muster. It took all that willpower not to throw it at the wall behind her.

"We should tell people." She ignored his questions and attitude to make her point clear, appearing to grow frustrated as she turned, trying to find someone to take her order.

"저기요!" she hollered.

"장난해?" He stared at her in shock. She was crazy, but he didn't think she would stoop to such levels for fame. He tried desperately to find any sort of tell that would indicate she was just trying to get a rise out of him. That maybe she did at one point like him and want to rekindle what they had. But he knew he would never see that in her eyes.

"We're in a new drama together, playing lovers. It would be a publicist's dream to promote the idea of us rekindling what we once had. Think of the buzz it would create. Your first big breakout role would be huge." Her face was brightening like it would only when she believed she had reached another level of fame. A new way to boost herself into the A-list she so desperately desired to be a part of.

"No," he said quickly, standing to make a quick exit. He didn't want to hear another twisted word from her mouth.

She wouldn't let him leave, however, and grabbed his arm harshly. She was surprisingly a lot stronger than he remembered.

"Hwan-Soo-ah, think about it. This is your first lead role. I've been doing this for a bit now. Being photographed together, telling them we did have something and maybe working together could bring back that spark we once had." She was really trying to convince him of her scheme. But she was no Jung-hyun.

"Again, no. I have no interest in using cheap tricks to get people interested in my work." He suddenly realized how perfect dropping the fake little bomb about Maria would be. Sure, it would be his own cheap trick, but it was for his sanity. If she thought he was taken, maybe she would back off. He turned back to her, mimicking her devilish smile and spoke as clearly as humanly possible. "I also don't think the girl I'm currently seeing would be too fond of bringing up the past either. She's proud of what I've accomplished without the need for meddling."

Her hand loosened on his arm, letting him escape her clutches. If he could've snapped a picture of her slack jaw, eyes glazed over trying to process the information, ears turning bright red with anger, it would've been the best photo ever taken of her. At least to him.

"Y-y-you're seeing someone? 누구? Do I know her?" Her hands gripped the edge of the table ready to flip it over.

And just like that, he had easily taken the advantage.

"I keep my private life private, Hae So. In fact, I think you said that to me the first time I suggested telling my friends about you," he chided, knowing if he didn't make his exit at that moment, he probably wouldn't have gotten out without a scrape.

Stepping out into the slightly chilly stairwell, he exhaled deeply. He had fought off the snake trying to strangle him and was finally able to breathe again. Shoving his hands in his pockets and feeling as if he could skip, he walked down to the street toward his car.

She burst through the door of the café, following him. "You honestly want me to believe you moved on so quickly?" she shouted. "When you screamed how in love with me you were? How you would do anything to keep us together?"

Looking around, he saw that of the business owners who were just opening their shops, only a few bothered to stop to look at her. She looked around as well and threw her sunglasses on. He laughed when the vendors didn't react to her loud protest, but instead went right back to what they were doing. They had no clue who she was, and he knew that was a great blow to her ego. She stormed up to him, hoping people would catch them together so she could achieve what she wanted in the first place. But he knew her game all too well and pulled her off the street and into the back entrance to the flower shop.

"So quickly?" he scoffed. "It's been seven months. Why would I pine for someone who chooses to use deception to gain celebrity status? I'll stick to actually having talent. And as for the woman I'm seeing..." He trailed off and pulled his phone out, finding the video of Maria from the night before.

As the video played, his heart beat faster, and a smile grew on his face as he remembered how much fun he had with her. When he caught sight of her embarrassed smile between her hand's attempt to hide her messy eating, images of how he possibly kissed her came flooding back and his body felt warm.

"I can barely see her face." Hae So tried to grab his phone, but he knew better than to let her get her hands on the device. She would stalk his contacts, social media, even call his manager to find out whatever she could about the new girl. He held the phone tightly, locked the screen, and threw it back into his pocket.

"Let me reiterate, my private life is private. I let you see that to show you that she is very much real and how happy we are. I hope you can respect that and give us privacy during this new budding relationship. I will fake a smile when I stand next to you, I will pretend to act as if I like you as a co-star. I will even kiss you when the script demands it. But I will not stoop to your level of theatrics to get people to like me. I hope, somewhere in that cold, dead heart, you will respect that." He never thought he would have the balls to say anything like that to Hae So in his entire life. As he turned to walk away, his heart was ready to rip out of his chest, and his hands, balled into fists in his pockets, shook violently with nerves.

"야!" she shouted, trying and get him to come back and face her. But he could barely hear her over the loud audience cheers that were playing in his head. He had survived seeing his ex for the first time in seven months and didn't leave wanting to curl into a ball and die.

He weirdly had Maria to thank. She never shyed away from speaking her mind, and confidently at that. As he thought about her, a level of guilt settled in his stomach. He was still using this girl as a fake girlfriend without her knowing it. He wanted to come clean. He had to tell her that night.

Korean Vocabulary:
오랜만이야- oraenmaneeya – long time no see
잘 진냈어 – jal jinesso – you've been good?
저기요- chogiyo – excuse me
장난해 – jangnanhae – are you kidding me?

Chapter 20 (스물)

"Val, you look stunning," Maria gushed at her friend in yet another flawless white gown.

"Are you sure?" Val clearly still was not sold. Hands on her hips, swaying the tulle of the dress side to side, squinting her eyes. "I'm just trying to picture if this is really the dress I'm meant to get married in."

"Literally every dress you have tried on makes you look breathtaking. Jung-hyun will cry with happiness at the mere sight of you in any of them. Hell, even if you walked down in sweats and a t-shirt I think he would die happy because he gets to marry you. Not the dress," Maria joked.

"You're right. Although I would never do that. I'm going to try on one more dress, and if it isn't the one, we have to hit up another store." Val walked back into the fitting room with a sudden burst of adrenaline.

"Maria?" Val shouted through the door.

"Yeah?" Maria shouted back, only to have the whole store look at her with judgmental eyes.

"Didn't Hwan Soo-ah seem a bit odd on the phone? Like he was hiding something?" Val had noticed it too.

Maria's stomach started doing that flip again.

"Not really. Why? What did he sound like to you?"

"He sounded kind of...I don't know how to put it... anxious, maybe? Nervous about asking you to hang out," she said loudly through the dressing room door.

That's because Maria and Hwan Soo shared a sleepy kiss that still had Maria's toes curling every time she thought about it. And he didn't even use his tongue. Crap. She was thinking about what it would have been like if he had used his tongue.

"You're crazy. He seemed normal to me. Maybe he was nervous about meeting his manager and that made it sound like he was anxious talking to us?" Maria continued trying to cover for the "illicit" moment.

"I think you're trying to deny that Hwan Soo-ah might have a crush on you." Val had brought the conversation to a head. One that Maria wasn't ready for and one she certainly didn't want to face at the current moment.

"What kind of crazy juice are you sipping in there, girl?" Maria's heart felt like it had stopped. Why was she excited about Val's ludicrous assumption? Was it that she wanted it to be true?

"I was simply pointing out something I noticed." Val opened the dressing room door and walked to the large trifold mirrors. When Maria looked up, her best friend's face said it all.

"That," Maria chose to put it into words, "is your dress."

Val's eyes started to water, and when they placed a veil over her friend's face, reality started setting in for both of them. Val was stunning and about to marry the man she loved. Her entire demeanor changed once the veil was on. Her smile could not only light up the room, but the whole city block.

Val nodded, confirming to the saleswoman that this dress was the one, and everyone in the vicinity started clapping and cheering for the happy bride.

Maria had never thought she'd want that feeling. The stress of finding a dress, wondering what a fiancé would think when she walked down the aisle. That was her mom's thing. But watching her friend experience the joy and anticipation, all leading up to a happiness Maria didn't think she would ever experience—suddenly Maria wanted that feeling.

"Wanna try one on?" Val said, obviously reading Maria's expression.

"Well, I should find a bridesmaid's dress. I need to make sure I don't embarrass you before you make your entrance." Maria stood from the couch to browse one of the many racks to keep her mind from wandering back to her unusual thoughts.

"Actually, I'm gonna have you walk in behind me. Like a lady in waiting." Val explained. Maria should've remembered Val's love of the English monarchy.

"Oh. That's different!" Maria smiled.

"That wasn't the dress I have in mind though. I meant a wedding dress," Val laughed. Maria had to turn back to her friend to see if she was serious. And when she saw Val's light up in excitement, Maria scoffed.

"And have my mom curse me and tell me that trying on a wedding dress when I'm single is a surefire way to never actually get married? No thanks." Maria continued looking at the colorful bridesmaid's dresses, her hands skimming along the multitude of fabrics.

"Your mom is thousands of miles away. She would never know!" Val jumped down from her pedestal, walked over to Maria, grabbed her wrist and walked her to the much larger bridal section of the boutique.

"You know my mom can sniff out poor single woman choices no matter the distance," Maria chided, trying her best to get back to the non-white dresses.

"If she does, I'll take the blame. Come on." Val was bopping up and down in her dress, pouting.

Maria couldn't say no to a face like that, and with a roll of her eyes, she allowed herself to be pulled into the dressing room with Val and was soon zipped into a dress. As the final hook was clasped and she looked in the mirror, Maria's mind went to Lee Hwan Soo and his lips against hers. Those thoughts mixed with her previous new desire for a wedding and she inhaled sharply.

She was in trouble.

~

Meeting up for dinner that night was even more awkward. When she saw Lee Hwan Soo, their bows were staggered, and whenever she looked up to his face, her eyes focused straight on his lips.

How was she going to be able to spend time alone with him after dinner? She kept avoiding looking at him altogether, but she could feel his eyes on her trying to find a reason why she was averting her eyes, and she would end up once again watching his lips, trying desperately not to touch her own in remembrance.

The waiter led them to a round table with what looked like a grill in the middle, where she was of course seated next to both Lee Hwan Soo and Val. When they all propped open their menus, she was lost once again. While she was picking up Hangul, she still was not sure what exactly she was reading. Some words stood out as being English words simply put into Hangul, while most were totally foreign to her. A long slender finger came into view and pointed to one of the words. When she followed the finger, it was connected to the guy she was hoping would put his lips back on hers at some point.

"Sound it out," he mouthed, making her focus on his lips even more. They were plump, soft, and a light dusty pink that make her cheeks match their color as she continued being plagued by her memories. *What the hell is he trying to do to me?*

Looking back to where his finger pointed, she sounded out the Hangul from what she remembered from the book.

"돼...지...갈비?" she said in a hushed tone, squinting her eyes

132

closed, scared he would tell her she was an idiot and didn't learn anything.

But instead she felt his hand on her head, patting her gently. Her eyes shot open to see him nodding with a bright smile. He pulled his nose up with his finger and very softly snorted and began pointing to his rib cage. She coughed out a laugh as she realized he was helping her understand what she had said. Nodding that she understood it was pork ribs, he then pointed to another item.

"김치찌개?" she said quickly.

"You've gotten better." He smiled brightly as a woman came around plopping small plates of food around the table. Hwan Soo grabbed one of the silver bowls, and handing it to her he explained, "김치 is a staple food group for Koreans. It's cabbage pickled in a red chili pepper sauce to keep it very simple."

"Sounds delicious." She grabbed the chopsticks and plucked a piece of the cabbage, bringing it to her mouth. It was tart, vinegary, sort of fishy, sweet, and spicy. While it tingled down her throat, she smiled trying to hide how it burned all her taste buds.

"Spicy?" he laughed.

She was afraid to talk. She quickly nodded.

"매워," he said.

Water finally came around to the table and yet again Hwan Soo was quick to pick up a glass and hand it to her. She bowed her head and quickly drank the water that only made it worse.

Hwan Soo noticing the water not helping, waved the waiter over to order something else. A minute later he was pouring a peach colored drink into her glass and bringing it to her mouth. *It taste like real peaches.* The relief was instant.

"괜찮아요?" he asked. She was about to answer when he reached out to wipe something off her cheek. She was now sweating for another reason.

Those slender fingers were so soft and brushing gently against her cheek. Looking back up to him, she saw he didn't seem fazed by touching her. Meanwhile her entire body had ignited with pleasurable burning all pooling between her legs. His attractiveness both physically and now through his kind gestures were getting to her, and she was getting frustrated with herself.

What sent her over the edge was when the thumb he had used to gently rub the red sauce off her cheek went to his mouth so he could lick the sauce. Her legs had to clamp shut so the flood gates wouldn't fly open.

"Do you want to see Maria in a wedding dress?" The voice of her best friend brought her out of her trance with a sudden realization that Val was about to embarrass the shit out of her to a man she was clearly getting sexually frustrated over.

"You said you didn't take a picture!" Maria exclaimed, trying her best to get the phone out of Val's hand.

"내가 거짓말 했다." Val shrugged, passing the phone over to Jung-hyun quickly out of Maria's reach.

"Why were you trying on wedding dresses?" Lee Hwan Soo asked, pulling a clear green bottle of what looked like water over to himself, pouring some for everyone but himself into tiny shot glasses.

Guess it's alcohol? Maria thought as Val reached over her and poured Lee Hwan Soo's glass. *Interesting...don't pour for yourself. Noted.*

"I tried one on because Val was begging and people were starting to stare," Maria said, full of spite and sending her friend a death glare that hopefully conveyed she planned to kill her later.

"And because her mother probably has started figuring out ways to have an arranged marriage when she gets home, I decided to help the process along," Val joked. Maria deemed a kick to the shin was the only acceptable payback in such a public place.

There was a slight yelp, which Maria rejoiced in but was quickly cut off by Jung-hyun coughing.

"우와! 너 정말 이쁘다!" Jung-hyun said as he was zooming in and out of the photo.

"그렇지?" Val gushed, leaning over to look at the photo with him.

"Whatever you just said—"

"He said you looked pretty and she agreed," Lee Hwan Soo said, cutting her off with a frown on his face. His eyes were focused solely on playing with the small glass of alcohol in his hand, spinning it on the edge of its curved bottom.

"You wanna see?" Val grabbed her phone from her fiancé and started handing it over to Hwan Soo.

"How about we just cheers to your upcoming wedding instead," he said, changing the subject and lifting up his glass, bringing it to the middle of the table.

While Maria felt relief, she could tell something was bothering him. Maybe he was trying to help her out, but there was definitely something else behind his change in subject. He was there physically, sitting next to her, looking fantastic in his crew neck sweatshirt and tight denim pants, with his hair in intentionally styled disarray, but mentally he wasn't present.

They all lifted their glasses and she heard the three of them yell, "짠!"

While she simply said "Cheers!", she watched all of them tilt their glasses to their lips and then thrust their heads back. She followed suit, taking in the liquid like a shot. If vodka had an older, more mature brother, it would be whatever the liquid was that had just gone down her throat.

"Holy hell! What is that?" she choked out, once again grabbing the water to chase the burn away.

"소주." Lee Hwan Soo smirked as he watched her struggle. At least his mocking was still a thing in his current vacant state.

"Well whatever that is, it's freaking potent. I'd be on the floor with one more shot." She grabbed the bottle, even though she knew she wouldn't be able to understand what it said.

"You're lighter than a lightweight. Even they can drink at least two bottles each." He motioned to the lovebirds as he went to pour her another glass, but she stopped him.

"I'm good. I need to stay sober and awake so we can study." She flipped her glass over but grabbed the bottle from his hand, pouring him and the rest of the table shots.

They cheered once again, and before Lee Hwan Soo could down the shot, Jung-hyun put a phone screen in front of his face. Suddenly the alcohol was leaving Hwan Soo's mouth and spraying onto the grill, causing a small fireball.

"야!" Val screamed, grabbing the phone from Jung-hyun.

Oh no. That was Val's phone. That means what made him choke...was Maria in a wedding dress.

She could hear her mother's voice in the back of her head screaming, "My forever single daughter! This is what happens when you don't listen to me! You've now embarrassed yourself in front of a potential husband!"

Korean Vocabulary:

돼지갈비-dwaejigalbi -pork rib

김치찌개- kimchi jjigae – kimchi stew

매워- maewo -spicy

내가 거짓말 했다- naega kogitmal haettda – I lied

우와! 너 정말 이쁘다 – oowoa no jongmal eepooda – wow you look really pretty

그렇지 -kurohji – right?

소주 – soju – the liquor of choice for most of SK

Chapter 21 (스물하나)

The fireball hid the redness of his face resulting from the shock at how gorgeous Maria looked in that wedding dress. It looked like it was made just for her and unlike anything he had seen in Korea before. Women in Korea are always told, "Legs are okay, but never show your chest." And so women's shorts could be so short that it would leave nothing to the imagination, but they would also be in a turtleneck sweater.

Maria had on a dress that was just the opposite. A full skirt exploding with fabric, while the top had a neckline, if one could call it that, that plunged all the way down to her navel. The fabric itself looked to be lace with some tiny gems or something shimmering against her olive skin tone. He couldn't see the full back of the dress, but from the mirror in the image it looked to be backless, which again caused him to choke, thinking about how easy it would be for just the right gust of wind to make that whole thing become a wardrobe malfunction of the best kind.

"Yeah, it was a bad choice, I know. Val rushed me to pick one, against my will I might add, and well, I just chose the one closest to me," Maria said as her face turned just as red as his and her eyes closed tightly. He could see she was biting the inside of her cheek. She was avoiding eye contact with him and the phone.

"No, I wasn't—" He tried to explain his blunder but was cut off by the waitress coming and dropping a pile of meat onto the grill.

The conversation would have to wait until later that night. The list of things he needed to tell her seemed to get longer as the day went on.

~

Wrapping up dinner took longer than expected with Val and Jung-hyun insisting on more drinks, but finally they walked out of the place into the fresh air.

"My car is a few blocks away. Do you mind walking?" he asked Maria, whose eyes went wide with what looked like surprise. Did she forget he was standing next to her? Had she forgotten they planned to study? She shook her head, saying nothing, looking back to the ground as she kicked her feet against the concrete, making loud scraping noises.

"That's fine," she mumbled quickly.

"이차?" Jung-hyun shouted as he made his way out of the restaurant, clearly feeling the buzz of the several bottles of 소주they had ordered and wanting to continue his fun.

"자기야, you know they had plans to work on her speech tonight," Val said, flirting with her fiancé, wrapping her arms around his waist. "But we can go for이차! 어디로." She began pulling him away and waving Hwan Soo and Maria off. He couldn't help but notice the little wink Val was throwing at Maria. He chuckled, as she was trying to be discreet and failing miserably.

Once the couple was out of sight, Hwan Soo felt how alone he and Maria were. He looked to his side, seeing that she was still kicking the ground, her cheeks puffed out like a chipmunk, and was slowly rubbing her hands up and down her arms.

"Are you cold?" He started pulling his light gray spring jacket off to cover her, but she reached out to stop him. Their hands touched ever so slightly and he felt a jolt through his whole body. Her skin was soft. He had felt it before but with this touch he was thrown back into the moment his eyes opened to Maria's hands on his chest and her lips playing a dangerous game with his.

She shot a glance over to him and shook her head vehemently as if she had the same vision as him. She quickly pulled her hand away from the touch and immediately changed the subject. "I'm fine. Which way is your car?"

"Let's hit up a 편의점 first. It will help fuel us for the long night ahead." He began walking up the street on a quest for something he knew she would recognize but would also never seen in such a magnitude.

"A what?" she asked, jogging a bit to keep up with his long paces.

"You'll see." He smiled.

~

"A 7-Eleven? A편의점 is a 7-Eleven?" she asked, confused as they arrived to the insanely lit corner store of a brand she was very familiar with.

"Well, it's a convenience store. You have this particular chain in the States as well, just nothing like this. Your mind is about to be blown." He laughed and entered before her.

"I meant to ask. How do you know so much about the States? And the fact that you speak English like a pro makes me believe you lived in the States for a time." She had been meaning to ask ever since she realized he spoke English at all.

"You're not wrong. When Jung-Hyun and I were young, our families moved to the U.S. for several years. They were both trying to grow their companies in the market and ended up not only in the same state and city, but our houses were on the same block. While our parents were and still are competitive, fighting to overtake the same or even bigger companies, Jung-Hyun and I chose to be friends.

Our parents didn't want it, but when you're the two weird Korean kids in school, you have only each other to rely on.

"My family moved back here when I was in what you call high school, so I assimilated back into Korean culture. Jung-hyun not so much. Hence why he chose to stay and take over his family's business in America. And how he met your best friend," he explained as they walked into the super brightly lit store.

The store was like nothing she had ever seen before. Aisles, more than the two or three she was used to, were filled with anything anyone could ever possibly want. Forget just chips, candy, and soda—one aisle was just ramen. Legitimately just hundreds of different types of ramen ranging from what looked to be soups to super spicy, to having actual meats, and so on. A long, narrow table along the whole front window, with high bar-like stools where people sat or stood eating food and watching the nightlife outside. There were tables and chairs, both inside and out, where groups of friends could spread out their food treasures to share. Fridges lining the entire store were filled with prepackaged food, side dishes for said meals, sodas and cold coffees, as well as large floor-to-ceiling enclosed glass refrigerators filled with alcohol Maria had never even heard of. But one clear green bottle caught her eye.

"Ah, 소주. Right?" She looked at all the different bottles of various brands and flavors.

"네." He nodded, grabbing one and handing it to her. "This one is a lot less painful than the one we drank in the barbecue place."

"Are we getting this?" she asked, shaking it with a puzzled face as to why he had handed it to her.

"네." He nodded, grabbing a small bin and filling it with snacks she had never seen before. "These will help with our studying tonight. Not only as fuel, but also these are standard foods you're going to need to know for the rest of your trip. And maybe even when you're visiting Val in San Francisco."

She had almost forgotten that Val hadn't brought up the idea to Jung-hyun, or anyone other than Maria, of staying in Seoul. And now his statement seemed to stick with her more. She was going to need to know the language for more than just the month of the wedding. She was most likely going to need it the rest of her life, for the times when she came to visit Val in Seoul.

She was pulled out of her daze when Hwan Soo tossed items from the shelves into the bright yellow basket. He knew exactly what he was doing, grabbing some foods she knew, like chips and ramen, and then oddities like what looked to be an entire preserved sea creature.

They made their way up to the cashier to pay. Hwan Soo quickly reached into his back pocket to pull out his wallet. Realizing he was about to pay, she stopped him. Hitting his hand away, the cashier looked at her like she had seven heads. She began rummaging through her purse.

"I owe you for all the stuff you bought last time we were together," she said, pulling out her wallet.

"I'd prefer to pay." He tried to hand his credit card over to the young man working behind the counter, who looked terrified that his hand would also get swatted away.

"And I'd prefer you didn't," she bit back as she gently placed her hand on his to push it down. Her heart couldn't stop pounding at the contact. She really enjoyed these small touches, like when she had stopped him from giving her his jacket. Her pulse raced like he had taken her in his arms and confessed his undying love, when in reality, all he did was pull a jacket off his shoulder. His hands were soft, knuckles rough, and his long fingers had her imagining what they could do to her body given the opportunity.

"I'm really uncomfortable with this," he explained but backed down, sliding his card back into his wallet.

She looked to the young man with a smile, handing him the amount of cash that flashed on the screen. *Phew.* She felt instant relief that she didn't actually have to ask how much everything cost. But she knew she was going to have to ask Hwan Soo how to say that at some point.

Korean Vocabulary:

<u>이차</u> – eecha – round 2. used to talk about going to another bar or club.

자기야 – jagiya – honey. term of endearment for couples

어디로 – odiroo- where to?

편의점 – pyeonhwijom – convenience store

Chapter 22 (스물둘)

They rode in his car in silence. Every time they ended up alone, an awkwardness fell between them. The only sound was the crinkling of the bags when he hit small bumps in the road. She figured it had to be the fact that he was still mortified because they kissed, followed by seeing her in a wedding dress, all in the span of less than twenty-four hours. He was now probably internally screaming to himself "marriage-crazy single lady". As these thoughts floated through her mind, her phone began ringing with the sound she had set for one person and one person only.

Like a true evil genius, her mother's name lit up her screen.

"Crap," she whispered. Hwan Soo's head turned to see what she was talking about and saw the name on her phone.

"Go ahead," he said, nodding toward the phone.

"If I don't answer she'll kill me. If I do answer I'll probably kill her," she explained, seeing a small smirk play on his face. At least that made those nervous butterflies in her stomach calm to a relaxing warmth. She took a deep breath and swiped to answer. "Hi, Mom."

"How has the wedding planning been going?" her mother quickly asked.

"I went to look at wedding dresses with Val today. Found her dream dress. I'll send you pictures later. You'll agree, it's totally made for her. So excited to see her walk down the aisle." She couldn't help but gush about how happy her friend was finding the perfect ensemble.

"One day I hope to see you in a dress as well," her mother said, her voice softening dreamily. If only she knew. Her mother followed up with, "And how is this Hwan Soo girl? Is she being nice?"

"You mean did she introduce me to any eligible men? You are forever probing to find me a man." Maria again saw where this line of questioning was going and was already over the conversation.

"It wouldn't hurt for you to at least ask her—"

"We already had this conversation. When I get home I will go on all the blind dates you want, and maybe, just maybe I'll even see one guy more than once. And to humor you, maybe I'll even get engaged to one of them." Rolling her eyes and silently begging for the conversation to end, she let out a huff of frustration.

A loud cough came from next to her and again Hwan Soo was choking. She started hitting his back while also trying to soundlessly shush him so her mother wouldn't hear.

"Where are you? That person sounds sick. Don't catch anything. You can't be looking all puffy and red for the wedding photos. I'm gonna use them in your online dating profile pictures." Her mother was again being the voice of odd reason.

"Don't worry, Mom. It was just someone passing. I'm headed back to the apartment right now. Can I call you tomorrow or something?" Maria finally got Hwan Soo to stop coughing, and he was staring at the road straight ahead.

"Sure, but don't forget. And before you hang up, I wanted to say the photos you've been sending make Seoul look gorgeous! Makes me wish I'd been invited to the wedding. You've always had an eye for getting the right shot."

"Of course I'll call, Mom. And thank you. I love you, bye." Maria quickly hung up and looked over to see Hwan Soo concentrating on the road. Every so often she watched the muscles in his jaw clench, showing off his impeccable bone structure.

"미안해요." She bowed a bit in apology.

"Ah. Another new word." He smiled, never taking his eyes off the road.

"Val taught it to me in my first like ten minutes of being in this country. Smart choice." She laughed at how sad that truth was.

"How's your mom?" he asked, his smirk growing into an amused grin knowing her answer was going to be a sarcastic one.

"She's my mom," she huffed, feeling how loaded the question was, and she slouched down on the seat.

"Three words and yet I totally understand what you mean," he scoffed.

"찐자요?" she asked.

His head snapped to her, his eyebrows raised, mouth slightly open with surprise. And then he smiled happily. "찐자요. Let me guess. She's proud of all your accomplishments. But she always wonders with everything you've done, who do you have to share it with?"

She stared at him in shock. How did he know exactly what her mother was like?

"Yeah..." He trailed off, the back of his head hitting his headrest with a small thud.

"So your mom is obsessed with getting you married off too?" she laughed, finding yet another thing they could relate on.

"The amount of blind dates that woman has set me up on would blow your mind." He started laughing harder, and it was loosening the tension she had been feeling since they met for dinner.

"Twenty-five this year." She raised her hand, owning up to the last several months of her mother's insanity.

"이십오? In a year? That's nothing." He started laughing even harder, making the corner of his eyes crinkle and glisten with tears as he raised his hand up with four fingers extended as he spoke. "사십... and that was just this last six months. I had been seeing someone befo

—" His face suddenly went dead. The smile had left both his lips and eyes. Stoically, he stared at the road ahead. Clearly this person was not a topic he enjoyed bringing up.

"사십...if 이십오is twenty-five, and you're saying yours is higher and resembling four, then do you mean...forty?! That's more than one a week," she said, attempting to get back to the original topic, since it was something they could both laugh about. She also wanted to take his mind off a topic he obviously hadn't meant to bring up in the first place. "Clearly none of them worked out. What? Did they get the initial Lee Hwan Soo-씨 first impression and chose to dip?"

"Lee Hwan Soo-씨 first impression?" he asked, scrunching his face in confusion, which made him look vulnerable.

"Well, yeah. Your first impression was definitely not the best. The whole pulling my collar and essentially calling me a tactless American wasn't the best way to get someone to like you. But the following day when you told me about how you haven't seen Jung-hyun in years, I was able to see that you're not the absolute worst and you care about the people closest to you." She laughed and continued, "Those girls only got the first impression. Not the second, which was a little better."

"Maybe. I mean, for the most part, they were nice girls...and one boy when my mom thought I might not have liked girls at all," he scoffed. "I was against the whole concept of blind dates, but I went on them to humor my mom, like you. I think the reason none ever progressed past the first date was the fact that they knew who I was. I'm not well-known in any way, but on my profile my mom exaggerated my career, so the first things out of my dates' mouths were questions about who I've met, worked with, posed with, filmed alongside. They weren't interested in knowing more than the sugarcoating. Not my actual personality. Just the benefits they could get from dating and potentially marrying me."

She could feel his disappointment and discouragement about the idea of real love. He probably felt a sense of hopelessness, like he would never find someone who would love him for who he was—that feeling settled into her too.

Her heart hurt for him and with him. Impulsively she grabbed his hand that was resting on the stick shift and gently squeezed it.

"I may not get the whole fame thing, but I totally get the feeling of people judging you for something. Your fame and my looks seem to get us both the same results. I'm not being conceited, but even you said in the cab that if I was just slightly less pretty, I would be treated totally differently. I've had some dates tell me they love the—and I'm quoting several men here—'trophy wife looks' I have." She laughed but it was filled with the same hurt in his voice. But she was comforted when his hand flipped around to cover hers and gently squeezed. When she looked up from their hands, she saw he was intermittently looking back at her with an expression of total under-standing.

"Maybe our moms should be friends," he said, trying to lighten the mood again.

"Are you crazy? If anything, they would gang up on us. They would possibly even throw us together." She was laughing hard but her heart skipped a beat at the thought. She knew her opinion of him had changed, but even with her newfound feelings, she didn't think she could joke about the serious subject they had just been having.

Why did he have to be the guy who pushed her buttons, yet also the man she enjoyed spending her time with, even enjoying his button pushing?

"Doubtful. At least on my end," he chuckled, rubbing his thumb against her knuckles. "You're not Korean."

That made it perfectly clear that they would never be a thing. Although she never thought that would be something she would feel disappointment about, she wasn't a fan of it being thrown in her face like a pie at a clown.

Korean Vocabulary:

이십오 : eeshiboh – 25

사십 – sashib – 40

Chapter 23 (스물셋)

They drove for what felt like hours and were finally in a much different looking area than Maria was used to in the few days she had been in Seoul. While she was usually surrounded by large skyscrapers, tons of noise, the hustle and bustle of city life, she was now in what looked like a suburb. The area was still cramped, but with houses instead of huge buildings and businesses. Actual homes, modern mixed with old, along tiny tight roads with small streetlights barely illuminating the road ahead, all leading her to a new Korean experience.

He turned the car toward a large wooden privacy gate and put the car in park. Letting go of her hand that he had been holding ever since they opened up to each other, he reached over her, his sweater grazing against her legs, to open his glove compartment and hit a button. She heard a loud thud as the gate began slowly revealing a driveway.

When the gate clacked to a halt, he pulled up into the driveway to a house that surprisingly looked like an all-American brick home Maria was used to seeing on her side of the world. Industrial-looking lamps that reminded her of lights outside most hipster restaurants lit a black front door and were above all the windows lining the two-story house; the windows were further adorned with black shutters. A small lawn had a swinging bench and a small table with metal chairs—none of this was what she expected. Even more surprising was the four-car garage he pulled into; to top it off, he parked next to another three cars. She had assumed he was rich by his clothing and mannerisms, but clearly being second lead paid well.

"Acting doesn't pay for this, if that's what you're thinking," he said with a smirk.

"That's exactly what I was thinking." She heard both of their seatbelts click and saw that he had undone hers as well.

"Remember how I said our parents were in constant competition? They both own large international companies. I lucked out being the second child, the 'spare', so I get all the perks of being a rich kid while following my own dreams because I don't have to work for the company. Jung-hyun, being an only child, had no choice. Luckily he was always the smart businessman and willingly chose to continue his family legacy." He spoke as he was typing a code into the door keypad similar to the one on Val's penthouse.

Her heart was thudding so hard, she was sure he was able to hear it. She was entering the lion's den. Willingly. She took a deep breath as the door opened and the entry light kicked on revealing a rather sparse entryway with a small shoe rack against one of the walls. Maybe he just put on airs and inside looked like a total hoarder's den filled with floor-to-ceiling ramen cups and 소주 bottles scattered on the floor while rats ran around picking up the scraps from his 편의점 visits.

He kicked off his shoes, she followed suit. He reached into a shoe cupboard she hadn't realized was hidden in the wall next to the rack, to pull out a pair of slippers for her that she slipped on quickly to walk into the actual house.

She couldn't have been more wrong about what she had hoped she was walking into. The living room was massive, with an L-shaped gray suede couch that was as large as some beds, across from which hung a TV nearly the size of the wall met with large floor to ceiling windows that had a view overlooking a large portion of Seoul. Even the Seoul Tower was in view, a focal point she had seen in several episodes of the dramas she watched. A romantic spot for a date, where couples would put locks with their names on the railing to symbolize their undying love. Cheesy, yes, but being a sucker for romance, she thought it was cute. As she admired the sprawling cityscape, she noticed that the lights of office building and apartments seemed miles and miles away. She hadn't realized they had driven up such a high hill.

"What a view," she gushed, grabbing her phone to snap a few photos to send to her mother. She would just be sure to leave out that she was alone in a man's house when she told her mother where they were taken.

"Yeah it's nice," he said in a monotone voice, and she saw his uninterested shrug in the reflection of the window. "Call me jaded, but I am so used to seeing it, I don't get much excitement from it anymore." He continued walking, flipping a switch and revealing a large teal island topped with a massive slab of marble. The wall beyond was lined with shiny white cabinets, a high-tech fridge with a screen that lit up when Hwan Soo walked toward it to toss several of their snacks inside, and a cooktop and oven off on the other side.

"Jesus! This house is gorgeous," she gushed, following him into the kitchen, dreaming she could have a house like it in the future.

"고마워요." He smiled at the compliment but then got right to the point. "Alright, let's get started. We can start the drama from last night. What episode did we leave off on?"

"I think seven or eight." She smiled and walked back to the living room, plopping down on the couch to wait for him.

When he followed her back to the living room, she could tell his nervous manner from earlier in the night had returned. With a bag of snacks in one hand, he rubbed the back of his head with the other, taking awkward steps toward the couch and choosing to sit on the far end. She wanted to speak up but he beat her to it.

"Something happened today," he said in a rushed whisper.

"Was it seeing me in a wedding dress? I know it was a hot mess, I looked horrible, most likely crazy, but please don't think that I'm some insane chick who thought our accidental kiss meant we were meant to be together. I just—"

"You looked beautiful in that dress." he said, waving his hands to cut her off. With a compliment that stopped her heart.

"What?" She blinked quickly trying to readjust her eyes to see if someone other than Hwan Soo was in the room. But it was him, looking right at her.

"너무 예뻐요. And I never thought you were that type of girl. After my many blind dates who were that type of girl, and knowing the power of Jung-hyun's persuasion, I can imagine Val's is very similar. So I knew you were not the one who made that decision. But know that you looked great in that dress." He softly smiled easing her nerves. "It actually has to do with me."

"What?" she repeated her question, not able to come up with anything else. He constantly pulled back his hair, making her nervous.

"I auditioned for a part before Val and you arrived here in Seoul. I didn't even know about this wedding until a few weeks ago. And in all honesty, I was shocked my management sent me to the audition since it was a lead role."

"Right. Forever the second lead." She nodded, listening carefully to what he had to say, waiting for the inevitable bad news.

"Well two days ago, while you were in the shower, I got a call from my manager telling me I got the part." He looked away from her down to his hands that were spinning their thumbs around each other.

Maria leaped off the couch and started jumping up and down. He looked up, surprised by her reaction.

"Oh my God! Lee Hwan Soo-씨! That's amazing! 축합니다! No more second-lead syndrome for all your fans. Me included!" She jumped around the living room with excitement over the new role she would get to see him in. Especially now that it would be a lead role. He would be more prominent on screen and be a total heart-throb. He was destined for success. She could feel it.

His eyes widened as his head bounced along with her, a surprised smile as he watched her jump up and down.

"고마워요. But that isn't all." Had he misled her? She immediately stopped her clearly premature joyous celebration.

"Okay, Lee Hwan Soo-씨, if you don't get to the damn point in the next sentence, I will slap you upside the head." She placed her hands on her hips and tapped her foot.

"Tomorrow is my first table read, and the lead actress is the ex who broke my heart seven months ago." He had listened well to the whole "fit it into one sentence" thing, but that was definitely not what she was expecting to hear.

"Fuck." She exhaled as she fell back onto the couch trying to process the information to find more appropriate words.

"Yeah, that's about how I felt when I found out." He fiddled his hands, rubbing them on his pants, and then went back to pulling them through his hair. "This morning when I called you, I was waiting to meet up with her because she asked to meet with me before we started shooting. I felt like my heart was going to fall out of my chest."

"Because you're still in love with her." Maria's stomach was churning as her heart began beating at an agonizingly fast pace waiting to hear his response. *Why? Why do I care what he has to say about this woman?*

"No. Not anymore. I thought I was. But when it all really ended and I realized she was using me just for her own personal needs, I started to hate her. Seeing her this morning made me nauseous. Pretending to have to be in love with her will probably be my most Oscar-worthy performance ever." He tried to laugh, but she could see that whoever this chick was, she had done him dirty and not only broken his heart, but messed with his head.

"미안해요," she said softly, worried that if she spoke any louder the world would come crashing in on both of them. As she watched him, she saw his eyes scrunch, his arms twitching as though he was trying not to run his hands through his hair again.

"Why are you telling me all of this exactly?" she wondered out loud.

"Because like I said, the first table read is tomorrow, and I was supposed to watch you for the next month. I was hoping that you would—"

"I get it. You can't watch over me anymore, and I have to fend for myself." She nodded, believing she understood. "Well then we better cram a whole lot into tonight and maybe we can just meet up when you have a free day or something to test me."

"You really love jumping to your own conclusions here, don't you?" he laughed, moving over to sit closer to her on the couch. He looked at her, seemingly attempting to gauge whether she would be willing to listen.

She puckered her lips shut waiting for him to continue. Oh boy, was she antsy for him to speak. Him moving closer had caused all the feelings she had been questioning to come back in high gear. She tried to keep her eyes from looking down to his lips, but looking into his eyes wasn't much better as they twinkled with the reflection of the lights. Heat was emanating from him and running right through her. Why was she getting so excited over his presence? She wasn't a fan of how quickly her body was growing full of want for a man she swore was a total prick just a few days ago.

"I don't want to not spend time with you. For one reason, Val and Jung-hyun would be pissed. Secondly, you wouldn't be able to practice your Korean as frequently as you should. Thirdly, and most shockingly to both of us, I like having you around, and I think you being around will help me keep sane while having to be near my ex."

"뭐?" she all but whispered. Was he admitting that he liked her? Even if it was a friendly like, her heart felt like soaring. Why? Why was this happening to her? She couldn't afford to like him. And what would come of it? He told her that his mother was strictly into him dating and marrying a Korean girl. Something she most definitely wasn't.

"I am asking you to tag along with me while we film. You would be able to watch a drama being made, learn Korean, and well, you would be helping me out immensely. So will you?" he begged, shifting even closer to her.

"What would I do exactly? I can't just be there, standing around awkwardly. What if someone asks me what I'm doing there? Even worse, what if they ask me something in Korean that I don't understand?" she asked, wondering if he had thought the idea through, because her mind was coming up with every worst case scenario.

"We can give you whatever title you want. I can say you're a new assistant, my American PR representative, an intern with my company, anything you want," He smiled and continued as if he thought she had already accepted. "And as for people asking you questions, I will make sure that you're always with either my manager or me so that if people do ask questions, we can intervene."

"So you have thought this out?" She leaned back on the couch again, which was more like a cloud than anything she had felt before, almost making her forget she was contemplating pretending to be an employee of Lee Hwan Soo.

"If it helps, you get some perks with the job. Like coming to the press parties and the set and all the photo shoots. Plus, all the food trucks that fans send to the set."

"Okay, while that stuff does sound cool, it sounds cool for you," she argued.

"It will all help you practice." He again gave a good reason.

"I really don't know why I'm arguing. I have no other option," she admitted. Everything he said was logical and since she didn't know the next time she would spend a whole day with Val again, she knew it was the best option to keep her from going insane. She nodded, finally coming to her decision. "Okay. I'll do it."

"감사합니다." He bowed his head several times with a boyish grin and jovial bop.

"You don't need to thank me. It's what Val and Jung-hyun would've wanted me to do. And well, I want to meet this woman. She sounds like a trip," Maria joked, but in all honesty, she wanted to give the woman a piece of her mind for clearly breaking the man in front of her.

"She's not someone you want to meet or get to know. Although you both might enjoy bashing me," he said in an apparent attempt to joke about the situation. But even having known him only a couple days, she knew that this woman had broken him down and ruined his self-esteem.

Reaching for his hand, like in the car, she gave him a gentle squeeze. "I'm on your side here. As much as I complain about you, I don't hate you. I won't bash you. I'm also not someone you loved."

Korean Vocabulary:

고마워요 – gumawwoyo – thank you

너무 예뻐요 – nomu yeppoyo – very pretty

Chapter 24 (스물넷)

He was speechless as he stared at her. Her hand was squeezing his once again in a comforting way. She had grabbed his hand in the car and it took everything in his power not to weave his fingers between hers. He had even thought about bringing her soft skin to his lips as they wove through the winding streets to his house.

He was growing way too attached to the girl who had given him the worst first impression he had ever experienced. But to be fair, he didn't give the best impression either, and she reminded him of that. And the way she was being so nice also made the thought of not telling her the whole truth about why he wanted her with him the next day sink into him with guilt.

He wanted to tell her, to be one hundred percent honest. He was about to come clean when she spoke first.

"I don't know what your ex did to become your ex, but I can tell it hurt you. I can see it in your eyes—you're still not over it. As a girl whose exes, and I mean all her exes, have cheated on her, the look you have is similar to the one I always had. By the fourth guy I don't even know why I was hurt by it anymore. But it doesn't get any easier. I will be there to support you in whatever capacity that is." She gave him one of the most reassuring smiles and it made his heart light, even as his head screamed to tell her the truth.

He had no clue what to say. How could he tell her that he wanted to use her? Maria was really starting to get under his skin, and not in a bad way. He was getting more and more worried about the feelings that were growing. Flipping his hand in hers to grasp it gently, he did what he had resisted doing in the car and slipped his fingers between hers, holding on tight. It was a powerful feeling being interlaced with her like that, a caring gesture he couldn't take his eyes off of.

That was until he felt something. Looking up, he saw her eyes on him, filled with warmth, lips parted, and cheeks flushed. What was she feeling? He wished he knew. Was it the same need of more contact?

He felt his eyes fall to her lips. Like hers had been doing all night. Yes, he noticed. What man wouldn't? His eyes had gone to hers just as much throughout the night. Those lips of hers smiled nervously, like they knew they were being watched. Letting go of her hand, he reached out to touch the ripe fruit. His thumb gently traced her bottom lip, noticing it was a lot less chapped than the day before. They were soft with a slight shine from a gloss they bought at that makeup store. He felt her breath hitch against his finger.

"Wh-wha-what are you doing?" she said against his finger, and he couldn't help himself from dipping his head closer to hers. But he was stopped when she pushed him away. Looking into her eyes, he saw them darting everywhere, her chest rising and falling at a rapid pace, and her hands pressed against his chest.

Why did he think she would let him kiss her? Why did he want to in the first place?

"미안해요. 정말 미안해요. I-I-I don't know what I was thinking," he said, quickly moving away from her.

"I know what you were thinking." She covered her mouth as she spoke, then dropped her hand to reveal a kind smile. "You were thinking that since I am being nice, you wanted to seek comfort...in more than just a reassuring speech kind of way. It happens to everyone." She was clearly trying to make him feel at ease, but his body was so revved up on sexual tension that he needed a change of subject and fast.

Moving away from her, he grabbed the remotes to begin the setup, ignoring everything that had just transpired as he asked, "Can you go grab the snacks I put in the fridge? They should be chilled again by now. I'll set up the drama for us to watch."

"네." She nodded with a slight pout as she got up and left the room.

Once she was out of his line of sight, he began flailing his legs and arms in frustration as silently as he could. What the hell was he thinking?

"여기." She dropped the bag on the table.

"우와. 잘했어요." He smiled at her ever-growing Korean vocabulary.

She pulled out a few of the things he had bought with a questioning look and, pointing to several of the bags of snacks, suddenly asked, "이거 뭐예요?"

"I'm impressed. Very impressed," he said, smiling as he grabbed one of the bags. "These have been popular here. The Hangul tells you exactly what they are. It's Konglish. 허니버터칩."

"Honey...butter...chip? You're kidding," she laughed.

"Try 'em. I promise you won't regret it." He plucked open the bag and angled it toward her. She hesitantly reached in to grab one of the rather large potato chips and slowly brought it to her mouth.

The mouth he was desperately trying so hard not to focus on let out a slow moan.

"What in the world? Who made these and where can I buy them in economy sizes to bring back home?" She dug her hand back into the bag, retrieving a fistful.

"See?" He smiled, passing the whole bag over to her and digging into the convenience store bag to grab his favorite food to have with soju. "I don't know if you're ready for this, but..."

He trailed off, pulling out the small bag of stringy fishy goodness.

"What in the heck is that?" She pointed, eyes wide with concern.

"Can you sound it out? If you get it correct, I will tell you what it means." He handed her the package.

"오징...오징어채?"

He was so proud of how quickly she was getting a handle on reading Hangul. He smiled brightly, reaching over and patting her head. Her hair was still as soft as he remembered from the previous times he had run his fingers through it.

Her eyes lit up and then he explained what she had just pronounced. "It's dried squid."

She threw the bag back to him like he had said it was a silkworm pupae that exploded in her mouth when she ate it. Which was actually a fairly popular snack in his culture, but he didn't think she was ready to try that yet.

"I'll stick to the honey butter chips." She cringed and shook with disgust.

"If you think this is bad, be glad I didn't try to feed you 홍어." He cracked open the bag, the pungent smell of salt, ocean, and fish filling his nostrils, begging to be eaten with a shot of soju.

"Don't even want to know what that is and I hope to never experience either thing. But let's get this drama started, shall we? I should probably get home at a reasonable hour tonight if you want me to look presentable tomorrow for your table read." She made herself at home grabbing his black and white plaid throw blanket off the back of the couch and flinging it around her shoulders while she dove her hand deep into the honey butter chips.

"Don't worry about that. You can just stay here," he said without thinking.

Loud coughs came from next to him, and Maria dug into the

convenience store bag for one of the small yogurt drinks to calm her throat.

"뭐라고?" she finally squeaked out.

"I said you can stay here tonight. Guest room is right over there." He pointed to the door behind the couch.

"But I don't have—"

"You can borrow something of mine to sleep in and I can get my manager to grab some clothes from Val's for you in the morning," he said, cutting her off as he gnawed on a piece of squid.

"Are you sure?" she asked just to reassure both of them.

He looked over to her and saw that she was watching him as if trying to get a read on the situation. He smiled kindly, nodded, and then grabbed the remote to start playing the drama.

He instantly felt regret when he looked at the screen to see the male lead pulling the female lead into his arms. They looked longingly into each other's eyes wondering what was about to happen next, when he threw his lips onto hers, raising one of his arms that was holding her so that his hand could lie on her cheek. After several angle shots from every camera the crew could possibly have, they pulled away from each other and his thumb started tracing her plumped-up, thoroughly kissed bottom lip.

How could he forget where they had left off? Oh right! He fell asleep and apparently kissed Maria while asleep.

"사랑해," the male lead said, looking around the female's face and waiting for her response, his finger never leaving the soft comfort of her lips.

"저도요," she slowly responded, and his lips claimed hers again.

How badly Hwan Soo wanted to skip the whole scene. He looked over to Maria, whose cheeks were flushed, her hand frozen as it held a chip to her lips, her eyes entranced by the couple on the screen. She was so into the moment, he was sure she wasn't even thinking that their almost kiss was eerily similar to the one on screen. And he was so into watching her, he forgot there was a show on the screen until she did a double take and caught him, making his head snap back to the TV.

"What did they just say to each other? It seemed hella important," she asked, looking between the screen and him, not wanting to miss a moment of the steamy make-out session. How could he forget this scene? It was talked about for weeks on all SNS and it was one that he had hoped to have one day. He used to dream of it being with Hae So...and now it might actually be and it no longer sent shivers down his spine, but rather horrible pains in his stomach.

How could he avoid added awkwardness to their situation? He was going to have to lie.

Add it to the list.

"He said that he missed her. And she concurred."

"Oh." She took the lie at face value. He watched as she began to mouth 사랑해 over and over again while watching the show.

Maria and Hwan Soo didn't speak after that. They silently shared the snacks and took sips out of their own 소주 bottles. That scene had done a number on Hwan Soo's mindset for the night. The awkwardness that had already started to fill the room had, at that point, fully encapsulated the room and was overflowing into the rest of the house.

"Hold on," she finally said near the end of the episode.

It shocked him out of his mindless gazing at the screen, and he jumped a bit, looking over at her with an inquisitive glare.

"뭐?" he asked nervously.

"I feel they keep switching between the word kiss and something else...뽀뽀? Am I saying that correctly?" she asked.

"Yes you are, and they're the same but different." He knew his explanation was crap, but he was trying to think of a way to explain the difference, since most people learning would see 키스 and 뽀뽀 were both defined as a kiss.

"How so? From what I can gather, they're being used in the same kind of situation," she argued.

"Not really. They're arguing about if what happened between

them was a 키스 which is konglish for kiss, or a 뽀뽀 which is also...a kiss." Another fantastic educational breakdown by Hwan Soo.

"Okay, that literally makes no sense. A kiss is a kiss. Plain and simple. And if in your culture that is not the case, you need to elaborate. I don't want to accidently say the wrong thing when I'm at the wedding. Like their first kiss as husband and wife—is that a 뽀뽀 or a 키스? Will I be shunned the whole night if I use the wrong term? Everyone will be saying, 'This is what you get with foreigners. Jung-hyun should've married a nice Korean girl. This would've never happened if he just followed the rules!'" She was speaking so fast, he was sure she hadn't taken a single breath the entire rant. Her face was turning bright red and her leg started bopping.

"야!" He grabbed her, putting his hands on her upper arms and pulling her to face him, her hands instinctively pushed onto his chest to keep a safe distance. But it wasn't safe. Not even close. Her eyes were wide, deep dark brown pools of nerves and curiosity, as they looked up at him, trying to figure out what was going to happen next. She pulled her bottom lip into her mouth, holding it between her teeth, and it drove Hwan Soo to act totally irrationally.

"The difference..." He barely spoke before bringing his lips gently to hers, not giving her even a second to react. Not moving his lips in order to gauge her reaction, he found she wasn't moving away or fighting him to stop. And while he wanted to press harder and poke his tongue way into the warmth of her mouth to dance with her tongue, he would've ruined what he was chalking up to a small lesson for her to spot the difference in kisses.

Pulling away, he looked to see her eyes still closed, lips still slightly puckered, expecting more. More he was willing to give.

"뽀뽀," he whispered.

Her hands that had once pushed on his chest were clutching his shirt. Her face was full of confusion, still watching him, looking as if she wasn't sure if he really kissed her or not. Waiting to see what he was going to do next. The lustful look on her face gave him the go-ahead to continue.

"키스." The word fell slower off his lips than he anticipated. One of his hands that had held her shoulder moved slowly down her spine, and his arm wrapped tightly around her waist, pulling her just about into his lap. The other hand went to the back of her neck, gently pulling her lips closer to his. Her eyes closed waiting for him to make his move.

His mouth had gone dry as he watched her eagerly awaiting his lips on hers. He smirked as his nose played with hers before moving his lips closer to hers.

Bzz. Bzz. Bzz.

Something vibrated between them causing both to open their eyes wide. They looked down to see his pocket gently glowing. When they looked back up at each other, it was like everything that had just transpired was done through hypnosis by an imaginary entity. They flew apart from each other like the same sides of a magnet.

He wanted to kiss her. A real 키스. So badly he was tempted to grab his phone and throw it at the wall so it wouldn't disturb them again. He was hooked on Maria's lips and everything those lips did. The way they spoke, the way they smiled, the way they felt against his, even if it was for the briefest of seconds.

He liked the rest of her too. She wasn't like anything he had experienced in a woman. She had her opinions and spoke them. She also knew when to admit she was wrong but also stood her ground when she had a point. She was gorgeous in more than her looks. A beautiful mind and heart. She loved her best friend and only wanted what was best for her. She was similar to him in that respect. They wanted the best for everyone around them and didn't focus much on themselves. It's probably why he felt such a pull toward her. She was going to get them both in trouble, and he didn't mind one bit.

Korean Vocabulary:

정말 미안해요 – jongmal mianhaeyo – I'm very sorry

여기 – yogi – here ya go

이거 뭐예요 – eego mwoyaeyo – what is that?

허니버터칩 – honey buttah chib - honey butter chip

오징어채 – ohjingohchae – dried squid
홍어 – hongoh – fermented stingray
사랑해 – saranghae – I love you
저도요 – joduyo – I do too
키스 – kisseu- kiss
뽀뽀 – ppo ppo – kiss

Chapter 25 (스물다섯)

He kissed her. Maria was sure that his lips willingly touched hers and were about to do it again, much more passionately, before his phone interrupted.

She moved as far away from him as possible, turning back to the TV. The episode had wrapped up, and she'd missed a large chunk of plot that she wasn't all too bothered to have missed. She had been thinking about his lips on hers all day and suddenly they were. How? Why? What was he thinking? He had almost kissed her when they first sat down together, then suddenly again.

Was he thinking about kissing her as much as she had been thinking about it? She looked over and saw him typing quickly. His eyebrows formed a scowl and his teeth were gritted as his jaw clenched. Whoever that text was going to was not going to be happy.

"누고세요?" she asked. His head snapped over to her, his glare instantly less harsh.

"I swear you pick up more and more in an abnormally short amount of time." His cheerful smile wasn't tricking her into changing the subject.

"Yeah, well I am just that good. That doesn't answer my question. 누고?" she repeated.

Instead of simply telling her, he handed her his phone. "Figure it out for yourself."

She gently reached for the phone to see the number that had texted him was not saved. Meaning whoever this person was, it wasn't someone whose number was worth saving. She started reading the Hangul.

Mystery Person: 어딨어?
Hwan Soo: 집. 왜요?
Mystery Person: 우리 같이 밥 먹어
Hwan Soo: 안돼요
Mystery Person: 보고싶어. 우리 먹자.
Hwan Soo: 미치냐?! 꺼져.
Mystery Person: 미안해 환스아

"Why is the person apologizing to you? Who is this?" she asked, confused. While she was able to read everything, it didn't mean she grasped any of it other than the end.

"Take a wild guess?" His ears were starting to turn red. There was anger in his tone that she didn't like, but she could see it was not targeted at her. Rather, it was directed at the person who had texted. When she started putting it all together in her mind, she had a pretty solid guess.

"Oh. Her?" That was all she had to say to ignite a heated grunt from Hwan Soo.

He shot off the couch and began pacing, running his hands through his hair. She wanted to comfort him, but she knew nothing she could say would help. But she did want to understand why what this ex-girlfriend had said set him off.

"Can you please explain to me what she said? I know you're heated right now, and I am sure you have every right to be, but I want to understand why. Please," she begged, standing to hand him back his phone.

He grabbed the phone and threw it at the couch with such a force, she flinched. Looking back to him, his eyes were growing red, his nostrils began flaring, and his jaw stayed strongly clenched. She went to pat his shoulder to comfort him, and instead he pulled her roughly to him, holding her so tightly to his chest she was struggling to breathe. This wasn't the Hwan Soo she knew.

"Let. Go," she hissed, struggling against his body. Every movement allowed her to feel his hard, taut body hidden beneath his sweater. She shouldn't be focusing on his body at such a time. All her woke friends would tell her that he was bad news and dangerous for the way he threw his cell and the way he was holding her. But when she looked up at him and his eyes met her worried ones, his mood changed. His hold on her loosened to the point that she could easily free herself of his embrace, and he looked apologetic. It was as if holding onto her calmed him, bringing him back to reality. She stopped fighting and once she did, his forehead rested on her shoulder. His breath heavy, heating her chest as he finally spoke.

"She asked where I was and wanted to meet up. Get something to eat. I told her she was crazy. And then said she was sorry, among other things. Not sure what for exactly. There's so much she did wrong. And here she is trying to act like what she did can be fixed over some 찌개 and 소주." He sighed, dropping his arm from around her and taking a few steps back toward the couch to grab his phone.

"Wow. She really sounds like a piece of work," she said empathetically. He was clutching his phone so hard she was worried he would crush it to pieces. Looking at the phone, she had an idea. Walking back over to him, she put her hand on his, feeling it relax, giving her the space to grab the device and swipe up to open the camera. Switching to selfie mode, she checked to make sure she looked somewhat presentable.

"What are you doing?" he asked, looking to the camera as well.

She needed to make it obvious they were in his house together.

And she pulled him down on the couch with him. Cuddling up to him and making sure he was most in frame, she used her finger to trace his jawline to make him face her.

She couldn't take her eyes off him. From his eyes darting from her eyes down to her lips to his tongue jutting out to lick his own lips, as his Adam's apple bopped with a heavy swallow, she knew what she was doing would cause confusion. But she wanted it the most in that moment and the consequences didn't matter.

"Seriously what are you—" he whispered, but she cut him off with a peck on the lips.

Click. She heard the fake shutter of the phone. Looking to check the photo in the preview album, she showed it to him.

"Send that to her," she said with a smile.

"네?" His face was full of confusion.

"You want her to leave you alone, right? Send her that photo. If she has any sense, she'll back off." She played with the photo zooming in and out, thinking it was a cute couple photo. She had never done one before and she didn't think her first one would be with a guy she wasn't dating and was confused about her feelings for.

"She won't." He shook his head, laughing a bit, which eased Maria's mind.

"Okay. She's one of those kinds of exes. More believable? Got it." She flipped on the live photo feature, fixing her framing and once again tracing his jawline. "Ready for this one?"

He didn't say anything, he just looked at her the same way he had previously. She leaned in, her lips against on his, gently moving them. Her tongue swiped his bottom lip as she hit the button to snap a photo. His lips latched onto hers, bringing her bottom lip between his and his teeth gently nipped, causing her to open her mouth. It was way better than that sleepy kiss they had shared and miles above what he had deemed a 뽀뽀. She wanted so much more. She needed to stop herself before she went any further. Pulling her lips away from his, she opened the live photo and turned it to him with a devious smile.

"I think that one will for sure do the tri—" She got cut off when she was pushed down onto the couch and straddled by Hwan Soo. She tried to sit up, but his hands pinned her arms to the couch. She let go of his phone and heard it thud onto the accent rug. "Lee Hwan Soo-씨. You don't want to do this." She tried to reason with him, unsure why since that kiss was so amazing and had set her entire body ablaze.

"You now know the difference between a 뽀뽀 and a 키스," he whispered, his nose dipping to meet hers.

His breath fanned over her face and neck, causing an electric shiver to run down her spine. His hand released her wrist, only to trace said area, and finally his fingers pressed gently.

"Your pulse is racing," he said as he pushed off her and stood to grab his phone off the floor. Looking to the phone he smirked, but it wasn't the same one that she usually found so sexy.

It had hurt and confusion behind it. He held the phone up higher for her to see the picture on his screen. "If I send this photo, it could cause a lot more problems than solutions. She could use it against me. And you could be thrown into the limelight. I'm not sure you know the possible repercussions of sending this image."

He cared. As much as he was trying to make it sound like he didn't. She watched him scowl as he told her what he knew could potentially happen. Unhappy with what he could foresee.

"If you don't want to take that risk, then why bring me to set in the first place?" She sat up. "Some random girl shows up with you to the first day of your new big gig, a person no one in the industry knows, who doesn't speak Korean, is most definitely not Korean, and you think that they're not going to question that? I may not have been in the acting world, but I have had jobs before. People talk."

She stood up, reaching over to place his thumb on the unlock button; the picture was there on the screen. Clicking all the right buttons, she finally hit the send button. It was done. And she chose to do it herself.

"You have no clue what you just did," he whispered again,

looking down at her eyes. His expression told her he wanted to kiss her again, and she wanted it just as much. But he took a step back and spoke at a normal volume. "I should get some rest. You can continue to watch the show. If you have any questions, make notes and I will answer them tomorrow."

He bowed and walked down the hallway to what she assumed was his room.

Korean Vocabulary:

누고세요 – nugusaeyo – who is that?

어딨어? – ohdisso? – where are you?

집. 왜요 ? – chib. waeyo? – home. why?

우리 같이 밥 먹어 – uri katee bap mogo- let's go eat.

안돼요 – andwaeyo – no way

보고싶어. 우리 먹자. – bogoshipoh uri mokja – i miss you let's eat.

또! 또!미치냐?! 꺼져. – ddu! ddu! michinya?! kojyeo. – again! again! are you crazy?! get lost.

Chapter 26 (스물여섯)

Who was he kidding when he walked into his bedroom? He wasn't going to be able to sleep with thoughts of Maria swimming around in his head. Why had she done that? She even knew the repercussions of what she had done and didn't feel any type of way about it. He'd underestimated her. And she seemed to be willing to be used in the game of keeping his psycho ex at bay.

I really do need to think of a better word than "use".

Falling onto his bed, he could hear the faint sound of the drama theme song beginning and the crunching of a bag of chips. She had gone on like nothing even happened. How?

She did that to help you out. Not because she likes you, his mind screamed. Then it said something even more concerning. *But you like her.*

~

She watched the screen, but she wasn't focused on a thing they were saying. Her mind was on the fact that she had kissed Hwan Soo and the fact that they both seemed to want to continue. She enjoyed that kiss way more than she thought possible. It was way better than the sleep-induced kiss or that peck to try to explain what a 뽀뽀was. It opened her eyes to what he meant by 키스. All those poor leading women who never got to experience such amazing kissing skills missed out big time.

Then a thought made her blood boil—his ex not only experienced it and most likely even more, but would experience it again. She was jealous. One hundred percent jealous and she was not going to try to deny it. She wanted to run into his bedroom and tell him that she hated the idea of him kissing his ex, even if it was just acting.

She had no right to say that. Or think that. She was just someone he was forced to spend time with. He might've enjoyed the kiss, but it could've been his idea of a fun way to pass the time. Maybe it was like a Stockholm Syndrome type of thing. Maybe she didn't really like him, but just thought she did because he was all she had.

Stop lying to yourself. He was rough around the edges, but kind, thoughtful, funny, intelligent, scarred, hurt, and just about everything else that made a human relatable. And when he focused his attention on her, it was something different. Sure, he was kind and thoughtful, but he went over the top, buying her 붕어빵 when she had to lie about eating, playing charades to teach her what words she was saying in Korean. And funny when he would bite back at her comments about things she didn't understand about his culture. When he opened up about his missing friendship, his insane mother, and even his horrid ex-girlfriend, she felt a kindred spirit in him she couldn't explain in any other way but...she liked him.

She heard rushing water from where he had just walked down the hall, and the thoughts of him in the shower fogged her mind.

"Shit," she puffed out, falling back onto the couch.

"일어나세요." She heard the voice that continued to plague her thoughts and dreams all night.

Thinking it was another one of her dreams, she pulled on the luxurious comforter that she swore was made of clouds, grumbling and rolling over.

"야, 일어나!" he shouted, pulling the pillow out from under her head and making it drop heavily onto the couch.

"What?!" she shouted, not looking at him.

"You have to get up. The first reading is in two hours. My manager will be here soon and we need to leave in less than fifteen," he explained. She heard a loud crunch as he cleaned up the bags of chips and snacks she'd eaten alone last night.

She had fallen asleep on the couch watching the drama. But in all honesty, the show was simply on in the background; she was focused on her total mental meltdown over the fact that she might like Hwan Soo.

She sat up, looking around to see him in the kitchen wearing a leather jacket, black denim jeans and Converse. If she thought he looked good from behind, when he turned to face her, she was not remotely prepared for his whole look. His wide-necked white cotton shirt made his collarbones protrude, and he was adorned with a long silver chain that hung midway down his chest. His hair hung slightly shaggy over his forehead and dipped just below his eyebrows, and his eyes were looking everywhere around the house—except at her.

When he stood in front of her, he handed her a small brown bottle that had a disturbingly energetic man on the label, saying nothing. Awkwardly grabbing it from him, she grumbled, "Good morning to you too."

Trying to cover up the fact that her face was flushed and her heart was racing a mile a minute just from the way he was dressed, she opened the drink and took a sip, spitting it out the second it touched her tongue.

"What is this? Onion juice?" She wiped her tongue to try to get rid of the taste.

"It's 모닝게어. I assumed you drank the soju on your own last night and you might need it to get through the day." He grabbed the bottle from her and tossed a napkin at her so she could wipe the juice off herself and his now ruined blanket.

"I didn't drink anything." She dabbed at her stained sweater and realized she now had no clean clothes to wear.

"Lee Hwan Soo-씨?" She looked over at him and finally his eyes met hers. "I don't have anything to wear."

"Don't you remember me telling you my manager would pick up some of your clothes on his way over? He said Val handed him a bag the size of a suitcase because she couldn't decide what she wanted you to wear," he laughed, grabbing a bottle of water for himself from his fridge. "But you should probably clean off yesterday's makeup. My closet is down the hall to the right. There is a vanity with everything you could need." He pointed as his eyes continued watching her, much the way she looked at him. The second her eyes were on him, they had no desire to leave. She would find more and more things attractive about him. In that moment she took in how long and slender his neck was, his Adam's apple bobbing up and down as he swallowed the water hard.

"You should also grab some masks," he added as she made her way down the hall.

"Grab what now?" She spun back around, looking at him like he had six heads.

The mood was instantly lightened with a small chuckle from him as he made his way past her and into his closet. When she followed, she nearly fell to the floor at how magnificent his "closet" was. It was a room. A full room the size of her tiny apartment. One wall was lined with suits. On top were blazers, suit jackets, and button-ups; below were the matching set of trousers. On the opposite wall were sweaters, t-shirts, jeans, and jackets, all hung and even appeared to be pressed. Several were still in the plastic from the laundromat. On the farthest wall from the door were floor-to-ceiling shoes. From dressy to casual, any shoe a man could want, he had.

He made his way to the center island—yes, there was an island in his closet—where he pulled out one of the drawers to reveal what looked like surgical masks, but they had drawings, studs, and they seemed to be made of cloth, not the usual medical material.

"These," he handed her several, "you're going to need to start wearing when we are out together. And maybe stick with the usual grunge look you wore before. Netizens won't think you're 'with' me," he explained, walking over to the wall with casual clothes and pulling one of his hoodies off the hanger.

"뭐?" She looked through the few masks he had given her, and she could've sworn one had leather piping around it.

"While most Western countries don't think these are normal everyday items, here and in a lot of Asia, we wear them for a multitude of reasons. I'm sure you've seen some people wearing them when we've been out. Courtesy if we are feeling sick. If we think someone is sick around us. And we sometimes have unhealthy levels of what we call yellow dust, which can be toxic if too much is inhaled."

"That's a thing?" She was so surprised by his explanation, but they all made sense.

He nodded. "Yes, but for now they are simply to keep your face hidden from—"

"Netizens?" she repeated as well as asked.

"네. Internet citizens. I'm sure you know about online fans and bullies? Well we made a name for them; they're people who scour the internet for something to like or hate. Netizens." He again taught her something new.

"It's a fun little name," she said, smiling. "And this means I can cut out the twenty-step face-washing process you had me doing."

"It isn't that much work. I do it every morning." He shrugged.

"You're joking, right? You can complete that entire process before you leave for work? On top of that, women have to put on makeup. You guys take your skin care hella serious." She pointed to his flawless face in mock anger. "I mean, look at that! Not a blemish. Perfection."

With that she saw a light rose color rise to his cheeks.

"어머! Are you blushing? Did I just make you blush? People are constantly praising you for your looks and you don't blush in front of them. Flustered, sure, like when that woman at the shop recognized you, but blush? Never." She moved closer to get a better look, and he tried to move his face away from her prying eyes. But when she got too close, she lost her balance, tripping and falling right onto his chest.

His hands didn't wrap around her, he was totally frozen, and the room went silent. All she could hear was his labored breathing, and all she could feel was the hardness of his chest.

Pushing off him, she looked up at him and cleared her throat. "I will use them as well as..." she grabbed the hoodie from one of the hangers next to her and smiled, "this."

Korean Vocabulary:

일어나세요 – irohnasaeyo -wake up

모닝케어 – mohning kaeo- morning care (a hangover drink)

Chapter 27 (스물일곱)

When Hwan Soo's manager, who she learned his name was Gi Young, came to pick them up in the usual black coach van, he saw what his manager meant about the suitcase Val had sent. It was barely staying closed, it was so full of clothing. Maria barely unzipped it before is burst open, seeing the chaos of her friend's packing, and rolled her eyes.

"We don't have time for you to change here at the house. You can get dressed on the way. The windows are heavily tinted, so no one will see you," he explained as he climbed in and put his hand out to help her up.

She reluctantly grabbed his hand and climbed in. Her eyes went wide looking at the interior. He followed her eyes scanning the large tan leather seats, the clothing rack for costume or clothing changes, and his small section of snacks in the back.

"This is like the size of my entire apartment," she chuckled, taking the seat next to him.

"Really?" he asked incredulously. He knew his life wasn't normal, but he didn't realize just how different it was.

"It's an exaggeration, but not by much," she joked as she began to rummage through the suitcase, pushing aside most of the clothing that still had their tags.

"Nothing to wear?" he mocked.

"None of this is mine. It's all the stuff from her closet she wants me to wear." As she said that, she pulled out a very skimpy undergarment that made him turn his head away and cough violently. He immediately had about thirty new images of her in his mind, all including the removal of the lace thong that was still hanging from her finger.

"Ah, finally!" he heard her exclaim. His head snapped over to see her unbuttoning the pants she was wearing to put on a new pair of pants. No shame in the fact that he was sitting in the chair next to her.

"Shouldn't you...eh-hem...maybe go to the back to change?" He again turned away from her. His mind didn't need any more inspiration for his inappropriate thoughts.

"You're probably right." He saw her reflection in the window as she maneuvered her slender frame past him and into the back seat. As he continued looking forward, he couldn't help but notice Gi Young glancing in the rearview mirror a little more often than needed. With a clearing of his throat, his manager got the hint he had been caught and kept his eyes focused on the road.

"Done," she exclaimed as she returned to the seat next to him, still wearing the hoodie she had stolen from his closet.

"Your top?" he asked, confused.

"Oh, well you said I should dress down and grungy. This hoodie fits that since it's oversized, and I can throw the hood up to hide my face," she explained, throwing the hood over her head to prove her point. When she looked over at him with the hood covering her eyes and a bright, show-stopping smile, he couldn't resist smiling and reached out to pat her hooded head once again with a laugh.

"귀여워," he whispered. Suddenly the van braked hard, sending

them lurching forward. Out of instinct his arm moved to hold Maria back against the seat.

"미안해." His manager bowed his head with an apologetic face.

"Be careful," Hwan Soo said, trying not to yell. When he looked over at Maria, her hands were gripping his arm for dear life; her eyes were closed and teeth clenched.

"You okay?" he asked, looking to make sure she didn't hit her head or anything.

She nodded and released her death grip on his arm.

He tried to remain calm on the surface but as the car got closer and closer to their final destination, his nerves kicked in. His leg tapped alarmingly fast as did his fingers on his thigh. And no matter how hard he pushed his hand down, nothing could stop them.

"You've done this before, right?" she asked out of the blue.

"네?" he asked, confused by her question.

"You seem really nervous. I wanted to make sure you're okay." She looked down at his leg that continued its nervous tapping.

"It's like any first day of a job. It's nerve-racking. On top of knowing who is going to be there," he explained.

"But you've done this kind of thing many times before." She shrugged, still not understanding how it could make him so nervous.

"Doesn't make it any less scary. What? You don't get nervous when you start a new job? Or even just a new project at work?" he said with a small waver in his voice.

"I've never been nervous about a job. I remember people always saying 'Don't be nervous', but I never was to begin with." She leaned back on the seat, closing her eyes, taking deep calm breaths he wished he could take himself.

"That's really weird. You know that, right?" He didn't mean to be harsh but he couldn't control his emotions around her.

"You're telling me you get nervous every time you audition?" She bit back with one of the most ludicrous questions he ever heard.

"Of course! A show can make or break you. All I've wanted to be was an actor. Since I was a teenager, girls told me I looked like a drama star they watched, and they wished I could be in dramas because they would watch them more. A very pubescent boy reason to choose a career path, just to get more girls, but it's true. And when I got my first very tiny part in a web drama, I ended up enjoying it. I got hooked. But whenever I went to auditions, I was turned down constantly. I never had 'the right look.'" He couldn't seem to stop confessing his life drama to Maria. He knew she was someone who could understand, or if not, she would still listen to let people get things off their chest. He saw then why Val kept her around.

"But one day, a director gave me a shot. Someone finally saw something in me. And from that day, every audition has me waiting for them to tell me my looks aren't useful anymore."

His leg had stopped fidgeting, and his heartbeat had gone from hummingbird fast to painfully, achingly slow. He'd never confessed how worried he was about his career. Jung-hyun had never even heard how broken Hwan Soo would feel after every "no" he got, about how he was ready to quit, and his now constant battle to stay relevant.

"You really love what you do," she said, her voice filled with calm admiration. She opened her eyes to gently look over at him. "That's obvious. Maybe that's why I'm never nervous. I've never cared about the jobs I've worked. It's a means to put food on my table and pay my rent."

"You've never had a passion you wanted to pursue?" he asked, befuddled by her own admission.

"Sure I did. But it wasn't a way to make money." She laughed dejectedly.

"Who the hell told you that?" he seethed, wanting to find whoever told her she wasn't good enough and beat the living crap out of them.

"Everybody." She smiled, but there was hurt behind her eyes. She was good at hiding it, but he saw it.

"I won't ever say that. I've been in your position. Knowing people don't and won't believe in you. Take my parents, for instance. They think this is a hobby until I finally decide to get a 'respectable' job. But this is all I've ever wanted to do and have no interest in doing something else. You should follow your dream as well. So, I believe in you. I might not know what your passion was and I hope still is, but I believe your passion will be your success." He reached over, grabbing her hand in his, easily weaving their fingers together.

"I can see why they chose you as the lead," she said, squeezing his hand with a much warmer smile than she had been wearing only seconds ago. It made her eyes glisten with happiness.

"We're here," Gi Young said from the driver's seat.

Hwan Soo quickly let go of her hand and looked out to see the cameras and fans squabbling to try and get a view through windows to get the first shots of his arrival to the reading.

"All these cameras for a table reading?" She looked out the windows nervously.

"It's good press to get people excited before the show starts," he explained.

"Smart." She nodded, impressed with the idea.

"Listen, you're going to need to put your mask on now. 팀장님 is going to drive you around back so you can enter with the rest of the staffers," he explained. "If they see you come out with me, there will be questions. Questions you won't understand and don't want to, in all honesty. And the director will be annoyed that I've caused non-drama-related press on day one. 미안해요."

"Don't be. I definitely don't want to be that kind of burden on you." She shook her head. "Good luck. I will see you inside."

He laughed at her positive attitude and felt his heart do a weird skip as it started pumping a little faster. All his nervousness had come back, but not because he was worried about failing at his job; instead, it was about how he was feeling about the girl sitting next to him trying to put on her face mask.

"I'll see you in there," he said as he smiled and flung open the van door. The camera lights were instantly brighter, flashing quicker, and the screams were substantially louder. What shocked him most was how many people were there with signs of appreciation for him.

Korean Vocabulary:

귀여워 – gwiyeowoah – cute/pretty

조심해 – jumshimhae – be careful

Chapter 28 (스물여덟)

H is manager didn't speak to her as they drove around the corner to the employee entrance. In fact, he barely even acknowledged she existed until they walked into a large room filled with cameras both video and photo, surrounding what she could just make out through the crowd to be a table, and he pointed to a chair where she could take a seat. Handing her a pass to place around her neck so she wouldn't be questioned about how she got into the reading, he then turned and walked away to greet several people with very deep bows.

Guess he has to suck up to those dudes for Hwan Soo's sake.

He was a slightly chubby man, with thick black-rimmed glasses that fell onto his cute little chipmunk-like cheeks. His hair, while styled, looked as if he had tugged on it, and his face showed a few small signs of acne. She noticed that the man was as stylish as the people he was surrounded with. A white crew neck sweater with what appeared to be a small blue stitched bear on his left chest, an expensive watch that shimmered as he shook people's hands, nice slim-leg jeans, and high-end sneakers made him fit the part of a young manager to a young artist.

She smiled at how he was blatantly sucking up to some people more than others, but as she was snickering to herself, lights flashed, shutters clicked, and murmurs began getting louder. Clearly, people of importance had entered. She couldn't see a damn thing, and while she knew she didn't need to, she desperately wanted to get a look at the woman who broke Hwan Soo's heart.

She sat anxiously, and suddenly a chair scraped on the floor and the room went silent.

"오늘은..." She could only make out the beginning of what the man had said before he began speaking quicker than she was used to. She assumed it must've been the director.

"안녕하세요. 저는 이 환 수입니다," she heard Hwan Soo introduce himself.

A female voice then followed. "안녕하세요. 저는 박 해 소입니다." Maria's ears strained to hear everything the woman said. She had to be the ex. And damn if she didn't have a gorgeous sultry voice that even made Maria shiver in enjoyment.

Maria's heart beat faster and then clenched hard multiple times throughout the read through. Whenever she heard an interaction between Hwan Soo and Hae So, she tried desperately not to cringe.

After three hours of reading through the script, there were loud claps that Maria followed along with, and suddenly everyone began packing up their cameras, tripods, etc. Some of the reporters tried to stay behind to ask questions but security continued to push them out the door. And that's when she saw Hwan Soo sitting at the table with another handsome male discussing lines from their scripts.

She looked around, but there was no sign of the leading lady anywhere. Bummer.

"So you're the 짜장면girl?" a familiar sultry voice said from behind Maria.

When Maria spun around, pouty pink lips, fair skin, minimal-looking makeup and hair perfectly set into waves cascading down her shoulders met her eyes. The woman's glare was dead set on Maria.

"I'm sorry, were you talking to me?" Maria pulled her ornate mask that had what she could only assume were real crystals down from her mouth and looked around just in case there was someone standing behind her.

"Yep, you definitely are. And the girl in the photo Hwan Soo sent me. I don't know how you sank your little foreign claws into Hwan Soo, but I'm warning you right now—" She stopped as one of the crew walked past them and bowed with the most fake kind smile.

Who the hell is this chick?

"If you cause any problems for my drama, I will make sure your precious Hwan Soo will never work in the industry again. I'll keep your little indiscretion from last night quiet for now, but try to test me and I will make it very clear how powerful I can be. Understood?" Her face had now gotten too close for Maria's liking.

It clicked who the woman was, and just as she was about to respond to her, a hand slid across her back, grabbing her waist and pulling her away. Looking up, she saw Hwan Soo, jaw clenched and eyes filling with rage as he looked at the woman across from them, which only confirmed her suspicion.

"이게 뭐야?" he spat. It was scary. This was the anger she saw in him last night. This was a volatile anger and she was worried about him going too far. But then he looked down to Maria, and his face softened instantaneously. The red in his cheeks subsided and his jaw released.

"괜찮아?" he asked kindly, bending down slightly to get a closer look at her. She noticed he had asked informally, which made her stomach fill with butterflies.

Maria's mouth went dry but she nodded, knowing he was asking if she was okay. His increased his grip on her hip slightly, which she took as a message that he was there to keep her safe. But he had no idea of the electricity and heat that was coursing through her body as he touched her.

"야, Hae So, next time you have to say something, speak to me." He tried to move Maria behind him and out of Hae So's line of sight.

"Calm down, Hwan Soo, I was just getting acquainted." That

fake smile she had fooled the crew with was not going to fool Maria and clearly wasn't fooling Hwan Soo either.

"You have no need for that," he said, his venom never ceasing toward Hae So.

"Why are you so mean to me? I just wanted to know your friend's name." She tossed her hair back, looking at Maria as if asking her to corroborate the story and extending her hand for a shake.

Maria was about to meet the woman's hand with a nice hard shake, possibly breaking her tiny little bird wrist, but Hwan Soo's hand covered hers and pushed it back down to her side.

"Didn't I say you had no need for that?" He raised an eyebrow and nudged his head to the door exiting to the hallway, "가자."

He pulled Maria into the hallway and once there, he released his hold on her hip.

"So that's the ex." She leaned on the wall and he spun toward her, his eyes wide as he quickly covered her mouth.

"You need to learn how to whisper," he murmured as he looked around the hall to make sure no one saw or heard them. She was, however, too focused on the fact that his soft, long fingers were rubbing against her lips, sexually charging her body like he had last night.

She shook her head not to only get rid of those thoughts but also his hand. "What's the deal?"

"The deal is, we have rules written into our contracts about dating. And since my contract is new, if they caught wind of a dating scandal, I could lose a lot more than just this role," he explained, pacing in front of her while trying to calm himself.

"Okay. I'm sorry. I won't bring it up again...in public, but I need to hear what went wrong. I mean, you may not be a sparkling personality on the regular, but damn, you were cold as hell to her." She tried to lighten the mood with her

Hwan Soo was clearly not in the mood for her antics at the moment. He looked over at her, rage subsiding but still there as he said in a monotone voice, "Go back inside."

"But—" She wanted to help him calm down but he cut her off.

"Don't," he said to stop her from continuing.

"Lee Hwan Soo-씨—"

"Seriously Maria, we're not having this conversation," he bit quickly.

"Okay, why do you get to call me by my first name but I have to call you by your whole damn name. It isn't fair." She huffed like a small child, not actually annoyed but trying to take his mind off his anger and put it toward something else.

"Maria," he said in a pleading tone, which only caused her to become more concerned.

"Are you okay?" She reached for his hand, but he quickly pulled away and began looking around the hall again.

"Can we not? Seriously, can we just not talk about it right now? Please go back inside." He was speaking calmly but sounded desperate in his pleading for her to leave him alone.

She chose to not say a word and walked back into the large room that had emptied even more from when she had been pulled out. She looked to the side, feeling that someone was standing there and worried it could have been Hae So. She was partially relieved to see it was his manager.

"어?" He pretended to act like he hadn't been lurking near the door to hear what he was saying. Most likely making sure his money maker was still in fit form. She bowed and began to walk away when Gi Young surprised her by saying, "She's a heartless woman."

She turned, surprised he could speak English almost as well as Hwan Soo.

"Sorry?"

He moved closer to whisper, "Hae So. His ex."

She looked him up and down thinking about how Hwan Soo mentioned that his contract contained a strict dating clause.

"Hwan Soo is like a brother to me. I would never rat him out to the higher-ups for simply seeing a woman," he explained, as if he had read her mind.

"Well good for you." She didn't understand why he had even told her any of that; he seemed like he couldn't have cared less about her.

"She cheated on him. With his last co-star several months back. She wanted a big scandal that would put her into the spotlight. Make her the name on everyone's lips. And since his co-star was the lead, she decided to make him her next mark. Get herself higher on the totem pole. She even told Hwan Soo that she never considered what they had all that serious, hence why she kept it to late-night rendezvous. That crushed him." The man had explained with almost as much disdain for the woman as Hwan Soo had shown. Clearly, he wasn't lying about caring deeply for Hwan Soo and she felt bad about her assumption of him.

"Shit." She let out a loud sigh as kindred feelings filled her heart again. As she looked back to the door leading to the hallway, wanting to run out there and give Hwan Soo the largest hug to tell him he would be okay, the man who plagued her thoughts came walking in.

"Ready for the rest of the reading?" Gi Young asked excitedly, hiding the fact that he knew and had now spilled Hwan Soo's dark secret to Maria.

"Always." The blinding smile from Hwan Soo was almost convincing enough for her to believe he had gotten over his anger. Almost. She still saw the hurt in his eyes and she wished that she could somehow take that pain away.

Korean Vocabulary:

오늘은 : ohnulun – for today...

저는 ... 입니다 – chonun ... ibnida – my name is ...

이게 뭐야 -eegae mwoya? -what's this?

Chapter 29 (스물아홉)

"Tonight we celebrate!" Jung-hyun shouted to the group as he lifted his soju glass for everyone to clink.

"짠!" they all shouted simultaneously as a bit of the liquid sloshed out of their glasses and they poured the shots into their mouths.

Maria still was not used to the strength of the soju, but she downed it anyway. She thought it was only right to celebrate the big news of Hwan Soo getting his first lead role. As she bit the inside of her mouth to hide her displeasure with the alcohol, a different bottle appeared in front of her.

"You didn't get to try this last night," Hwan Soo whispered. "It's a lot easier to handle." He waved the bottle in a circular motion, forming a small liquid tornado in the bottle before tapping the bottom to his elbow and finally twisting the cap off to pour some in her glass. She watched this bartender-like technique in amusement, which made him laugh. "It's a Korean thing."

He was about to pour some for himself, but she knew he shouldn't and she reached for it, pouring the shot for him. With wide eyes, he watched as she poured the fruity-scented liquid. She lifted her glass to him which he clinked with his own, eyes never leaving hers, making a pleasurable shiver run through her body They then drank their shots together.

That was magic. She looked the glass wishing there was more in it. The sweet, fruity flavor totally overpowered the strength of the alcohol.

"맛있어요?" he asked with a knowing smile.

She nodded her head excitedly as she held the glass out to him for more.

"You gotta pace yourself. You're not used to the strength of this stuff. Even if it's fruity, it's potent," he said as he poured the liquid into her glass anyway.

Jung-hyun then butted in, handing Hwan Soo the stronger-tasting stuff. He skipped her glass, pouring it to the other two, while switching up to pour her the sweeter stuff for their cheers. He was being extremely generous, which was making it harder for her to deny that she was attracted to more than just his face and physique.

At the third stop on their tour of drinking and eating through Seoul, Maria had cut herself off. She knew her limit and wanted to sober up in case Hwan Soo had some random Korean lesson in store for her the next day. Hwan Soo, on the other hand, was pounding the soju back like it was water. She tried to stop him at one point but between his nearly lidded eyes, red cheeks, and the grumbles coming from his puckered lips, she decided it wasn't her problem. It didn't help that neither Val nor Jung-hyun were in any better of a state.

"미친년," Hwan Soo slurred out.

"야!" Jung-hyun shouted while Val opened her mouth wide in shock. "Don't say that about Maria."

"Excuse me? What did he say?" Maria looked between the two for an answer.

"You don't want to know." Jung-hyun dropped his head to the

table with a thud, and Val quickly reaching over to make sure he hadn't bruised his forehead.

"Not her. The other one." Hwan Soo flung his arms around nearly slapping Maria in the face. Luckily, she ducked out of the way.

"Oh, you mean..." Jung-hyun mumbled as he sat up, slumping to lean his head against Val's shoulder.

"Why bring her up during such a happy occasion?" Maria groaned, now realizing whatever he had said was about Hae So.

"Because she ruins it," he groaned, stomping his feet on the ground like a child who didn't get his way, causing people in the small bar to look over at their group with annoyance.

"She shouldn't." Val finally spoke up like she had been in a total daze until that moment.

"Of course she should!" Hwan Soo yelled. "You don't get it."

Maria looked over to him. "She broke your heart. We get it. Pretty sure billions of people around the world get it. But it doesn't stop them from enjoying the happy moments in life. Wanna know why? Because we refuse to let it. Sure, there are days one struggles. You don't want to face the day ahead, but you still get your ass up. You just got a role that you yourself said could make your career. Are you seriously going to let her kill that for you? Ruin your dream? She's a speed bump you need to move slowly across, so she doesn't mess everything else up in the car. 알았어?" She shouted the last bit, deciding she needed a shot to calm her overt jealousy. She hated him thinking about that woman. About any woman, for that matter.

She continued her rant by saying, "Your first read through sounded like you did great. People laughed appropriately, seemed awed, even had some of the women reports blush a little, so clearly your animosity toward the chick hasn't come out. Leave it that way and you should be all good."

They all stared at her—Val with surprise, Jung-hyun with a devious smile, and Hwan Soo with a slack jaw and a small amount of drool about to fall out of his mouth. She rolled her eyes at all of them and slammed her elbows on the table, which startled them all, making them sit up straight.

"야." Hwan Soo grabbed everyone's attention, including some people who were not part of their group. Those people, however, were clearly not amused by his drunken state. "Do you wanna know why I choshh acting?"

Maria, Val and Jung-hyun all stared at him and shook their heads. He had told Maria a large part of why he wanted to act. Girls in school told him he was attractive enough to be on TV, but she knew he wasn't that vain and had a suspicion there was more to it than that.

"Because I wanted to feel love." He grabbed Maria's shot glass and took her shot. As she watched his Adam's apple bob, she was confused as to why he felt that way; Val and Jung-hyun appeared confused too.

"뭐? People have always loved you. You were the most popular kid in high school. I didn't even live here and I knew that." Jung-hyun reached over to grab his friend's hand in comfort.

"It wash all fake love," Hwan Soo huffed and pouted, exaggerating his sadness.

"Being an actor is full of fake love," Maria blurted out, and all eyes turned to her as she continued. "You didn't want real love. You just wanted love you knew wasn't real so you wouldn't fall for it...again."

Hwan Soo stared at her more intently than the other two. He scooted closer to her, eyes never leaving hers as he brought his hand to her cheek. It was a bit sweaty, probably from a mix of the alcohol and the warm grills they had been around for most of the night, but it still made her clamp her legs shut to keep from giving in to her lust.

"You're the first—" He didn't even finish the sentence before his body fell limp into her lap, his head falling into her chest. Val and Jung-hyun burst into fits of laughter, holding onto the table so they wouldn't fall off their own seats as Maria looked at the now passed out man on her lap.

Even through her slight buzz she could make out how calm, soft, and warm he looked when he slept. He looked...

"Lovable."

"뭐라고?" Val shouted through her laughs, bringing Maria out of her thoughts.

"Huh?" Maria looked away from the slumbering man in her lap.

"You said something. I couldn't hear you." Val was still trying desperately to contain her laughs.

"No, I didn't." Maria wasn't sure what she had said out loud and was not about to repeat any of it. Putting on her mask to hide the blush that was rising to her face and making it known she wanted to leave, she tried pushing Hwan Soo off. "Are either of you gonna help get him off me?"

She tried desperately to lift him even the slightest bit, but he was total dead weight. She slumped and he stirred, wrapping his arms around her waist and pulling her closer to him, making their stools move together with a loud scrape.

"That's all yours 친구," Val stood grabbing at Jung-hyun.

"뭐? 왜? If anything, he's actually your friend so you guys should be taking care of him!" she shouted as she tried to stand and again failed miserably.

"True...but this is a great bonding moment for you guys. Plus, he's in your lap. Which means he wants you as his drunk companion for the night." Jung-hyun's cunning smile remained plastered on his lips. She knew he was thinking something nefarious and she wanted to know exactly what it was.

"Is this some other drinking tradition I don't know about?" Maria asked.

The happily engaged couple looked at each other as if corroborating their story, then turned to her with happy nods.

"Take him home and make sure he doesn't die. See you tomorrow!" Val pulled Jung-hyun even harder to get them out of there as fast as possible.

Maria didn't even have enough time to argue as they bolted out the door.

"Great," she huffed again, trying to get even the littlest movement out of the man in her lap. He was so peacefully asleep she felt bad that she was about push him off her when a voice scared her from behind.

"도와 드릴까요?"

Her head snapped around to see who was talking to her, and she was surprised to find a very handsome waiter looking to her lap with his finger pointed at the slumbering Hwan Soo. While she was pretty sure he had offered to help, she also worried he could've been asking if Hwan Soo was an actor he recognized, and so she gently began stroking his face to keep it obscured.

"Ah. English?" he asked.

"네." She nodded her head as she sneakily pulled Hwan Soo's mask from his pocket to put it over his face.

"Do you need help?" the man asked with a thick but understandable accent.

Relief washed over her face. "Oh God, yes please."

The young man smiled, showing blinding white, straight teeth and thick lips that when stretched looked as if they could actually go ear to ear. He reached down to peel Hwan Soo's arms off Maria's lap. But then he came to life, fighting with the stranger and holding Maria even tighter as he screamed, "싫어!"

"What?" she asked. Realizing Hwan Soo wouldn't answer, she looked to the young man to explain.

"Umm...it means 'hate'. I'm assuming what he means is he hates letting you go. I mean if I were your boyfriend, I would shout it if someone was trying to separate us as well." He again smiled cheerily, cheekbones high and sharp, almost like Hwan Soo's jawline, and dark brown hair pulled back and off to the side, gelled to stay exactly in place.

Did he just hit on her? While also assuming she was with her boyfriend? A boyfriend that was Hwan Soo? She had to give the guy some major ball points for the attempt.

"Oh, we're not...he's a friend of a friend," she felt the need to explain.

"Good to know." He now had a devious smirk playing on his lips. Finally, with all his gusto, he pulled Hwan Soo off Maria, leaving her legs feeling a chill, as well as calming her arousal.

"도와주셔서 감사합니다 ," she said, combining what she had learned from him with bits of what she knew previously. She stood, regaining feeling in her legs, and bowed.

His eyes lit up at her response to which she explained. "아...한국 조금 할 수 있어요"

"Well for only speaking a little, you've picked up on pieces quickly. And very well, I might add. Let's get you guys a taxi." He threw Hwan Soo's arm over his shoulder and dragged him out of the restaurant.

Whoever the waiter was, he was strong, handsome, and a total flirt. She found it fun.

They walked to the side of the road and she put her hand out as several cabs came down the street. One finally stopped in front of them. She pulled the door open quickly so that the waiter could toss Hwan Soo into the back seat.

She turned to the handsome stranger once again with a smile and bowed. "감사합니다."

"천만에요," he replied, bowing back.

She was about to close the door when his strong hand stopped the door from closing. "Before you go, can I get your name...maybe even your number?"

"뭐?" Her jaw dropped at his blunt flirtatiousness. She shouldn't have been as surprised as she was since he had shown some interest in the restaurant, but even so, she looked at him with wide eyes and a slightly parted mouth, unable to respond.

"You said he wasn't your boyfriend, so I thought maybe I could take you out sometime." His smirk was not sexy like Hwan Soo's.

"Oh...wow...um...well I am only here until the end of the month," she explained nervously, undecided if it was to inform him of her timeframe or politely turn him down.

"That's several weeks away," he said with a smile, making her giggle. "제발?" He pouted those lips that were so plump she could bounce off them, and he squinted as if throwing a little tantrum.

She looked around, not knowing what to say or do, and she saw Hwan Soo slumped on the window of the cab starting to drool. *When did he get his mask off?* She moved to block the window from view of the waiter.

The guy seemed to be nice enough, but she wasn't about to risk getting Hwan Soo and possibly herself in trouble with his manager by it getting leaked Hwan Soo got sloppy drunk. And if anything she could at least have some fun with wasn't like she was expecting to fall madly in love. Turning to back, him she smiled and gave a small nod.

"Sure," she replied. to which his eyes lit up with surprise and delight. He pulled his phone out of his pocket and she quickly entered her number for him to save.

"제 이름은 Kim Sul Bin 입니다. Maria반가워요." He smiled before bowing and shutting the door for her.

"어디 가세요?" the driver asked.

"Shit," she breathed out. She didn't know Hwan Soo's address. She nudged him but he didn't move. She then slapped his shoulder hard and his eyes flew open, looking around in surprise.

"Where is your house? What's the address?" she asked slowly.

He grumbled, his eyes starting to close once again, but he pulled out his phone, swiping it open and dialing a number. He sloppily pulled the mask from his face and waited for the person on the other end of the phone to answer.

"Oh, 형, 왜 갔어요? 네?" He was talking to Jung-hyun as his eyes began closing and the phone started to fall from his face.

Grabbing the phone before it could fall completely, she put it to her ear. "여보세요? Jung-hyun?"

"Yeah. Maria, you okay?"

"저기요! 어디 가세요?" the taxi driver repeated more aggressively.

"Ah. Give the man the phone," Jung-hyun huffed, out of breath. And she could hear Val whispering in the background. Hwan Soo had clearly interrupted something with his phone call, and she would definitely make him apologize the next day.

Handing the man the phone, there were several quick네's. The phone was then back in her possession and the cab took off. As the cab trudged along, every time it hit a bump, Hwan Soo's skull would smack on the window. Finally, after having enough of the frightening sound and concerned he would end up with a bruise and possibly a concussion, she pulled him to her so that his head rested on her shoulder. Once he got comfortable, he rubbed his head against her, his cheek against her shoulder and his hair tickling her neck. When he stopped rubbing, his head lifted off her shoulder and his chin then dug uncomfortably into her collarbone.

She was about to push him off when his hand went to her opposite shoulder, pulling her closer to him so that his lips connected with the skin of her neck. She had thought about that moment more than she wanted to admit in the short amount of time she'd known him, but the actual thing was even better than all of her fantasies. His soft lips on her open neck were even more pleasurable than when they were on her lips, and the feeling stirred a lot more pleasure below.

He pulled away only to dive right back giving her the feeling of floating in the calm ocean with the enjoyment he was causing. His tongue traced down her throat as she closed her eyes, relishing the electricity she felt. Her head fell to the opposite side, giving him the access he desired. His teeth nipped as his lips gently sucked her skin, but she pushed away so he wouldn't leave a mark.

When she looked down at him, his eyes were clouded over with a drunken haze, and his smirk was lopsided at best. His head fell back down on her shoulder, and that's when her ears perked up. He had begun to lightly snore.

This man really enjoyed making moves on her in his sleep.

Korean Vocabulary:

미친년 – michinnyeon – crazy bitch

도와 드릴까요 – dowah rilkaypo- do you need help?

싫어 – shiro – hate (in context it means I hate it)

도와주셔서 감사합니다 – dowahjuseoso kamsahabnida – thanks for your help

한국 조금 할 수 있어요 – hanguk jogum hal su issoyo – I can speak a little Korean

천만에요 – cheonmanaeyo – you're welcome

제발 – jaebal – please

제 이름은 ... 입니다 – jae eeroomoon ... ibnida – my name is

반가워요 – bangawoahyo – nice to meet you

왜 갔어요 – wae kassoyo – why'd you leave

Chapter 30 (서른)

P ulling up to Hwan Soo's house, she looked to the cab driver and said with a nervous smile, "얼마예요?"

He smiled and responded, "삼만 원."

She tried desperately to figure out the amount she owned him and with a smile of encouragement, the driver put up three fingers.

"Three?" she questioned, and the gentleman nodded. "만? I have no clue…원is the currency," she whispered to herself.

"Thirty thousand," Hwan Soo mumbled, his head rubbing on her shoulder to wipe the sleep from his eyes.

She pulled out her wallet and paid the man, adding a tip. He waved his hands, refusing the excess money. Tipping, she concluded, was not a normality.

"Lee Hwan Soo-씨, we're at your house." She nudged him, trying to wake him up.

"집? 어디?" He sat up, looking out the window like a child and bounced in his seat, making the car shake as he bowed to the driver saying, "감사합니다 ."

He climbed out of the car. As Maria slid to exit through the same door, he closed it on her and continued bowing to the man.

"Hey!" she shouted.

"I'm fine." Hwan Soo waved her off with a hiccup and stumbled.

Instinct kicked in and she jumped out of the car, running to his side.

"You're not fine. Let me help you." She put her arm around his shoulder and saw the cab hadn't moved as the man looked at them with concern. She bowed, letting him know they were fine and turned slowly to get Hwan Soo into the house.

"I don't need your help," he groaned. "I've done this walk many times."

"Call it a motherly instinct, but I'd rather know for sure you make it to your bed than just hope you do." She wrapped her hand around his wrist a little tighter so he couldn't sway too far away, and she felt his pulse beating rather quickly.

He giggled lightly as he mumbled, "Motherly instinct."

She rolled her eyes, still lugging him to the front door. Seeing there was a passcode that needed to be entered, she nudged him. He looked at her and she indicated the door with her eyes. He followed the line of sight, wobbly, and reached out to enter his code. A small ding went off and a loud thunk of the lock opening gave her relief.

Getting into the entryway was an even bigger relief. He pulled his arm out of her grasp to pull off his shoes and stumble into the living room. She followed behind, making sure he didn't stumble too far to one side as her hand clutched the back of his shirt to stop him from toppling forward. He pushed open the door at the end of the hallway and almost ran in.

His room was immaculate. The three long white bookshelves on the wall held plants, a smattering of books, and what looked to be little robot toys. The recessed lighting was dim, creating a relaxing, almost spa-like atmosphere, which matched the smell of eucalyptus and pine. Across the room were the floor-to-ceiling glass doors that opened to his own private veranda filled with plants that looked to be well taken care of.

Horticulturalist? Hwan Soo? Who would've known? His bed

was nearly on the floor, just barely encompassed in what looked like a bamboo box. His sheets were shades of white and gray all flowing together, and when he fell onto the mattress, it gave a little bounce as he was enveloped by the comforter. If she didn't know this was his house, she would've thought she was in a five-star hotel room.

"You can stay here the night since you were too worried about me to grab the cab back to yours," he mumbled into the comforter, shimmying it down to cover him.

"Wow, what hospitality." She rolled her eyes and walked over to him to make sure he laid on his side in case he vomited.

"Don't get too used to it," he laughed, snuggling more into his blankets.

"잘자요, Lee Hwan Soo-씨," she whispered.

"잘자, Maria," he said informally. She was surprised by the sudden change, but she blamed it on the alcohol.

She hadn't had a good night's sleep the night before, due to a kiss that caused her toes to curl and Hwan Soo almost taking it to the next level, so she was very excited to be able to crash on an actual bed. Although he thoughts of Hwan Soo devouring her neck were brought back to the forefront of her mind. His lips had the most powerful influence over her body. She craved more and more of the feel of them and it was getting harder to keep herself in check. Especially when he chose to act out her naughty thoughts like they were also his own.

Confusion sank in as she walked into the guest room. Looking nothing like the room she had left, the walls were stark white with no added decoration. There was a small shelf in one corner that again held some small plants, a few books, and some photos. The bed was well raised off the floor, almost as if she would have to take a running leap to land on it. The bedding itself looked like a plush cloud that would cradle her softly to sleep, and the headboard was a white iron-work piece of art.

Following her own idea, she ran toward the bed, jumping up to fall gently into the bedspread. It was even more luxurious than she thought. Her body was melting into the fabric when she felt the buzz of her phone in her pocket.

Thinking it was a text from Val asking if she had gotten home okay, she was all set to give a quick answer. But instead it was an unknown number.

Unknown: Make it home yet?

She realized that it had to be Sul Bin.

Maria: Just got to the friend of a friend's house. He's been so generous to let me crash in his guest room *eye roll*

Sul Bin: 아. You sure you guys are nothing more than friends?

Why that questioned bothered her, she didn't know. While Hwan Soo had a lot of redeeming qualities and she seemed to find more and more as their time spent together went on, she was mad at the fact that a man and woman couldn't just be friends. And they weren't even that.

Maria: Yes. In fact, we aren't even friends. We're civil for the sake of our friends.

Minus when they had a steamy kiss on his couch to make his ex-girlfriend jealous and also him making out with her neck not even twenty minutes ago.

Sul Bin: That's good. Otherwise it would've been a real bummer.

Maria: "Bummer"? You must've lived in America at some point.

Sul Bin: ㅋㅋㅋ. Yeah. I lived there up until I was fifteen. My mom moved back to Korea when her and my dad split and she took me with her. Not that my dad

minded. Wow...already digging into my past? You're good. ㅋㅋㅋ

She smiled, snuggling even more into the sheets. He had his charms.

Maria: What can I say? I'm just that good.

Sul Bin: Pretty and smart...I must've done something in a previous life to deserve such luck.

Blush filled her cheeks, and she was no longer the least bit tired as they continued to chat throughout the night.

"일어나세요!" A loud knock came from the door.

She grumbled, snuggling into the sheets, covering her face from the morning light. She couldn't remember when she fell asleep, but it was most definitely too early for her to be waking up.

A click of the door, and a swooshing sound of curtains meant that Hwan Soo had entered her room most likely trying to wake her up. She, however, was not in the mood to even get out of bed.

"야," he grumbled, and she felt the comforter get rumpled and suddenly tugged cleanly off her body as the cool air of the room hit her skin. She sat up angrily, about to let him have it when he dropped the covers to the floor. His eyes flew open wide and his cheeks flushed as he covered his mouth and suddenly turned away from her.

"어머." She looked down, realizing the cause for his reaction. She still didn't have her own clothes to wear and chose to sleep in just her underthings. She grabbed a pillow to cover what he had basically already seen and screamed, "Get out!"

"Be ready in fifteen," he said, barely audible before leaving the room and shutting the door behind him.

She hopped up and grabbed her clothes, which were technically still his clothes that he let her borrow the day before, and walked out to the living room.

Looking around she saw him in the kitchen standing at the stove, pouring egg into a pan. He was cooking? How was he even functioning? He was beyond the valley of drunk the night before and there he was, a fully functioning adult ready to get on with his day.

When he turned to plate the food, he jerked his head for her to come into the kitchen. Placing the plated meal on the counter, he handed her utensils and said, "먹어요."

"How...what...how—" she stumbled.

"I don't get hangovers, if that's what your confusion is about. I also couldn't get much sleep since all I could hear were your giggles down the hall. This house echoes, so laugh into your pillow next time," he bit. "Also I'm sorry for this morning. I didn't think you would be..."

As he trailed off both their faces went bright red with embarrassment. She shook her head as if to say it's nothing and quickly dug into the omelet. The egg was fluffy and even a bit sweet and filled with veggies that gave each bite a little crunch. She was surprised at how well he could cook.

"This is delicious," she said through her mouth full of omelet.

"맛있어요," he repeated as he put an omelet in front of himself and quickly dove in.

"Again, I wasn't planning to spend the night here—"

He cut her off, saying, "My manager kept the suitcase Val gave us yesterday. We thought if there were late nights of filming and you would have to spend the night here again, we would be somewhat prepared."

Like a scene out of a drama, 팀장님 walked in with a bag of clothing and a bright smile.

"좋은 아침," he said excitedly.

"좋은 아침," they both responded.

"여기," he said, handing the large bag to Maria and then focusing all his attention on Hwan Soo. Maria had become invisible and chose to walk away to change into Val's clothing.

Letting out an exhausted huff, she knew she had no other options and went back to the guest room to change.

Korean Vocabulary:

얼마예요 – irlmayeyo – how much is it?

삼만 원 – Samman won – 30,000 won (roughly $30USD)

집? 어디 ?- chib? odi? – House? Where?

잘자요 – Jaljayo – goodnight

일어나세요 – eeronasaeyo – wake up

어머 – omo – OMG

먹어요 – mogoyo – eat

Chapter 31 (서른하나)

H e could barely remember she had brought him home, but what he did remember was every so often when he woke up, head spinning slightly, he heard a faint giggle coming from his guest room.

Waking up with only a mild headache, he started to flash back to those laughs and decided to check who was in his guest room. At first, he snuck in to see Maria, probably the most angelic he had ever seen her sleep. A smile with lips parted so she could breathe deeply, her hair only slightly matted to her cheek, her phone facedown on the bed but still in her hand. He tried to wake her up gently. Walking up to the bed, sitting beside her, brushing the hair out of her face which was buried in the pillow, making him chuckle. But he saw the time and realized she had to get up ASAP.

And so, he made his second 'entrance'. Making all the noise in the world to get her up he shut the door loudly, stomped over to the curtains where he pulled them open to have the bright light of the morning flood in stomped back over to her with impatience.

When he pulled the covers off her, he hadn't expected to see those great legs he had seen barely covered by a towel only a few days prior spread over the mattress. Or that butt he had previously enjoyed watching walk ahead of him, in a thin piece of maroon cotton fabric. He most definitely didn't expect to see her chest bounce in its slightly crooked bra, and her toned stomach with skin that looked so creamy smooth that called to be touched.

They sat side by side in the managers van, not saying a word, but one thing continued to gnaw at him.

"What were you laughing about so much last night? Did you start a new drama or something?" He spoke in a monotone voice as he pretended to scroll through absolutely anything on his phone to mask his curiosity.

"No. I didn't even know that room had a TV." She shrugged, leaving him still needing to probe for an answer.

"Oh, did Val call to check up on you?" he asked.

"It wasn't Val. Pretty sure she and Jung-hyun were in the middle of something when you called and interrupted them last night. By the way, you should call to apologize to him."

"They haven't slept together yet. I know you know that much." He did feel bad for potentially ruining the possibility of his friend getting laid. But he still didn't have an answer, and he had to push further.

"A friend from home then?" He finally looked over at her to gauge her reaction.

She shook her head, then spun violently toward him. "Why do you want to know so badly?" She smirked, eyeing him up and down.

"You want to give me an attitude after I let you stay in my house and eat my food?" He crossed his arms defensively.

"You were too drunk to even tell the driver where to go last night, and I had to lug you from the cab to your bedroom. The least you could do was offer me a place to crash. As for the breakfast, 고마워." She dipped her head in feigned gratitude.

"You're seriously going to dodge the question?" His blood was beginning to boil.

"I answered all your questions, Lee Hwan Soo-씨." She was

relentless with the sass, leaning her elbow on the armrest of the seat, eyelashes fluttering, smile feigning innocence. So different from her pure smile he saw while she slept.

"Who were you talking to?" He spoke as calmly as he could through gritted teeth.

The smirk quickly became one of total pleasure etched across her face as she responded, "Just someone I met last night who helped me get you into the cab since you chose to fall asleep in my lap at the restaurant and I was unable to get out of there without help."

He had no recollection of that happening. He did, however, vaguely remember a dream in which he was kissing her neck and leaving a mark on his territory. Could it actually have been real? No way. She wouldn't have let him make such a move on her.

"You met someone?" His eyebrow raised as he tried to get a look at her neck without arousing suspicion.

"I did. He seems like a nice enough guy. We made plans to have dinner tomorrow night," she giggled.

She likes this douchebag. He didn't even know the guy, couldn't even recollect if he saw the guy's face, but he already didn't like him.

"You can't go," he commanded.

"Excuse me? Who are you to tell me what I can and can't do?" She looked ready to throw off her seatbelt and climb over to strangle him.

"I'm not. That's the night of our best friends' engagement party," he pointed out.

As she looked at him, he watched as she was trying to piece what he said together when realization dawned in her eyes, a lightbulb going off. A sick sense of satisfaction filled him from head to toe as she grabbed her phone.

"What a shame..." he said with fake pity in his voice.

"It's fine. I can reschedule for the following night." She shrugged, quickly typing out a message to who he assumed was this mystery guy.

"너 미쳤어?" he spat.

"뭐? It's not like I have much time to hit him up," she said, looking over at him like what she said wasn't surprising.

But it was. She liked this guy and she had only met him the night before. How could he have wormed his way into the playing field so fast? What field? There was no field. Why did Hwan Soo get mad about this guy so quickly? He had never been jealous when it came to women being with other men. They fawned over him; he never felt the need to. When one lost interest another would fill her place. However, hearing Maria excited about seeing another man sent him reeling.

Ding. Her phone's text alert.

She went back to texting him. With every ding, Hwan Soo was losing his ability to stay calm. Her reactions went from excitement to giggles to concern to contemplation. She hung on that contemplation one a bit too long, which had him worried about what this boy had said.

"What are you thinking about so hard?" He didn't even think about it as he ripped the phone out of her hand to see what had gone on in the conversation to warrant her perplexed face.

"Hey!" she shouted, trying to grab the phone out of his hand. He deflected every lunge as he read through the messages and his stomach sank. They were laughing, he was speaking Korean, explaining the meaning, and then finally asking if he could be her date for the engagement party.

"What nut job wants to have their first date at an engagement party?" Hwan Soo criticized.

"Give it back!" She unbuckled her seatbelt, charging over to his seat. With her hand precariously close to his crotch, she grabbed the phone out of his extended hand. Their noses almost touched and as he looked down at her lips, they pursed. Looking slightly farther down to her neck, he saw no indication his hickey dream was real. Relieved, he focused on what was happening—her hand was slightly twitching near his crotch, causing him to close his eyes, trying to imagine everything sad and boner destroying before he got both of them in trouble.

That's when he felt a vibration under her hand and realized she was pressing his phone, which was alerting him of a phone call. She moved away from him, and he pulled out his phone to see Jung-hyun's name light up the screen.

"어 형. 잘 지내?"

"네. Wanted to call and check up on you and Maria. Both still in one piece?" Jung-hyun joked.

"Yeah. Question—would you be okay with Maria bringing a stranger to your engagement party?" he asked, making sure every word was enunciated so Maria, who looked on with mirth, heard.

"I can't say I know any people she does, apart from my gorgeous fiancée, so anyone she's planning to go with would be a stranger to me," Jung-hyun validly claimed. *Damn him.*

"He was our waiter last night. So she's known him maybe a total of four hours. You still okay with it?" He had to have someone side with him on this, and he was sure Jung-hyun would pick up on that.

"Well he was checking her out the entire time we were there. I give him credit for making a move when you were slung all over her," Jung-hyun laughed.

The phone was ripped out of his hand and when he looked over it, was at Maria's ear.

"He actually thought Hwan Soo was my boyfriend," she scoffed, giving Hwan Soo the once-over, clearly being able to hear both sides of the conversation. "But when I told him we weren't even really friends, he asked for my number," she explained.

Leaning a bit closer to hear his friend's response, he was shocked to hear, "I mean, if he is comfortable coming to the party, I see no reason why he can't. You do have a plus-one for every step of the wedding."

That bastard! How could Jung-hyun allow it?! Especially after he was the one who told Hwan Soo to make it look like he and Maria were a thing in public. Her being with another guy would ruin the whole plan!

She handed the phone back to Hwan Soo as Call Ended blinked and his screen went black.

"I've got to get a totally new outfit now. Oh, and what am I going to do with my hair? Ah! I gotta text Val!" she gushed, blush rising to her cheeks as she prattled on.

He hated it. Because he wasn't the one who caused it.

Korean Vocabulary:

잘 지내 - jal jinae - How are you? or You've been good?

Chapter 32 (서른둘)

"So this Sul Bin guy is meeting us at the restaurant?" Val inquired as she helped with Maria's hair and makeup.

Maria could tell that Val was probing for something. She had a similar way of asking roundabout questions like her mother. And after yesterday, she realized so did Hwan Soo.

After Jung-hyun gave Maria the go-ahead to invite Sul Bin to the party, Hwan Soo ignored her completely. She sat and watched another read through of the script, but her mind was unfocused and preoccupied with what she was going to wear to impress Sul Bin. When her mind would come back into the room, it was only because she felt someone watching her. Looking around, she found two people's eyes on her.

Not only did Hwan Soo look at her, eyes filled with a heat she was unsure of, but also a blatantly jealous pair of female eyes that were attached to the gorgeously evil Hae So. And when their eyes met, all Hae So did was sneer. Maria was going to have her work cut out for her if she was going to be around this woman for the month she was set to be there.

When they wrapped up for the day, she saw Hae So trying

desperately to cozy up to Hwan Soo, who was clearly trying to get out of there as fast as possible. Maria stepped in by walking over to them, grabbing Hwan Soo by the wrist and pulling him away with an excuse that he had another engagement as they ran to the van for their quick escape. While he hadn't spoken to her for most of the day, he mumbled his gratitude as he dropped her off at Val's for the night.

∼

"Helllllloooo?" Val was waving her hand in front of Maria's face.

"네?" Maria looked up at Val in the mirror.

"Where was your mind just now? You looked...the only thing I can come up with is, turned on." Val brushed a pretty pink gloss on Maria's lips as she spoke. Maria said nothing, as what her friend said seemed so far off base. But was it? Maria knew she was attracted to Hwan Soo, not that she would ever tell a living soul. But now she was about to go on a date with another attractive and interesting guy, yet her mind kept yelling about Hwan Soo.

"Are you that smitten with this waiter already?" Val smirked.

Clearing her throat, Maria responded, "Yeah, I guess so."

∼

When the luxury service car pulled up to the restaurant, there was an onslaught of cameras flashing to see who was in the cars.

"What the hell is this?" Val spat. "Jung-hyun said he kept this whole thing totally out of the public eye. No one should be here but invited guests." Val looked ready to rip someone's head off.

And then a knight in shining armor came to open the door.

"Ladies," Sul Bin smiled brightly, "I'm here to get you through all this."

His smile was reassuring, and even Val's face appeared to calm down as he put his hand out to help them out of the car while keeping the cameramen out of the way.

"고마워," Maria whispered to him as his hand wrapped around her waist. He kept his other hand in front to give them a clear line of entry.

"You forgot to mention that your friend is marrying one of the largest CEOs in South Korea, and your drunken friend of a friend is a fairly well-known actor," he whispered.

"미안해. If you're uncomfortable being here, I totally get it. I can meet you afterward or something." She felt horrible. She didn't think anything like that would happen.

"Are you kidding? This is gonna be the talk of my friends for at least a month," he laughed, pulling her waist closer to him as they finally got to the front door.

When they walked in, Val immediately ran over to have words with Jung-hyun, leaving Maria with her date. And suddenly it was awkward.

"You look amazing in that dress," he said, looking her up and down with an appreciative smile. She had actually spent several hours rummaging through her clothes, only to figure out nothing she packed was impressive enough to go to her best friend's high-end engagement party. Val willingly let Maria raid the penthouse closet. The sleek black number she chose hugged her body but still flowed enough to sway as she walked. The high neckline, which Val told Maria was the best bet, let her arms stay exposed as well as the top half of her back.

She bowed her head and complimented him back. He was a bit more casually dressed, since he couldn't have known what he was about to get himself into. Navy dress pants that accented a very nice peach bottom she hadn't noticed the night they met, a nice light-blue button-up that had some added details of what looked like a safety pinned receipt where a breast pocket would be, and a nice pair of tan Oxford shoes.

"How've you been?" he asked nicely.

"Good. I appreciate all your help teaching me Korean. I've mainly been binging dramas," she answered, smiling appreciatively.

"It's not a problem. I'm shocked they asked you to learn a whole new language so quickly, so any way I can help, I'm more than happy to oblige. Especially if it's you." He winked.

She giggled, feeling an ease settle over them as a man serving champagne came around. Sul Bin grabbed two flutes, handing one gracefully to her.

"I have to run to the restroom real quick, can you hold this? I will be right back." He smiled and she nodded, and before she knew what was happening, his lips were on her cheek. Her eyes went wide and he gave her a wink as he walked off.

That was smooth. Almost too smooth.

"I swear my mother didn't do this, Valerie." Jung-hyun vehemently denied Val's accusation.

"Then who would want our engagement party on display?" Val bit back.

The truth was, Hwan Soo knew exactly who.

"It was Hae So," he said quickly.

"Eh?" both Jung-hyun and Val responded, snapping their eyes to him.

"Yesterday at the read through, she saw my text asking what to wear and so on and she asked what it was for. Before I could stop myself, I told her it was your engagement party. She didn't know I had such 'well-to-do' friends, so she tried to invite herself as my date so she could talk herself up to get more connections. You know, true Hae So. When I denied her and told her I already had a date, she made an eerily cryptic statement about how happy 'mystery girl' looked with whoever was on the phone." Hwan Soo looked over at Maria, who was just being pecked on the cheek by the dude who'd made her smile like crazy the day before. Hwan Soo was disgusted and had to put his glass of champagne down before he smashed it in his fist.

"So she sent them here to what?" Val asked.

"Well, I'm hazarding a guess she believes that your 'relationship' with Maria is fake. And with another guy wrapping his arm around her and smacking a kiss on her cheek, she's probably going to get her way and expose the lie and potentially threaten you with it," Jung-hyun very logically concluded.

"You say that so calmly. When it was your idea in the first place to make it look like we could possibly be a thing," Hwan Soo huffed as he looked around and saw that Maria was alone, looking like a lost puppy. Her eyes were wide, darting all around the room, while she kept her lips on her glass which was, what he could only assume, a way for people would think she was drinking and not try to talk to her. She may have feared that someone would come up to her and ask her a question in Korean that she wouldn't be able to understand. She had learned so much in the short amount of time she had been there that he was almost positive she could answer anything. But his heart clenched, knowing she was uncomfortable in her environment.

"Okay, I'll go over there and somehow convince her to stay away from the windows." Val nodded and was about to make her way over to her best friend when someone interrupted.

"And then what?" a different voice spoke from behind them. A voice he didn't recognize but knew he already hated.

Sul Bin.

"Do you enjoy eavesdropping on private conversations?" Hwan Soo turned to see the man in question and distaste filled his entire being. Sure, the guy was attractive, and that was probably the main reason Maria swooned over him, but something behind his eyes told Hwan Soo this dude was trouble. He had that look that Hwan Soo had heard several Americans even refer to him as on his Instagram. "Fuck boy".

"When the conversation involves the girl I came here with, I believe I have the right to eavesdrop when her name is mentioned. And as for your ex, what could Maria possibly do to make her bring an onslaught of paparazzi here?" Sul Bin looked over at Maria and

Hwan Soo's eyes followed. He saw the still nervous girl standing alone waiting for her date to return to her. "Okay, I get it. You have Maria to help make your ex jealous. To maybe get her to come running back to you or something like that?"

This guy had formed his own conclusions and Hwan Soo was annoyed. "It's nothing like that. Don't go making your own assumptions."

"Then should I go and give my date a nice big kiss in perfect view of the cameras? Maybe wrap my arms around her waist and whisper sweet nothings in her ear. I've already seen how easy it is to make her blush. Imagine what would happen with all of that. Where would the blush lead? I might not be able to control my curiosity." Sul Bin grabbed a flute of champagne and took a small sip, then flashed a cocky grin, not once taking his eyes off Maria. Hwan Soo had just watched this man undress the girl Hwan Soo liked in his little "fuck boy" mind.

Hwan Soo wanted to deck him right there, but knowing the cameras were outside and people inside also had cell phones, it wouldn't end well for him. But worst of all was picturing Maria's face when she would see who was knocked out on the floor.

"What do you want?" Hwan Soo hissed.

"I guess what every 나쁜 남자wants. 돈." He rubbed his fingers together in front of his face.

"How much?" Hwan Soo's skin was crawling.

"Well, now that I know who Maria's friends are, I can't help but feel inclined to ask for just a little bit more." His cocky smirk had turned into an all-out evil grin.

"Just give me a damn number, 쓰레기," Hwan Soo bit.

"삼백만 원 should be a nice start." he smiled.

"You little piece of—" Jung-hyun was about to deck the guy for Hwan Soo but Val held him back.

"Fine," Hwan Soo said.

"친구야!" Jung-hyun looked at Hwan Soo with shock.

"If that's what it takes for him to go away, I will gladly pay. Send me your information and the money will be in your account by end of today," Hwan Soo said simply.

Tilting the glass and polishing off all the champagne inside, Sul Bin replied, "Pleasure doing business with you."

He walked away to the large tables of food, leaving Hwan Soo free to go over to Maria. And his heart nearly stopped when she looked at him and he saw the tension instantly dissipate from her body. She was comfortable with him.

"Your date abandon you?" He smirked, trying to play it cool.

"I thought he ran to the bathroom, but he's been gone a fairly long time. I mean, when nature calls..." she joked, but he could tell she was worried she had been ditched, and that made him feel bad.

"I just saw him walk over to the food. Maybe he's grabbing you guys some things to eat," Hwan Soo covered for the douchebag.

"Oh," she looked toward the food, where Sul Bin was chatting with someone as he put food on a plate. He looked over to them and gave a kind nod and wink.

"Would he mind if I stole you to introduce you to a few people? Jung-hyun's family and mine are here," he asked, putting out his hand for her to accept.

"You want me to meet your family? This is so sudden." She feigned nervousness, drawing her hand lightly to her chest. But when he followed that hand which was gently shaking, he saw her chest rising and falling quickly. She was nervous.

"I feel this is at least a fourth date kind of thing," she joked.

He laughed, which made the last few strains of tension release from her. With every bit of tension she released, his tension built. He wanted Maria badly. But there was no way he could say that out loud and not sound crazy. They'd only known each other a week. How could he have such strong feelings for her?

He liked her. He had admitted it to himself the second he saw her walk in the door of the restaurant in the black silky number that had a slit so far up, he was reminded of her half naked in bed two nights prior.

"You should probably meet them all because while they're rivals in business, they basically had to become friends since their sons were inseparable, and since we are part of the wedding his family should probably meet you. As for my family, I haven't said hello to them yet, so you will help ease the tension and hopefully help steer the conversation away from my lack of business professionalism and decision to be an actor." Her hand slipped into his as he spoke, weaving her fingers between his and making a different kind of tension build. Her hand fit perfectly, like it was meant to be in his.

"You're right. We are part of this wedding. And how dare you not say hi to your parents yet. You got here before us!" She jokingly hit his shoulder.

"I wanted to introduce you to my parents," he admitted. He hadn't thought about it until she mentioned it, but he really did.

"가자," she said as a blush dusted her cheeks and ran up to her ears as she shouldered through the large swarms of people.

He nodded, feeling a complete sense of happy terror as he began introducing her to people with shocked eyes, confused crinkled noses, and the worst part, disapproving frowns.

Korean Vocabulary:

나쁜 남자 - nabboon namja - bad guy

돈 - money

쓰레기 - ssooraegi - trash

삼백만 원 - 3,000,000 won – roughly $3,000USD

Chapter 33 (서른셋)

S he could tell people were not fond of her. Whenever he introduced her, their eyebrows would raise and then look to her with surprise as their eyes raked over her and stopped at their entwined hands. She had tried to release her hand multiple times, but he held on tight. She wasn't sure how he was introducing her to people, but they weren't happy.

"Ready for my parents?" he whispered as he began heading toward the back of the restaurant where all the bigwigs of the party were with Val and Jung-hyun.

"Maybe introduce me differently than the way you have been," she whispered back, "Whatever you're saying is not going over so well."

"I'm more or less telling them you're someone I'm seeing," he said calmly.

"뭐라고?" she hissed, pulling him to a halt.

When he looked over to her, he looked confused as to why they had stopped. How could he not realize what he said could have major repercussions not only to them, but to their friends and even his career? He seemed totally unbothered by that.

"Why would you say that?" she asked, feeling heat on her cheeks that she was trying desperately to hide by keeping her head down.

His free hand slipped under her chin, pulling her head up so their eyes meet. As his eyes scanned her face, their dark color, like a night sea, had such a calming effect on her. She could look up into them like she was looking up into the night sky to count the stars. He smiled, making every part of her body melt, her knees wobbling as the knot below her stomach was growing tighter with need.

"It's a lot easier to explain. Like Val and Jung-hyun said, our titles of best man and maid of honor are very Western. Not too common-place here. 걱정하지마. I won't tell my parents such a lie. They will know that we are simply partners in the sense of working together for the common good of our friends."

"So eloquently put." She smirked as his thumb hovered over her lips, as if he wanted to touch them but knew he shouldn't. She wanted more than just his fingers to touch her lips. And she wanted her lips to touch a lot more than his fingers.

Did you forget your date?

When that thought came to her mind, a large sense of guilt took over the pleasure and she looked around to see where he could've gone off to while she was being introduced to all those people. Maybe he left? If he did, she would've understood. She, in a way, ditched him. She would need to apologize profusely later.

Hwan Soo stopped in front of a small group of people who were chatting in polite conversation. Suddenly all conversation halted and she felt like cowering behind Hwan Soo. He pulled her forward and two people whose backs were to them turned around.

Hwan Soo's parents. No doubt about it. He had the hair and lips from his father and the nose and flawless skin of his mother. They stood, heads held high, posture that even had Maria stand straighter, and wearing designer clothing she could only dream about wearing.

The woman's eyes slowly, calculatingly looked Maria up and down, and she sneered very slightly. Enough to make it known she did not enjoy the company her son was keeping.

"어머니, 아버지, this is Maria, Valerie's best friend and maid of honor at the wedding. Maria, these are my parents," he said, smiling brightly, openly excited to be introducing them to one another. Not only did her heart flip, but her stomach did a whole gymnastics floor routine.

"만나서 반갑습니다." She bowed deeply to them.

While his father looked impressed and even slightly amused, his mother still held a look of disgust.

"아들." Her mother looked to Hwan Soo and with a disappointed tone asked, "Why have you chosen to associate yourself with her?"

"네?" He seemed baffled by her distasteful and rude question. Maria was not as surprised but couldn't stop herself from squeezing Hwan Soo's hand when he suddenly pulled her gently closer.

"Are you trying to follow in the footsteps of your friend Jung-hyun by shacking up with this woman? At least he is running a company and can cover up for such...indiscretions." She pouted and made her eyes go all puppy-like.

"Shacking up? 어머니, I don't under—" He stopped himself. "You had me followed again?"

"Again?" Maria asked, surprised.

"I'm all for you pursuing your dream of being an actor, but you still have to take our family's name into consideration. If you want her to be a plaything, at least keep her away from your work and your house." Her voice dripped with fake concern.

"여보." Her husband looked just as shocked as Maria felt.

"어머니!" Hwan Soo shouted.

Maria's blood ran cold at the sound of his voice. He was annoyed with her, maybe even a little angry. Even when he had to coldly acknowledge Hae So, he held some semblance of decorum. But the way he looked and sounded when he spoke to his mother made Maria concerned. His face was bright red and his breathing was erratic; his hand was squeezing hers so hard, his knuckles were growing white.

She held his hand tightly to show she was there to keep him calm.

She bowed to his mother. "It isn't like that, ma'am. I am sorry for any confus—"

"And what if it was?" He cut her off, not looking at her, keeping his eyes dead set on his mother. "She's smart, she's picked up more of our language and culture in the week she's been here than you even tried while living in America for years. She is beautiful—just look at her, most of the men and women here are. She deserves just as much respect as she has shown you."

Hell had frozen over. Surely. If not, she had fallen asleep and woken up in a Korean drama dream. But the pressure of his hand holding hers nipped that idea in the bud. Lee Hwan Soo had not only come to her defense. He came to her defense against his own mother.

"Lee Hwan Soo-씨 it's—"

"No, it's not okay." He cut her off as if he knew what she was going to say. "We're here to celebrate our friends' happy engagement, and she insults you and me in the process. 어머니 사과하세요."

His father's eyes went wide, looking at his son like he had sprung an extra head. His mother's face was ghostly white.

"What did you say?" Maria whispered.

"She needs to apologize for being rude to a guest," he explained, finally looking down to her. His eyes that were once as calm as a night ocean were filled with the turbulence of a wild storm, but they calmed slightly as he looked at her, giving her butterflies in her stomach that fluttered so erratically she was afraid they would fly out.

"Are you insane? These are your parents. They have every right to look after your well-being. However ill-mannered it might be," she whispered before turning to his parents, bowing over and over again. "죄송합니다. 죄송합니다"

"Why are you apologizing?" he snapped.

"Because you're being ridiculous. We aren't what they think we are, so let her say what she wants. It hurts, but it won't kill me." She tugged on his hand, desperately trying to let go and separate them with a massive amount of distance, but with every tug he pulled her closer much more strongly.

"I don't accept that." He turned back to his mother expectantly.

"Hwan Soo-아." His father begged to stop him from making more of a scene.

"미안해," a soft female voice said, and all eyes went to the beautiful older woman whose head dropped with embarrassment.

Maria heard the woman loud and clear, regardless of how quietly his mother had mumbled. She'd apologized.

"Louder, 어머니," he commanded.

The woman's head popped up to meet his face and then looked over to Maria, bowing her head once again, but lifting her eyes to meet Maria's as she spoke. "미안해, Maria."

Maria simply stared at the woman, at a total loss for what to say or do. Hwan Soo bowed and, saying nothing, pulled Maria away and walked them down to what looked to be a service hallway.

"Why the hell would you do that?" she asked, finally feeling able to breathe.

"I defended you. Was I supposed to let my mother belittle you?" he asked, looking shocked by her anger toward him.

She had only just started watching K-dramas, but she had learned quickly enough that rich parents don't like poor girls who hung around their well-to-do sons. Even if it was just in a friendly way. She was also willing to accept that fact considering she and Hwan Soo had refused to even discuss the fact that they'd kissed multiple times but never spoke of the incidents. Yet there he was defending her like she was his actual girlfriend. Her heart was a jumbled mess of emotions. Happy, confused, scared, and most of all, protected. He might not have done what he did because he liked her, but he was a gentleman who wasn't going to allow anyone to be looked down upon because of where they came from.

"You didn't have to do that," she mumbled as her thumb grazed the back of the hand it was holding. His grip on her hand was slowly loosening and she was regaining full feeling. She had almost forgotten how tightly he had gripped her as he spoke to his mother.

"And why not? Because it's my mother? No one should be

treated as if they are less than someone else. She doesn't even know you or what we are, and she came at you with her claws out ready to tear you to shreds. If that happens again, I won't shy away from defending you and me." As he finished speaking, his hand released hers completely to scratch the back of his head roughly.

She moved to stand in front of him thinking over everything he had just said, and something stood out most. "'What we are'?"

He looked over at her with confusion, but his expression quickly lightened with realization.

"We're friends. She doesn't know what we are. That's all I meant by that," he said rationally.

"Right," she agreed.

Before she could say more the door next to them flung open and Val and Jung-hyun came running over.

"괜찮아?" Val looked her friend over to see if Hwan Soo's mother had done anything to her.

"I'm fine. For real. All of you are making such a huge deal over this. It's your party, guys. You should go back out there. I am sorry if I caused any ruckus." She bowed in apology.

"Hwan Soo, can you help her home?" Val said, looking over at him as he leaned on the wall behind Maria. When she turned around Hwan Soo stood straight, nodding his head.

"Val, I'm fine," Maria argued.

Val said nothing, looked to Hwan Soo and simply walked away with Jung-hyun. What the hell? Did her friend just ditch her? Like ditch her, ditch her?

Hwan Soo put his hand on Maria's elbow to lead her to the service exit, but Maria struggled, trying to fight for her right to be at the party.

"I'm not leaving," she hissed.

"If you go back out there, it will cause even more of a scene. You really want to do that to your friend?"

"This is all your fault! Why should I have to leave?" she argued.

He stopped to look at her. Studying her face, he shrugged and squatted, wrapping his arms around her waist. Then standing straight, he lifted her clear off the ground. Déjà vu set in as she began to kick and scream.

When the door flung open, the stench of garbage hit her nose and she tried very hard not to gag as she was plopped down back to her feet.

"I don't get you, Maria," he said angrily.

"When did you ever have any interest in 'getting me'?" she spat back, not understanding the reason he seemed so frustrated.

"You're right. I can't say I ever did. But when your friend says to leave, clearly there's a reason. She's a damn good friend," he said, slowly creeping over to the exit of the alleyway.

"What?" She looked him over as he walked away, realizing for the first time that day how well-dressed he was. A well-fitted electric-blue suit, black button-up, and patent leather dress shoes. Not to mention his hair, which was combed up and away from his face. He may not have been the man to take over his family's company, but he sure could look the part.

"That flood of paparazzi in the front. If they were allowed to see anything going wrong, I could lose my job. On top of you being mixed in the drama, your face would be plastered everywhere. Which, if you remember, we are trying to avoid. Val asked me to take you home to save both our asses, Maria." He was trying to explain her friend's rationality; she would be damned, but he made sense.

"Fine. But I should at least let Sul Bin know I have to leave. Maybe he could meet me at a coffee shop nearby or something." She reached into her bag for her phone, and when she finally found it, she saw Hwan Soo's feet right in front of her own.

Shooting her eyes up, she saw how close he was to her, his eyes searching her entire body and making her lips his home base.

"I'm sure Val or Jung-hyun let him know what was going on. We should probably get going," he whispered. Like it was the hardest thing he ever had to say.

"Still not the same as if it comes from me. He is, after all, my date." When she said the words "my date", she saw his jaw clench and unclench several times, and he exhaled sharply enough for her to smell the faint hint of champagne.

"질투해?" she asked, raising an eyebrow, egging him on to give an honest answer.

Instead giving her a rational answer, he hit the wall on the side of her head with one hand, and just like in the elevator their first time alone, his other hand followed on the opposite side. Taking a step closer to her, she was trapped.

"Jealous? Me? Of what? A waiter who clearly has a screw or two loose to come to an engagement party with a chick he just met? Please." He rolled his eyes, then stared at her lips. It made her heart race. She wanted to kiss him. An actual kiss to get rid of the weird attraction she had to him. If he kissed her when he wasn't asleep, maybe he would be horrible at it and she would realize he was just that douche she met the first night.

Even her mind laughed at that idea.

"If I was the jealous type I would ask what you two were doing," came a familiar voice from where they had exited the restaurant. "Luckily Maria explained your relationship to me, and I don't think I have much to worry about on her end. Your end, however..."

Sul Bin began to make his way over to the two of them with a swagger Maria had only seen in the K-dramas. It was like slow motion—him slipping his one hand in his pants pocket while the other one brushed at his lip, indicating his willingness to fight Hwan Soo. While her eyes lingered on his slender frame, her mind was barely processing that he was there. Hwan Soo's closeness still had her body's full attention.

"I'll take her home," Sul Bin said as he reached the two of them. Maria smiled kindly as Hwan Soo let his arms drop from the sides of her head.

"It's fine," Hwan Soo responded. Maria snapped her head back to him.

"I believe I choose who takes me home or not." She defensively crossed her arms. Looking between the two men she knew who she should pick, but she wasn't sure in that moment he was the right choice. So she bowed to both of them and made her way to the end of the alleyway.

"야 Maria," they both shouted, but she continued walking. She would figure it out. Texting Val to ask for the address to their apartment, she began walking, avoiding the front of the restaurant. She snuck around the smaller alleyways until she could finally breathe. The only problem was that her feet were screaming at her in the insanely high heels she borrowed from Val.

Why did this have to happen to her? A choice between two very attractive male protagonists? When did she become the lead in a drama?

"Maria?" Her mind was pulled out of its whirlwind of questions when she heard Sul Bin's voice. Looking up, she saw he was standing right in front of her.

"Sul Bin? How did you find me?" she asked, looking around but seeing nothing that looked remotely familiar.

"Call me old-school, but I didn't feel comfortable letting you walk alone. Even if you kind of ditched me back there." He laughed but she could see it actually hurt his feelings.

"I'm so sorry. I'm just...ugh. I don't even know what I am." Putting her hand to her forehead, she wished she could just smack some sense into herself. There was Sul Bin, concerned about her, following her to make sure she was okay, and all she could think was she wished it was Hwan Soo.

"I get it. You're feeling a lot of different emotions right now. Hence why I was worried you would get distracted by your own thoughts and not realize you were going to walk into the middle of traffic." He smiled, putting a hand on her shoulder, giving her a small bit of comfort.

"Like in a K-drama," she laughed, feeling even better as her stress and uncertainty lightened. Sul Bin was a really nice guy. And he cared about her enough to make sure she made her way safely to Val's apartment.

"Sure." He shrugged. "But mostly because, well, I like you."

"What?" She tried to get a read on how he meant what he had just said.

"I like you, Maria. 좋아해요," he repeated, taking a step closer to her.

She didn't move away. She just continued to look up at his well-formed features while at the same time questioning his motives. Why would she question him? Maybe because of the points Hwan Soo had brought up the day before.

She barely knew Sul Bin, and he was so willing to come to an engagement party with her. He'd hit on her in front of a man he had also assumed was her boyfriend. While sweet and willing to help her, when he made the swift-peck-on-the-cheek move, even then she felt that he was just a bit too smooth.

"Sul Bin, I—" She didn't know what to say. She was never one to let someone down. And could she truly fault him. She'd jumped into some of her past relationships rather quickly. Maybe he was the same. But there was a nagging little devil on her shoulder who sounded a lot like Hwan Soo, screaming that there were too many red flags.

"You don't have to give me any sort of answer today, or even ever. I just thought I would make my feelings known. I like you, and I hope to spend some more time with you before you leave Korea." He grabbed her hand, his fingers gently pressing in on her palm. "Can I please take you back to your place? So I know you got home safely."

While she was still at a loss to say anything, she was able to give a smile and a nod. And just then, her phone buzzed with a text from Val with the apartment address.

Korean Vocabulary:

걱정하지마 - gokjonghajima - don't worry (informal)

어머니, 아버지 - omoni ahbuji- mother, father

만나서 반갑습니다 - manaso bangapsoobnida - It's nice to me you (formal)

아들 - adul - child (in this context specifically 'son')

어머니 사과하세요 - omoni sagwahasaeyo - mom apologize

죄송합니다 - juisunghabnida - I am sorry (slightly more formal than 미안해요)

좋아해 - johahae - I like you (informal)

Chapter 34 (서른넷)

He followed her too.

But Sul Bin beat him to her. Apparently he was good at that. Hwan Soo watched as Sul Bin confessed that he liked Maria, taking her hand and walking her to a cab. They got in and drove off to God knows where.

All Hwan Soo could hope was that they weren't going to a Love Motel to spend a few hours together; then she'd probably come to his shoot the next morning with hickeys all over her neck.

Just the thought caused his stomach to churn. He wanted to follow them just to make sure, but then he would look insane when he ran out to stop her. So he simply drove home.

But thoughts continually plagued his mind: Sul Bin's hands running over Maria's body, his lips on hers, her moaning his name as they experience ecstasy together.

Hwan Soo slammed his palm hard onto his steering wheel as he let out an exasperated husky grunt. The screen in the center console suddenly came to life with an unknown number. One thing was for sure. It was not a Korean number.

"Hello?"

"Hwan Soo-씨?" Maria's whispered, scared voice came through the speakers of his car.

"Maria? Where are you? What's wrong?" He pulled his car over immediately to wait for her to explain what was happening.

"I'm fine, but it seems that Hae So might've also figured out where Val lives. I don't have any kind of mask to cover my face. I didn't think I would need one, and I'm worried that if the paparazzi see me and know that I am living with Val but also seen with you they might get the wrong idea and harm your show. So Sul Bin dropped me off a few blocks away and I just—"

"Calm down, Maria, you're going to be okay. Tell me anything you see so that I can find you," he said calmly as he turned his car in the direction of Val's apartment.

"Ummm...there is a 포장마차 like the one where you got me that bread, and a 편의점 at the corner. Not a 7-Eleven though. E-mart?"

"Go to that store. Wait for me there. 걱정해지마. It's going to be okay. 약속해." He knew exactly where she was. That area was familiar to him and Jung-hyun in their younger years.

"Okay. I'll see you soon." While there was still some fear in her voice, a slight relief also filled his ears. Hanging up, he sped as fast he possibly could in Seoul to her location.

As he approached, the roads became more winding, and he had to give Sul Bin credit for picking a spot not easy to access by car or paparazzi vans. How or why he knew that only made Hwan Soo more suspicious of the guy. He parked his car and ran up the winding street until he saw exactly what Maria described. A green and blue tarped structure with steam coming out, people sitting with their bowls and plates covered in 떡볶이 and its hot red sauce that patrons dipped their 김밥 and 튀김 into. And just down the road was the E-mart.

His heart raced as he took longer strides so he wouldn't look as if he was running, but he would still get there as fast as possible. When he looked in the window his heart felt like it had stopped. Maria sat at the window on a stool with her purse on one side, her phone in one hand and chopsticks in the other, with noodles held just above the plastic cup to cool down as she read whatever was on her phone. She brought the noodles to her mouth, eating almost all of them in one big bite, and he was so shocked at how well she fit in. Even in her fancy dress and high heels, she fit perfectly in the world that was Korea, and more importantly, he found she fit perfectly in his.

Smiling, he walked into the store, sneakily purchased a bowl of 라면 and all the other food he would use to make it his own, then quickly and quietly made it. He was able to do all of it without her knowing, as she was so enthralled with whatever was on her phone screen.

When he walked up behind her he saw exactly what had her so enthralled. His last drama. He had to stop himself from saying anything even though he wanted her to quit watching, but she seemed so happy that he couldn't.

And then the screen froze and the credits started rolling.

"아 진짜 ?!" she whispered.

"진짜," he responded behind her.

She jumped high, nearly flinging the 라면 cup off the small ledge that she had perched all her things on.

"Lee Hwan Soo-씨, why the hell would you scare me like that?!" Her hands flew to chest as if to calm her heart, but his still felt like it was stopped. Why and when did he become so attracted to her and the little things she did?

"미안." He bowed as he put his bowl, still piping hot and cooking the noodles and sausage he added to it, and moved toward a seat.

"When did you get here?" she asked, seeing all he had done before she even realized he was there.

"A little while ago. You were so invested in your phone, I wondered what you were watching," he joked, taking the seat next to her.

"I wasn't sure how long it would take you, plus I didn't get to eat much at the party since I was kicked out only a half hour or so into it.

And I happened to have some cash on me. So here I am. You caught me. Addicted to your drama," she laughed, finally sitting down again.

"You like the show that much?" He raised an eyebrow. Not that it was a bad show, but it didn't do that well in the ratings, and a lot a fans bashed the lead actors for choosing such simple roles.

"How do I say this without sounding like an ass? The plot is a bit simple but there is something about it that makes me keep watching." She picked at her fingers as she avoided eye contact with him.

He smiled at the fact that she wasn't sugarcoating her opinion to make him feel better.

"Your character is honestly the reason I keep watching. He is such a good person through and through. He has his faults, sure, like everyone, but he would do anything for the people he loves. Even if sometimes it could be misunderstood. I'm mad knowing you're not the one who gets the girl. This lead male is a total douchey rich guy." She pointed to her phone, frozen on the image of his co-star.

The smile couldn't leave his face even if he wanted it to. But he didn't. She liked him. Well, his character.

"I'm surprised you didn't get a lead role sooner," she said, smiling back at him. "From only watching this drama I can tell you have a knack for this kind of thing. And despite what your parents might think about your choice, I think you made the right one. I wish I had your courage to follow my dreams." She looked away from him, suddenly very interested in her cup of most likely cold noodles at that point.

He wondered what her dream was. She had brought it up before but never actually told him what it was.

He looked at his own cup, feeling his stomach grumble as steam poured out of the sides of the lid. Pulling off the brightly colored lid, the cheese was bubbling at the top, indicating it was ready to eat. Trying his best to focus on his food and ignore the fact that his heart had started beating at such an alarmingly fast rate because of the woman sitting next to him, he began swirling the cheese into the noodles and sausage.

"Whoa! Which 라면 was that? I didn't see any with cheese and meat," she said, looking over at his bowl.

"Please tell me you didn't just eat the plain bowl of 라면?" He slumped, trying to look into her bowl.

"Plain bowl? What do you mean?" she asked.

Rolling his eyes, he pushed his bowl over to her, commanding, "먹어."

She looked down at the bowl with an insatiable hunger. Her tongue ran across her lips as she grabbed the wooden chopsticks and wrapped the noodles and cheese around them, poking one of the sausages and shoving the whole thing into her mouth.

Her eyes lit up as she looked between the bowl and Hwan Soo, and she continued chewing as she wrapped another bite around her chopsticks. He leaned his elbow on the ledge and watched her. She was enjoying such a simple meal with the pleasure of what most women he knew could only get from a five-star hotel's most expensive meal. He thought of Hae So, and how the one time he tried to cook for her, she smiled and said, "At least you tried."

"This is seriously the best 라면 I've ever eaten. How do you make it?" she asked through a mouthful.

He laughed, grabbing a napkin and dabbing away the sauce on the corners of her lips. Her smile faltered a tad as his finger traced her lip. Clearing his throat, he removed his finger from her lip. He never wanted to stop touching the damn woman. He was in so deep; meanwhile all she saw him as was her best friend's fiancé's best friend. Not even her own friend.

"It's all just stuff from here." He waved his hands around, indicating the entire store. She nodded her head with understanding.

His mind was still questioning what her dreams were. As he watched her put another large mouthful past her lips, he chose that most opportune time to ask.

"What's your dream?"

She looked up at him, noodles still spilling out of her mouth, eyes wide, cheeks flush from the heat of the steam...or was it something more? Biting the 라면 enough to swallow the mouthful so she could speak, she gulped, biting her bottom lip leaving them in a lingering silence.

"Maria?" He leaned closer to her, which only made her eyes go wider as she leaned back away from him.

"Why do you want to know?" she asked coldly.

It made him back away a bit. What was that sudden change in her mood? She was so happy, like a bright ray of sunlight, and then all of a sudden a chill filled the air and a storm rolled in, clouding the sky in gray.

"It was just a question." He shrugged. "You know my dream. And you had mentioned you had one a couple days ago. I was just curious as to what your dream is."

She looked out the store window, watching the one or two people walking by. As he watched her, he saw a sadness cloud those golden-green eyes he enjoyed looking into so much. She had said people told her that her dream was not worth pursuing—maybe that's why she wasn't a fan of him asking about it. But he wanted to know for the total opposite reason.

He wanted to support her. While he had no clue what her dream was—for all he knew it could be that she wanted to be a clown in a freak circus—he wanted her to know there was at least one person who would stand behind what she wanted.

"I didn't mean to make you upset," he apologized.

"Don't start apologizing, please." She laughed, but he could see she was still at odds with herself, deciding how to respond to him.

"I was just asking. If you don't want to answer, that's totally fine." He wanted out of the situation and quick.

Digging into his jacket pocket, he found the mask he'd grabbed from his glove compartment and handed it over to her. "We should probably get you up to Val's now."

She said nothing, bowing her head as she grabbed the mask and put it on.

He struck a nerve when all he wanted to do was get closer to her. 시발.

Korean Vocabulary:

약속해 - yaksokhae - promise

먹어 - mogo - eat

시발 - sheebal - fuck (this is a very strong word to not be used lightly.)

Chapter 35 (서른다섯)

The next morning when Maria woke up, she saw Val was still slumbering with a small bit of drool coming out of her mouth. Laughing, Maria got up, knowing she had to be ready for Hwan Soo to pick her up in a couple of hours.

"What's your dream?"

She heard his voice echo all throughout the night and again as she scrubbed her face with the pear-scented foam soap Hwan Soo had purchased for her. The question was simple, but it was question that haunted her.

After her parents had told her she had no future following her passion, she never told anyone what she really wanted to do with her life. And when she felt she could trust someone again and told them, they laughed and told her that it was a pipe dream. She had never even told Val, the one person in whom she confided everything.

"What's your dream?"

She heard his rich, soft voice ask in her head once again.

Splashing water on her face, she looked at herself in the mirror that hung from nearly invisible wire so it looked like it was floating in midair. She watched as her mouth tried to form the word. Several attempts and still no sound ever left her vocal cords.

"What's your dream?"

Ugh, shut up, will you? Her subconscious shouted at the sexy voice in her head.

Looking away from herself, she continued her new morning skin care routine.

~

As she walked into the cool morning air, she was thankful for another one of the masks Hwan Soo had given her. She had started to see them as accessories to her ensembles. No matter how "grungy" she dressed.

The van was already waiting outside, puffs of smoke coming from the tailpipe, making her crave the warmth that was inside. As she got closer she saw Hwan Soo's manager get out of the driver's side seat and run to open the back door for her.

She quickly ran up to try to stop him, but it was too late. She bowed her head and looked inside to see Hwan Soo's immaculate profile, head leaned back against the headrest, eyes closed, lips parted, his Adam's apple gently bobbing with his steady breathing.

"He had to work late last night on an ad campaign shoot. He's been asleep since he got in the car," his manager whispered to her.

She watched his sleeping frame, so calm. Meanwhile her heart was racing, her mind was a flurried mess of anxiety and all she wanted to do was scream.

Bzz. Bzz. Bzz.

Her phone vibrated on her hip in her fanny pack. Reaching to get it, she saw Sul Bin's name pop up.

Now she added the feeling of total guilt to the list.

Sul Bin: I hope you were able to get back to your apartment last night. I wanted to text you but got called into work and just got off. I am so sorry I had to leave

you there. Please let me make it up to you. Tonight my friend got a bunch of us into this new club that opened in 이태원. It's probably not your friends' scene but they are also more than welcome to come.

A club? Hmm. She hadn't been out clubbing in a while. Mostly because her clubbing partner moved across the country and found herself a handsome, wealthy, good-natured man to marry. But now they could go together again.

Maria responded, telling him she was interested in going and would let her friends know they were invited as well.

"Must be Sul Bin-씨," a groggy voice croaked out.

Spinning her head to the side, she saw Hwan Soo had almost completely turned his whole body to face her. His eyes were slowly blinking to adjust to the light as he let out a yawn, stretching his arms out in front of himself, leaving her to admire another Korean fashion masterpiece. A large black crew neck sweater, the front tucked into a pair of tight dark blue jeans with a designer belt, leading down to an ornately designed pair of slip-on loafers.

"응? 뭐가?" She pretended not to truly hear what he had said, but she also wanted to hear it again just in case she misheard the undertone of jealousy.

"You've been smiling like an idiot looking at your phone for only one of two reasons lately. The first, when you were watching a drama, like at the 편의점 yesterday. The second is ever since you got that waiter guy's number. Since I hear no speaking and you don't have headphones in, I assumed the latter." He dropped his arms to his sides, his eyes finally meeting hers for the first time since the day before. The second they landed on her, all she could hear was:

"What's your dream?"

Coughing as an excuse to look away from those piercing brown eyes, she felt her phone buzz again.

Sul Bin: Great! I know you'll look gorgeous in anything you wear, but I did hear this place is a bit on the judgy side. Let your friends know too.

She responded with a simple "ok" and began thinking of what he meant by the statement.

"And now she's gone to the pensive phase of the conversation," Hwan Soo sleepily narrated.

"He invited all of us to go to a club tonight," she explained, "and he said it's 'judgy.' What does that mean?"

"It means if you're not in designer gear from head to toe, you won't be able to step foot into the place. And count me out of those festivities." He finally turned away from her to close his eyes again.

"뭐? 왜?" While she didn't expect him to make an appearance, she was bummed he had declined the offer so quickly.

Instead of him answering, his manager did. "He has another shoot tonight after the costume fittings today."

"So when exactly do you get to rest?" She looked over at Hwan Soo, concerned that he could be wearing himself too thin. She knew he worried about staying relevant but to her, staying alive was more important.

Neither Hwan Soo nor his manager answered her. She grabbed Hwan Soo's sweater, pulling him to look at her.

"내 말을 듣고 있다?" Her voice raised as she became very concerned about what his working conditions were like.

His eyes went wide, his lips tried to answer but he said nothing. Looking to his manager, his eyes had the same wide-eyed expression even as he kept them on the road ahead.

"I'm listening, but I don't have an answer for you," Hwan Soo finally responded. "I sleep when I can. Days without sleep are not unheard of. And I was sleeping just a few minutes ago, before you woke me up with your giggle."

"I didn't giggle." She let go of him, pushing him back onto his own chair as she fell back into her own.

"You did," both Hwan Soo and his manager responded with smirks on their faces.

"닥쳐!" she yelled, crossing her arms and then looked back to Hwan Soo. "Go back to sleep."

"네." The smirk on his face didn't leave even after he fell asleep. She watched as his eyes closed once again and his breathing steadied, his plump lips still quirked to the side with amusement.

Something she hadn't felt in ages stirred inside her. This. This moment was a moment she wanted to capture. And quietly she lifted her phone to take a sneaky picture of him sleeping. Even the lighting was perfect. The tinted windows made the interior dark, but when they were stopped at a light and the tree leaves outside blocked bits of the sun's rays, it left shadows playing among the outfit she had already admired.

"Perfect," she whispered with a smile as he continued to sleep soundly the rest of the car ride.

I want to be a photographer, Lee Hwan Soo-씨.

Korean Vocabulary:

이태원 -Itaweon - an area in Seoul

내 말을 듣고 있다? - na malool doodgu issda? -Are you even listening to me?

닥쳐 - dak chyeo - Shut up

Chapter 36 (서른여섯)

Pulling up to the monstrously high office building, she saw more of the usual cameras and fans waiting outside ready to do anything they had to for an opportunity to see the cast members. Maria tossed on her mask once again and when the manager stopped the car at the entrance, she decided she would take her "intern/helper/whatever-she-was role" more seriously.

Punching Hwan Soo's shoulder, he jumped a bit and was about to argue, but she pulled open the door, climbed out, and bowed to have him leave the car so she could follow after him. Clearing his throat with a scowl, he shifted over to climb out of the car. Several fans began to scream and bright flashing lights surrounded them. She helped his manager hold people off as best she could to make their way to the front door.

She saw him look down at her every so often, seeming to make sure she was okay, to which she would give a small nod and continue pushing people aside for him to get closer to the door.

His manager pulled the door open for him and they made their way into the silence of the entryway. They could still hear fans screaming faintly beyond the glass, but it was nothing compared to the noise going right into her eardrum. Her ears were still ringing a bit.

"Why did you do that?" he asked as the manager went to check them in and get badges to go upstairs.

"If I am going to supposedly be part of your team, shouldn't I act like it?" She smiled, not that he could see it behind her mask. She wanted things to be normal between them. And they seemed to be just that. The previous day had not been brought up and she was thankful that he didn't try to apologize again.

They were waved over to the desk to take security photos and then were whisked past the security barricades and to the elevators. When the doors shut and the elevator began to climb, she thought of their first encounter when he offered to prove he wasn't gay. His lips so close to hers. And when she thought of his lips, her mind went to the moments when they were on hers, and more recently when they were sucking on her neck.

"괜찮아?" The voice that had groggily greeted her in the car pulled her out of her thoughts.

"응?" She looked up to see his eyes were scanning her face and neck. Had she said her thoughts out loud?

"You look flushed. Your ears are turning bright red. You feel okay?" he attempted to put his hand on her forehead but she quickly ducked away, not wanting to feel those soft, long fingers on her skin, which would cause her even more issues.

"I'm fine. Just excited to see another cool step in your acting process. When else can I say I shadowed a celeb for a month?" She laughed it off awkwardly but looking up at him, she could see he wasn't buying it.

When the doors opened, her eyes were assaulted by chaos. People were running around everywhere, rolling racks full of clothing that were lined up like aisles in a supermarket, names largely printed and hung on the end racks.

Seeing Hwan Soo's name she walked toward them, his manager following. He, however, walked over to greet the director and other cast members. Another man stood with them whom Maria didn't recognize.

The man, tall and lanky, with disheveled hair and a goatee that was patchy at best, smiled with crooked, slightly yellowed teeth and bowed slightly to Hwan Soo, who was taking a deep bow toward the man. Clearly, he was important. But his weird patterned clothing just made him look like a hot mess.

"That's the main photographer for this shoot. They're having clothing tests while also doing promo photos for the drama. They can kill two birds with one stone, and also the production team can start editing promotional posters." As his manager explained, a team of cameramen and women charged past them, making their way over to the chatting group. "Ah, the behind-the-scenes team."

"There's a whole team for that? I always assumed it was a singular person with a small camera." She watched as Hwan Soo was handed a mic set.

"Not here," his manager laughed. "Thanks for before. There were a lot more people than I was expecting. I am happy to see him becoming more popular, but I'm starting to think I can't handle him on my own."

"No problem. I will help however I can while I am here."

"Will you help him run lines?" The manager didn't take any break in starting to dole out requests. "Hwan Soo said you needed to learn the language. This will help you and him."

He pulled out a large bound book from his massive backpack and tossed it to her. She looked at the novel-sized package and saw the name of the drama.

나랑 같이 있어

"What does it mean?" she asked.

"Stay With Me," Hwan Soo said from behind her. Spinning quickly, she saw how close he was as the lapel of his jacket skimmed her mask covered nose.

Grabbing it to keep it up and hide the heat rising up her face, she stepped back, giving them distance as she looked up to him.

"Why are you giving her my script 형?" Hwan Soo asked with a clenched jaw.

"She wants to help you. And you want her to learn Korean. I thought it would be the best of both worlds." His manager smiled the brightest yet most suspicious-looking smile as he walked away to talk to some of the other managers.

"If you don't want me to help—"

"It's fine." He cut her off as he walked past her to begin looking through his clothing options. A stylist walked over to help him begin pulling pieces while Maria walked off to the side to take a seat in one of the folding chairs set up for everyone who wasn't involved in the current happenings.

Pulling open the script, she began reading what the story was about as best she could. As she was reading about a man who loved a woman from afar and finally made the move to show her how he truly did love her, a sound hit her ears. An extraordinarily contagious laugh that had almost the whole room laughing along with it. Looking up, she saw the lightest smile on Hwan Soo's face, his eyes nearly completely closed, as he patted the guy in front of him on the shoulder. They were having a grand time. He looked so happy and in his element. She couldn't stop herself once again. Reaching for her phone, she began snapping photos of him laughing and enjoying himself. She planned to show them to him later that night so that he could possibly use them on his social media platforms.

Swiping through to find some of the best ones to edit, the photo disappeared, and a name popped up.

MOM

"Crap," she whispered.

Looking around, she saw no one was paying any mind to her and so she swiped the little button to answer the call.

"Hey, Mom—"

"You haven't called or texted in *days*! I have been worried sick about you over there and you just go AWOL. You better have the best excuse ever as to why I haven't heard from you." She could practically hear foam forming at the corner of her mom's mouth as she ranted.

"I'm sorry, Mom. Hwan Soo-씨 has been keeping me really busy with all the educational aspects of this trip. I've been studying like crazy. And yesterday was the engagement party, and I am really sorry. I will explain to Hwan Soo-씨 that I need some time to call you from now on throughout the day." Trying to calm her mother's nerves, she spoke slowly and with a sweet voice.

"You can stop telling me Hwan Soo is a girl. I know," her mother huffed out.

Maria panicked. How could she know possibly know Hwan Soo was actually a handsome man? *A handsome man that I can't stop thinking about even though there was another perfectly good-looking man pursuing my affection?* What a first-world problem to have.

"Wh-wha-what?" Her tongue was tied as she stuttered out the question.

"Yeah, you keep saying Hwan Soo *she*. I get it. She is a she," her mother explained.

Maria's panic instantly turned to relief, and she let out a small chuckle.

"What the heck are you laughing at? Nothing I said was funny. You ignoring your mother is no laughing matter," her mother said, reprimanding her again.

"Mom, I'm laughing because 씨 is a formal term. Kinda like Mr. or Mrs. or Miss. I am not calling her a she all the time." She couldn't contain the smile at her mom's unknowing play on the word.

"Oh. Well is this 씨 introducing you to anyone while you're spending all this time together?" her mom inquired.

"Didn't we talk about how you were going to set me up when I got home? Why are you asking for me to be set up in a foreign country?" Maria leaned back in the chair, her head hitting the wall with a loud *thunk*. She closed her eyes and was trying to keep her breathing steady as her mother started the conversation yet again about why Maria was still single.

"Sweetheart—" Before she could hear anything more, the phone was ripped from her hand. She shot her eyes open and saw a differently dressed Hwan Soo.

He was in a gorgeous dark cherry-red suit jacket, with a black turtleneck, black dress pants, and patent leather black dress shoes. He looked flawless.

"너 미쳤어?" he hissed.

"미안해요." She looked around to see several sets of eyes on her, including his manager's.

"You're taking a call from him while you're at—"

"It's my mom," she cut him off, but the damage had already been done. She knew her mom heard all of that, including simply hearing Hwan Soo's voice.

His face contorted from enraged to embarrassed as he looked at her phone screen to see it read "Mom."

"Take it outside...지금," he ordered as he handed her phone back to her.

She grabbed it as she shot up, bowing until she was out of the room.

Putting the phone back to her ear, she said, "Mom I really need to—"

"Who was that sexy voice attached to and what 'him' was he talking about? Have you not only met one man but two?" The hopeful tone in her mother's voice made Maria feel bad for what she was about to say.

"That was Hwan Soo's employer. I'm tagging along while she works so I can be immersed in the culture. And the 'him' he was referring to was a competitor to their team, who I didn't know was a competitor when he was hitting on me at a dinner they always go to at night."

Wow. She might need to cut down on the drama binging. That was too easy to make up.

"Jesus. Well the devious one sounds like a total scumbag and you should ditch him real quick, but that voice I just heard sounded like an angel who was trying to watch over you. I like that voice. Keep close to that voice." Her mother's tone went to that soft kind of lovey dovey timbre that she only got when she thought she had found the perfect man for Maria. Which had only happened about five times, but Maria recognized the tone from the first time she heard it. Her mom liked the guy.

And the guy she currently liked was Hwan Soo.

If only she knew I like him too.

She slapped herself to get that thought out of her head immediately.

"Mom, I really need to go. He was being kind by letting me leave, but I know for a fact he's going to chew me and Hwan Soo out when I get back in. Please let me go," she begged through her lie.

"Yes sure, of course, but please think about that man with that voice. I think he has your best intentions in mind." Her mother sounded concerned but in a weirdly happy way.

"I promise to call more. I love you. Goodbye." She hung up before her mom said anything and walked back into the room.

When she entered, she looked around to see there were only one or two people inside.

Where did everyone go?

She heard another door open, where music was playing and multiple voices were heard. Looking toward the sound, she saw what appeared to be another manager running out to grab something from one of the racks.

She followed him back into the busy room where there were three completely different sets for photo shoots. One looked eerily similar to the bar where they first met. Dark, with interesting lighting, high-top tables with stools, glasses and bottles filled to all different degrees everywhere, and square in the middle was a large velvet emerald-green couch in the middle of the scene. Clearly that was the focal point.

Another set looked like a stereotypical rich person's large entryway. Marble floors, ornate emerald-green wallpaper with gold trim, and a sizable crystal chandelier hanging above the whole scene.

The last wasn't truly a set. It was a white backdrop with some stools, and it looked as though they were changing out the seats to match the image they were trying to portray.

She loved that place. She never wanted to leave. She walked around to the sets that were not currently being used to take her own pictures of the objects that made up the spaces. They may not have been real locations but taking the shots of them made up for not being able to take many pictures throughout her stay. She tried but would get bombarded with different issues.

Her body began to tingle, the memory igniting a warmth just below her stomach, and her lips pouted, feeling swollen from just the thought of his kiss. She needed to cool down immediately.

"Maria," she heard the manager call for her. Looking up, she saw a man on the verge of a breakdown. Cheeks flushed, breathing appearing erratic, sweat forming over his eyebrows and upper lip as his eyes darted around the room trying to find her.

"여기." She waved her hand so he could see where she was.

He practically sprinted over to her, something she never thought she would see the pudgy man do, and pulled her closer to the set.

"What's wrong?" she asked, concerned as to why this man seemed one step away from the loony bin.

"I need you to just stand here and calm Hwan Soo-야 down," he said in a hushed tone.

"What do you mean calm him down?" When she looked over to Hwan Soo, the question she asked didn't even need to be answered in words.

He was tense as he held onto Hae So. His grip on her waist wasn't soft, it looked like he was touching a stove top and couldn't let go because he wanted to be cool in front of his friends. His eyes weren't shooting arrows of adoration at Hae So, but rather daggers and poisonous darts. His jaw was clenched so tightly shut that his

段 skip

jawline, while very sexy, looked as if it were about to slice the woman into pieces.

"Shall we take a break?" The photographer spoke kindly, but anyone could tell he was getting more and more frustrated.

The second Hwan Soo let go of Hae So, he ran off the set. Maria tried to follow, thought better of it thinking he might want some time by himself. With that in mind, she went back to the dressing room area to take a seat in the chair she had previously occupied and began scrolling through the photos she had taken on set, hitting the little heart to favorite the ones she would edit later. She came to the ones of Hwan Soo laughing with some members of the staff, which made her smile at how natural he was in that element. He needed to be exactly like that on set, and she contemplated how she would be able to help get that kind of smile out of him for the shoot.

"You're full of surprises." She was pulled out of her thoughts by the voice of the man she had just been thinking about right next to her. Spinning, she saw him sitting beside her with a smirk like the one he had in the car.

"Huh?" she barely choked out, still anxious at his close proximity.

"You have an eye for capturing people." He gestured to her phone screen.

When she looked down, she realized that she'd zoomed in to his face so close, she could see every hair on his head.

"Not really. I just thought I could help with your social media following. I always see a lot of actors post behind-the-scenes shots and such. I just pointed and clicked." She tossed her phone into her bag, trying desperately to not have her heart jump out of her chest if he saw the photo of himself asleep.

"That just proves you even have more than just an eye, you have talent." He stood up, pulling her up with him and walking back into the room of sets. Everyone had cleared out for their break, so it was just the two of them. Hwan Soo walked over to the table of cameras and lenses, plucking up a camera nonchalantly, which made her heart panic as she knew how expensive those cameras and equipment were. She took a nervous step forward to stop him from making a huge mistake and breaking thousands of dollars' worth of products.

"Ever use one of these?" he asked as fumbled around with the camera.

"Of course, just not of this caliber." She took another step forward and jerked her hands out to try to prevent him from destroying the camera.

Once he noticed her slow approach, he held out the camera. "Take it."

She grabbed it quickly to stop her heart from racing. Looking down at the camera in her hand, she silently thanked him for giving her the opportunity to hold such a camera. It made her heart pound as she looked at all the different buttons marking the various settings.

"Now," he grabbed her attention again and when she looked up his smirk had become a bigger smile, "take my photo."

"뭐?"

"Take my picture." He walked over to the bar setting, plopping down on the emerald-green couch. His outfit complemented the scene rather well.

"I'm not sure they'd be happy with us—"

She was cut off by one of the staff walking in. She hid the camera behind her back as Hwan Soo began speaking to the woman, whose unease seemed to subside immediately as Hwan Soo spoke. He was always charming to other women. She found it funny that their first few meetings were so opposite of their current state. She would even dare to call them friends at this point.

The woman gave a small nod and walked out of the room, and Hwan Soo looked at Maria.

"All good. Now take my photo," he joked and leaned back on the couch, striking the poses he should've been in when he was with Hae So. But she just stood there watching him. He seemed so natural, but Hae So ruined his natural charm. There had to be some way to help keep him at ease.

"Are you gonna take the picture or not?" he asked, still posed.

258

"When you give me something more to work with," she teased.

He stuck his tongue out like a child and it made the tension in the room evaporate. He fell back, throwing his head back with laughter and she began snapping photos. His natural smile made the photos feel all the more real. When he brought his eyes back to the camera, his smirk exuded a fun but sexual allure with a desire for the camera like it was his lover.

Was he looking through the camera?

Her heart was pounding so hard, the flush that covered her cheeks felt like it had embraced her whole body. She kept the camera to her face to make sure he couldn't see how much she was blushing.

"난 귀엽죠?" he joked, his smile growing wider with his flirtatious remark.

"Shut up." She kept the camera to her face as he laughed.

He then shot up from his seat and as she was just about to take another photo, the camera was ripped out of her hand. Turning, she saw it was the actual photographer, who was red in the face for a whole different reason.

He was fuming. He started yelling at several of the staff who had entered with him, pointing to Maria with a finger she thought was going to take out her eye, he was so close. Hwan Soo walked over quickly trying to explain what she was doing, but suddenly they weren't the only two talking.

Murmurs came from behind and when they all turned they saw several of the staff surrounding the computers. The photographer pushed aside the staff members and froze as he looked at the screen. Hwan Soo followed to see what was on the screen, then looked back at Maria with the brightest smile on his face.

"여기와," he whispered as he waved his hand.

She took timid steps to the front of crowd and saw what they had all been staring at. Her photos of Hwan Soo were being run through by the photographer who was supposed to be shooting the whole cast.

She looked to the photographer who was saying nothing as he scrolled through the photos with no sign of emotion on his face.

"미안해요. 정말 미안해," she whispered as she bowed over and over again to the man who still hadn't said a word.

"일하러 돌아 가라." The man turned to everyone, who quickly cowered and hurried to their stations.

"Hwan Soo, are you ready?" Hae So walked over to the small group that was still at the computer. When she looked at the screen, she smiled. "Wow. You look great in those photos. He really got your personality."

Hwan Soo covered his laugh as the photographer shot the woman the evilest look. She looked around with wide eyes, her lips opening and closing as she stumbled to find the right thing to say.

"What? What did I say?" she asked.

"Maybe compliment the right person next time," Hwan Soo laughed and gestured to Maria, who really wished he hadn't told Hae So anything and let her stay oblivious.

Devil horns sprouted on Hae So's forehead. Maria swore it. The woman's eyes narrowed and steam was practically coming from her ears when she turned to face Maria. Everyone had walked away, leaving the two women alone.

"Didn't I warn you about meddling with my drama?" the woman hissed.

"I didn't meddle—"

"What do you call taking pictures of my man?" She spat as she spoke, the dewy substance hitting Maria square in the face.

"Your man? 바보야?" Maria wasn't intimidated by the heated yet stunningly attractive woman trying desperately to get under her skin.

"What did you just say?" That steam coming out Hae So's ears had become full flames.

"I said, 바보야? Hwan Soo doesn't even want to be in the same room as you and cringes whenever you call his name, and you call him your man? Hae So-씨, accept he doesn't care about you anymore. It might actually help your working relationship and make this drama a very popular one." Maria bowed, leaving the speechless actress to collect herself before the shoot continued.

She walked over to the set, tucking her hands into her jean pockets and hoping not to cause a scene.

She watched the lights being adjusted and the cast walked onto the set to listen to the director explain the game plan of the photos. When he had completed his explanation, he turned towards Maria causing nerves to rise but choosing to stand her ground if he decided to try and kick her off the set. Instead he held something out to her. Looking down she saw a camera. The one she had been toying with taking photos of Hwan Soo.

Looking to see who was handing her the camera she was surprised to see the photographer who looked furious when he saw her taking pictures.

"You're good." He spoke calmly but avoided looking at her.

"네?" She wasn't sure what was about to happen, but nerves hit her like a brick wall.

"I said, you're good. If you choose to change professions from the management profession to photographer, I would like to have you work with us. You have raw talent. We would simply need to teach you some of the more advanced ins and outs." He was gritting his teeth a bit, but she could tell he was being genuine.

"Wow. That means a lot to me. But I am only here for a few more weeks," she explained.

He finally looked at her. "Well, if you decide to make Seoul your home again, don't be afraid to reach out." He handed her a business card with his information. She bowed to him and he walked toward the set, then turned to her and said, "You helping or what?"

She looked at the three leads of the drama: Hwan Soo was looking directly at her with the brightest, most dashing smile on his face; the second lead looked indifferent; and Hae So looked about ready to rip Maria's head off.

Which egged Maria on. Walking up to the front of the set, she began snapping pictures, her shutter clicking as she tried new angles. She and the main photographer even discussed different types of shots they wanted and how the actors should be positioned throughout the different sets.

After several outfit changes and set switches, the production wrapped up. Maria continuously thanked the photographer for his amazing offer and kindness, and with a subdued smile he thanked her for her help.

~

Hwan Soo couldn't believe that he heard the photographer offer her a job because of the pictures she took when they were just playing around. He wasn't lying when he told her he thought her pictures were good, and when she had the professional camera in her hand instead of her phone, she looked like a natural-born artist.

They climbed back into his van and when he looked over at her, there was a smile he had never seen before on her face. Sure, he had seen her smile before, but this one held something behind it that was both positive and nervously questioning.

"Is your dream to be a photographer?" he blurted out. Her smile quickly disappeared as she looked over at him with eyes wide, the depths of green and gold filling him with a fear that he might make her angry again. But he still couldn't stop himself from saying, "사진 작가? From what I've seen today and even that night..." He didn't know where he was going with that statement, but he knew he probably shouldn't bring that night up. Clearing his throat, he chose to stop talking.

"네," she responded calmly, her eyes never looking away from him.

"설마...I didn't think you would give that up so easily." He leaned back in his seat continuing to face her, and once again he saw that smile reappear on her face. And he couldn't stop himself from asking, "Why did you tell me?"

"It's not a secret."

"Seemed like one yesterday when I tried to ask," he argued back.

"I don't see it as a dream anymore. It was a thing I liked to do. I knew it wouldn't take me far, and I faced the facts. I went to school for something I knew would get me a decent job so I could live comfortably." She leaned back in her seat, turning her gaze to the window.

"You just had a highly respected Korean photographer not only tell you that you're good, he offered you a job and had you work with him today. I would say you have the potential to make it a career." He was proud of her. Genuinely proud.

"Hwan So-씨, I'm not sure how it works in your world but in mine it's simple. Don't follow dreams, follow money," she said darkly.

"That can't be what you really feel?" He reached out grab her hand from the armrest but she pulled it away and faced him again. Her eyes were no longer sparkling with excitement but with pools of water threatening to fall onto her cheeks.

"It's how I was raised." She shrugged.

The conversation died after that. He didn't want to start an argument, and he knew that the way he was raised was very different from her, but he felt guilty that he had the luxury of choosing what he wanted to do. All because he was the second son in a well-off family. He wanted her to follow her dreams. She'd helped him continue following his.

"팀장님, can you drop me off at Val's apartment before you guys go to your next shoot?" she asked his manager.

"네," he responded gently as they continued their drive.

"Try to get some rest after your shoot tonight, you have another packed day tomorrow." She spoke to him like his actual manager.

He bowed his head, knowing if he tried to say anything it wouldn't end well.

They had stayed silent the rest of the car ride, both scrolling on their phones. He could feel her eyes on him, but when he looked up she

263

was no longer looking at him. He wanted to talk to her about how he thought she had such raw talent that she should drop everything back home and stay in Seoul to work as an assistant photographer until she built her own following and became a world-renowned artist.

He finally slammed his phone on his lap and worked up the courage to say something when they pulled up to Val's apartment building. There were no longer paparazzi outside, clearly having found something more interesting to use to make money. Maria said nothing as she climbed out and bowed to the two men.

"Have fun tonight," his manager said with a bright smile, cheering her on.

Hwan Soo was about to ask what he meant when he remembered she had brought up going to some club with that douchebag Sul Bin. She was going to look drop-dead gorgeous in some designer piece that Val dolled her up in, and that worm was going to wiggle his way all over her.

"I will." Her face turned that blush-red that grated on Hwan Soo's heart when he wasn't the one to cause the reaction.

And apparently Val and Jung-hyun were okay with this group date. Why? They had witnessed the piece of trash get paid off by Hwan Soo to keep him out of the way at their engagement party. He was in his own world when the door shut and she was already running in the front door of the building.

"You really hate that guy," his manager said with a smirk.

You have no idea.

Korean Vocabulary:

나랑 같이 있어 - narang gateessoh - stay with me

일하러 돌아 가라 - eelharo dulah gara - Go back to work

바보야? - paboya - are you an idiot?

사진작가 - sajinjakka - photographer

설마 - solma - no way

Chapter 37 (서른일곱)

"**Y**ou're sure you want to go to this club?" Val's questioning tone matched her worried, pinched face.

"Why do you keep asking me that?" Maria tried to laugh off the vibe Val was tossing her way. But she couldn't shake the feeling that Val didn't like the idea of going. Which was surprising. The thought of going to the club reminded her of their college days, when they would dress provocatively just to get free drinks out of men. They would get home from those nights, wipe the makeup off each other's faces, snuggle up together and laugh about the night until they fell asleep.

Maria held another skimpy dress up to her body, not finding it to her liking.

"I'm just making sure you really want to go. I mean, Hwan Soo won't be there—"

"Exactly." Maria cut off her friend's train of thought, rolling her eyes and tossing another failed attempt at sexy on the bed. She needed to finally spend time with Sul Bin with no signs of Hwan Soo around. She needed to see how she felt about the guy, without Hwan Soo interrupting in some way.

Val huffed, tossing her makeup brush on the counter. "What about him is so unappealing to you, Maria?" Aggravation built in her voice.

"I never said he was unappealing, Val," Maria sighed as she fell into the pile of rejected dresses.

"So are you saying you like him?" Val's interrogation was starting to sound very similar to the ones she had with her mother.

"As a friend and, weirdly, my boss, yes. He is not as horrible as I initially thought. He's been very helpful throughout all this stuff going on," Maria explained.

"So your heart didn't flutter when he came to your defense with his parents?" Val raised an eyebrow.

If Maria said yes, Val would lose her mind. But if Maria said no, Val would also lose her mind. As she contemplated her losing battle, a question arose.

"Why would you want it to? Why are you talking about Hwan Soo-씨 so much and how I feel about him?" Now it was Maria's turn to raise a quizzical brow.

"W-w-what are you—" Val choked, unable to even ask her own question.

"She called you, didn't she?" Maria shot up and went over to Val's phone. Sure enough, one of the last logged phone calls was from Maria's mother. She waved the phone accusingly at her best friend, who tried to hide her actions.

"Fine. She called earlier today," Val confessed. "Something about how Hwan Soo's boss sounded like a stand-up guy and that she wanted you to get to know him better. She said something about him sounding like he had your best intentions in mind. At first, I was confused, forgetting you told her Hwan Soo was a girl. That's when I realized she must've actually been talking about Hwan Soo." She stood to grab a gorgeous white and pink lace dress, that while short, was still elegant.

Maria couldn't believe Val had gone behind her back and talked to her mom. "She's unbelievable," Maria huffed. "I already told her that I would go on all those damn blind dates when I get back in just under three weeks, and she's still trying to hook me up with men here. She will literally do anything to get me married off. How could she go to you to try and convince me?"

"미안. That woman could sell sand in the desert. She's so convincing." Val grabbed a dress from her closet and passed it to Maria like a token of penance. Another short black silky dress with spaghetti straps, which flaunted her chest. She was surprised that it was so revealing, but it looked like club culture in Korea had a similarity to American culture. The sexier the better.

Sitting up, Maria smiled at Val and accepted the cute dress. "As always, it's the perfect fit," Maria said, slipping into the sexy number.

"I just know your style." Val smiled knowingly before becoming serious once more. "I'm sorry for trying to meddle in your love life."

"It's okay. While it drives me up a wall when my mother does what she does, I know she means well. And you're the same. Just know I love myself and can also fend for myself. Let's enjoy tonight, okay?" Maria hugged her bestie as they finished getting ready.

Their car pulled up to the corner of a very densely populated street in Itaewon. People flooded the street, going into and stumbling out of the numerous bars and clubs.

"We're gonna have to walk from here," Jung-hyun explained as he climbed out of the front seat to open the back door for Maria and Val.

Maria looked around at all the fashionably dressed people and admired the different styles they daringly mixed and matched. She took mental photographs of the busy bars, the couples holding desperately onto each other, the groups of friends who were cheering each other on to have more drinks. The air carried an odd smell. A mix of different foods from the vendors, cigarette smoke, and alcohol from the people passing by.

She slowed her pace a little, taking in the atmosphere as she watched Jung-hyun and Val holding hands, walking up the street to the club like they were the only two people in the world. Maria once again felt the pressure to make these memories last and realized she couldn't let any more opportunities pass. Grabbing her phone as quick as lightning, she took a round of photos to nail the romantic shot.

Once she got several pictures, she ran to catch up to Jung-hyun and Val, who had stopped in front of the club Sul Bin had invited them to. A small neon-green sign hung inconspicuously outside a large black metal door. The man standing beside the door looked like a bouncer who could crack someone's head open like a nutshell with his biceps. Unlike other clubs they had passed, there were no people waiting in a queue, and no music was flooding out of the place.

"이름이 뭐예요?" The man spoke with a higher-pitched voice than she expected to hear from such a bulked-up figure.

"아...잠깐만요." She grabbed her phone to text Sul Bin that they were outside.

Not even a minute later, the door flung open, music pulsating from inside, and Sul Bin walked out dressed to kill. Maria couldn't stop her eyes from wandering as his oversized button-up was only being held closed by three little buttons, leaving his firm, toned chest on display. A pair of tight black jeans hugged all the right places, giving her a nice idea of what he was working with, and his high-end sneakers were stark white. Finally coming back up to his face, a smirk played on his lips, which looked as though they had a slight gloss on them. His eyes looked her over with a similar appreciation as his hand ran through his hair, tousling it perfectly.

"와." He smiled, extending his hand in invitation. She dropped her hand into his, his slender fingers gripped hers and gently pulled her into the club. He nodded to the bouncer, who simply turned back to the empty street.

"This place is very deceptive from the outside," she shouted over the music.

"That's why it's great. Only certain people know about this place.

It makes it that much more fun." He winked, letting go of her hand and wrapping his arm around her waist, pulling her closer to him.

He seemed so comfortable with touching her. Normally that wouldn't throw her off, but since being in Korea and watching all the dramas where 스킨십 meant so much more to people, it was odd that he seemed so unfazed by touching her.

"You look gorgeous, Maria." He brought his lips to her ear as he spoke. Her body reacted to the touch, but she wasn't moving closer to enjoy the vibration of his lips on the shell of her ear. She was more so jerking her head from the sensation of her eardrum feeling it was about to burst.

"You look great too," she responded with a small bow. She looked around the club. Fifty or sixty people crammed onto the tiny dance floor, where at the far end a DJ was spinning and bopping to his beats on a small stage hidden behind a cage. The lights were an epileptic's worst nightmare of flashing multi-colors as laser lights scanned the crowd. Surrounding the dance floor were sections filled with large tables and black leather booths. In the middle of the tables were large bottles of all types of alcohol. Groups sitting around the tables would grab the bottles, popping them open and pouring themselves drinks.

Getting to their own private booth, Maria saw two other men and a woman chatting and drinking. When Sul Bin entered, they all looked at him, obviously impressed. He had mentioned that knowing Maria's friends would be the talk of his friends for at least a month. He clearly wasn't joking.

"This is Maria. And these are her friends who are getting married at the end of the month," he explained. The group all nodded quickly, grabbing bottles of beer and tossing them to each new arrival.

Dipping her head, Maria popped the top off and began to drink. It barely even tasted like beer. More like water. If PBR had a brother, it was whatever Korean beer she was just handed. She looked to the table to see a familiar green bottle. 소주. Reaching over she grabbed the bottle, and without even asking the rest of the group if they wanted any, twisted the top off and took a large swig.

Jung-hyun and Val seemed to fit in immediately, befriending Sul Bin's friends rather quickly, while Maria looked out to the crowd of dancing people, desperately wanting to join them.

"가자," Sul Bin shouted a bit, grabbing her hand and pulling her up to head to the dance floor. He seemed to know exactly what she was thinking, and she mentally thanked him for that.

Mingling with the crowd, his hands grabbed her hips, pulling her close as they started to sway with the music. She loved these moments. Just like in college, she never felt guilty when dancing in the clubs. She was free to let out all her good feelings and enjoy the moment.

Maria closed her eyes to feel the bass through her body. It felt like ages since she'd last been to a club. In fact, the last time she went was with Val when Val had come home for the holidays. As she reminisced about the good ol' clubbing days, she was brought back to the present when something brushed her neck.

Lips. Lips were on her neck. Her eyes sprang open, and she pushed Sul Bin away. He really didn't spark any kind of heat in her. But the sleepy kiss on her neck from Hwan Soo caused her insides to melt. Sul Bin's eyes were trying to read her expression. She tried to keep it neutral to not hurt the poor guy's feelings.

"아, 미안. You startled me," she explained.

He nodded his head but didn't move any closer to her. Great. She just killed the mood. Attempting to salvage it, she grabbed his hand, placing it back on her hip. Her arm wrapped around his neck and gently tugged him closer to her again as she started to sway. He smiled and exhaled a tense breath. She felt his body relax, and he began swaying with her once more.

They danced for ages. Even laughing and making up silly dances in between coming together to sway their bodies in rhythm with one another. It felt comfortable. Friend comfortable. Boring comfortable. A Korean pop mashup that she was going to have to ask Val to find for her ended and, panting, they headed back to the group for drinks.

They must've been gone longer than she realized. Jung-hyun and

Val were snuggling even closer than before, their eyes half lidded as they leaned in for pecks that escalated into a full-blown make-out session. When Val started unbuttoning Jung-hyun's shirt, Maria shuffled over to intervene before they did something they'd regret. They were in public! But maybe if drunk enough... Maria stopped her train of thought. If her friend wanted her and her future husband's first time to be special, a drunken mishap was definitely not that.

Sul Bin's friends weren't in much better shape. They screamed and swayed back and forth unsteadily, their eyes unable to even stay open.

"Should we try and get them all home?" Sul Bin shouted.

"Probably," she screamed back, wondering the logistics of how two sober people were going to get five very inebriated people out of a bar and into taxis.

Wrapping one arm of each of her friends around her neck, Maria steered them toward the exit. She glanced back at Sul Bin to see him holding his three friends up. He shouted something to her about doing something together after they got their friends home safely, but she was too focused on getting her friends into the fresh air.

Once outside she remembered that getting a taxi wasn't going to be easy, and Maria didn't have Jung-hyun's special car service on her favorites list to help get them home. Looking down the busy pedestrian street, she was going to have to walk the long distance to the main road to grab a cab.

"Can you wait here with your friends? I will get these guys into a cab and then help you get your friends home. Then we can grab some 라면 and hang out some more?" Sul Bin asked as he held onto all three of his stumbling friends with ease.

She struggled to nod with two arms draped around her neck as he began tugging his friends down the road to grab them a cab.

He looked back to her and shouted, "기다려."

She watched him disappear down the crowded sidewalk and leaned Val and Jung-hyun against a wall to relieve her aching back muscles. They seemed comfortable leaning on the cool concrete and drunkenly smiled as they slid down to sit on the ground. She would've argued that the ground was dirty and would ruin their nice clothes, but she was happier knowing they weren't planning to run away anywhere.

Waiting for Sul Bin, a cool breeze danced across her heated skin and she felt her body relax a tiny bit. The aches in her back subsided as she rubbed her neck and massaged down her spine.

"Why are you here alone with our two drunk friends? Where's your boyfriend?" Maria heard Hwan Soo reprimanding her in her head. She couldn't even have one night free of the deep timbre of his voice? Rolling her eyes, she shook his voice out of her consciousness.

"Did you seriously just ignore me?" His voice had become annoyed.

Wait. That sounds like it's coming from behind me.

Korean Vocabulary:

이름이 뭐예요 - eeroomee mwoyeyo - What's your name?

스킨십- sookinshib - skinship.

기다려- keedaryeo - wait

S pinning around, Maria's eyes were surely playing tricks on her. Hwan Soo stood casually in front of her on the bustling sidewalk. His black hair was mussed as it fell across his forehead in loose waves. His billowing white shirt accentuated his long neck, but the sexiness was offset by an oversized blush cardigan with large brown buttons tucked delicately into his dark jeans fastened with a designer belt. He looked ready to hit up any bar or club in the area and be the center of attention. With one glance, her heart began racing and a flush she knew he would be able to see crept into her cheeks as heat spread down the rest of her body.

"W-w-what are you doing here?" She rubbed her eyes to make sure he wasn't an alcohol-induced illusion thanks to her slight buzz.

"The shoot ended earlier than expected, and I thought...that doesn't matter. Why are you here alone?" He pulled off his cardigan and draped it over her shoulders before brushing past her to where their two friends sat, legs kicked out straight as Val's head leaned on Jung-hyun's shoulder. He seemed to be checking the severity of their intoxication.

The smell, his smell, wrapped around her, reminding her of his home. His bedroom, more specifically, and its calming eucalyptus scent. She threaded her arms through the massive sleeves, surreptitiously bringing her sweater paw up to take a deeper inhale to get her body to calm down.

"It's not that I'm alone..." she started.

Assured their friends were settled, Hwan Soo turned to look at Maria. "Really?" He stood, knees cracking. Impatiently his hands went to his hips, making his shirt pull and offering a glimpse at his toned chest. He looked around possibly trying to find who she should've been with, but as luck would have it, Sul Bin was nowhere to be found.

"Yes, really. Sul Bin had to get his three friends a taxi, and then he was coming back to help me get these two into a cab back to their places," she explained. She couldn't tell who Hwan Soo was annoyed at more, Sul Bin or her.

And before she could ask, the person in question arrived.

"Hey, you ready?" Sul Bin asked, ignoring the latest addition to their party. When Hwan Soo turned around, Sul Bin's attitude changed drastically. A cocky smirk overtook his calm face, and his head fell with a shake. But what unsettled Maria the most were his eyes. An evil glint took the place of his charming laugh lines.

"Why am I not surprised?" Sul Bin scoffed.

"Was I not included in the friends you asked Maria to invite?" Hwan Soo stood straighter, puffing his chest out and broadening his shoulders.

What is happening right now? Maria looked between the two men like she was suddenly watching a safari documentary. The British voice in her head explained how two males entered the ring to fight over the female.

She stepped past Hwan Soo to get Sul Bin to calm that evil stare in his eyes.

"Sul Bin, I did invite him this morning when you invited me and my friends," she explained. "He had something earlier tonight but was able to get off early and just showed up."

Sul Bin looked to her, his eyes not softening their fiendish glare, and it made her take a small step away from him.

"I'm sure that's the case," he bit back at her.

"It's the truth. You should believe her," Hwan Soo said, coming to her defense.

"Yeah, and I trust anything you say," Sul Bin said, sizing up Hwan Soo.

"What the hell is going on here? You two need to calm down." Maria looked back and forth between them as they stared each other down. Neither man spoke. Their eyes never left one another as they continued to puff out their chests, nostrils flaring, jaws clenching, and fists staying to their sides. Were they going to fight? How could they hate each other so much? Had they even spoken before?

Sul Bin was the first one to speak. "Since the white knight makes his appearance once again, I should go and make sure my friends get to their place safely."

"Sul Bin..." She didn't want the night to end so harshly and reached out to him, but he took a step back, avoiding her touch. Maria pulled her hand back to her chest.

"Call me when you get home, okay?" he asked.

Before she could stop him, Sul Bin stalked off into the ever-growing crowd.

"Let's get these two home." Hwan Soo turned back to their drunken friends, brushing off the heated exchange that had just happened, but Maria couldn't let it go that easily.

"What was that?" She pulled him back to face her.

"It was nothing, Maria," he huffed out. They were close enough that she could smell his minty breath. Looking back at their friends, he said, "We need to get these guys up and into my van before the cops come and start asking questions."

Fearing being arrested in a foreign country, Maria ran over to lift Val, putting the nearly dead weight of her drunk friend on her side, and began trudging them down the sidewalk.

A crowd that had previously amplified her excitement and had her pulse racing with euphoria had become a nuisance, full of annoying babbling idiots, stumbling into her way to freedom.

"비켜!" Hwan Soo's muffled voice shouted from behind her. When she turned around, she saw he had covered his face up to his eyes with his shirt. His commanding voice did the trick, parting the drunken masses like the Red Sea.

They got to the street with ease after that. Like a rabbit out of a hat, Hwan Soo's van appeared in front of them. His manager popped out of the driver's seat and pulled open the doors to help them lift their friends into the car. Pushing them into the farthest back seats, like magnets Val and Jung-hyun wrapped each other up in their arms, snuggling closely and continuing to sleep.

Maria's annoyance subsided seeing the love those two shared even when not conscious. She smiled back at them as she heard the doors slam shut and the car begin moving.

"We can't take them to Val's or his place. His mother would find out and freak," Hwan Soo explained. "형, take us home."

His manager nodded and continued driving.

"We can let them sleep in the guest room, and you can crash in mine," he explained.

"I am not sleeping with you." She quickly shot him down and crossed her arms, falling back onto her seat.

"Calm down. I'm not staying the night. We start filming tomorrow." He looked down at his watch. "Technically later today. It starts really early, so I will just head to the set once we drop you all off. Take the day off tomorrow. Keep watching some dramas or even venture out on your own if you dare." His head fell back onto the headrest, eyes closing, and he sighed loudly.

"미안해," she mumbled as she looked down to her hands, picking at the cuffs of the warm pink sweater. Suddenly her well-manicured hands had become the most fascinating thing in the car.

Maria heard the squeak of leather and from the corner of her eye, she saw Hwan Soo's head turn toward her. He didn't speak at first, making her look over to see what had made him hold his tongue. He was just staring at her. No anger on his face, no animosity, no confusion. Just watching her. Instead of being uncomfortable, it was causing her emotions to get the better of her. She focused on calming her breathing and trying desperately not to blush.

"Why are you sorry?" he asked languidly.

"Because you came all the way out here during your packed schedule hoping to have a relaxing, fun night with your friend, only to have to help me carry two drunks to your van and take them home." She turned away from him, unable to keep her eyes from roaming his fit frame.

"Don't apologize for our friends over-drinking. I expected it, actually." He laughed lightly. "Just thought you would still be in the club."

"I thought so too, but Sul Bin said something about getting everyone home and then getting some 라면 or something like that. I couldn't totally hear because I was trying to keep Val and Jung-hyun standing." At the thought of food, her stomach gave a hearty gurgle.

"He said what?!" Hwan Soo bolted up in his seat, scaring her with the sudden movement.

Why does he look like he is about to rip someone's head clear off?

"He wanted to grab some 라면," she repeated carefully. His face looked like a cherry; it was turning more and more red by the second.

"Don't ever do that with him. Do you understand?" he commanded.

"Umm...you are not the boss of me and who I eat with. And what's the big deal? You and I ate 라면 just the other day," Maria reasoned. Suddenly, they were flung forward as the manager slammed on his brakes. He swung around, glaring back at them with crazy eyes.

"형, don't worry. It's not like that. We were in a 편의점," he explained, which didn't seem to make his manager any less frantic.

"What is so wrong with eating 라면 with someone?" Maria asked, feeling more confused by the second.

"It's not the act of actually eating the food. It's what it can imply when asked a certain way. And the way that Sul Bin was asking..." Hwan Soo trailed off, leaving them all in an uncomfortable silence.

She could tell the conversation was not going in a direction she was going to like, and pondering what Sul Bin really meant was making her squirm uneasily in her seat. Hwan Soo looked to his manager, who began driving once again, but their movement didn't last long as they got stuck in bumper-to-bumper traffic.

"오늘 최인이다," Hwan Soo huffed out, leaning back in his chair and closing his eyes once again. Maria could tell he was tired and chose to let him rest instead of asking for a translation.

Half an hour later, they had only moved a mile. Maria was relieved Hwan Soo was getting time to sleep and watched as the steady rise and fall of his chest caused his pecks to crease his shirt in a way that shouldn't have been sexy but was.

She turned to check on the ones in the back, who were still fast asleep, entwined in each other's arms. Jung-hyun's nose kept twitching from Val's fluffy beautiful top bun of curls he had been using as his own personal pillow. Maria's heart swelled seeing her best friend in total comfort with someone else, and she wished she could find someone she could share moments like this with.

Maybe her mom wasn't totally crazy in wanting Maria to find some-one. Her mother's method for finding "the one" may be insane, but she only wanted Maria to be loved by a special someone. Comfortable but still excited to see and do new things together. To explore new places, travel the world, and continue falling in love with each other. Her heart told her that she should have a serious talk with her mom about finding "the one."

As her mind began to run through those romantic scenarios, her eyes wandered back over to Hwan Soo. Why? Why was he the one she looked to? Why was he the one she had begun to picture in those scenarios with her? She liked him. She could admit that. He was handsome, caring, a great friend, driven, and she could see he was going places. But him? "The one?"

He's asleep, right? She watched those steady breaths, his Adam's apple protruding from his neck like a delectable fruit ready to have a bite taken. His hands sat in his lap, long fingers laced, palms resting against his—most likely—six-pack abs.

Maria glanced toward his manager driving. Eyes focused on the road. She returned her focus to Hwan Soo, who was still making her heart act without conferring with her mind. She reached over to move some of his hair away from his eyes. Gently tracing her fingers through his hair, she could feel the slight coarseness of the hair spray remaining from the shoot. His head lolled toward her, and she snapped her hand back to her chest, nervous he had woken up. Holding her breath, she watched as he tried to bury his body deeper into the seat, wrapping his arms around himself.

Is he cold? She looked down at herself, remembering she was wearing his sweater. Pulling it off quickly, she draped it over his torso so he could sleep more comfortably. She smiled as he grabbed it, bringing it up to his face to snuggle.

Maria leaned her head on her headrest continuing to watch him. Frowning, she realized he still had his makeup on. She knew that leaving it on would ruin his perfect skin. Sitting up, she looked for the bag his manager always carried around.

"팀장님," she whispered. The man turned slightly to hear her better. "Do you have makeup remover in your bag?"

"네." He gestured to the passenger seat, where his large bag sat open filled like a diaper bag with everything one would need for any kind of situation.

She shuffled forward to grab the bag, digging around to find wipes and lotions used for his skincare routine. Pulling out two wipes to start, she reached out and began wiping his cheeks. He flinched, and Maria paused. When his eyes didn't open, she figured she was in the clear. As she continued to gently wipe, his bare face came into view. She could see the tiny freckle on his nose and was mad that they hid one of her favorite features of his face.

Having wiped all the foundation off, Maria moved on to his eyes, focusing on the liner and light-brown-colored eye shadow. He hadn't moved a muscle since she started, and it made her happy that she could help him in the smallest amount.

The last thing she had to remove was the light tint on his lips. She looked at his plump, soft-looking mouth and swallowed hard. His lips were part of many thoughts that cursed her mind and plagued her dreams. She reached over with the last clean wipe and began swiping across his bottom lip. Continuing to wipe with a laser-like focus, she noticed a very faint freckle near the corner of his bottom lip. She moved closer to get a better look at the freckle.

Maria hadn't realized how close she had gotten until her nose brushed his.

"어머," she whispered, pulling her body away. She stopped short when her wrist was caught in the firm hold of the man below her, eyes unopened.

"기분이 이상해," he said groggily. She believed he was talking in his sleep.

"뭐?" She tried to twist her hand free from his grip, which only made him hold tighter. Hwan Soo pulled her hand closer, pressing it to his chest, where she could feel his heart beating as fast as hers.

"마음." His eyes opened to look at her.

His gaze met hers, her hand still in his, her heart beating quickly.

"What is—" She couldn't choke out the final words before he closed the distance between them, bringing his lips to hers.

Korean Vocabulary:

비켜 - pikyo - move

오늘 최악이다 - ohnul chuwoakeeda - today is the worst

기분이 이상해 - geebuonee eesanghae -it feels weird

마음 - maoom - heart (but in a feelings way)

Chapter 39 (서른아홉)

S omeone pinch me. This has to be a dream! Instead of a pinch to her skin, Maria felt his teeth nip her bottom lip. Hwan Soo's tongue, which gently toyed with her, sent a refreshing minty tingle to her mouth, exciting her. Making it apparent that she was most definitely awake.

Oh God. She pulled her lips away from his, her bottom lip tugged as his teeth held their grip. When she was able to look over his whole face, she saw his eyes had closed. Not reopening.

Seriously? Is he still asleep? She huffed out an exasperated breath and tried to move back to her seat, but something stopped her.

A hand caressed the back of her head, returning her lips to his pleasingly plump ones. His other hand released hers, allowing her fingers to skim the soft cotton of his shirt before resting at his cold belt buckle. He leaned forward, not letting her lips leave his for a second, as he wrapped his free arm around her waist to pull her onto his lap.

As his lips moved over hers, Maria tried to solve the puzzle of what the kiss meant. She wished there could be some profound answer. Like how it was in the dramas. A kiss that told her what he felt. What she felt.

When his hand slipped from its gentle hold on her head, fingers tracing the bare skin of her back and finally landing on her bottom, she pulled her lips away for a second to catch her breath. His lips looked ravaged, her gloss smeared against them, making all the work she had done obsolete. While her breathing calmed and she looked at his handsome bare face, a glimmering light of realization hit her. She liked Hwan Soo. A lot. More than a friend, and more than a one-night kind of fling. Her mother would even call what she felt close to love.

His hand that had been resting on her butt gave a gentle squeeze and before she could let out a small yelp, his lips covered hers again. His tongue slipped into her mouth, and while her mind was racing with what her feelings were, her body kicked into overdrive. Her arms closed around his neck, crushing her body against his chest so their racing hearts battled it out.

The second she admitted her feelings to herself, she was an uncaged animal. She ground her hips down to feel a rather large package greeting her, and his hand moved from her bottom, skipping down the side of her dress that was nearly up at her waist. His lips left hers, trailing searing hot kisses along her chin, her jaw, making his way to her neck. Her head lulled back as she let him take what he wanted of her. And she wanted all of Hwan Soo. She wanted every single itty-bitty piece of the man. Her hands raked through his hair to pull him closer. She could still feel the coarse stickiness of hairspray, but she didn't care. Her breath was becoming ragged as the heat of his lips on the skin leading to her chest threatened to cause her internal combustion.

Her hands crept across his chest, the hard muscles twitching as her fingers tripped over the cotton and the indents of his abs. When she reached the cotton shirt's bottom seam, she didn't think twice about slipping her hand underneath to finally feel those delicious abs she knew existed. He clearly approved of the move because his thumb had begun circling to the inside of her leg making her grind against him again. It took every bit of her willpower not to moan. There were people asleep in the car.

But wait! He's asleep! Stop making out with a dude who's not conscious.

She pushed off him with such force, she fell off his lap with a loud thump to the van floor. She didn't look up. She didn't want to see the face of the man she just inwardly confessed her feelings for, who was sleeping soundly as if nothing happened.

The silence in the car became deafening. An all-too-clear reminder that what she had just done could never be repeated. She would have to erase it from her mind, and desperately try to extinguish the feelings in her heart.

With a few small squeaks of the leather, she was safely back in her seat, eyes staring straight down at her hands until they arrived at Hwan Soo's house.

Was she embarrassed she kissed Hwan Soo back? Why did she push away from him? And why couldn't she look up at him when she fell onto the floor? When he went to reach out to help her up, she had already moved back over to her seat and looked down at her hands the rest of the car ride to his house.

He had woken up the second the cool makeup-removal cloth touched his skin, but he enjoyed her touch so much he wanted to feel it however he could. As she continued to wipe away the caked-on foundation, he heard her tiny little tuts of disapproval. He had to clench his jaw tight not to laugh. When the cloth began to scrub softly on his lips, he heard a louder tsk.

She had moved a lot closer. Her breath was fanning over his dampened face, cooling him as well as spreading a warmth throughout the rest of his body.

When he felt her nose against his, he couldn't hold back any longer. He confessed to her how her being near him made him feel, and he kissed her. She kissed him back. Nervously at first. He could taste the soju she must've drunk in the club, which fueled his need to kiss her harder to make her forget that douchebag Sul Bin. Her lips were made to be pressed against his. They dueled for dominance, but he wanted to make it clear that he was going to take charge.

When he pulled her onto his lap, a very faint squeak left her lips, and her legs straddled him, making him want her to feel how aroused he was by her touch. He wanted her to be as excited as he was. His fingers played up and down her spine like a fine piano, and he felt her quiver against his chest. And when his hand reached that perky butt he had admired since he first met her, he was done for. Her body reacted as he had hoped, and her pelvis rolled against his sexually frustrated body. After giving a gentle squeeze, he moved his hand around to her thigh; the bottom of her dress had risen so high on her leg he was desperate to look and see what kind of underwear he would have the joy of ripping off soon. If his memory was correct, she had pulled some pretty sexy little numbers from her suitcase that Val had packed a few days ago.

As his lips finally left hers to bury themselves in her neck, her pulse beat at a bewildering pace on his tongue before he gently nipped her neck. A fuzzy drunken dream shot through his mind. He had done this before. With her. Was he sure it was just a dream?

His thoughts returned to the present when her hand moved under his shirt. Her nails scratched gently down the path from his navel to the metal of his belt buckle. His body ignited. He needed more skin-to-skin contact. He moved his thumb to graze the bare skin of her inner thigh, and her body pressed down on his manhood harder than before. The "Hallelujah Chorus" practically sang in his head. This woman was going to drive him madder than any woman ever had. He took the chance to slip his hand farther up her milky thigh, his hand about to touch the clothing covering her most sensitive area, when suddenly she jumped off him like he was on fire and she didn't want to get burned. Why? He almost groaned aloud in frustration.

When they arrived at his house, he chose to pretend he had fallen asleep again so as not to make the situation more awkward. His manager climbed out of the car, and he heard them shuffle to get the two drunks out of the back. The door slammed shut and he jumped, opening his eyes. If he thought it was silent before, the eerie calm that had taken over the car in that moment unsettled him more.

He grabbed his phone to try to take his mind off what he was going to say to Maria the next time he saw her. What could he possibly say to her?

"Hey, enjoyed making out with you. Wanna do it again?" Cross that off the list immediately.

"Should we talk about our feelings for each other? I think I'm really into you and want to take this to the next level." Jesus. He wasn't trying to have them pick out dish towels and china patterns.

Before he could have another idiotic thought, his manager climbed back into the car and pulled out of the driveway.

"바보," his manager mumbled. But it was clear enough for Hwan Soo to hear.

"알아요," he responded, exasperated.

The contour brush tickled his cheek as he took a deep breath. The first day of filming was about to start, and nerves were getting to him. His stomach was churning, and even with the tea his manager provided and the gifts of red ginseng from his small number of fans, nothing could calm the rumbles. As he picked at his fingernails, his thoughts strayed to the memory of wrapping them around the soft curls of Maria's hair. How his lips, which were now receiving a glossed tint, had played along Maria's supple ones only a matter of hours ago.

What the hell was he going to say to Maria when he saw her next? Why was kissing her so different than anyone else he's ever kissed? And the big question that plagued his mind: Why did she push away after such an amazing kiss without even looking at him?

"어때?" A squeaky female voice pulled him from his thoughts.

He looked over to see Hae So in a loose canary-yellow blouse tucked into a burnt-orange floor-length pleated skirt. Her makeup was light, flaunting her natural beauty, and her long sun-lightened brown hair was pulled into a ponytail that bounced and twirled as she moved. If he didn't know her personality, he would say she looked pretty. But that wasn't the case.

"양의 탈을 쓴 늑대," He smirked mischievously as he watched the makeup artist cover her laugh with her brush-filled hand.

Hae So didn't find his comment or the makeup artist's giggle very funny. She crossed her arms and dropped a hip, her skirt flowing with the movement. She said nothing, but he could feel in his gut that something bad was coming.

"What did you end up doing last night?" she asked casually, ignoring his insult.

"I had a commercial shoot..." he answered suspiciously, knowing very well there was a reason for her question. His stomach sank as his heart beat against his chest like a jackhammer.

"And after?" She raised an eyebrow as she took a step closer. The makeup artist backed away as the evil emanating from Hae So shrouded them, becoming almost tangible.

Hwan Soo stood to keep the sparring match between the two of them. Pulling his shirt straight, he looked down to Hae So with a commanding stature.

"What exactly are you getting at?" He lowered his voice an octave to make his point very clear. He was not going to play her game.

"I saw you were with that 'assistant' of yours last night. 짜장면 girl." She leaned closer, her body nearly flush against his.

"Well she is my assistant. Why wouldn't I be seen with her?" he retorted simply.

"Ruining her date doesn't sound like something you needed to be there for. To be fair, Sul Bin clearly wasn't cutting it. She still ended up going home with you. Why is she staying in your house, Hwan Soo?" She turned her head, her ponytail flying and hitting his face.

"Sul Bin had his own friends to take care of, and he was about to take her home to a situation she had no clue she signed up f—" He stopped dead. That tangible evil had encompassed him, and his heart was no longer a jackhammer. It had ceased movement altogether. He wasn't sure he was breathing.

"How do you know his name?"

Another whip of the ponytail to his face, and he was ready to chop it off, but he needed to hear her response. Or did he? Was this woman like his mother? Having him tailed to see all his whereabouts and who he was with? At least with his mom there was some sort of excuse. But with Hae So, he couldn't wrap his head around her motivations. She tossed him aside like he was a piece of trash. She didn't consider that they had a relationship yet was sleeping with other people while he obeyed her like a puppy, believing that she was as loyal to him as he was to her. Yet now she wanted to know the ins and outs of his life? Just how sick and twisted was this woman?

She smirked, reaching a bony, long-fingered hand out to adjust the chain of his necklace. He grabbed her bird wrist, pulling her cold fingers away from his heated skin. It took everything in him not to push her away.

"How do you think I know?" she whispered icily.

"You followed me." He tossed her hand, sending her body back a bit with the force.

"Please. You think I have time to follow you around like a lost little puppy? That was always your job," she said coldly. The smug look on her face spoke volumes more than her words, which didn't hurt him like they once did.

He knew her. On several levels, he knew what kind of person she could be when she didn't get what she wanted. She was like a Mafioso. She gave a warning, and when that warning was disregarded, she made her power known. If someone dared to defy her after that, well, one could figure out where it led.

She'd never killed anyone...at least he hoped. How he ever thought he was in love with someone so maniacal was baffling. Finally taking a step away from her, keeping his temper under control, he looked down at her.

"How do you know Sul Bin, Hae So? Don't make me ask again," he threatened. He could see for a split second he had frightened her.

Covering up her alarm with a shake of her head, she looked around to make sure no one was close enough to hear her.

"Your little girlfriend threatened to ruin my show. I couldn't let that happen. Those silly innocent loved-up eyes were always being thrown in your direction. Even some of the staff noticed during that first read through. So, I made her look somewhere else. He's newly signed to my agency. I offered him something he couldn't refuse," she explained calmly. "But since he failed to even keep her occupied for a week, that won't be happening."

"Your show? *Your* show?!" he spat. "Who do you think you are exactly? You offered Sul Bin what? Sex? A role in our drama? What? All to keep a woman I like out of your hair? To make sure your popularity is higher than the rest of us working here? Your logic is so twisted, Hae So. I like Maria. She's a hard worker, she's a good friend, and she has several things you don't have."

Hae So didn't back down, but her next words made him see a side of her that he had never seen. "What could that little girl have that I don't?"

Jealousy.

"A heart, a conscience, friends..." He trailed off, turning away in an attempt to end the conversation before their words turned more spiteful. But he realized needed to say something more to put a final stop to all this because he knew Hae So wouldn't let it go anytime soon if he didn't go straight for the kill.

"Oh, and one more thing she has that you don't?" He turned back to her, her face redder than 김치. "She has me."

Korean Vocabulary:

양의 탈을 쓴 늑대 - yangoi tarool ssoon nookdae - a wolf in sheeps clothing.

Chapter 40 (마흔)

Maria couldn't sleep in his room. The second she walked in, all the memories of what had happened in the car came flooding back. His scent was so strong that she could feel his hand creeping up her thigh again, causing an involuntary shiver up her spine.

Jesus, Maria, 정신차려.

She walked out of his greenhouse-like bedroom and strode into the kitchen. Grabbing a bottle of water from the fridge, the cool sensation down her throat soothed her heated skin but did nothing to calm her racing heart. She went to the couch, lying down and stared up at the blank white ceiling, reflecting on her inner turmoil. Not only did she like Hwan Soo, but she wanted to be with him. If her mother heard these thoughts, she would be on a plane, wedding dress in hand, ready to throw her daughter down the aisle with Val and Jung-hyun. "A two-for-one deal," her mother would boast proudly.

Maria should tell him. She knew she should. But the problems it could cause him and his career could be detrimental. If someone overheard her, they could leak it everywhere. If he rejected her, he could be marked as a playboy just looking for cheap thrills. But if he actually had feelings for her, and she really hoped he did, he was under a strict no-dating contract. He could lose everything he worked so hard for.

He had warned her when she sent Hae So the photo of them that even fake kissing could be used against him if the evil bitch decided to share it. At the time, Maria had no clue about Hae So's wickedness or what Hwan Soo's life as a Korean actor entailed. But since working alongside Hwan Soo, Maria worried just how low Hae So would go to keep her fame status elevated.

How he could've dated her, kissed her, loved her...

Maria! Focus! she scolded herself.

Her phone buzzed at her side. Grabbing it and hoping to see a text from Hwan Soo, her heart clenched, guilt now replacing every happy tingly feeling she had.

Sul Bin.

Sul Bin-이: Was traffic really bad? I'm sure by now you got home ok? You're probably really tired so I'll just talk to you later. 오늘 일은 미안해.

He always seemed to text her at the perfect time to make her feel the guiltiest.

Taking a deep breath, she decided to respond.

Maria: Hey. Sorry. Just got my friends into bed. Who knew traffic could still be so bad at this hour? I don't know what exactly you're apologizing for, but you don't have anything to be sorry about.

Sul Bin-이: I shouldn't have gotten so angry when I saw Hwan Soo. I just got...jealous.

Maria: Jealous?

Sul Bin-이: Maria...I'm not stupid. I see the way you guys look at each other. I mean, you told me he wasn't your boyfriend. And you asked me to go to your friend's engagement party with you. I thought I had a fighting chance. I hoped I could change your mind and have you like me instead. But I know when I've lost.

Maria's guilt was at an all-time high. How could she apologize for being such a horrible person to Sul Bin? He had been nothing but a good guy to her, and he was so honest with his feelings.

Maria: It's not like that.

She lied. She liked Hwan Soo. She knew it, and apparently Sul Bin did too. She wasn't about to kick the guy while he was down. But Hwan Soo liking her? She had nothing to offer him. Other than some mediocre Korean, American tact, and his family disowning him.

Sul Bin-이: I hope we can still be friends. I know you're only here for a short while, but I would really like to stay in touch. Maybe even take you around to where the not so rich and famous hang out. 남산 서울타워 is gorgeous at night. Total tourist trap but you should see it once in your life.

She smiled as a wave of relief washed over her. She had never been the one to end a relationship. And once again she was spared the mess. At least this time he wasn't cheating. Actually, she was kind of the one who had cheated. Even though she and Sul Bin weren't together.

Maria: I would like that 😊

Putting her phone down, her mind became somewhat at ease. Sure, she still had the problem of her feelings for Hwan Soo and their steamy make-out session in his van, but with one issue knocked off her to-do list, she could feel exhaustion slowly taking over her body. That was, until the door to the guest room opened and Val stumbled out. Jumping to attention, Maria ran over to try to help her friend.

"Val, you need to go back to sleep." She tried turning Val around to head back to the guest room, where she could see Jung-hyun completely sprawled out and hugging a pillow instead of his soon-to-be wife.

"물. I need 물." Her voice was scratchy as she pointed to her throat, and Maria ran to the kitchen, grabbing the bottle of water she had been drinking from.

"Here." She brought the bottle to her friend's lips, and Val took the bottle like a baby begging for sustenance.

When Val pushed it away from her face, Maria tried to get her friend to go back to bed to sleep off the rest of her drunkenness and maybe even some of the hangover she knew was sure to follow, but Val had other plans.

Pushing past Maria, she wobbled over to the couch, and as she fell onto the cushions. She patted the empty space on the couch next to her. Maria laughed at how nostalgic she felt at that moment. This was going to be one of their usual late-night drunken chats. Maria was happy that this conversation was going to be in person after all their time apart. These were some of the moments she missed the most. And now that her friend was considering staying in Korea after the wedding, it was going to be even less frequent. She had to make every moment count.

"So..." Val started, turning her head to Maria with a glare.

"You okay, Val?" Maria asked.

"I'm hoping you mention it first." The vague and very confusing statement Val led with made Maria sit up in her seat a bit more. What could she possibly be trying to lead into?

"I'm not sure what you mean," Maria said, baffled by her answer.

"So you're not planning on telling me that you and Hwan Soo have been seeing each other?" Val's glare had become unbearable.

"뭐?" Maria didn't know where to start. "No, I'm not dating Hwan Soo" would've been the right starting point, but her mind had gone as blank as a hard drive that got a virus.

"While you thought we were all asleep in the car, you made your move with your boyfriend. You two were getting very frisky. I guess my dress choice worked. Is that why you like staying at his house lately? So you guys can do the nasty and not have any of us know?" Val leaned over trying to nudge Maria's shoulder, but because of her drunkenness, fell hard onto Maria's lap.

Oh. My. God. Val saw them making out. How the hell was she going to explain that? She wasn't.

"I think you're seeing things, Val. How much did you drink?" Maria gently brushed at the tight ringlet curls that had fallen out of her friend's bun.

"Oh please,." Val shot up to look Maria dead in the eyes. "I didn't drink enough to start hallucinating. You and Hwan Soo were about to have sex in the middle of his van!" she shouted.

Maria slapped her hand over Val's mouth so she wouldn't wake the woman's drunk sleeping fiancé.

"Fine. Fine," Maria said, easily caving. "We made out in the car. But that means absolutely nothing because the guy was asleep. He tends to do tha—"

Shit.

"What do you mean he tends to do that? This has happened before? You guys have been doing this a lot?" Val's eyes lit up like fireworks on the Fourth of July.

Maria scratched her forehead. She hadn't told Val about the other times because they never came up in conversation. Now that it was out in the open, Maria couldn't lie.

"The night you went out with Jung-hyun and Hwan Soo-씨 ordered us 짜장면, he fell asleep and when I went to give him a blanket to sleep on the couch with, he pulled too hard and I kinda fell on his lips," Maria explained.

"That was like the third day you were here!" Val's smile had nearly stretched from ear to ear.

"And then—"

"Oh my God! How many times have you kissed him?!" Val was gushing and looked like she was about to melt into a puddle on the floor.

"Tonight would be the third time. Well, the third time he was asleep. I did kinda kiss him to make his ex jealous too." Maria blushed at the thought. She was excited to tell her friend. Especially now that she had been able to admit her feelings to herself. But there was still the problem of him being asleep and not remembering these things happened.

"Hae So. Yeah, I think I remember Jung-hyun telling me about some scheme involving you and Hwan Soo. I didn't think it would go that far." Val shrugged. Maria now had a lot of questions to ask but couldn't, as Val continued thinking out loud. "Wow. If you've been hooking up with Hwan Soo, why did we even go out with Sul Bin tonight?" Val asked. "That guy is a total dirtbag."

"Hwan Soo-씨 and I aren't hooking up, Val. We've kissed a few times. And Sul Bin is a friend. At first, I thought he could've been a nice guy to maybe bring to your wedding, have some fun with...something like that, but we've agreed that friends is where we are going to stay," Maria explained, and again more questions began arising in her head.

"Sul Bin said he wants to just be friends?" Val cringed as she spoke about him. What was so wrong with Sul Bin? Why did Val have such an animosity toward him? Dirt bag? Why did everyone around her not like the guy?

"Yeah...he agreed. In fact, he was the one to make the suggestion. Why don't you like him? I don't get it. You've been mixed about him since your engagement party. Did something happen that I missed? What are you not telling me? And what scheme did Jung-hyun plan?" Maria finally had the time to process and form all her questions.

Val seemed to be having an internal debate. Her cheek was pulled in between her teeth as her eyes looked all about the room trying to not land anywhere near Maria.

"Val, did something happen that I don't know about?" Maria probed.

"여보." A groggy low voice came from the guest room. Val's face filled with relief.

Saved by the drunk, needy fiancé. Jumping from the couch, she ran with her half full bottle of water to help her man.

Maria laid back down on the couch, looking to the stark ivory ceiling. The feeling of once having something crossed off her list was overshadowed by the several large questions now buzzing in her head.

Korean Vocabulary:

정신차려 - jongshincharyeo - get a hold of yourself, come to your senses

오늘 일은 미안해 - ohnul eeroom mianhae - I'm sorry about today

남산서울타워 - Namsan Seoul Tower

물 - mul - water

Chapter 41 (마흔하나)

Hwan Soo deserved an award for being able to put a smile on his face around Hae So the whole day. Not only did he keep a smile, but he also pretended that his skin didn't crawl when he looked at or touched her as they filmed.

Especially the scene where he sees her for the first time and he's supposed to be blown away by her beauty.

As the director called "cut" on the last scene for the night, Hwan Soo's callous, deadpan stare returned instantaneously. His manager handed Hwan Soo a mask to cover his displeased face from all the fansites that had started to gather at the filming locations. Hwan Soo was shocked that several of them were for him. He had only ever seen one or two when he first started acting. He even looked for them online to see their photos and thank them for their kind words of encouragement and kind gestures. But now he saw at least five girls with large cameras following him as he walked back to his van.

When the door finally shut and he was able to be himself, he let out an exhausted sigh, feeling the minor fatigue of his poor rest schedule. As he leaned his head back to relax before he went to his next obligation, his manager gently interrupted.

"You've got several texts," his manager whispered as he passed Hwan Soo the phone.

Watching the screen light up, he saw several bubbles but none were from the person he wanted to hear from the most.

Had he really messed up that badly?

Jung-hyun 형: This hangover is going to kill me. I didn't even know you showed up last night. How drunk was I?

Jung-hyun 형: 고마워 친구. Val and I appreciate you letting us crash in your guest room.

Jung-hyun 형: Maria slept on the couch though. You really couldn't let her sleep in your room? You aren't even here.

Jung-hyun 형: Val and I just left. We have a meeting with the second venue location all day. Maria said she was gonna venture out on her own.

She slept on the couch? Why would she do that? Was she that repulsed by him now that she didn't even want to sleep in a bed that he had previously slept in? He kept reading through his messages. Most were from Jung-hyun trying to remember the night before, some were the company sending his most updated schedule, but one at the very bottom of his list caught his eye.

An unknown number with two words, and that was it.

Unknown: 니가 이겼어.

After doing some major shopping to keep her mind off what was going to happen with Hwan Soo when he got home, Maria patted herself on the back for figuring out the public transportation system with ease. Sure, it wasn't all on her own. It was also binge-watching the dramas and being immersed while listening to Hwan Soo work that helped the most, but she was still proud she was able to figure it out all by herself.

Humming with a spring in her step, she rounded the corner back to Hwan Soo's house and froze. Cameramen and what looked to be fans were all huddled outside his house. They were trying to peer over his very large cement wall and into his yard.

Crap. Had they seen them last night?

She grabbed her mask, quickly covering her face, and made her way to the front door. Her heart raced as she entered the small collection of people. The second they noticed her, cameras were flashing, questions were being screamed—none she could understand—and she felt her clothing being tugged. She pushed as gently as she could to get out of the hoard, opening the gate within the fence and slamming it shut so none of the crazies could get in.

Even after she got inside, her mind went wild with thoughts as to why they had been waiting outside. What had she missed that made the press gather outside his door? She dropped all her bags to the ground and went to grab her phone. The pocket was empty. Did they seriously steal her phone?

Oh hell no.

She walked back out to the group; more than half of them weren't even facing the door anymore. Slamming the gate, they all jumped to attention and charged her once again.

"Which one of you stole my phone?" she asked, trying not to shout at the total invasion of privacy. Not one of them answered. They continued to snap pictures, the flashes blinding her as they got closer to her face.

Holding her hand up to her brow to cover whatever she could of the light, Maria asked the question again, with a little more force in her voice. Some of them turned to look at each other, apparently understanding what she had asked.

"핸드폰!" she then shouted. Shockingly, instead of taking more photos of her throwing a tantrum, they looked around, and one older man rummaged through his bag, pulling out her phone. He looked apologetic, as if he hadn't meant to take her phone in the first place. She wanted to tell him she understood, but she also didn't want the rest of the group to think what he did was okay. She wanted to get away from them to figure out what had happened for her to be jumped the second she made her way to his home. She bowed several times after taking her phone back and ran to the safety the gate held.

When she got inside, she tossed all the bags on the countertop and went straight to the search bar on her phone to find out what had happened. Nothing popped up. She searched in Hangul and English, yet all she could find was news about Hwan Soo getting cast as the lead for the show. He must've been gaining popularity with his new role. Which made her feel very proud. And anxious. She knew she would probably need to start going back to Val's every night. Even if staying with him was more convenient, she didn't want those people outside to get the wrong idea.

Sighing as a small weight of worry lifted off her, she unpacked all the food she had bought to fill his empty fridge. She was concerned that his diet consisted only of things he would eat out. Which, while delicious, was seriously unhealthy. She looked up some simple recipes to cook and leave in his fridge for when he came home late.

She chopped the 양배추, marinated the thin slices of 소고기 before grilling it on an indoor grill she found in his cupboard, and boiled some 떡 for her 떡볶이. Her phone dinged across the counter, pulling her out of her enthusiastic little dance number with the spatula.

It was from Hwan Soo's manager letting her know that Hwan Soo would be coming home late again. Was he telling her so that she had a reason to leave? Or a reason to stay? A sinking feeling settled into her stomach. He had to have seen what transpired in the back of the van. Or at least heard as he kept his eyes on the road. She stared at the phone for what felt like hours, but the blaring of the smoke alarm brought her back to reality. She had burned some of the 소고기. Damn.

That'll be my portion.

Four in the morning, and Hwan Soo was so ready to climb into his bed for the few hours of sleep he could get. His manager came to an awkward slow stop a block away from the house, turning his head to look at Hwan Soo with concern. He was about to ask why they had stopped when he looked through the windshield to see several cars lined up with people sitting inside, some on their phones, others with cameras hanging around their necks. Several young women sat outside against the brick privacy wall, some falling asleep, while others looked up and down the street, apparently checking for cars. They weren't part of his parents' team of private investigators. Those guys were so stealthy, the only time he knew they had been near him was when his parents threw the photos in his face.

"무슨—" he began, but was cut off by his manager.

"Looks like you're getting popular." There was a hint of delight mixed with worry in his voice.

Hwan Soo continued looking at the people waiting by his home.

"We should probably get you up there so you can see if your friends are okay. I'm sure Jung-hyun is used to all this, Val too, but Maria—"

"Jung-hyun and Val left this morning. He texted me." Jung-hyun's text about Maria venturing out suddenly popped out into Hwan Soo's mind.

"Get me up there. Now," he commanded as he pulled out his phone to call her to see if she was okay. When she didn't answer, his hand was already on the door handle ready to jump out and see if Maria was inside and if she was okay.

As they got nearer, his manager said, "If she is inside, make sure she is okay. And you should probably talk to her about what happened last night. I like her. I think she is good for you, and I know I should be deterring you from any kind of relationship, but I wanted to give my honest opinion."

"I will talk to her and let you know how it goes." Hwan Soo

ripped open the door and jumped out. Car doors slammed and lights began flashing. The girls who were huddled around the gate looked starstruck as they pulled out their phones to snap photos. Cameras were shoved in his face as questions were being hurled his way. While most of them were pointless, simple questions about the drama, one question caught him by surprise.

"누가 여자야?" A scruffy voice pierced through all the other questions.

He started to turn and respond, but before he could, a jacket was pulled over his head and his manager was by his side, pushing him toward the security gate of his house.

"고마워 형," Hwan Soo whispered.

"I'm not about to leave the company's hottest commodity, and my friend, to fend for himself." He smiled as they finally got through the gate and onto his property.

Hwan Soo typed his code into the door and flung it open to take a nice relaxing breath.

"Something smells delicious." His manager kicked off his shoes and ran to the kitchen.

Hwan Soo had more pressing matters to attend to. Where was Maria? He walked into his living room and didn't see anyone. The only light he saw was from the kitchen where his manager was diving into some food.

He looked down to the hallway to the bedrooms, and he could hear faint voices coming from the guest room. A small smile stretched across his face as the joy of seeing her again filled his heart, he began walking toward the room. A thin sliver of light leaked through the bottom of the door.

Slowly pushing the door open, he was surprised to see himself on the TV hung on the wall and Maria asleep, snuggled deep in the comforter. Her hand, the only thing other than her head that he could see, hung off the edge of the bed and held the remote, which looked ready to fall. He couldn't let it make a loud noise that would wake her up, so he crossed the room to stand beside her. He looked at her face.

Hwan Soo couldn't stop himself. He used to complain about how horrible she looked when she slept, but as his eyes traveled over her face, he realized how wrong he was. Her deep almond hair was sprawled in waves across the pillow, and her lips, which were plumper than he remembered, were slightly parted as she took slow, steady breaths. Her cheeks were flushed, probably from being so warm engulfed in his comforter. She was adorable.

"아이고," he whispered and bent down to her level as she shifted around in the massive comforter.

"가서 먹어," she mumbled in her sleep.

"네?" He was sure she'd just spoken perfect Korean in her sleep.

"먹어," she mumbled again before turning away from him.

Leaving her to sleep, he went to the kitchen where his manager was still snacking away on whatever was on the counter. When he finally saw exactly what was on the counter, his jaw hit the floor. 밥, 소고기, 떡볶이, 김치, 라면, 오이무침, 김치순두부찌개, the works.

"What is all this?" He walked over to grab one of the cucumbers and was shocked that it was almost perfectly seasoned. It just needed some more spice. It reminded him of the first time he saw her eat kimchi. Clearly she tried to avoid being unable to eat it herself.

"I'm pretty sure she made all of this for you." The manager handed a note to Hwan Soo.

잘 먹었습니다!

Her writing was rough and showed signs of pausing several times, probably to make sure what she was writing was correct, which made him smile even brighter. His manager pulled out one of the stools at the counter and plated a bowl of rice, passing it to Hwan Soo.

"Come on. Let's eat before we get some rest." His manager grabbed his own bowl of rice as he picked up several of the side dishes and ate like a man who had been starved half his life.

" 'We'? What do you mean 'we'?" Hwan Soo ate a small bite of the plain rice. Fluffy and perfect. Damn, she's good.

"Think about it. If we are going to tell the press at your door tomorrow morning that she is nothing but someone on your team, we have to make that believable. If I stay, it'll look like she is in fact a nobody and also makes you look like the nice, amazing, caring guy who takes great care of his employees. It's a win-win," the man explained, his cheeks even more chipmunk-like than usual.

"알았어요." Hwan Soo bowed his head as they ate the rest of their meal in silence.

I guess I'm not going to get to talk to her tonight.

Korean Vocabulary:

니가 이겼어 - naga eegyeossoh - you win

핸드폰 - handoopone - cell phone

양배추 -yeongbaechu - cabbage

소고기 - sugogee- beef

누가 여자야 - nuga yojaya? - who's the girl?

가서 먹어 - gaso mogo - go eat

밥 - bap -rice (can also mean food)

오이무침 - oui muchim - cucumber salad

김치순두부찌개 - kimchi soon dubu jjigae - kinmchi soft tofu stew

맛있게 드세요 -maseetkae deuseyo - enjoy the food

Chapter 42 (마흔둘)

Maria grumbled as light poured into the room, ruining her enjoyable sleep as she buried herself in the luxury of the comforter surrounding her.

Wait...this comforter...crap.

Bouncing up, she realized she had fallen asleep while cleaning Hwan Soo's guestroom. The comforter was just so luxurious, she wanted to enjoy it for a little while before she went back to Val's for the night. Apparently she had gotten too comfortable and fell asleep. There was nothing she could do about it now.

Throwing the comforter off her, she walked out into the living room. Hwan Soo's manager was asleep on the couch, lightly snoring as he curled up with a tiny blanket and pillow. Why was he there? Then she heard the refrigerator door close, and she looked to see Hwan Soo—hair unkempt, which made him appear even sexier than normal, in an oversized white t-shirt, leaving his collarbones she loved looking at exposed—running around the kitchen.

"일어났어?" she asked, her voice still groggy from just waking up.

Startled, he spun around, almost dropping one of the Tupperware containers filled with her homemade side dishes, and stared at her briefly before unloading the food in his arms onto the counter.

"네. I got up early to make some breakfast for all of us before we head out this morning. Luckily, someone decided to go food shopping yesterday, and we have enough food to feed an army." He laughed, running his hand over the back of his head, which only drew her eyes to the bulging lines of his well-built arms as he flexed.

"I saw your fridge was scarily empty, so I thought this was one way I could repay you for everything you've done to help me," she explained, walking into the kitchen to see his t-shirt was loosely tucked into the front of his denim jeans. She swallowed hard thinking about what she had felt on her leg two nights prior.

"아... Thank me? For what? I'm simply doing as I was told. Jung-hyun and Val needed someone to help you out." He continued setting up all the food on the counter.

Of course, he was just doing his "job." Why would she think anything else of his kindness? Why did she want there to be more meaning behind anything he did to help?

Because you like him...a lot. And if he were just doing a job, would he have kissed you the way he did that night? Was that part of his job?

He had been asleep, she argued with herself. She tried to pull herself from her thoughts as Hwan Soo's head tilted to the side, eyes crinkled in thought. She had gone silent for a little too long.

"Right. Sorry. Umm...why is your manager sleeping on the couch?" She finally pointed to the man whose snores still quietly floated in from the other room.

"I'm sure you saw the people outside." Hwan Soo jerked his head to his front door.

"Saw them? How about one of them took my phone," she said. Before she had time to explain, she saw Hwan Soo's eyes filled with rage. He threw down the chopsticks in his hands, his nostrils flaring, fingers flexing, and he turned to storm out of the kitchen, ready to go outside.

"I got it back!" She rushed to his side of the counter with her hands up to keep him from doing anything rash. "I don't think the man meant to take it in the first place," she explained quickly. He took a deep breath and turned back to the counter, grabbing the chopsticks again to dish out more of the food.

"Last night we weren't sure if you had been here or not, but when one of the reporters asked who the girl was, we realized you had been seen. We decided to use 팀장님 staying here as a cover story. If he stays, then we simply say that my employees stay with me on occasion. It was better than him leaving, you staying, and the public thinking that there is something going on between us." He spoke calmly, averting his eyes. When she tried to grab the bowl from him, he recoiled his hand as if she was a flame he was worried would burn him.

Confirmed: he has no feelings for you.

Her heart felt like it was sinking into her stomach. And all she could do was play a part.

"Oh wow. Yeah, definitely don't want that happening." She grabbed the rice as quickly as possible and shoved a bunch in her mouth to stop the conversation from going any further. She didn't want to hear any more confirmation of the answer she had feared.

"맛있는 냄새가나." A new, groggy voice entered the conversation.

"팀장님 좋은 아침입니다," Maria mumbled through the rice in her cheeks, thankful for the distraction from her feelings.

"You don't have to be so formal with me, Maria. Just call me Gi Young 오빠." He smiled brightly, grabbing one of the bowls of rice.

Both she and Hwan Soo choked on their food.

"형!" Hwan Soo exclaimed, his mouth so full of food that some fell out.

"뭐?" his manager asked, seeming surprised that what he said would cause any issues.

Silence fell on the group as they sat and ate. Maria looked up every now and again to see that Hwan Soo was trying to have a silent conversation with his manager. She wished she could understand Korean when simply mouthed, but her level of understanding was not that good. She decided to focus on eating and ignore the awkwardness hanging around them.

"Don't forget, you need to take Maria to get a dress for tomorrow night." His manager's voice cut through the quiet sounds of chewing, taking her out of her own thoughts.

"Huh?" She looked up, trying to figure out what Gi Young was talking about.

"Jung-hyun 형 is hosting an event tomorrow night. His mother forced him into being the host a while back. Anyway, a lot of well-known people in the Korean entertainment industry are going to be there and since I'm his best friend, I'm expected to be there. And since you're his fiancée's best friend, you're allowed to be there. Please don't take that the wrong way." He ended his lengthy explanation in a pleading tone.

"I get it. I am not in the entertainment industry. I'm not insulted." She understood he wasn't trying to insult her and smiled to ease his nerves.

"Well it's this big to-do, and we need to get you a dress for the evening," he explained.

"I can just go back to Val's. She has an entire closet of dresses," she argued. "I don't want to waste your energy on something like that."

"The company wants to style you," his manager said.

"네?" She snapped her gaze over to him to see what he meant.

"They are friends with that photographer who you shot with," Gi Young explained. "He will also be at the event tomorrow. Guess he talked you up, and they sounded interested in working with you."

"You didn't tell me that," Hwan Soo said, clearly just as surprised as she was.

"It didn't involve you, so I didn't think I needed to. But now I'm apparently her manager as well," Gi Young joked.

"I don't even know what to say." Her face filled with heat and her stomach twisted with nerves. She was asked to be styled by a designer? Her? She would admit it was a serious ego boost, but what did it mean for her as a "fake" employee of Hwan Soo? Was she no longer in that position? What was she?

"Say you'll work with them." Gi Young smiled reassuringly. She looked at Hwan Soo, who also seemed to be at a loss for words. She gave a simple nod, and his manager smiled. "Great! I will call them now and tell them to expect you later tonight!"

Gi Young stood from the counter and walked into the living room, phone in his hand to make the arrangement.

She and Hwan Soo stared at each other in an awkward silence. She desperately wanted to know what was going on in his mind. Was he happy for her? Jealous? Nervous? What?

As filming for the day wrapped, Maria and Hwan Soo were whisked away to her dress appointment. Gi Young 오빠 drove through some sites she had already seen, but then they pulled into a shopping area that she knew was way out of her league. Brands she knew like Louis Vuitton, Dolce and Gabbana, and Chanel, among others that were unfamiliar but looked just as lavish, lined the streets.

"Hwan Soo-씨, I know for a fact I can't afford even a keychain on this block," Maria whispered. "I can't possibly afford a dress from here. You and Jung-hyun might have money to burn, but I am on a very tight budget."

"You're not paying for anything," he explained quickly, going back to his phone for entertainment.

He had been distant the whole day. When the director called "cut" on his scenes, he had turned off like a robot. He sat silently in his chair, read through the lines for the next scenes and walked back in front of the camera to turn himself back on. She had so many things she wanted to talk to him about, but he acted as if she wasn't even there.

His manager eased the van to a stop in front of one of the stores. A beautiful man opened the door for them, and Hwan Soo climbed out and spun to help Maria out of the vehicle as well. As Maria stepped onto the sidewalk, her jaw dropped. She was greeted by a large Grecian-like entrance adorned with cream-colored columns three stories high. The man who held their car door was one of many beautiful men standing between the columns, ready to greet customers. Gazing through the large glass windows that made up the façade of the building, she saw massive crystal chandeliers hung high above the showroom floor. On the ground floor were golden racks adorned with clothing that looked so elegant, she was scared to even breathe near it.

"Hwan Soo-씨, these people may want to work with me, but I think they believe I am someone I'm definitely not. I also can't expect you to pay for it either," she said, tugging on his sweater sleeve nervously.

"Maria," he sighed, "you're not paying, and I am not paying. You are going to wear the dress for the event, then we are going to return it." He looked at her for what felt like the first time since that morning. "They just want you to wear their name and drop little hints about who designed it while we talk to people at the event. It will funnel more customers their way."

As they walked through the entry, her nose was assaulted with a potent floral scent. Not overly sweet, but reminding her of something a grandmother would wear. Before she had time to process what was going on, several people rushed to greet them. One handed her a glass bottle of water, while another started tugging on her oversized clothing in an attempt to size her and began pulling her toward racks of dresses.

"잠깐만요." She tried to speak over their many voices, but they overpowered her. Pulling dress after dress, they pushed her up a large spiral staircase she hadn't even noticed when entering. Turning around to find Hwan Soo in the throng of attendants, she could see an amused smile on his lips. While it annoyed her, it was the most emotion she had seen on his face in her presence all day.

As she was pulled up onto a round platform, she met her own

eyes in the mirrors that surrounded the dressing room. One employee after another walked in with dresses. Large ball gowns, satin draped gowns, twinkling sequin gowns, every type of style she had seen walk across Paris runways and at American award shows on the brightest stars of the world's stage.

Self-consciousness made her stomach churn, and her fingers played with the hem of her hoodie. She didn't even have enough time to comprehend her own feelings when one of the women walked up to Maria from behind. Tall, extremely skinny, and dressed in all black, she had a look on her face like she was entering battle. In one movement, she yanked Maria's hoodie up and over her head, the cool air from the AC chilling her bare flesh.

Maria tried to cover herself, but this woman was no-nonsense, pulling Maria's hands down to her sides, lifting her chin and pushing her shoulders back. She pointed to Maria's legs.

"바지." She spoke like a commander in the military.

"네?" Maria asked, looking down.

The woman began miming unbuttoning her pants and removing them. Begrudgingly, Maria followed the woman's directions. She stood nearly nude as several other employees sized her up. Their faces blended and transposed with those of the paparazzi who had swarmed her the day before, trying to figure out who she was. A sudden fear sank deep in her stomach as she stood on a pedestal, half naked, leaving her more exposed to the scrutiny of their questioning glances.

Who was she to Hwan Soo? Why was he here with her? All questions she would've loved to ask herself.

"가," the woman commanded, and all the other people in the room left in synchronicity. "Better?"

"Much." Maria smiled appreciatively at the woman, who she had at first thought was very cold.

"Any particular style you are more comfortable with?" The woman walked over to the wall of dresses that had been selected.

"The last time I wore any kind of fancy dress was prom in high school," she joked as her eyes fell on all the beautiful fabrics of the dresses.

"Prom 무엇입니까?" The woman blinked rapidly as if unable to accept there was a fashion event she was unaware of. Waving off her own question, she went to the wall and pulled one of the dresses, spinning it to show off the flow of the large sequined skirt. Maria's eyes danced along with the shimmering garment. The woman unzipped it and plopped it down for Maria to step into it. Once the dress was lifted up, she took a deep breath and the woman began to use large clips that reminded Maria of a chip bag clip to pull the dress tighter on her form. Before she could even get a good look, the woman grumbled disapprovingly, pulling the clips and causing the dress to slump and fall unflatteringly to the ground.

"다음." She snapped her fingers and a younger woman came back in through the large curtained entrance, picking out one of the other dresses hung up on the wall as Maria was being pulled out of the one she hadn't even really seen herself in.

The next dress she was actually clipped into as the woman did a small walk-around, gauging if she liked the garment or not. Maria was shocked how much a dress could change her mood. She had been so scared of all the prying eyes on her, but the second she slipped into a pretty dress, she felt fabulous.

"Wow," she exhaled, touching the small beads sewn onto the tulle at the waist of the elegant garment.

"Eh. We can do better." The woman shook her head in disapproval and quickly peeled the dress off Maria.

Several dresses later, they seemed to agree they had found "the one" for the occasion. Giving little claps of success, the dress was removed and the women left the dressing room with a single bow.

Maria hopped off the pedestal and ran over to her clothes. Since she was alone, she grabbed her phone first, wishing she had an actual camera to capture the opulence of the room, but accepted what she had to work with and began taking photos of every angle.

Nearly leaning against the mirrors, she tried to shoot the substantial, deep blood-red velvet curtains that closed the dressing room off from the rest of the store. She didn't feel like she was in a clothing store, but rather the dressing room of a large castle in Europe. As she snapped a few photos that simply couldn't do the curtain color any justice, she attempted one more shot.

"What is taking so lo—"

Click.

Hwan Soo walked through the curtains at the exact moment she had snapped the photo. When she looked at her phone's gallery, she was surprised at how flawless he looked as he pushed the curtains aside, as if he had been in a real photoshoot.

"Whoa, you should totally use this for one of your SNS posts." She walked over to him to show him what a great shot it was. When she looked up at him, he was staring at her, mouth agape, and cheeks turning red.

"They said you were done. I—" he closed his mouth unable to finish his sentence.

"What?" She worriedly ran her hand over her face, thinking she had somehow gotten some glitter from the dresses all over her, but then she looked down. To her body. So distracted by her excitement of the photos she hadn't finished getting dressed.

Scampering back to her pile of clothes and erratically tugging on the hoodie and jeans, she kept bowing in apology. What made her heart race was the fact he wasn't looking away. He didn't even try.

"For a guy who nearly lost his mind when he saw me in my underwear a few days ago, you are extremely calm right now," she whispered frantically as she fixed her clothing.

"Three days ago, I would've been. But then two nights ago happened, and I feel as though these kinds of run-ins are in the range of our norm," he laughed, rubbing the back of his head.

"Two nights ago?" Her head lolled to the side as she tried to think of what he could mean. It didn't take long for her to piece two and two together. Her cheeks pinked. Her head instantly filled with the feel of his hands sliding up her bare thigh. His lips gently sucking on her neck, and her body leaning into his for more pleasure.

"Y-y-you were awake?" She stumbled with her words as her thoughts continued to plague her. His eyebrows knitted together; his lips puckered as he took a step closer to her.

Her breaths were quick, trying to keep the oxygen flowing into her body, but with every step he took, she became more breathless. Her skin tingled, begging to be touched by him again.

"Did you think I was asleep?" His nervous smirk made her knees weak, and she stepped back to find the wall for balance.

"It wouldn't be the first time...or the second..." She trailed off, his eyes questioning her. She watched as his eyes seemed to reach an answer all on their own.

"Well...I was awake and not drunk for this one." He took another step toward her.

"I'm not sure this is the best place to talk about this." She looked around, hoping that no one would walk in on them and cause a problem for him.

"I wanted to talk about it last night, but you were already asleep, and then this morning my manager was there. This is the first time we've been alone. I think this is the perfect place to talk about it." He stepped back, taking a seat on the upholstered ottoman that matched the large curtains at the entrance of the dressing room.

"Are you su—" She was cut off by him speaking over her.

"미안해."

What was he apologizing for? Kissing her? Was he really that repulsed by the action? He didn't seem to mind when he pulled her onto him and rubbed his hard length on her leg. His apology made her feel worse than if she had continued to think he was asleep.

"I shouldn't have done it. You were being nice by wiping my makeup off, and I knew you were upset with how Sul Bin walked away. I may not like the guy, but I took advantage of the situation." His hands formed fists as he spoke, his knuckles whitening when he spoke Sul Bin's name.

So he wasn't apologizing for kissing her with no feelings, but because he was sorry he made such a move when he believed she was with someone else. Could that mean...did he have some sort of romantic feelings for her?

"Sul Bin and I are just friends. You didn't take advantage of anything. And why do you not like him? Even Val has been saying she doesn't like him. What did I miss? What party was I not invited to?" She dropped down onto the other ottoman next to him with mixed feelings of confusion and relief. When her eyes met his, they looked away from each other immediately, laughing. Leaving her to wonder what would happen next?

"Did you—"

"What is taking you two so long? The staff are starting to ask questions." Gi Young's voice came in a whisper behind the curtain, cutting her off once again.

"We should probably go," Hwan Soo whispered with a smirk. His shoulder bumped hers as he stood to leave.

"Yeah, let me just grab my shoes, and I'll be right out." She stayed seated until he was no longer in the room.

Her head fell back, hitting the wall softly as she tried to take her first full breaths since Hwan Soo had entered the dressing room. Her feelings were getting the best of her, but she made a major decision.

Tell him you like him. Tonight.

Korean Vocabulary:

맛있는 냄새가나 - mashitnoon namsaegada - something smells delicious

바지 - baji - pants

Prom 무엇입니까? - Prom muosibnika - what is prom?

다음 - daoom - next

Chapter 43 (마흔셋)

"Why are we at Val's apartment?" Maria looked out of the tinted window and saw they had pulled up to the massive skyrise that housed a place that had started to feel foreign to her. She had been staying in Hwan Soo's house more often than Val's.

"You haven't seen her in a few days," Hwan Soo said. "You've been following me around, helping me with my job. I think you need some girl time, don't you?" He was stretched across his armrest to look up at the skyscraper, causing her body to tremor in pleasure as his crisp clean cologne filled her nostrils.

"You should also start staying here again. I didn't think the press would be a problem, but more of them will sit outside my house if we are continually seen together. And 형 needs to stay at his own place as well. We will come to pick you up when it's necessary." His callous words were so different from their conversation a little over an hour ago in the dressing room. He had shut down again.

She wanted to ask what he meant by "when it's necessary," but she knew whatever response she would receive, she wouldn't like.

"그럼..." she tonelessly responded as she unclicked the seatbelt and tossed it off her body to get out of his vicinity quickly.

She stormed into the lobby of the building, her heart racing as her brain tried to keep up with what she was feeling. She slammed the up button for the elevator numerous times, desperately needing a place where she could be alone, even if it was only for the minute it took to get up to Val's apartment.

Ding. The doors slowly—too slowly for her—opened, and she bolted in, slapping the button for the top floor so the doors would close behind her.

The doors were about to slide shut when a hand thrust between them, triggering them to open again.

Maria pulled her gaze from the floor to see that it was exactly who she hoped it wasn't. His chest rising and falling quickly, his cheeks flush, his mouth parted slightly, and his eyes staring deep into hers, Hwan Soo's broad-shouldered frame filled the doorway.

"Did I forget something in the van?" Her voice sounded calm, but her insides were doing all sorts of dance routines.

He walked into the elevator, saying nothing, his eyes never leaving hers. The doors closed behind him, and they were totally alone. The silence was deafening. She needed to say something, but he took the lead.

"I need to know what you were about to ask me before my manager interrupted us in the dressing room. 'Did you regret it?' 'Did you enjoy it?' 'Did you want to stop?'" She opened her mouth to try to respond, but her emotions got the best of her and all that came out was a squeak.

"I will answer all of those," Hwan Soo said. "No, I don't regret it. Yes, I enjoyed it. And finally, hell no! I didn't want to stop." His soulful brown eyes bore into hers. It was like his stare could strip her down and bare her real self to him. A self she felt even she didn't know completely and didn't expect someone else to see.

And while she liked every answer to the questions he had thought she was asking, they didn't answer the real question she had been trying to voice. She had decided back at the store she was going to tell him that she felt something for him, and this seemed like the perfect opportunity.

She smiled as she dropped her head, hair cascading in front of her face, tickling her cheeks as it fell. Nerves were getting the better of her. She wanted to speak. She wanted desperately to tell him her feelings, but then the trauma of every other man prior came flooding into her body. Every time she had told a guy she was starting to grow more attached to them, they fled. Usually into the arms of another woman. While she couldn't picture Hwan Soo doing such a thing, she also knew there was a woman who had her arms wide open for his return.

Maria closed her eyes and took a deep inhale. Before she could exhale, long soft fingers brushed under her chin, giving it a nudge for her to look up at him. But she couldn't let her eyes meet his. They could look right through her.

"바라봐," he whispered with his gentle deep voice that she couldn't deny.

She slowly drew her eyes up to meet his, pausing for a few seconds at his lips, which were still parted, making their heart shape more prominent. His breathing had slowed to calm, patient exhalations that fanned her face with a gentle mint scent. He took a step closer, his gaze dropping to her lips, making her bite the corner nervously because she knew this was the perfect moment to say what she needed to say.

"Did I answer the question properly?" His voice was still low.

"You answered the questions you believed I was going to ask. But they weren't what I wanted to ask." Her voice was a lot softer than she had expected, but nerves were getting the best of her. His eyebrows scrunched as if questioning where she was leading. She reached up to take his hand off her chin, holding it in hers, and then asked the question she had really wanted answered.

"Did you feel something?" The hand she had been holding grabbed hers and squeezed it tightly. He rocked on his feet, eyes ablaze as he looked behind her every now and again. She contemplated moving farther back into the elevator, wondering if that would cause him to press his toned six-pack against her chest. Her heart raced, and her breath caught in her chest as she waited for his answer.

He finally took a step closer, and she mirrored his movement, taking a step farther into the elevator. "What did you want me to feel?"

Her heart sank into her stomach. That wasn't the answer she hoped for. She didn't expect a confession of love, but she hoped for confirmation that their feelings were mutual. Instead, he answered her question with another question.

Maria removed her hand from his, shifting to the side so that they were no longer face to face, and it would be easier for her to focus and respond.

"I can't tell you what you felt, Hwan Soo-씨. That was the question I wanted to ask, and now I have your answer." She stared at the door, watching the number of her floor approach. Like the elevator knew the conversation was over, there was a ding, the elevator settled, and the doors opened. Stepping into the hall, she turned to look at him, but unable to look at his face, her gaze fell dully to his torso. She bowed politely and retreated to the safety of Val's apartment.

Hwan Soo hadn't wanted to bring Maria to Val's that night. He had every intention of taking her back to his place so they could spend more time together and talk about what really happened that night in the van. But Jung-hyun texted him asking him to bring her to Val's, as she really needed to talk to her about something.

The elevator door closed, cutting him off from the girl he knew he wanted but was too afraid to ask out on a damn date. He fell back on the cool metal of the elevator wall behind him, his head making a rather loud thud. He closed his eyes and replayed what had happened.

He had turned off his emotions around her. To protect her from Hae So trying to use any interaction they had on set as possible ammunition. She already had a photo of them kissing, even if at the time it was fake. He knew she was waiting for the perfect time to strike. If Maria did anything to pull the spotlight away from Hae So, there was no telling what the woman would do.

"Did you feel something?"

The question played on repeat in his mind. Of course he felt something. But what kind of answer did she want to hear? She thought he was asleep the whole time. Did she think he was picturing someone else? That his reaction was based on that? But now that she knew he was awake, was she worried that the feelings she thought were for someone else were actually for her?

He knew she had a crappy dating past, so did he. In fact, he had sworn off women after Hae So, and seven months later was falling for Maria.

Falling for? Well, he knew he was attracted to her and liked spending time with her. He even got jealous that she was seeing another guy.

"Did you feel something?"

Is that what she was asking? Was he feeling love toward her? Was he? Jesus. How he was playing a strong male lead in a drama baffled him. He was a bumbling idiot when it came to expressing his feelings to or for Maria. His current drama character would've known exactly what to do when that question was posed. He could picture himself not letting her leave the elevator, kissing her, telling her that he wanted to be with her no matter what sacrifices they had to make. He would do anything if it meant he could be with the woman he cared so deeply for.

But he wasn't his character. He was Hwan Soo. The constant second lead who just dipped his toe in the lead role world he didn't fit into.

"And once again I mess it up," he huffed out, hitting his head multiple times against the elevator wall.

Maria entered the apartment, wishing she could just curl into a ball and never be heard from again. She made a fool of herself in front of Hwan Soo again. How many times did the world plan on doing this to her? She had to mentally thank whoever was looking over her for not letting her tell him how she felt. Maybe there was some fairness in the world. But she still had more than half a month to go before the wedding. Dropping her head in shame for having any kind of feeling other than friendship for Hwan Soo and planning to drown her sorrows in a bottle of 소주, a bowl of 라면, and binging a drama with Val, she kicked off her shoes and slipped her feet into the pink fluffy house slippers provided.

Val came running to the entrance with a happy but nervous grin on her face. She was biting the inner corner of her cheek. Maria knew something was wrong. In two quick strides, she was wrapping her friend in a hug and rubbing her back in comfort.

"What happened?" she quickly asked, knowing she needed to remedy the situation in either food, alcohol, or a mix of both.

"It's a long story. And well...one I've been meaning to share with you for a while now. We should sit." The wariness in Val's voice was even more concerning. She always had a bubbly voice, like it was impossible for her to speak without the corners of her mouth turning up in a smile. She could turn anyone's bad mood into a good one by simply talking to them. So when she would get serious, it was blatantly obvious something was wrong. Whether she was scolding someone or breaking bad news to someone, her voice became slow and her words were much more well pronounced.

"I'm grabbing some 소주 and snacks for this...I have a feeling I might need them." Maria left Val's embrace to run to the kitchen for some "safety gear."

Returning to the living room, she saw Val sitting with her legs folded like a pretzel, holding a big fluffy throw pillow in her lap, picking at the strings of faux fur. Maria plopped down next to her, twisting the bottle top open. Without wasting time pouring a glass, she took a sip straight from the emerald bottle.

"I've wanted to tell you this from the beginning, but I wasn't sure exactly how to explain. It's about Jung-hyun," Val started off.

"What the hell did he do to you?" Maria was ready to throw hands if he hurt her bestie.

"He didn't do anything...well..." Val was getting more worrying by the second.

"Wait, are you actually pregnant and lied to me? But you've been drinking so that can't be it. Is he holding you against your will and forcing you to marry him? That wouldn't make sense either because he wouldn't have let you have your own place to live while you're here. Hwan Soo-씨 has told me I like to jump to my own conclusions, so girl, you better start explaining before I come up with even more bizarre ideas." Maria took a much larger swig of the 소주, which burned going down.

"Our relationship didn't start the way I told you it did. Yes, we met while I was asked to decorate his apartment, but it wasn't like we worked together and grew attracted to each other. He bribed me into being his girlfriend to get his mother off his back. In return, he would pay me a large sum of money that I could invest in starting my own interior design business." Val spoke with the speed of a humming-bird's wings.

Yep. 소주 definitely needed.

After another gulp burned her throat, Maria nodded for Val to continue. She decided she would wait until the end to ask questions.

"While pretending, things started to feel real. And while we both felt the connection we were trying to be way more loved up in person. And then one night, to make his already furious mother explode like a bomb, he got down on one knee and proposed. I knew I had to say yes. So I did. Afterwards some stuff happened that is not totally important, but we did end up 'breaking off' the engagement. That was when I called you and you flew to San Francisco. I wanted to tell you then, but he and I still had to work together and you would've let him have it. Worse than you did," Val laughed nervously.

"But then he came to me one night while I was working late and told me that he felt our relationship was real from our first 'date' when we met his mom, and that I had learned more about him from decorating his home than she had giving birth to him. And I realized I had fallen totally head over heels—the crazy expensive heels he purchased for me—for him. And maybe two or three months later, he proposed for real. A nice, new, real-love ring. And I said yes." Val rolled her eyes as her shoulders slumped, looking relieved to finally tell Maria the true story.

"And so now you're getting married. For real?" Maria asked.

"네." Val's eyes were quickly pooling with tears.

"Well then..." Maria took two more large swigs of 소주.

"That's all you have to say?" Val asked with eyes wide and mouth agape.

"Well what exactly do you want me to say? Do I wish you told me sooner? Duh. But you had your reasons, and I am glad you finally did tell me. We're best friends, Val. Forever and always. And look what came out of this! You're getting married, girl! To a man who loves you and you love. What did you expect?" Maria grabbed Val's hand to stop it from picking at the faux fur on the pillow.

Everything Maria said was the truth. She would've been annoyed and most likely furious with Val two weeks ago. She would've packed a bag and stayed in a hotel for a night to cool off. They had gotten into arguments before. They'd been friends for nearly twenty-five years, they were bound to have fights. But because they were best friends, they knew exactly how to handle each other during these situations. Maria usually needed space and would come back when she had calmed down. Val would go out with her other friends to help her forget the argument. But after letting out all the anger with some kind of adrenaline rush, she would run to Maria to tell her everything she did, and they would make up.

But all the moments she had with Hwan Soo-씨 and all her time spent watching all the dramas had changed her view on some things. Specifically, how "love" worked. After figuring she would forever be the single friend who met guys who ended up screwing her over, she had a very skewed view of what "love" was. While she believed in love, she believed it would never happen for her. And she was fine with that. Even if her mother wasn't. But now...now she had Hwan Soo-씨 breaking down that wall around her heart. She had almost confessed to liking him! What kind of insanity food were they feeding her?

김치. It had to be the 김치.

Luckily, he shot her down, bringing her back to reality and rebuilding the wall.

"I don't know. I guess I expected you to be mad and say that I'm being crazy for marrying a man who had pretended to love me and now says he's really in love with me." Val put her free hand on top of Maria's.

"Two weeks ago I probably would've. But you brought me to Korea. A place where television shows have taught me that these things are the totally perfect setup for romance. K-dramas have really skewed my view of reality," Maria laughed, holding out the 소주 bottle to Val, who gladly accepted it and took a large gulp herself.

"That went way better than I expected it to." Val rubbed her forehead and looked to the television.

"Wanna watch some more dramas and talk about what we are gonna do to get ready for tomorrow night's event?" Val asked, pulling the remote from behind her and waving it happily. They both laughed as they started a new show while Maria described the dress she had been asked to wear for the next night.

Korean Vocabulary:

그럼 - kurom - well then

바라봐 - barabuwa - look at me

Chapter 44 (마흔넷)

"I'm coming out," Val shouted from behind the closed bathroom door. Maria was getting her hair done by a stylist hired by Jung-hyun when she looked into the vanity mirror to see the bathroom door opening and her stunningly dressed best friend walked out.

A simple light baby-blue ballgown with a slit from the floor almost to the waist showed off one of Val's toned deep-bronze legs. The off-the-shoulder sleeves accentuated her collarbones, and a stunning platinum choker with diamond teardrop strands falling elegantly against her skin completed the look.

"어때?" Val asked as she spun slowly to show the full effect of the dress.

"너는 너무 아름다워," Maria gushed, leaving the chair to see her friend's true beauty. Reaching out to grab her best friend's hands, she saw the massive oval-cut diamond, set in white gold with smaller diamonds on the rest of the band. She had never noticed how large the diamond on her friend's ring finger was, but it radiated on Val's skin. After finding out how they really became a couple, Maria could understand the thought behind the diamond and how Jung-hyun had to prove his love in a large way.

"Your fiancé is going to have his breath taken away more than once tonight." Maria choked out the words, happy to see her friend filled with such nervous joy.

"Well, Hwan Soo-아 will faint at the sight of you from what you've told me about your dress. When is it supposed to arrive?" Val squeezed Maria's hands, looking to the clock on the opposite wall.

"Hwan So-씨 and his thoughts on how I look are none of my business. I told you we just kissed. It was nothing more than that," she tried to explain to a friend who was starting to sound like her mother when it came to finding her someone to settle down with. Her mind and heart still weren't ready to have that conversation. Speaking of her mother, she had started to miss her and made a mental note to call the next morning.

As Val was about to argue, the doorbell rang, giving Maria the perfect excuse to flee the conversation.

Hwan Soo had adjusted his black bow tie in the mirror as Jung-hyun walked out into the living room of his family's home. Hwan Soo hadn't been in Jung-hyun's family home in years. The crazy part was that it looked as if nothing had changed. The한옥-looking home boasted all the appearances of a modern living space on the inside, while still maintaining the Joseon Dynasty design on the outside. Hwan Soo always enjoyed walking up to the house and seeing the black tiles laid along wood beams, while the lightly stained wood that the entire house was constructed with sat upon an elevated stone foundation.

"Val said they're almost ready to be picked up," Jung-hyun announced. "Are you ready?"

"As ready as I'll ever be," Hwan Soo huffed, struggling to make his bow tie go straight.

"친구야, you know I tried to tell them Hae So shouldn't be invited. But she has grown in popularity over the last few months and when I told them you were in a drama together, they thought it was perfect publicity for you as well." Jung-hyun looked more apologetic as his apology went on.

But that wasn't the reason for Hwan Soo's trepidation. He hadn't spoken to Maria since the previous night. Not a word from her, while all he wanted to do was text her or call her to hear her voice and understand the question he had clearly answered incorrectly. Her words echoed in his mind.

"I can't tell you what you felt, Hwan Soo-씨."

Could it have been that she wanted her feelings reciprocated? Would that mean that she in fact felt something similar to the affection he felt for her? Could she possibly be attracted to him as strongly as he had become to her? Tonight's event wouldn't be the place to have that conversation but at some point, he knew he would have to tell her how she made his heart race, his palms clammy, and his mind question if he truly had ever been in love before meeting her.

"형 걱정마. Your parents made the smart move. And I will be a respectable gentleman the whole night. But if I am forced to introduce her to my parents, I might lose my mind," he joked. In all seriousness, he had no intention of having her meet them. Or his older brother.

A panic hit his chest the second he thought of his brother. He hadn't thought about a scenario with his older brother before. What if Hae So tried to dig her bony little bird-claw hands into his brother?

"친구? Hwan Soo? 야!" Jung-hyun was waving his hands around trying to get Hwan Soo's attention.

"네?"

"What the hell was just on your mind? You looked and still look freaked out." Jung-hyun reached out to help Hwan Soo with his bow tie.

"My brother. Hae So and my brother. We need to keep them apart. At. All. Costs," Hwan Soo commanded.

"아. Yeah, I hadn't thought about that. We will keep them away from each other one way or another," Jung-hyun tried to reassure him.

"I know a way. I just know I am going to hate it." Hwan Soo looked Jung-hyun in the eyes, and like a telepath Jung-hyun took a step back in shock.

"You're not taking one for the team like that," he argued.

"I have to. Otherwise it's guaranteed she will run off to find him and do whatever she can to seduce him. My brother, while smart when it comes to running a business, is easily persuaded by pretty women. My parents have had to bail him out more than once, and since Hae So knows who my family is now, she knows about my brother." Hwan Soo was going to have to stay by Hae So's side all night. If Maria didn't already hate him, she was going to by the end of the night.

"시발," they both muttered under their breath.

"Our men are on their way." Val jumped up from the stool at the kitchen counter and walked over to Maria, who was putting on her final bits of jewelry to complete her look.

"Your man and his friend. Please stop trying to pair us up," Maria begged. She knew she was going to have to tell Val the whole story, but this was a fairytale kind of night for her friend and she wasn't about to ruin it with dumb boy drama.

"Alright, alright, but I'm just saying that you and Hwan Soo make an adorable couple. And could you imagine you and me? Power couple best friends? Yas!" Val did a little prance, her stiletto heels clacking the title floor.

"Valerie," Maria chastised with a disciplining tone.

"Alright, alright, I'll stop. Let me say that if his jaw doesn't drop at the sight of you tonight, I will let this gut feeling go once and for all." Val waved her hand up and down at the gown Maria was decked out in.

Maria had to laugh at her friend's excited behavior. Even though she was filled with turbulent feelings inside, she did hope that Val was correct in her assumption of Hwan Soo's reaction when he saw her in the dress. After all, the company had literally sewn her into it since they only had one day to tailor the delicate lace and trim of the dress.

Val looked down at her phone and her already giddy smile began to spread from ear to ear. More little clacks of her heels as she reached for her tiny clutch bag.

"They're here." She put her hand out to grab Maria's and make their way downstairs.

Sighing and giving one final look at herself in the mirror across the room, she grabbed her matching clutch, her best friend's hand, and they proceeded downstairs to meet Jung-hyun and the man she was nervous as all hell to see again.

When they walked out of the building, Maria saw Jung-hyun dressed to the nines in a gorgeous black tux that was slim, trim, and most definitely tailored-made for him.

She looked over to Val, whose eyes were hungering for the man standing by the large van. Val was undressing him with her eyes.

"You want me to not come home tonight?" Maria nudged her elbow into Val's side.

Val's eyes went wide as her head snapped to look at Maria. The blush on her cheeks was growing ever redder as her subtle pink lips fumbled to try to say anything. While Val was unable to form words, Maria pulled her friend closer to her betrothed.

"와, Valerie you look...와." He put out his hand to hold hers which, she happily obliged.

"너도," Val responded, and her cheeks had become nearly as red as a lobster.

"Maria, you look very pretty as well," Jung-hyun said, trying to pay some attention to Maria, but she laughed, telling him he didn't need to flatter her with compliments.

He opened the door for them to climb into the van, and when Maria entered, she saw Hwan Soo with his eyes closed taking deep breaths. She had hoped for some kind of reaction to her in her dress, but instead he took her breath away as her eyes took in his soft, creamy skin and eye-shadowed lids. His lips, which were pursed, had a glossy sheen to them, and his hair was pulled away from his face in a pompadour with a freshly manicured undercut. Not to mention the tux he was wearing wasn't some ordinary black tux. The deep green color made his skin even more vibrant.

"Love the tux, Hwan Soo-아," Val said kindly, but he didn't even react.

"He's not being rude. He is trying to get in the mindset of having to be nice to Hae So all night," Jung-hyun explained.

"Did you have to say her name?" Hwan Soo said, his eyebrows creasing in displeasure.

"Hae So is going to be there?" Maria's stomach sank at the thought.

"Unfortunately," Hwan Soo grumbled.

"We won't let her ruin the night. I refuse to let that skank cause any kind of trouble," Val said threateningly.

"여보." Jung-hyun grabbed Val's hand, rubbing gently, and gave a gentle kiss to her knuckles.

"Yeah, yeah." Val sat straight and looked forward as the van finally started to drive.

When they pulled up to the venue, large spotlights shooting straight into the air lit a path into the entrance of the building. Maria could hear loud screams of fans, while flashes of cameras were nearly blinding from behind the tinted windows of the van. When she looked farther past the entrance she craned her neck to see the tallest building she had ever seen. She could see the reflection of all of Seoul on the glass windows that reached up to the sky.

"What is this place?" Maria gawked at the sheer size of the building.

"롯데월드타워," Val said with the same awe that Maria had spoken with.

"Time to make our entrance." Jung-hyun grabbed Val's hand as the door of the van swung open.

Like Maria had guessed, the camera flashes were blinding the second the door opened. Squinting, she stayed seated waiting for the door to close.

"What are you doing?" Hwan Soo asked beside her.

"I'm waiting for you to get out so I can go through the other entrance." She looked over at him to see his eyes were locked on her. Unmoving. His lightly glossed lips were parted as he leaned forward.

She leaned away, about to put her hand up to stop him when she saw him turn to move to the door of the van. He jumped out, and the screams intensified. She relaxed a bit, feeling the relief of not being next to him any longer, but when the door didn't shut she looked and saw he was standing there facing into the van.

"Why aren't you leaving?" she asked.

"You're an invited guest tonight, Maria. Not an employee. I may not be able to walk you into the venue, but I can at least be a gentleman and help you out of the car." He extended his hand back into the car.

"나 기분이 이상해," she mumbled, lifting the skirt of her dress so she could shuffle closer to the door.

"Strange?" He shifted on his feet, his hand still waiting to take hers.

"This is not a normal thing for me. Celebrities, gowns, high-profile events. I don't fit in here." The second her hand touched his, he grabbed it tightly as if he didn't want to let go.

When she glanced at him, the look in his eyes sent shivers up her spine. Goosebumps appeared on her arms, but the gown's long sleeves hid her reaction to his deep stare and touch. He helped her take the small steps to climb out of the van, his hand squeezing hers every time she moved to gain balance. It was a comforting feeling, but she wished it could last longer.

When she was finally out and fixed the short train of her dress, she looked at him for assurance that everything was going to be alright. Instead she was met with a kind bow before he quickly stepped away.

The camera flashes at the red carpet erupted as Hwan Soo made his appearance. Maria watched as he took his place in the center of the red carpet to make small waving gestures and smiles. But his smile wasn't real. It didn't show how bright his eyes could be when he was experiencing true joy, or how when his smile would grow from ear to ear, his cheeks would bunch up and almost close his eyes completely. He was displaying a smirk at best. She wanted to walk over and tell him to smile more but before she could, a scrawny arm decorated in a gorgeous sapphire bracelet set wrapped around his and pulled him closer. Maria didn't need to look past the bony hand to know who had wrapped her claw around Hwan Soo's.

Hae So.

Under her breath, Maria whispered the one word she had remembered Hwan Soo had used to describe that woman.

"미친년."

Korean Vocabulary:

너는 너무 아름다워 - nonoon nomu aroomdawa - you look stunning

롯데월드타워 - lotte world tower

나 기분이 이상해 - na gibunee eesanghae - I feel weird

Chapter 45 (마흔다섯)

S tanding on the red carpet doing everything in his power not to run back to Maria only made Hwan Soo think of her more. The word gorgeous never could do Maria justice. But when he saw her that night, words had disappeared completely.

Hwan Soo had been looking out the window of his van as she walked out of the lobby of Val's apartment building and his jaw hit the carpeted floor. White lace embroidered to look like delicate leaves shimmered with beaded accents and made her more dazzling than a twinkling night sky. The deep nude-colored fabric under the white lace looked to be a silk that clung to her every curve. And while the beaded lace tried to cover up the sexy silk, it drew his eyes to the way she walked and how delicate she was. As she got closer to the car, a thin sparkling line brought attention to her collarbones. The necklace slid along her skin, reflecting the city's streetlamps like a halo around her neck.

He swallowed hard, putting his finger into the collar of his shirt to give him some space to cool down and breathe before she got into the car.

He wanted to jump out of the van and escort her himself. But he knew what his night was going to entail, and he needed to get into the proper headspace for it. Leaning his head back on the cushion, he took one last look at her beauty before closing his eyes.

"웃어라," an evil voice whispered, snapping him back to the reality that he was walking the carpet with Hae So attached to his arm.

"네." He looked down to his side.

She turned to look up at him with doe eyes that he knew would get the internet buzzing with stories of a budding romance between the leads of the most anticipated drama of the summer. She was so damn good at what she did.

She covered her mouth to keep the press from reading her lips.

"죽을래? 웃어라," she hissed. Before he could respond, her hand was joining her other one on his arm, pulling him ever so subtly closer to her. She was always desperate for all the attention, and sadly he knew he was going to have to give it to her tonight.

Putting on his best smile, he waved and laughed at the press, who were eating out of the palms of their hands. He continued walking her down the red carpet, even helping her when her heel got caught up in the underskirt of her dress. A true knight in shining armor.

Once inside the lobby of Lotte World Tower, she dropped her hands from around his arm and maneuvered herself in front of him. It was the first time he could take in what she was wearing. A black halter-neck evening gown that hurt her figure more than it helped, as it was so loose it looked like a nightdress his mother used to wear. Her bracelets and rings made her wrists and fingers look excessively bony and more like talons than human hands.

"You seriously came with her? 여기? To a public event that will help us promote our drama? 너 미쳤어?" Her whole face was turning as red as 고추장 as he could see her trying to control the urge to stomp her foot.

"She was invited to be here. Not by me. And not by the family who is running this whole thing. Which, just to remind you, is my best friend's family. The same best friend who is supposed to marry Maria's best friend." He pushed his hands into his suit pockets.

"말도 안돼," she scoffed, clearly not believing Maria could get into the event without them.

"진짜. Remember those photos you loved so much?" He leaned down making sure his point was being made loud and clear. "They weren't taken by who you think. And you weren't the only one impressed with how well they looked."

While he was desperate to get away from Hae So, he pulled her back to his side when he saw their director headed in their direction.

"같이 해도 돼요?" The man walked over to the two of them with a big, goofy smile to join his lead couple that was garnering him and his drama attention.

They both smiled awkwardly and bowed to their boss.

"You two look marvelous together. The perfect pair on-screen and off..." He nudged Hwan Soo on the shoulder and as his stomach churned at the thought, Hae So tugged him even closer to her.

"Oh, Jang 이사, you are too sweet!" she giggled, pushing his chest as she continued to latch onto Hwan Soo like a leech.

"It's so great to see such chemistry. I know you guys had worked together in the past, obviously not as closely, but it must be great to see each other again." The director's smile continued to get broader.

He was poking a sleeping bear, and Hwan Soo flinched every time the director spoke. When he felt a pinch on his arm, he looked down to see that Hae So had done something to try to help him stay in control of his feelings.

"Jang 이사, will you excuse us? I know Hwan Soo-씨 wants to say hi to his family and friends, and I have been dying to meet them myself." They both dipped their heads, and she dragged Hwan Soo farther into the venue.

When finally out of view of the man, Hae So let go of Hwan Soo once again and grabbed a glass of champagne from the tray of one of the many servers walking around the event. Not even batting an eyelash, she threw back the bubbly liquid in one gulp. He scoffed at her surprising lack of manners.

"You could at least say thank you. I didn't do that for my health," she sneered. "I would've let him keep talking about us if I didn't feel like you were about to deck the guy who will make us household names." She dropped the empty glass on a nearby table and grabbed another one, taking a small sip this time. One of the elevators opened and a man ushered a small group on. Hwan Soo pulled Hae So to get them to the party.

"고마워요." He bowed his head, and Hae So actually laughed. An honest laugh that he had never heard from her before. Maybe the night wouldn't be a total disaster.

"I guess it's me throwing in the towel. Sul Bin told me he waved the white flag on trying to seduce your woman. Of course, I'll have to destroy his career before he even gets a real gig, but you know how it goes." Just like that, she was the same most hated person in his heart.

"You truly are the ugliest person on the entire planet," he spat but with a smile to make it look as though their conversation was pleasant.

She said nothing of the insult and grabbed his arm again. "I believe you have to show me off to your parents. From what I heard, they aren't fond of your little American peasant either."

Maria wasn't surprised by the spectacular view of Seoul from the event's venue. Once she had entered the lobby of the building that had chandeliers as large as the home she grew up in, and when groups were whisked away onto elevators that shot up into the sky while displaying a virtual reality of the tower being built around them on LED screens that covered the walls and even the floor, she knew she was going to see something spectacular. When the doors opened, the opulence of the room's granite floors, fine table center-pieces and decor were all outshined by the windows that showed her the city she was starting to feel more and more comfortable staying in.

She understood the name of the building more and more as she looked out the windows at the other side of the room. She felt as though she was on top of the world where nothing and no one could bring her down.

She loved the panoramic scenery of the city below and could've spent the entire night looking out the windows, but a scratchy, high-pitched laugh cut through the daydream. Turning toward the awful sound, she saw Hae So laughing and smiling with Hwan Soo, their arms linked. Hae So playfully hit his chest with one bony hand and then covered her mouth and cheeks in feigned embarrassment. Maria felt the ugly green monster trying its best to claw its way out.

"I'm sure he would much rather have you on his arm than her," a familiar voice snuck up on Maria.

After standing alone by the windows for what felt like ages, Maria was startled to find the photographer who had supposedly asked for her to be invited to the event standing behind her. He looked like a totally different person. His hair was pulled back in a small man bun and a few loose wavy strands sat cleanly around his chiseled face. Had his jaw always been so pronounced?

His suit, while in keeping with his quirkiness, was an iridescent, dark blue fabric that shone when the lights hit it to reveal a jacquard pattern. If she was being honest, he looked like he should've been in front of the camera rather than behind it.

"어? 안녕하세요," she greeted him with a the smallest of bows. It was all her tight bodice would allow.

"No need to be so formal with me, I went to university in London and actually worked there for close to twenty years. I only recently came back to Korea. 편하게 말하세요." They laughed as he used formal language to tell her to speak comfortably with him.

"Well, thank you for inviting me to this event. Otherwise I probably would've been home alone watching more dramas," she joked as a server came by with glasses of wine.

He quickly grabbed two glasses and handed one to Maria. Gently tapping them together, they each took a sip. His kindness put her at ease among the clamor of the ballroom.

"I doubt Hwan Soo-아 would've allowed that. He seems very fond of you. Like I said, he'd much rather have you next to him than her." His lip curled with distaste as he looked over at Hwan Soo and Hae So.

"Not a fan of hers?" Maria sipped the wine, trying to hide her amusement that someone else could possibly find Hae So as vile as she did.

"You could say that. I worked with her on a shoot in New York a few months ago and well, one thing led to another..." That snarl suddenly turned to a frown and disappointment.

"No way. You...and her?" Maria couldn't believe he was telling her something so personal the second time she had seen him. When she looked closely, she saw his eyes were telling her a much bigger story.

"It's not that you don't like her, it's that you do," Maria speculated, but deep down she knew it to be true.

"뭐? 아니." He shook his head, the little bun shaking with the force. But when he looked over at Hae So, his tension melted, his eyes went dreamy, and a small smile played on his thin lips.

"Is it that obvious?" he asked.

"Honestly, until right now I had no clue. You didn't seem fazed by working together. And you were even mad that Hwan Soo and Hae So's chemistry lacked for the shoot," she said honestly.

"Work and personal lives are different. I know her job is to be 'in love' with her co-stars. And when Hwan Soo seemed more interested in his new manager than his co-star, I was a tad frustrated. How could he look at you and not her? Now seeing you all done up, I get it," he laughed while she stood there feeling awkward after the backhanded compliment he had tossed at her.

"Please don't take offense. You obviously know I have feelings for her. It's simply me being jealous and frustrated. But then you actually came in handy. I wasn't lying when I said you should come work with me. I would be happy to have you on the team," he said, reiterating his sentiments from the photoshoot.

"I see what you did there. Nice subject change." She smiled. "But I couldn't pack up my life and move out here for such an unstable career. And don't think this gets you off the hook for telling me about your encounter with Hae So."

He laughed before taking another sip of his wine.

"While I would agree that in other countries photography might be unstable, here you have a lot of opportunity to grow and build. We have so many avenues. Besides promotional shoots for dramas, we have countless promotional shoots for beauty products. I'm sure you've seen the amount of makeup, cleansers, and so on we offer. And our music scene is also a massive market full of new bands debuting and countless new albums coming out monthly. You will never be starved for work," he explained.

He turned back to the room, watching Hwan Soo and Hae So work the crowd. Glancing at Maria sideways, he added, "And you would have the power of Hwan So-아 to help."

"I believe you have our relationship mistaken. We are friends of friends who were forced to be together. I only ended up working with him because he got a role for a drama while I'm here, and he is in charge of helping me learn Korean." She was sure her feelings weren't hidden even though she tried. And with that in mind, she emptied her entire glass of wine at once. His laugh almost made her spit out some of the wine.

"You're almost as obvious as me. But then again, you're lucky in that it seems like Hwan Soo has feelings for you as well." He chuckled, taking her wine glass from her to get a refill.

"You love talking crazy, don't you?" She looked over to Hwan Soo and Hae So, who were attached not only by linked arms but by their smiles and laughter with everyone they greeted.

"We're hopeless, aren't we?" Her defeated voice caused her shoulders to drop.

"Yeah probably, but that's what could make us a great photography team." He nudged her shoulder.

"You're not gonna let that go?" She laughed.

"Not until you give me a real answer to my offer." He handed her a new glass of wine.

When she looked up at him, she saw his eyes demanded a response. A real one. But she didn't have a real answer. All her life she was told her aspiration wouldn't lead to success. It was a pipe dream, and she should get a real life skill that would keep her comfortable. Could she throw everything she was taught aside, follow her heart, and have the chance at true happiness?

"I can't give you a real answer right now. But can I make you a deal that I will seriously consider it and get back to you before I leave in a few weeks?" she truthfully responded.

"콜." He put out his hand for her to shake, and she graciously accepted the hand.

She was laughing and drinking and having an all-around great time. She had been nervous about the event for no reason. After a few more glasses of wine, she was feeling a lot more confident about mingling with all the rich and famous at the party.

"It looks like I'm being beckoned." Her small safety net of a friend was waving to a small group of gorgeous people who gestured for him to join their conversation. "Are you going to be okay by yourself?"

"네." She bowed her head with a tipsy smile. "I really want to take a few pictures of the view. Who knows when I will see it again."

"그럼." He bowed, stepping away from her and joining the group of people.

She wandered carefully toward the glass window. The view was intensified with a glass floor, and she felt as if she were nervously teetering on the edge of the abyss. Her heels were also too high, and her feet were screaming for them to be taken off, but she knew she had to bear with it for several more hours. As she went to grab the railing, she lifted her dress to take the few steps up to the glass, maintaining her balance, but her hand landed on something that felt like someone else's hand.

Looking down she saw it did in fact land on another person's hand. Pulling away quickly to not cause a scene, she bowed apologetically. When she looked at the person, her stomach sank with concern. A man with an evil smirk and devious eyes looked her up and down like she was the perfect prey.

When his eyes came back up to hers, he licked his thin lips and said, "당신의 눈이 정말 아름다워요."

His breath hit her nostrils, and it reeked of hard liquor. She looked at him with confusion as to what he had called beautiful, and she felt a shiver ran up her back telling her to get away from him quickly. She smiled as she tried to walk away, but his hand snatched her wrist. She looked at the hand on her wrist, then at his other hand holding a glass of a deep caramel-colored liquor.

"뭐라고 했어요? 잘 모르겠어요," she tried to explain calmly to get him to release her hand.

"우와 너 한국어 정말 잘한다." His grip on her arm got tighter as he approached her, a hungry look filling his drunkenly glazed eyes.

Maria looked around to see if anyone was seeing what was happening, but not a single eye was on them. She could see Hwan Soo taking a sip of his drink as he continued talking to a small group of people, and Val and Jung-hyun were also invested in a group conversation.

If she made a scene, not only could she ruin the event her best friend was hosting, she would cause Hwan Soo trouble as part of his management team. Not to mention, she could lose a potential job offer. She was trapped. She tried to take steps away but ended up pinned to the cold glass window looking out on Seoul.

With her pinned to the glass, his hand trailed from her wrist up her arm. Maria shivered in disgust. He caressed her cheek, pulling her face to look at his. There was some stubble around that thin thing he would call an upper lip. When his smirk grew, she saw his smoke-stained yellow teeth.

She smiled nervously, her eyes scanning for anyone who could see her situation. But his hand grabbed her chin to pull her attention back to him.

"당신의 미소가 정말 아름다워요," he said, leaning his face closer and closer to hers.

She couldn't let this creep get what he wanted. And she wasn't a girl who was about to get taken advantage of. She pushed him hard, making him stumble back.

"야!" he yelled, which garnered several people's attention.

"Sir, I think you misunderstood my action," she tried to explain slowly in English, which only seemed to enrage him more.

He started speaking too quickly for her to understand. His hand holding the liquor kept pushing into her personal space, and then his finger jabbed hard into her shoulder. She snapped, pushing him away again, which only infuriated the man more.

He reached for her one more time, and she slapped his hand away with a stern, "손 대지 말아요!"

In an instant something cold and wet hit her face. As it burned her nostrils and eyes, it dripped down her cleavage and soaked into the dress she had borrowed for the night. She was barely able to open her eyes, worried the alcohol would get in, but she could feel every eye in the room now on them. The one thing she didn't want to happen had just become a reality. Why was she always in the middle of making scenes that would cause problems in front of people she was trying to keep a low profile for?

She heard him snicker, which caused her fists to clench. She already made a scene. She might as well go for the total destruction of her future. But as she was about to give him hell, there was a loud thud followed by lots of gasps. When her eyes opened, a dark shadow blocked most of her view, but what she could see was the man who had thrown the liquor at her was on the glass floor, his lip bleeding and fury in his eyes.

Looking back to the tall figure in front of her, she realized the shoulders were rising and falling rapidly. He turned around and her breath caught.

"Hwan Soo-씨," she whispered as she took in his face, reddened with anger, and his clenched fist that was white with his rage. She looked at the man on the floor, and her stomach sank. If Hwan Soo had punched that man—which she was one hundred percent positive he had—it was in front of people he worked with as well as potential future co-workers.

"괜찮아?" He got closer to her, his eyes scanning to make sure she wasn't hurt.

Words failed her. She watched as he inspected her, and when his eyes met hers, she couldn't properly convey how sorry she was to him. Sorry she had become like a child he had to babysit, sorry she didn't fit into his life easily, sorry she constantly put him in positions that could possibly ruin his career, and most of all sorry for falling in love with him.

Love?

Something wrapping around her shoulders stopped her from answering her internal question. Hwan Soo had taken off his tuxedo jacket and covered her now sopping wet torso.

"I-I-I couldn't understand what he was saying. But he started touching me a-a-and I panicked and then he threw his drink and—" she stammered. The heat from her cheeks was starting to creep toward her eyes. They were watering, and she knew she needed to get out of the room to keep from causing more of a scene, but her heels were glued to the floor in shock.

"가자," Hwan Soo whispered, but when he wrapped his arm around her shoulder to help her leave, she still was unable to move.

They faced each other and she said, "발."

He looked down to her feet before swiftly lifting her up into his arms. The gasps heard around the room were deafening. Not to mention the flashes of cameras blinding her. She had no time to react or try to stop him. Her arms wrapped around his neck, and she buried her face in his neck to hide her face from more scrutiny.

347

In true drama fashion, an elevator dinged, announcing more people were arriving to the party, but Hwan Soo carried Maria into the elevator even as people were hurrying out, having missed the juiciest part of the evening.

She could feel the doors close silently, and when they were finally alone in the elevator, she opened her eyes. Still Hwan Soo didn't put her down, his fingers tense around her body. Their body heat melded together at their closeness.

"You can put me down," she whispered.

His eyes met hers at her weak request, his mouth trying to form words but failing. He simply bent down a bit and put her feet to the elevator floor.

"I'm sorry, Hwan Soo-씨. I am so freaking sorry." She didn't try to hide the tears from falling. She let them fall. She had ruined the evening once again.

"울지 마," he responded in a monotone voice. His hand, however, reached down to grab hers and held it tightly, offering her a small amount of comfort. With his other hand he grabbed his phone and called Gi Young, asking him to pull the van around back for them.

His hand never let go of hers even as they reached the ground floor and walked to the van. She couldn't stop her tears from falling. She tried to wipe them away to stop them, which only made her cry harder. When the back door of the building opened and she saw Gi Young at the open door, a sense of relief and guilt washed over her. Relief that she could be alone, and guilt for ruining another special event.

Hwan Soo helped lift her into the van but when she was about to sit, she saw he was closing the door without getting in himself.

"What are you doing?" she asked.

"I...I-I have to go back up there. I need to sort some things out," he explained, trying to leave again but she reached out to stop him.

"Hwan Soo-씨." She tugged his white collared shirt.

He turned back to face her and climbed into the van, his caring eyes meeting her saddened ones for a split second before he brought his lips to hers. The salt from her tears mingled on their lips. Her eyes widened, unsure that he was actually kissing her. But when his hand came up to her cheek, she knew it was real.

Her eyes fluttered closed, and she let their lips dance gently before he pulled away.

"아. You can call me Hwan Soo-아."

Korean Vocabulary:

웃어라 - oosora - smile (a command to smile)

죽을래 - jugulae? - Wanna die?

같이 해도 돼요? - gatchee haedu dwaeyo? - Can I join you?

이사 - ee sa - director

편하게 말하세요 - pyeonhagae malhasaeyo - speak comfortably (comfortably = informally)

콜 -cool - deal

눈이 정말 아름다워요 - nonee jongmal arumdawoyo - you have very pretty eyes

뭐라고 했어요? - mworago haessoyo? - what did you say?

잘 모르겠어요 - jal murooguessohyo - I don't understand.

우와 너 한국어 정말 잘한다 - ohwha no hangukoh jongmal jalhandda- wow your korean is really good.

당신의 미소가 아름다워요 - dangshinee misuga arumdawoyo - your smile is beautiful

손 대지 말아요! - sun dajee malayo! - get your hands off me!

발 - bal - feet

울지 마 - ouljima - don't cry

Chapter 46 (마흔여섯)

H wan Soo slammed the van door shut, running back into the venue, leaving Maria alone to take in everything that transpired between them. Bringing her fingers to her lips, a prickling sensation ran through her body and her cheeks heated. She could still feel his lips on hers.

Hwan Soo-아. He wanted her to call him Hwan Soo-아. Which gave her the hope that her feelings toward him were mutual. If a chaste kiss didn't help that realization enough.

"That smile tells me you're not upset anymore," Gi Young said as he glanced through the rearview mirror to her, his own relieved smile growing.

"I wouldn't go that far," she giggled. She was able to laugh. After having a near mental breakdown about ruining another event, Hwan Soo had made her capable of giggling like a schoolchild.

The van pulled up to Val's high-rise apartment building, and Maria's reality started setting in. She couldn't be seen at Hwan Soo's house. If by chance his feelings were mutual, their relationship could never be normal and would most likely have to remain hidden. Gi Young had told her about his contract and the rules about dating. Would she really want to be someone's dirty little secret? Even if that someone was Hwan Soo?

The door swung open, and Gi Young extended a hand to help her climb out when she caught someone running toward them. Her heart started to race, thinking it was potentially a crazy paparazzi that had followed them from the venue, but as the figure got closer, she realized who it was.

"Sul Bin?" she questioned, unsure what he was doing in front of Val's building.

Gi Young stepped in front of her like a protective older brother and asked, "여기서 뭐하세요?"

"오빠 괜찮아요." She gently pushed him aside to see Sul Bin's eyes widen as they roamed up and down before finally meeting hers.

"오빠?" Sul Bin asked, looking at Gi Young.

Gi Young turned to Maria, warning her with his eyes, but she gracefully walked over to Sul Bin.

"Sul Bin, it's great to see you, but why are you here?"

"I tried texting you, but you didn't answer. Guessing from the gown you must've been out somewhere with your friends. I was worried something happened, so I came to check and see if you were okay. I was just about to leave when I saw the van pull up and you coming out. Have you been crying?" He reached out to touch her cheek, but she flinched away.

"아 미안, I'm still not used to not wanting to touch you." He stuffed his hands into his pockets.

"Um...Sul Bin—"

"I was wondering if you were free? I have some things I need to tell you." His tone was apprehensive.

She looked down at her formal attire, still sticky and reeking of the booze that had been tossed on her, and then back at him.

"I can wait for you to get changed," he offered, rocking on his feet.

"Sul Bin, what's wrong?" She took a step toward him and grabbed the loose fabric of his shirt sleeve.

He didn't speak, but his eyes grew in size and she could tell that he was internally battling his emotions like she had been doing earlier in the evening.

"Come upstairs, let me take a quick shower and get changed and then we can go to a café or something to talk." She tugged his sleeve, pulling him toward the lobby entrance.

Maria stared up at another extremely high building. This one, however, was more like an oversized water tower than a skyscraper. It reminded her of pictures she had seen of the Space Needle in Seattle.

"Where exactly is this café you had in mind?" She studied her surroundings, taking in a small line that was forming for cable cars leading up to the large structure.

"남산 서울 타워." He smiled as he gestured up at the massive needle in the middle of Seoul. "I had mentioned I wanted to take you here before you left, and well, I guess this might be my only chance."

"Sul Bin, what's going on?" she asked warmheartedly as her concern grew. He had said nothing as she showered and got dressed. Even in the cab ride over, he kept his eyes to the window, watching the world pass by them, lost in thought.

"Once we get up there, I'll explain everything." He gave her a broken smile. Her heart clenched as the pit of her stomach dropped. Whatever he was going to say was not going to be good.

They climbed into the cable car, and as it started to move Maria looked through the panoramic windows taking in the night view of the city. Seoul had an affinity for boasting a beautiful view from every angle. While she had just been up in the lavish 롯데월드타워, the current view seemed more obtainable, more comfortable, more her.

She took several photos, even some of Sul Bin taking in the view. His forlorn demeanor spoke volumes and even through the photos, one could relate to his heavy heart.

When they reached the top of the hill, but only the bottom of the tower, she saw tons of people walking around taking pictures of the view. Small attractions spread throughout the forested area, like cute baby panda statues, the floral arrangements, and the large love lock trees and railings. The happy scene was a stark contrast to Sul Bin's miserable demeanor.

"We better head up, the café closes in a couple hours." He tilted his head to the entrance. Paying their entry fees, they were whisked all the way to the top in a large elevator, where once again she had a panoramic view through floor-to-ceiling windows. Even that late at night, families with children of all ages were out taking photos of the city behind them, loved-up couples as well.

He walked them into a café which gave off a basic coffee shop aesthetic with its metal chairs, small square wooden tables, and ambient music playing, but when she peered farther inside, she saw the same amazing night view of Seoul.

"Grab a seat, and I will get us some coffee." He extended his arm to the tables by the window and made his way over to the cashier to place their order.

She took a seat as she cast her gaze out into the night and fell more in love with Seoul. A city in a country she had never thought of prior to her trip, and for the first few days was ready to leave, had quickly become a comforting place she could never get bored of exploring. She understood Val's desire to stay.

"You seem to be feeling a lot better than when I first saw you tonight," he said, placing a tray on the table with two large coffees and an even larger slice of cake.

"I am, actually. I still have a lot on my mind but this little impromptu trip has already helped." She smiled as she reached for one of the drinks.

They simultaneously took sips of their coffees and after savoring the bitterness, their eyes met nervously, unsure of who should speak first. Once he placed his coffee back on the tray, he dropped his hands between his thighs and squirmed in his seat.

"Sul Bin, you've been pushing back the inevitable all night. There is clearly something you want to say. You wouldn't have been waiting outside my friend's apartment if you didn't need to talk to someone," she said, trying to comfort him with her tone.

"There is so much on my mind right now, I don't know where I should start." He looked up at her and a tear quickly fell from his eye. She wasted no time in standing up and moving her chair to his side to offer solace.

She wrapped an arm around his shoulder and pulled him closer to her as any friend would do.

"Whatever is going on, you can talk to me," she whispered.

"Did I ever tell you why I moved back to Korea?" he asked.

"Your parents split up, and you came to live with your mom," she responded.

"That's one reason. Another reason is I wanted to get into acting. Asian actors barely get screen time in the American market. So I chose to come here where I had more of an opportunity. I got signed to an agency, but they rarely sent me to casting calls and I still had to make ends meet, so I started working in the barbecue restaurant I met you in," he explained as he moved away from her soothing hold on him.

"I thought you were cute right off the bat, let me say that. So I hit on you. But I also knew who your 'friend' was," he nervously continued. "Yes, I was a total dick and made my move hoping that you would introduce me to him so I could make the connection.

"But during that night we were texting, I realized you were an amazing person with a good heart, and I was instantly attracted to you. The next day I had to meet my 'manager' and he was meeting with his real moneymaker. He was talking about Hwan Soo. And so I mentioned I had met him and his friends the previous night. I thought that maybe if I said I had made friends with someone well known, the company would give me more casting options..." He trailed off and Maria's gut sank. She was hoping he wasn't going where she thought he was, but it seemed all too likely she wasn't going to like the end of this story.

"I think you know what I'm about to say. But I need to say it to get it off my chest and explain myself. Hae So was suddenly interested in me and what I knew about you and Hwan Soo. She paid me to continue pursuing you. She promised me more photoshoots and acting gigs if I was able to seduce you and have you break up whatever it is between you and Hwan Soo. I had been ready to throw in the towel until she came along and offered me the one thing I wanted. Well, one of the things. After I started seeing you, I wanted something else. But I got jealous when I saw the way you looked at Hwan Soo, and I saw the way he looked at you and looked after you. I tried to be an asshole and ruin your relationship." He pulled her arm off him completely and engulfed her hand in between his.

"But after my few attempts of acting like a total piece of shit, I realized I couldn't do it. I told Hae So I wouldn't continue with what I was doing. I started to care about you too much, and I couldn't ruin your chance at happiness for my own selfish gain. Hae So didn't take that well." His eyes started watering again, and she released her hand from his to embrace him again, assuring him he could continue without her getting angry.

"What did that bitch do?" Maria was trying to control her anger, but seeing Sul Bin so upset made her want to go back to the party and deck the woman.

"They canceled my contract with the company saying that Hae So said I had made her feel 'uncomfortable' several times in the office. She's their biggest star, I knew I stood no chance in arguing. They offered to cut my contract, and they wouldn't get the police involved. I walked out and the next thing I knew I was at your apartment building." He swiped at the tears before they actually fell.

"I will talk to Hwan Soo about it. I'm sure there is something he can—"

"I'm going back to America." He cut her off with even more shocking news.

"뭐?" she asked.

"I'm going to move in with my father for a bit until I figure out what it is I want to do with my life now. I think getting out of Seoul is a smart move for me. But I wanted to see you before I left and tell you everything because I do care about you and would like to still talk to you. I know you can probably never forgive me. I wouldn't." He finally leaned into her comforting hug, and the tension in her body melted away.

"You're a great guy, Sul Bin, even with the whole trying to use me to get to my friend," she joked and felt him laugh in their embrace.

"I'm not thrilled about that, but I never got the impression you were a bad guy. The fact that you came clean to me, face to face, is more than I can say for some of my other relationships. You seem true to you, and you were forced into a situation that caused you to lose what you dreamed of doing. I can't be mad at that. I understand why you did it. I wish you would let me help you with the whole losing your contract thing. But maybe going back to America will be something you need. And depending on where you end up, maybe we can meet up when I get back from this wedding and we can drink, bond and become real honest friends." She pushed him away to see his face. While his eyes were puffy and his cheeks were red, he looked relieved.

They smiled weakly at each other, acknowledging their pains and sympathizing with one another. A new friendship had formed between them. And she was glad to be able to keep him in her life.

"I laid out all my shit. Now I think it's your turn. Why were you crying while wearing that gorgeous gown tonight?" he asked as he forked a piece of the cake into his mouth.

"Where do I even begin?" She slouched forward, getting a whiff of the cake and knowing they were probably going to need a second piece.

"I had a great night tonight. Probably one of the last ones I will have here. The next couple of days I'll just be packing, so thanks, Maria. I'm happy I got to see you one last time to explain myself." Sul Bin laughed as he walked Maria up the front door of Val's apartment building.

"Tonight was a very interesting one, to say the least. I had a lot of fun. And thanks for telling me everything that's been going on. I promise I won't tell Hwan Soo about what Hae So was up to—"

"Oh, he knew," Sul Bin said, cutting her off.

When her head snapped to look at him, his eyes were wide with fright and his lips were pursed. It seemed like he hadn't meant to let that slip.

"What do you mean he knew?" she asked as calmly as her nerves would allow.

Before he could answer, his eyes darted behind her, and he bowed very formally to someone. She looked behind Sul Bin to the reflection in the apartment windows and saw a tall figure dressed in a tux missing its jacket, hair disheveled, and eyes filled with hurt and rage. She turned around to see Hwan Soo, his fists clenched so hard down at his sides that his knuckles were white.

"Hwan Soo-야," she said for the first time. Saying it out loud was the weirdest sort of accomplishment, but internally her heart was doing somersaults at the sound of his informal name.

"Why is he here?" Hwan Soo spoke like a ventriloquist. His lips had barely moved as he spoke.

"He was here when I got back from the event. He came to talk. We went and grabbed coffee and got some stuff off our chests," she explained calmly.

It didn't appear to make him any less irritated.

"I should probably go." Sul Bin bowed as he stepped away from them.

"Before you go, can you finish what you were telling me before

Hwan Soo-아 showed up?" She pulled at Sul Bin's shirt sleeve. Sul Bin looked from her hand to Hwan Soo and back to her with a nervous twitch in his eyes.

"I think it's better if I just leave now. I'm sure Lee Hwan Soo-씨 would rather explain it himself." Sul Bin gulped as he pulled her hand off his shirt, bowed once more and started speed walking away from what was bound to be an argument.

Maria turned back to Hwan Soo, eyes narrowed. "You knew about Hae So paying Sul Bin?" she asked.

"If I told you, would it have made a difference? You were so smiley, giddy, and loved up with him, would whatever I had to say have mattered?" he argued. She couldn't be one hundred percent sure, but the malice in his statement sounded laced with jealousy.

"I wasn't loved up with him. I just enjoyed the company of someone I felt I could be normal with. I haven't been able to feel normal this entire trip!" She fought to control her voice, which was almost a yell.

"What the hell does that mean?" he asked, clearly frustrated.

"Are you kidding? Since the day I landed, I have been a fish out of water. I can still barely speak the language and get strange looks from everyone around me. And to top it off, I've been balancing living in a penthouse provided by a well-to-do family for their son's bride and working for an actor whose fame is growing constantly and who is also the son of a super wealthy family. I've been going out to eat at insane restaurants, going to gown-required events, where more well-to-do people are judging me for everything I do. How is any of that normal?!" She walked away from the entrance of the apartment, breaking free from Hwan Soo's piercing stare.

He grabbed her wrist, his hold strong but yielding enough that if she wanted to break free, she could. She peeked at his hand, its veins protruding against the creamy skin.

"That isn't even the point of this conversation," he said, bringing his tone down and tugging at her wrist so she would look up at him.

"맞아... It's about you knowing that Sul Bin was trying to deceive me because of your psycho ex," she replied, pulling her arm free of his hold.

"I only just found out. And at that point, he had stopped what he was doing. I didn't see a need to hurt your feelings. I felt so relieved he was out of the picture. I thought after paying him off at the engagement party he would've gotten the pic—" He stopped himself short.

"You what?" She took a step away from him. She was staring at a stranger. That wasn't Hwan Soo in front of her. It couldn't be.

"설명해줘." He ran his hand through his hair, taking a step closer to her.

"You better." She scanned him up and down, crossing her arms as she desperately tried to calm her heart that felt like it could shatter at any moment.

"You brought him to our friend's engagement party, and the paparazzi were swarming the place. I didn't want them getting the wrong idea." He took another step closer.

"'Wrong idea'? What idea was that?" Her fuming heart pushed her to take a step closer to him.

"That you were with him and not me. You're the one who sent that photo to Hae So of us kissing. Which worked at keeping her at bay just like Jung-hyun had planned. But that's not the point. The point is, if she were to see you were with someone else in photos, then she would've known we weren't together and that would've made working with her more unbearable. I didn't know at the time she knew Sul Bin." His eyes were roaming all over her face while hers roamed his body to see how tense he was.

Maria was still trying to wrap her mind around everything Hwan Soo was saying. Questions arose. Like, what plan did Jung-hyun come up with that Hwan Soo followed through on? Why did he think paying off Sul Bin was the right option? Was any of their time together real?

He used her. Just like all the other guys she had been with. How could she think he would be different? Just because it was a different country didn't mean the men changed.

360

"Yes, I didn't want to explain to Hae So why you were with someone else and have her try to get back with me just for the sake of making headlines. But also, no, it wasn't just because of Hae So." He reached out, taking her hand and bringing it to his lips. "Maria, I like you. A lot. What I did was unacceptable, and I know that, but I had no intentions of hurting you. Jung-hyun and Val assured me that this plan wouldn't backfire. But I'm an idiot. I've known Jung-hyun for so long, his schemes always have a way of backfiring. I mean, look at him and Val." He smiled.

If he thought that would make me feel better, it did just the opposite.

"You knew about Val and Jung-hyun?" She finally found the words but more of her world was crashing down around her. She pulled her hand out of his grasp. Feeling the soft skin leave hers was a sobering effect. His eyes widened as he pulled the corner of his bottom lip in between his teeth.

"네. Jung-hyun called me a while ago. Something had happened at work, and he had fallen for the girl he hired to date him." He explained.

"와...I've been deceived by all of you for so long, it seems. Thanks for letting me know, Hwan Soo-씨. I'm glad I traveled all this way for the same shit I could've gotten at home." She was done talking to him. She was done talking to anyone.

She stormed past him, into the lobby of the apartment complex and slammed the up button on the elevator. It arrived instantly, like it knew she needed to get away from Hwan Soo before she could no longer control her emotions and came off even more pathetic.

The doors closed, and she broke. Falling to the ground, she thought of everything that she had found out in the last few days. Her best friend had lied about her relationship, and Hwan Soo knew about it. Sul Bin had been paid to seduce her, and Hwan Soo knew about it. Hwan Soo even paid Sul Bin to stop. And apparently Jung-hyun and Val had something to do with Hwan Soo and her being 'together'.

Her breathing grew more rapid, her body fell limp on the floor of the elevator, the walls felt like they were caving in, and her eyes couldn't focus. Her anxiety had gotten the best of her.

She closed her eyes and the world went black.

Korean Vocabulary:

여기서 뭐하세요 - yogiso mwohasaeyo - what are you doing here?

맞아 -maja - right

설명해 줄게 - solmyonghae julgae - let me explain

Chapter 47 (마흔일곱)

I f Hwan Soo could scream without making a scene, he would've. He settled for his nails digging into the skin of his palm, and his teeth nearly grinding into a fine powder with how tight his jaw was clenched.

He knew chasing her would only hurt her. He had just destroyed their entire relationship and possibly several friendships in the span of a few minutes.

Walking to the curb to hail a cab, all he could think was that the day did not go as planned.

As he settled into the back of the cab, his eyes closed in frustration. Hwan Soo knew Maria had no clue who he had punched at the event that night. But he did, and he knew that with that one move, he'd most likely ended his career. For her. And he didn't regret it.

Park Joon was one of the biggest casting directors in the drama world. He cast actors who had little to no following and turned them into household names. And Hwan Soo had decked the guy.

When he worried Maria was having a panic attack for the scene that was caused, Hwan Soo had kissed her. For many reasons. To try and stop her panic attack, to show her he had no regrets for what he did, to finally prove that him kissing her meant something. Even with the brevity of the kiss, his mind had reeled, his heart lightened, he felt unstoppable. He would finally be able to tell her exactly how much he cared about her. How he wanted to spend all his time with her as more than just their friends' friends.

But that would have to wait.

When he went to clean up the mess he caused at the gala, he had been surprised to run into Hae So in the hallway outside the event. Eyes wide and lips gaping like a fish, she had struggled to come up with some excuse as to why she was there.

He knew why. She had wanted to either yell at him for causing such a fuss that their drama was ruined or she had wanted to spy on him to see what she could use against him if his career didn't completely go down the tubes.

Hwan Soo didn't have time for her crap, but something about the worry in her eyes—something he had never seen from her, even when acting—had given him pause.

"You shouldn't go back up there," she said nervously. Once again, something he had never heard from her. He looked past her but she reached for his arm, her grip not forceful or harsh, but of genuine concern.

"진짜, Hwan Soo. Val and Jung-hyun are handling what they can, and so is your family. Your brother sent me down here to tell you to go home." She squeezed his arm.

"가."

He had nodded, grabbing her hand on his arm and giving her a light squeeze of thanks before running back out the door to take a cab to Val's apartment—to the woman he loved.

Yes, he loved Maria. He wasn't sure when it happened, but he had known in that moment that love was the only way to describe the way his body shivered in anticipation of seeing her, his heart felt like it would thump out of his chest, and a smile overtook his face when he thought of her.

사랑. The word he thought he would never utter again was now the word he wanted to scream at the top of his lungs over and over.

But then he had seen her with him. Sul Bin. 미친새끼.

He thought the guy had finally left the picture, but there he was, and they were all smiley and happy, which enraged Hwan Soo to no end. How could she not see what a total scumbag the guy was?

And that's when everything came out into the open. Hwan Soo confessed to everything that had been going on behind Maria's back. When he said it all out loud, he realized just how fucked up everyone around her had been to someone who was supposed to be a friend.

She ran away from him with eyes on the verge of tears, her fists clenched at her side. He knew chasing her would only hurt her. He had just destroyed their entire relationship and possibly several friendships in the span of a few minutes.

--

The cab pulled up to his house to even more camera flashes than had been at the event. The lights hypnotized him, and he clawed through them in a daze, ignoring all the questions thrown his way about why he punched one of the most famous Korean casting directors.

As he pushed through the gate of his security wall, he leaned against the cool metal, shutting his eyes to get the spots to go away while trying to catch his breath. Like he hadn't been breathing since he watched Maria walk away from him.

"How is she?" a calm feminine voice asked, shocking him out of his daze.

Opening his eyes, there stood Hae So, leaning up against his front door, heels hanging in between her fingers, her small purse under her arm, and her dress billowing in the night breeze. He was surprised at how relaxed she looked for someone whose drama was most likely destroyed.

"너 한 테 조심하라고 말하지 않았나?" she whispered, still scarily unagitated. But the question itself was one that carried a lot of weight.

"네. But you saw what he was doing to Maria. You can't deny it. I saw your eyes jump over to the scene. And when I heard what he said...to her...I couldn't let that slide. She couldn't even understand what he was saying," he argued.

"Hwan Soo, what you did was commendable. And I came to tell you that you're coming out on top." She pushed off the door to walk over to him. With some jingling and snaps from her digging through her tiny purse, she pulled out her phone, began typing, and handed the phone over to him.

@kdramaloverrr: #TeamLeeHwanSoo That man deserves all the roles he gets in the future! No more second lead syndrome for me!

@leehwansooizdaddy: 대박! Knight in shining armor! That chick is lucky af.

@kdramaprincess: #leehwansoo is a god among men! Protect him.

@ifuknowuknow: Now even more excited for Lee Hwan Soo's new drama! #나랑같이있어

"이거 뭐야?" He looked up at her in between his scrolling through all the posts.

"Those are your fans. Apparently, someone in the party tweeted about the heroic act you performed before the press could even think to write up degrading articles calling you a violent thug." She laughed and bent to read along with him.

"아 그래?" He still was in disbelief.

"헐... You really are never on your SNS, are you?" She ripped her phone out of his hand and typed away again before thrusting it back under his nose. His brain couldn't believe what his eyes were seeing.

"Your Instagram alone has grown over 200,000 followers in the last two days. Now that you're a hero, I can see you getting even more," she joked, nudging his shoulder.

While he was surprised to see how large his fan base had grown, like Hae So said, he was never on his social media. He didn't have much control over what was posted anyway. His management was in charge of making sure he maintained a specific image. They would show him what had been posted if he was going to be interviewed, but he hadn't been in many interviews recently.

Hwan Soo's jaw went slack. There were tons of posts from the last couple of weeks he'd never seen before. Him talking to the costume designers, him practicing lines, behind the scenes of his photoshoot, even one of him sleeping in his van. From the angle of the photo, he knew exactly who had taken the photo and that fact made his heart clench.

"Maria," he whispered.

"Ugh, really?" Hae So's voice didn't sugarcoat her feelings for the girl. "I never thought you would actually fall for the American."

"What?"

"Did you think for a second I thought you two were a thing?" she scoffed.

"We we-were," he choked on the words, and she laughed.

"알아." She rolled her eyes. "Friends of friends fall in love in a few days? Come on. But even after doing my digging, using Sul Bin and all that, I'll admit I got a little jealous."

"A little? You paid the guy to hit on her to try to break us up." Hwan Soo tossed her phone back to her. "Why are you even here, Hae So?"

"I came to give you the good news that your career is saved, and our drama will most definitely be the talk of the year!"

"That is such bullshit." He turned to his front door, hoping she would take the hint and leave.

"Well, I also came because..." She trailed off, watching him with those doe eyes that once made his heart melt. She glided closer to him, pinning him to his door. She pressed against his body and forced her mouth over his.

Her lips were wet and cold. He tried to keep his lips sealed tight but could taste the alcohol on her breath. Grabbing her arms, Hwan Soo pushed her off him, and she stumbled back, her lipstick smeared around her lips.

"What the hell is wrong with you?" he shouted, trying to wipe all the lipstick off his face.

"Do you really feel nothing toward me anymore?" Her eyes filled with tears, and they looked believable.

It was Hae So, after all. The woman could cry on the spot. It was what made her a great actress. But these tears, they were genuine, and he hated to see people crying.

"Come on, Hae So—"

"말해봐!" she shouted, tears falling to her cheeks.

"I feel nothing toward you. What would you expect me to feel after the hell you put me through? You used me and broke my heart. I was mad, hurt, and yeah, I did hate you, but if I stayed that way, what would that accomplish? So instead I used it as an incentive. Actually, now that I think about it, I did feel something for you." He watched her eyes light up with hope. "I felt grateful."

She took a step closer again, but his hand went up to keep her away.

"That was until you hired someone, who I think actually likes Maria, as your own little personal spy to make me either jealous or prove we weren't together. And in the process, you hurt him, her, and me. Again. And now you just tried to shove your tongue down my throat. Why I'm surprised is beyond me." He started to enter his keycode and glared at her to get her to leave.

Her shoulders that always had perfect posture now slumped, her head that was usually held high had drooped in defeat. And his kindness got the best of him.

"Do you want to come in for a drink?" he sighed.

Her head shot up, those eyes that had lost their pride only a few minutes ago were eager like a kid offered candy.

- -

"So you really like 짜장면 girl?" Hae So slurred as she took another shot.

"I think I love her," he responded. The 소주 clearly loosened his lips.

"What are you gonna do about it?" she asked.

"What do you mean? She hates me. I told her that her best friend had lied to her, Sul Bin lied to her, I lied to her, and that we all ganged up to use her." His head was spinning from unloading all this to someone he knew he shouldn't. But the alcohol had disconnected his mouth from his brain.

"That shouldn't stop you from fighting. If you really love her, you should show her."

"Are you honestly giving me love advice?"

"Hey, you may not like me, but we have both worked in this industry long enough to see how our shows play out." She poured him another shot and handed him the bottle.

He poured her another shot. "Maybe it isn't really love. I mean, I thought I loved you." They clinked their glasses and downed the shot. "Sure, she makes me smile. And her presence when we're at work settles my nerves and makes me a better actor. And when I kiss her I never want to stop."

Hwan Soo's eyes started to burn. He refused to cry in front of his ex, and so he ripped the bottle off the coffee table and took a large swig.

"바보." She grabbed the bottle from his hand and slammed it back on the table, making him jump.

"You can't sit here and say that what you felt for me is even close to what you feel for her. And that's coming from the woman who should be insulted by that fact. You would never do the things you've done for her for me. The lead always fights for the girl. He doesn't back down. He makes mistakes on the way, but he proves his love. You've always been the second lead. You only know how to give up and repress your emotion. But guess what? You're not the second lead anymore. You got that lead role!" She jumped to her feet, jostling the table and spilling 소주.

"It's time for you to take that lead role in real life, my friend." She slapped his shoulder, clearly on a roll with her speech.

It wasn't anger, but in total support of him. She was either an amazing actress even when drunk, or she was truly supportive of his following his heart to get the girl he was in love with.

"친구? I would like that." He stood up to gauge how she reacted to the term. Her face turned bright red.

"아, 진짜? 친구? You could actually call me that? After all the shit I've put you through?" She sounded shocked that he even made the suggestion.

Hwan Soo was surprised himself, but if they could be civil long enough to finish filming their drama and maybe even continue a friendship after, he might have a friend in the acting world. He gave her a nod of his acceptance.

Her eyes sparkled like a child's. "And as a friend, you'll let me crash here since I am in no shape to drive." She turned on her heel, teetering precariously for a moment before bolting down the hall.

"Yes, but just not my ro—" He didn't have time to finish the sentence as his bedroom door was slammed shut and the lock clicked. Letting out a deep sigh, he stumbled over to the guest room so he could get some sleep before their shoot the next morning.

Falling into the bed, he felt the comforter wrap itself around him. His mind jumped straight to the time he found Maria bundled up sleeping soundly after making him and his manager a massive meal.

His thoughts spiraled from that moment to all their laughs, their bonding over interests and family, to their heated kiss he hadn't wanted to stop after showing up at the club, and his kissing her as he got her safely away from the pandemonium he had caused to keep her safe.

Why did he agree to Jung-hyun's stupid idea? After only a few days, he had stopped pretending. He may not have noticed at first, but it was obvious after seeing her with another man that he was jealous it wasn't him and he desperately wanted to be by her side.

How was he going to recover from the total fuck up that was the past four hours? He had not only told her that he paid some guy to stay away from her, he also admitted he was trying to use her to keep his ex—who was at this moment sleeping in his room—away. And he let slip her best friend had been lying to her for a long time.

Hwan Soo grabbed onto the comforter hoping to seek solace from the thoughts that made his mind spin faster than the alcohol. He took a deep breath and could imagine Maria being wrapped up with him as they tried to fall asleep but getting distracted by talking about each other's days, his hands tripping through her long hair as her fingers traced around his chest. Bringing up their friends in between pulling each other closer, leaving light kisses on each other's bare skin, and talking about how much they loved each other.

Warmth spread through his chest and the corners of his mouth curled up as he drifted to sleep, lured by the prospect of Maria's sweet kisses. And like that, his world went black.

Korean Vocabulary:

너 한 테 조심하라고 말하지 않았나? - no han tae jushimharagu malhaji anhatna? - Didn't I tell you to be careful?

바보 - babo - idiot

Chapter 48 (마흔여덟)

here am I? Maria tried to move but her body was in a weird state of paralysis. She fought with her brain to open her eyes, but once again her motor skills failed to do their job.

What the hell happened?

The last thing she remembered was being on the elevator to Val's apartment after having her heart ripped out of her chest and stomped on by the one guy she thought wouldn't be a repeat of her past crappy choice in men.

Since she couldn't peel her eyes open, her other senses would have to do their jobs ten times better. The air around her didn't just smell clean, it smelled clinically clean. Bleach and sanitizer. It stung her nose to the point that she wanted to sneeze. The fingers on one hand touched a rough gauze-like cloth while the other was being held and stroked comfortingly by a soft, dainty-feeling hand. The bed beneath her was thinly cushioned, and a coarse blanket covered her torso and legs, not doing its job of providing warmth judging by the cool breeze she felt on her bare legs. Bare legs? Yup, she was no longer in her jeans, but rather an uncomfortably thin dressing gown.

Definitely not the elevator. A hospital?

Beeping electronics, going off at all different rates, made her ears ring, her palms sweaty and her heart pump faster. It was hard to hear which one could be attached to her. Lots of footsteps of all speeds. Different voices, some grumbles of discomfort or pain, some distraught, while others sounded like they were trying to calm down those who were upset.

That's when her ears caught a familiar voice.

"What was she doing in the elevator? Why was she alone? Didn't Hwan Soo go with her?" Val's crushed voice caught Maria's attention.

"I've tried calling him close to fifteen times. 안 받네. The phone goes straight to voicemail," Jung-hyun responded.

"Why did your mother invite Park Joon in the first place? We all know what a disgusting person he is! How did he end up near Maria? How the hell did this happen?" Val asked angrily. Her breathing sounded shallow, and Maria started to worry Val might begin to hyperventilate.

"I don't know, Valerie. I wish I knew all those answers to help you calm down." Jung-hyun's voice became muffled. "But she's going to be fine. The doctors said she needs some more rest and once she wakes up, we can get her home to rest comfortably for another day or so."

"Yeah, I should probably stay with her. She's been here for close to a month and I've barely spent any time with her. I have no clue what's going on with her and I come home to the lobby attendant telling me she was rushed to the hospital? What kind of friend am I? What have I been doing this entire time?" Her friend's voice cracked, and all Maria wanted to do was sit up and hug her. No matter how mad she was, Val was still her best friend in the entire world.

"I'm sure she understands with the wedding and everything that you couldn't be there with her all the time. It's why we had Hwan Soo there to keep her company. In more ways than one," he chuckled.

"We knew they would be a match made in bickering heaven,

didn't we? And it definitely worked in our favor that his crazy ex ended up being his co-star in that drama." Val's breathing slowly calmed to a steady pace.

"Made it a lot easier to convince him to 'pretend' date Maria," Jung-hyun said calmly.

"I think it stopped being pretend a long time ago. Did you know they kissed? Not just once either." Val's voice filled with gossiping joy, as she excitedly spilled the beans about their friends' possible relationship.

Maria felt her body become more alert by the second, desperate to scream that Hwan Soo was a liar. That Val and Jung-hyun were no better. But she also wanted to see where their conversation would lead.

"진짜? 언제?" he asked.

"Apparently once was because of Hae So. He also kissed Maria when he was asleep. She said he did that a lot," Val snickered. "The last time was when Hwan Soo came to pick us up after the club with Sul Bin. I actually caught that one with my own eyes. They thought we were both drunkenly passed out, but I woke up to see her in his lap, the two of them going at it." Val spoke so fast that Maria wasn't sure she even took a breath.

"Wow. Can't say we haven't been in similar situations," Jung-hyun joked. Maria strained her ears to see if he would expand on that tidbit, but he changed the subject. "So if they do end up dating, do you think it would be easier for us to convince Maria to move here? You could even have her move into the same building like that show *Friends* you like so much." Jung-hyun laughed.

Had Val finally told him about wanting to stay in Seoul?

"Move here? Like to Seoul?" Val asked.

Guess not.

"Valerie," he chuckled, "I saw you getting texts from realtor apps almost every day since Maria got here. At first, I was confused because I thought you were happy in San Francisco, but then I started to notice how much happier you've been since being here. It's a good thing because I've wanted to talk to you about moving here. I love seeing all my family and friends more often. But you would be moving so far away from all those same things, so I decided to not bring it up."

Maria heard a small nervous chuckle from Jung-hyun as he continued. "That was until I saw you seemed to have a similar idea. I can easily convince my mother to let me bring HQ back here, and you wrapped up all your loose ends at work before coming so I'm sure you could move here and maybe start up Tina's international design firm or hell, open your own design business!" Happy chuckles came from the couple.

"I'm positive our life here will be more than we can imagine in San Francisco." His voice was so sincere and filled with love that Maria could feel tears welling up behind her closed lids.

"Jung-hyun..." Val's voice was choked up again.

"사랑해, Valerie. Forever," Jung-hyun whispered.

"나도 사랑해," Val echoed, her voice cracking.

사랑해. She had learned long ago that Hwan Soo had lied to her about what it meant. After watching so many dramas and reading through his script, she realized it was actually a confession of love. That should've been her first red flag about him and his ease with lying. But since she could understand why he had said it when they were about to have a heated make-out session after only knowing each other a few days and the drama they were watching was showing an eerily similar scenario, she had let it go. After everything that happened, maybe she shouldn't have.

Maria cracked her eyes open, squinting against the light, and saw her best friend kissing her fiancé.

"I can help you house hunt while I'm here," she whispered, her throat scratchy.

The partners' lips popped apart, and Val looked over at Maria.

"Oh my God, Maria. You're awake!" Val jumped up, her face full of joy.

"You can go back to kissing your fiancé. It's fine, I'm still a bit sleepy," Maria joked.

"I'll leave you two. I'm gonna find the doctor to see if we can get you discharged," Jung-hyun stood, making his way to the nurses' station in the ER, but Maria's reflexes kicked back in and she grabbed his arm.

"Thank you. For treating Val so well. I get why she loves you so much." Maria wanted to know what his plan with Hwan Soo had been, but she didn't think her queasy stomach could handle another shock.

Jung-hyun gave her a small bow, her hand retreating from his wrist before he walked off.

"Maria, I was so worried. I came back to the apartment as soon as I could and the front—"

"I heard," Maria interrupted as she tried to sit up, her body still weak from whatever meds they were pumping through her.

"How much did you hear?" Val's entire face puckered with fright.

"Everything from 'How could Hwan Soo let this happen?' And for your information, I wasn't with him for a multitude of reasons. Some of which you also brought up while I couldn't fully wake up." Maria gave one final push, her arms helping lift her to sit up with a loud huff.

"What do you mean?" Val nervously reached behind Maria to adjust the pillow, trying to help her get comfortable.

"Hwan Soo mentioned to me that you and Jung-hyun had something to do with us being together more often than initially intended. As well as the whole pretend-to-date-to-get-Hae-So-off-his-back thing. Something you didn't mention, but Hwan Soo did, was the fact that he's known since the beginning about how you and Jung-hyun were really brought together." Val looked defeated as Maria continued, "He also might've mentioned he paid off Sul Bin at your engagement party among other things that if I think about anymore, my mind will explode again." Maria's head and heart were already starting to feel that similar stab.

"Maria, I am seriously so—"

"Don't apologize." Maria didn't want to hear another lie.

"Why were you alone, Maria?" Val stood from the small stool at Maria's bedside and changed the subject, her eyes starting to water.

"I walked away from another man who was going to hurt me." Maria shrugged, trying to play off how her heart ached, but the stupid monitor started to beep faster.

"Everything he did was to make sure you didn't get hurt," Val argued.

"Using me to make sure Hae So stayed off his back was for my own good?" Maria bit back.

"At first no. It was very much for his own. But when he started to care about you, nothing else mattered. He protected you from her wrath constantly. And protected you from Sul Bin, who was a pawn in the whole thing," Val explained.

"Sul Bin told me everything. You knew. You knew, and you didn't tell me. What the hell, Val?! How long have you deceived me? Are we even really friends?" Maria raised her voice, desperate to cover up her heart rate beeping faster on the machine beside the bed.

"Grow up, Maria!" Val flung her hands in the air, making a loud clap on her thighs as they dropped back down to her side. "Even if I told you that Sul Bin was no good, you wouldn't want to hear it. You're like your mother that way. She will still try to set you up no matter how much you protest. You would still date him even if I told you he was trash." Val had one hand on her hip while the other was tugging her hair in frustration.

"And the reason I didn't tell you about Jung-hyun and me was because I was afraid of what you would think. I thought that you would hate me for not having that crazy Jane Austen novel type of romance we used to talk about. So, yeah, I lied about our relationship. Jung-hyun, on the other hand, didn't feel the need to sugarcoat it with his friend." Val looked around to see people had begun to stare. She took a deep breath and lowered her voice.

"We thought Hwan Soo had handled Sul Bin when he paid him at the engagement party, and we wouldn't have to bring up what he was doing. Then you invited us out to the club with him. I wanted to tell you then, but Hwan Soo kinda kept you busy. And don't act like you haven't been lying to yourself and to all of us about Hwan Soo! You really want me to believe you feel nothing toward him?" Val wrapped up her speech posing a question that hit Maria where it hurt.

Maria was speechless. There really wasn't a stone Val didn't over-turn and back up with a reason. And Maria knew the truth of the matter was Val was right. On all accounts.

Bowing her head in defeat, Maria said it out loud, "I like Hwan Soo. For the first time in a long time I found someone I connected with. And I liked him even more knowing my mother had no part in it. She didn't catfish him. She didn't hand him my photo and leave him my number. I met him by myself, I went out with him myself, I spent time with him by myself, and I fell hard for him."

Her heart ached, and her lungs felt like they were collapsing again as she tried to take deep breaths. When she finally had herself in control, she spoke again.

"But none of that's true now, is it? I met him because of you and Jung-hyun. I went out with him because we went out with you or he had to keep his ex away. I spent time with him once again, because of you and Jung-hyun."

"Maria—" Val started, but stopped herself.

Maria didn't want to be there. She wanted to be alone where no one could find her. Which was impossible for her in a city she didn't totally understand.

That was the perfect time for Jung-hyun to come back with the good news that after a final check-up from the doctor they could leave. Maria thanked him as the doctor came to take out the IV in her hand and handed her the clothes she had worn when she was admitted. He requested she take it easy the next few days and rest as much as she could, but all Maria cared to hear was that she could leave.

"I'm going to grab a cab. I'll see you guys later for dinner. Let me know where I need to be. I'll make sure to dress properly so as to not spoil another night for you." Maria bowed, and she could see Val was holding back the urge to stop her from leaving. Val and Maria knew that a day or two apart to let them both think would be the best move.

The hospital doors parted, Maria stepped out and took in a deep breath of the crisp morning air. The sun just was starting to come up over the horizon, casting a pretty purple and pink mosaic on the glass of the tall skyscrapers.

As she stepped away from the cold interior of the hospital and into the daybreak, a taxi cab pulled up at the curb. She ran to flag it down when a familiar face stepped out.

Maria froze, rubbed her eyes, and blinked hard a few times, unsure if the person standing before her was real or if the drugs were still in her system.

"엄마?"

Korean Vocab

안 받네 - an badnae - he's not answering

언제 - ohnjae - when

엄마 -ohma - mom

Chapter 49 (마흔아홉)

Hwan Soo woke up to his head pounding like a jackhammer. He should not have drunk that much. As he attempted to sit up, not only did his brain feel like it was being bounced around his skull like a tennis ball, but his body ached like he had run a marathon and begged him never to leave his bed.

Bang! Bang! Bang!

That wasn't his head.

Hopping up way too fast, his head spun and his stomach churned. He heard the loud thumping again followed by a familiar voice yelling for him to open the door.

"형?" Hwan Soo croaked out, his throat feeling scratchy and in desperate need of water. Wrapping the blanket around his body, he shuffled out into his living room.

"문 열어!" The man was pounding on Hwan Soo's bedroom door.

But didn't I just leave my bedroom?

Looking behind him, he saw the stark white walls with a small bookcase, meaningless books and random familiar photos on the shelves. He looked down at the blanket he had wrapped around him

—it was white and fluffy, like a cloud. He had slept in the guest room because Hae So—

"Shit."

His mind sobered up immediately and he shuffled down the hallway to join Gi Young at his bedroom door.

"야! What are you doing out here?" Gi Young yelled, his face as red as a lobster, his breathing so labored Hwan Soo was worried Gi Young was on the verge of passing out.

"What do you mean? I woke up to you trying to knock down my bedroom door," Hwan Soo shouted back.

"I mean why are you not in there? Where is Hae So?" Gi Young screeched.

"Hae So is in there. I slept in the guestroom. How did you know she was here?" Hwan Soo rubbed his head, relieved the real banging had ceased but the hammering in his head had gotten worse.

"How did I— How did I know?" Gi Young was frantically searching his pockets, his phone nearly flying out of his hands. He swiped it open and typed madly before shoving the phone in Hwan Soo's face.

Lee Hwan Soo Saves Young Woman Then Spends The Night With His Costar!

Kim Hwan Soo sent netizens into a frenzy last night as he hero-ically saved an unidentified young woman from being sexually harassed by another partygoer at a charity event hosted by close friends, Park Jung-hyun and fiancée Valerie Parker.

"Of course, they don't mention Park Joon's name. That smarmy bastard deserves to be publicly shamed for all the crap he has done to the women in the industry. When will our media start posting that kind of article?" Hwan Soo slammed the phone down on his leg, annoyed he would have to read any further.

"Agreed, but that isn't the point here, Hwan Soo-야." Gi Young brought the phone back up for Hwan Soo to continue reading.

After disappearing from the party, Lee re-emerged at his house, where his co-star Park Hae So waited behind the large gate. We are unable to confirm how she got in, however as of this morning, neither one has been seen leaving the house. Is there a romance building on the set of their new drama 나랑 같이 있어? Could this be the start of the latest string of drama couples? Neither of the stars' agencies have not responded to requests for comment. What do you guys think? Are Lee Hwan Soo and Kim Hae So a new power couple?

"This can't be real," Hwan Soo tossed the phone back to Gi Young with an incredulous look on his face.

"Hae So, 나가." Hwan Soo pounded on his bedroom door, ready to break it down if necessary.

"야!" Her shrill yell sounded from inside the room as loud stomps approached the door.

The door swung open and both men screamed in shock, Hwan Soo jumping into Gi Young's arms at what stood before them.

Hae So looked like a swamp creature with her hair tangled and pointing in several different directions. Her makeup was still on her face, just not where it was intended. Her lipstick was smeared onto her chin and cheeks, her eyes were surrounded in dark circles from the smudged eyeliner and eyeshadow, and little black specks of dried mascara were sprinkled along her cheekbones.

"뭐?!" she shouted as she stomped her foot.

Hwan Soo climbed out of his manager's arms and faced the nightmare in front of him.

"Hae So do you know where you are?" he asked.

"What are you saying, Hwan Soo? I'm in my—" She stopped herself, her eyes opening wide as one of her false eyelashes popped off.

"I'm...I'm...I'm in your house...I spent the night here. Oh crap." She threw her hand to her mouth. Her cheeks puffed up like a blowfish and a gag came up from her throat.

"Bathroom is behind you." He pointed to a large wood door at the back of his room as she bolted like the wind, disappearing from their sight.

"She seems to realize the severity of this issue," Gi Young huffed out as he patted the back of his neck with more force than necessary.

"형, I know the issue." Hwan Soo exhaled loudly, rolled his eyes, and his head fell back into the cushion of the blanket still wrapped warmly around him.

"No, I don't think you do. Not only did she stay the night, you have a strict no dating policy in your contract, and if there are rumors of you having a relationship, you could potentially lose everything!" Gi Young frustratingly pushed Hwan Soo.

"But it isn't true!" Hwan Soo pushed him right back.

"You know just as well as I do that means nothing to the paps or the world of social media! Okay. Fine. Let's say they believe you and say it isn't true. Now all eyes are on you and your drama," Gi Young stated like it was a bad thing. Hwan Soo wasn't seeing how this could be an issue once they made it clear that the two leads were not an item.

"헐, you really don't get why that's a problem." Gi Young's jaw dropped as he gave Hwan Soo a shocked once-over.

"Maria. Maria is always with you. Maria, the woman you were making out with in the backseat of my van not even a few nights ago. Maria, the woman you just saved last night from Park Joon. Maria, the woman you're in lo—"

"그만해! I get it!" Hwan Soo shouted to make Gi Young stop before he said something they would both regret.

"What are you going to do? Huh? If now, all eyes are on you?" The worried tone in Gi Young's voice settled in Hwan Soo's stomach. His nausea was back as fear filled the atmosphere of the house.

Thinking about his feelings for Maria was what he had been drinking to forget. He had ruined anything they could've had together in only a few short minutes. Thinking about her face, those gorgeous eyes that he had caused to well with tears, her pillowy soft lips that trembled with rage and sadness, and her cheeks that burned red with anger, as he told her that being together was a tactic drawn up by their friends and how he paid off Sul Bin, had him slumping against the wall.

"Luckily she hates me now. So we won't have to worry about that anymore," Hwan Soo said dejectedly.

He didn't expect another shove from Gi Young, but the man's face was once again red. Possibly redder than it had been.

"What did you do to her?" he hissed.

"형, 진정해요." Hwan Soo put his hands up to stop another shove.

Before more was said, Hae So came back to the door; her makeup was fixed, hair up in a bun and outfit changed into clothing she had stolen from Hwan Soo's closet.

Maria looks way better in my clothes.

"I called my agency. I told them that we are not in a relationship. In fact, I said we have been friends for years as we both started acting around the same time, and I came over to make sure you were okay after everything that happened at your friends' event. They are making a statement in the next half hour or so. You should probably tell your team the same."

Both men stared incredulously. Had she just done the noble thing? The right thing? Without it benefitting her in any way?

"뭐? 왜봐?" Her voice was fearful as she stepped back, her eyes were wide while her mouth clenched.

"Why did you do that?" Hwan Soo asked.

"어? Do what?" She shook her head, her concern turning to confusion.

"Save my career," he said.

She let out a small laugh that quickly grew to slapping her leg in hysterics. Her short breaths more small wheezes as she tried to get air into her lungs so she could speak.

When she finally gained control of herself, she wiped the tears from her eyes and patted each man's shoulder.

"I didn't do anything for you." She tilted her head, eyes big with mock sadness, and her lips pouted. "If you lost your contract because people thought we were together or your beloved 짜장면 girl, you would cause the entire production to shut down. A production in which I am the lead. I am not about to lose this and start from square one."

She walked past them toward the living room.

"나 간다." She waved back to them, grabbed her purse off the couch and disappeared into the entryway.

They heard the beeping of the door unlocking, the thud of it closing and silence filling the house.

The two men turned toward each other, jaws dropped with the same dopey expression of shock as Gi Young grabbed his phone to dial the agency.

After taking a hot shower and downing several bottles of water, Hwan Soo tried to get some sleep in the van on the way to filming. His van had been swarmed by reporters with cameras as he left his house, and as they arrived at the filming location, he saw the same fate awaited him. Hwan Soo sighed and pulled on a mask before pushing through the crowd to get to set.

Walking up to the makeup tent, he saw Hae So sitting in her chair already getting her blush applied.

"How you feeling?" she asked kindly.

He sat down in the chair next to her and responded in the same pleasant tone, "Much better. Thanks for asking."

The makeup artists halted, looking between the two of them with surprise. Their reactions weren't all that bizarre considering Hwan Soo avoided being in the same room with Hae So until they had to start filming.

"Glad to hear. I see Maria isn't with you. Shouldn't she be working right now?" Hae So asked.

Hwan Soo knew she was asking to get a reaction from him. But he still hadn't spoken to her, and he needed to. Pulling out his phone to text her, the screen remained black.

"Crap. 누구 폰 충전기 가지고 있는 사람?" He lifted his phone showing how desperately he needed to plug it in.

The makeup artist took his phone and plugged it into her charger.

"고마워요," he said, thanking her as she resumed dabbing foundation on his face.

They wrapped for the night on filming. Hwan Soo's mind was not fully in the shoot, and the director noticed, cutting the late-night shoot short and telling Hwan Soo to come back with a new attitude. He couldn't focus. How could he? Besides the whole Hae So mix-up, which the director quickly brushed aside after both her and his agencies denied the relationship, he hadn't been able to talk to Maria. He needed to go all-out in his confession of his feelings. It was a do or die situation. He would walk up to her, plant a passionate kiss on her lips and tell her he loved her and wanted her to stay in Seoul with him.

He scoffed at his own crazy drama-like idea. If he took one step into her personal space, he would be receiving a slap to the face and a knee to the groin. He wouldn't blame her. He really fucked up. And even though his body was calling for him to rest, his mind was telling him to go and see Maria. Hwan Soo climbed into his van when he heard someone shouting his name.

"Lee Hwan Soo-씨!" He turned to see the makeup artist waving his phone around frantically. She caught up to him and handed him his phone.

"I can't believe I almost forgot it! Thank you." He accepted it from her and bowed his many thanks to the young woman as she tried catching her breath.

Hitting the home button, he was alarmed to see over thirty missed calls from Jung-hyun and several voicemails. Not all that surprising, however, considering the scene he had caused at the event the night before.

Instead of listening to any of the voicemails, he pulled up Jung-hyun's number and called. The phone barely rang a full tone before there was a click.

"형, I am so sorry. My phone died, and I drank a little too much last night. I need to talk to you about the craziness that went down. I just finished filming, and the makeup girl who was charging my phone—"

"그만!" Jung-hyun shouted, cutting Hwan Soo off. Jung-hyun's tone was frightening and made Hwan Soo feel like a child about to be scolded by his father.

"We need to talk."

Korean Vocabulary:

문 열어 - mun yoloh - open the door!

나가 - naga - get out

헐 - hul - omg

그만해 - gumanhae - stop

왜봐 - wae bwa - why are you looking at me?

누구 폰 충전기 가지고 있는 사람 - nugu pone chungjon gajigo issnoon saram - does anyone have a phone charger?

Chapter 50 (쉰)

Maria sat across from her mother in a large café near the hospital. To say she was dumbfounded to see her mother would be an understatement. She couldn't believe it when she walked out of the hospital and saw her mother climb out of a taxi. Maria had slumped into her mother's arms and sobbed, all her emotions hitting her at once. Distraught with betrayal from everyone around her, enraged by what Sul Bin had tried to do to her, heartbroken by Hwan Soo's lies, frustrated by the fact that she still yearned for him. It had all combusted into a storm of tears and screams on her mom's shoulder. And her mother had cooed calming sentiments, hugging her daughter tight and stroking her back, trying to ease whatever was troubling her.

Now as she sat puffy-eyed in a coffee shop across from her mother, Maria was again shocked by her mother's attitude. Her mother had never left the comfort of her own town for longer than a day. And here she was in South Korea, sipping on an 아메리카노 and looking out the windows to the large, crowded streets of Seoul like a native.

Her mother was in Seoul. How? Why?

"Mom, what are you doing here?"

"I was invited to the wedding too, ya know." She leaned back in the distressed brown leather chair. Maria, in fact, didn't know this. Val had never mentioned it, but she wasn't shocked. Val was the daughter Maria's mom wanted. Smart, talented, and getting married.

"I hadn't planned to attend. You and Val know my feelings on travel, but it was nice of her to think of me and your father. I hadn't heard from you in a while and well, call it mother's intuition, but I felt I needed to be here. I only chose to come a little earlier so you could show me around the city. Your dad was more than thrilled to let me go alone."

Her mother's face had a forlorn, uneasy look about it. Her usual thin-lipped magnificent smile that could make anyone around her grin was nowhere to be seen. In its place was a rather scary frown. Her bright brown eyes seemed to have lost their luster and had deep bags underneath.

"Mom—"

"Did you really think lying to me was necessary?" her mother blurted out, a weight clearly lifting off her shoulders. Maria's brows furrowed in confusion.

"What?"

"I landed early this morning, thinking I would get to the hotel, rest a bit and surprise you later. When suddenly, all over these big screens in the airport is a video playing over and over of a handsome man carrying this phenomenally dressed woman with a blurred-out face out of a fancy building."

Maria could see where this was going, and she knew the other shoe had finally dropped.

"Even if they blur out your face, you think I can't tell what my own daughter looks like? All your little freckles, especially the little scar on your ankle from when you tripped on a rock in the ocean? What kind of cameras do these paps have? Those photos were 4K quality." Her mother laughed almost hysterically. "And to top it off, I find out Hwan Soo isn't a woman. But rather a very attractive, very strong man who came to my daughter's rescue and is some kind of celebrity here. And you've been traipsing around with him all this time doing God knows what." Her mother's voice was strained trying not to yell in the middle of the large café.

"Mom, if I told you who Hwan Soo really was, what would you have done?" Maria asked rhetorically. They both knew the answer, which only made Maria's point clearer. "The guy is a handsome, arrogant, backstabbing, generous, caring, entitled, charming, lovable idiot who was forced to be around me and I, him," Maria explained.

She tried not to remember what had really happened last night after he had saved her. Finding out he had been using her, paid off a guy who was already paid to ruin her, and knew about their friend's relationship from the beginning had done a number on her. Enough to put her in the hospital with a panic attack.

Her mother's eyebrows lifted inquisitively. She opened and closed her mouth several times before choosing to take a sip of her coffee and the asking, "And is he the reason you came running out of the hospital crying?" she asked.

"I didn't come running out crying. Geez, Mom, you know how to turn everything into something insanely dramatic. I cried because I saw you after coming out of the hospital. I was elated to see you after what I had been through." She reached over the small table between them to take her mother's hand. It was soft, her fingers strong as they squeezed Maria's fingers back with adoration.

Maria knew she complained about her mother's constant state of marital mania, but she also knew it was because she wanted her daughter to be happy. It was her way of showing love, and Maria knew that no matter how infuriating it could get, it was coming from a good place. And in that moment, she needed her mom's compassion.

"That leads to my next question. Why were you in the hospital? I called to check on you, and Val answered telling me she was with you in the hospital!" Her mother's eyes welled, turning red as her hand squeezed Maria's with worry.

"엄마..." Maria's throat painfully closed as she tried to hold back another round of tears. "Where do I even begin?" she questioned, more to herself than her mother.

"The beginning," her mother pleaded.

Hwan Soo ducked his head as he made his way through the false refrigerator door that hid their favorite bar. It was dimly lit with candles on the few bar tables and the strings of lights hung in the back garden. The place had always been where Jung-hyun and he would go to get away from the hecticness of their families, their jobs, and any other problems they were faced with. It was where they came up with the plan to deceive Maria in the first place. Weirdly it seemed like the perfectly depressing spot to meet Jung-hyun.

Maybe that was the point. After Jung-hyun had told Hwan Soo where to meet him, he said nothing regarding what they needed to talk about. But Hwan Soo had never heard his friend so furious. That was what scared him the most.

He surveyed the bar to find his friend already a bottle deep in 소주 and pouring himself a second. Hwan Soo rushed over and grabbed the green bottle, offering his friend a fake smile he hoped hid his nerves.

"형save some for me," he laughed, waving at the bartender to get a second shot glass for himself.

"쓰레기," Jung-hyun hissed, glaring at Hwan Soo. His tone was bitter and filled with animosity. Had something happened between him and his mother? Hwan Soo knew she probably still had her issues with him marrying Val. Maybe she had pushed his buttons again.

"형 무슨 일이야?" He put his arm around Jung-hyun in their usual playful way, but Jung-hyun shoved it off quickly. It wasn't his mother he was infuriated with. It was Hwan Soo.

"형—"

"니가 뭔데?" Jung-hyun cut him off, yelling so loudly that the few people in the bar turned toward them.

"According to you, I'm trash." Hwan Soo stepped back from his friend, unsure of what was about to happen.

"Hae So? Really?" Jung-hyun spat.

Hwan Soo's heart sank. Jung-hyun must've seen the articles. To be fair, they were everywhere, and the internet had already latched onto the idea that the two of them were together. Even with both agencies denying the relationship, fans had already started creating couple names.

"What are you talking about?" Hwan Soo needed to know what Jung-hyun saw or heard about the situation.

"You should be glad Maria was in the hospital and didn't see any of it. Well, she hasn't as far as I know." Jung-hyun grabbed the emerald-green bottle back from Hwan Soo, pouring them both shots.

"What do you mean hospital? Why was she in the hospital?" Hwan Soo sat down immediately awaiting the response. His palms had gone clammy, and his heart pulsed at such an alarming rate, he thought it might explode.

"You tell me. You were the last one with her. Why was she found alone passed out in the elevator of Valerie's apartment building? And why in that same time frame were you seen with your freaking ex at your house?" Jung-hyun's voice carried throughout the small bar. The bartender gave them a warning glare.

"형, let me explain." He grabbed Jung-hyun's shoulder, trying to get him to understand. His best friend's glazed-over eyes met his.

"I put Maria in my van to take her back to Val's while I tried to sort out the situation at the party," he explained as he spun his tipped shot glass under his finger. "But Hae So came down and told me that I should just leave and take care of Maria. And that's what I did. I grabbed a cab to Val's and found Maria with Sul Bin. They were hugging, and I nearly decked the guy, I was so furious."

"Sul Bin? What did that bastard want?" Jung-hyun asked.

Hwan Soo was grateful for his friend's patience. No matter how angry Jung-hyun was, Hwan Soo could always count on him to take the time to listen to every side of the story. It was what made him a good businessman as well. Learning all angles before making a decision that could make or break a relationship or a partnership.

"I'm not sure, but they apparently went for coffee and talked. He told her everything. Including the fact that Hae So had hired him to try to figure out the real relationship between Maria and me," he explained.

"장난하냐?" Jung-hyun's eyes widened at the shocking new information.

"Not kidding in the least. But I spilled the fact that I had paid him off at your rehearsal dinner and that your plan to use her backfired because I fell for her. Truly." He admitted it. He came out and said it to her. He might as well tell his friend his true feelings as well.

"I knew you would like her!" Jung-hyun's smile was a drunken, dopey kind of grin, but it eased some of Hwan Soo's nerves. "Valerie knew it too. We conspired before you and I even came up with that plan," Jung-hyun admitted.

"You what?"

"Let's get back to the point." Jung-hyun waved him off. "Why was Maria alone in an elevator, passed out, and rushed to the hospital? And why are you now sleeping with your ex?!" His temper rose again.

"I don't know why she was passed out," Hwan Soo said, exasperated. "She stormed away from me. I wanted to chase after her, but she looked so crushed I couldn't think of anything to say that would make her feel better. I thought she could use some time, and I could try again the next day." Hwan Soo needed a drink to continue the story because even to him it seemed unbelievable. After taking the shot—which burned the whole way down his throat—he continued.

"When I got back to my house, there were dozens of paparazzi blocking the entrance. When I was finally able to push past them all and get into the safety of my yard, who did I see?"

"이런 쌍년," Jung-hyun spat.

"When I saw her, I thought the same thing, but Hae So told me why she came. Netizens had come to my rescue and told the real story of what happened at the event and that Hae So wanted to check how I was doing." Hwan Soo laughed at the crazy turn of events.

"We shared drinks, I told her the truth about Maria and how I am totally head over heels in love with her, and that I messed it all up. Hae So actually told me to man up. Be the lead in my life. We ended up...oddly as friends. The only problem is we got so drunk, she passed out in my house, and that's when everything went to shit." Hwan Soo looked over at Jung-hyun, who had his chin in his hands, watching Hwan Soo as if he were telling a children's story.

"와... So now we don't hate Hae So?" Jung-Hyun questioned, making Hwan Soo laugh again.

"No. We don't hate her anymore." He wrapped his arm around his friend's neck, bringing him into a comfortable side hug.

"Is Maria okay?" Hwan Soo asked, desperate to know.

"I guess. She and Valerie got into a fight, and she stormed out of the hospital. Valerie went back to the apartment, but she wasn't there. She said that's pretty normal after they fight. They need their space but will come back to each other eventually." Jung-hyun poured them more shots ignoring the standard protocol.

While Hwan Soo wanted to enjoy the time with his friend, his heart told him he needed to find Maria and try to fix the damage he had done. And hope to God she hadn't seen anything about him and Hae So before he could explain. But he couldn't leave his buddy, now happily drunk, alone in the bar.

An idea struck. He could get his friend home and find Maria.

"형, let's get out of here. I know somewhere you would much rather be." He pulled Jung-hyun from his stool at the bar, tossed a large wad of money on the counter, and pulled his friend outside to hail a cab to their final destination.

≈

They pulled up to the familiar skyscraper, and Jung-hyun looked out the cab's window in confusion.

"Why are we here? Valerie is probably hashing things out with Maria right now. You really want to be there for that?" Jung-hyun grumbled.

"Sorry, but I need to see Maria." Hwan Soo apologized rather unapologetically. He got out of the cab, pulling Jung-hyun as fast as he could to the elevator.

When they arrived at Val's floor, he wasted no time. Ringing the doorbell and entering the code, Hwan Soo pushed the door open and rushed inside.

"Maria!" he shouted. Running to the kitchen, he found it empty.

"Maria?" he hurried to the living room. No one was in there either.

"She isn't here, Hwan Soo-아." Val's irritated, sleep-laden voice came from the doorway of her bedroom. She rubbed her eyes, adjusting to the light of the living room as she walked toward Hwan Soo.

"여보!" Jung-hyun stumbled into the living room. After seeing his fiancée, he waddled over like a penguin to wrap her in a hug. Her face, which had "pissed off" written all over it, slid into a mask of horror.

"What are you two doing here? I don't have any makeup on and my hair is a mess, Jung-hyun." She playfully slapped his back, begging for him to release her so she could cover her face.

"You're beautiful always. I love seeing your bare face because you don't share it with just anyone, and I am lucky to have seen it many times before. And soon every night for the rest of our lives." He brought his hand to her cheek and kissed her sweetly.

Hwan Soo watched his best friend be the mushiest, loved up version of himself, and for the first time didn't have to fight a cringe. The man who was always so straightlaced and business-focused had become a lovestruck fool. *I want that.* Hwan Soo had felt jealousy before, but usually for people who got roles he wanted. Never in matters of the heart.

Val pushed Jung-hyun away a bit to scowl at Hwan Soo. "Why did you bring Jung-hyun here exactly?"

"I wanted to have a buffer for when I saw Maria," he joked.

"Well, like I said, she isn't here," Val spat. Clearly, she had heard about Hae So, which didn't bode well.

"여보, 괜찮아. It wasn't true. Hae So is apparently a good person now." Jung-hyun shifted behind Val, wrapping his arms around her waist and resting his head on her shoulder.

"Do you know where Maria is?" Hwan Soo asked.

"If I tell you, what are you going to do?" Even while being upset with her best friend, Val stood at the defensive line and guarded her friend's wellbeing.

"I want to tell her that I know everything I did was fucked up. I wish I could take it all back, but I also don't. If we hadn't been thrown together by you two or by the weird disaster that is my ex as my co-star, we wouldn't have found out all the things we did. Like the fact that she loves photography, and it was her dream to become a photographer. Did you know that?" Hwan Soo asked.

Val's eyes went wide. "She told you that?"

"She told me about how she gave up on it. How people convinced her it wouldn't give her a comfortable life. I asked her to shoot me to try to get her out of her shell. She impressed one of the top photographers in Seoul. He offered her an apprenticeship on the spot." Hwan Soo's heart swelled with pride, his eyes brimming with tears, remembering how proud he was when he heard the offer.

"When I heard that, my first thought was, 'She can stay with me. We can work together. We can spend all our time together.' I have probably been in love with your friend since before I even knew it, but I know now. And I have to make this right." Hwan Soo had given a monologue fit for any drama. His hair probably stuck up in every direction from where his hands tugged as he tried to catch his breath, and he was practically wearing a groove in the marble floor from his pacing. The rush of adrenaline from finally letting everything go was enough to make him believe he could solve all the world's problems. But he only needed to solve the one he caused. Maria's pain.

Val's eyes welled with tears, and when he looked to his best friend whose head was still resting on her shoulder, he saw tears in his eyes as well.

An obviously still tipsy Jung-hyun cried out, letting go of his fiancée, and tumbled into Hwan Soo's arms. "That was beautiful, man."

Val quickly stepped up to remove her fiancé from Hwan Soo and looked Hwan Soo dead in the eyes.

"She is not going to forgive you easily, and I'm not sure she saw the whole Hae So thing all over the news. But considering it was all over the internet, I'm sure she has, which only narrows your chances of forgiveness even more," Val explained, trying to keep Jung-hyun from grabbing onto Hwan Soo again.

"Thanks for the pep talk, Val." Hwan Soo had lost all the confidence he had gained during his profession of love.

"But..." she began and the sighed deeply. "She is staying with her mother. I dropped off some of her clothes a little while ago. And if you've heard the stories about her mother—"

"I have been there when they were on the phone together." He cut her off, needing her to explain faster.

"Well in that case, your chances of survival just got higher. A young, handsome suitor coming to win her daughter's love? She will be on your side." Val winked.

"고마워요. Where is she staying?" Hwan Soo excitedly stepped forward, unable to contain his hopeful exuberance.

"It's a hotel a few blocks from here—"

He didn't wait for her to finish before he turned and made for the door.

"I'll text you the address!" she shouted, which made him halt. Val helped him, so he had to help her.

Hwan Soo remembered a random conversation he had with

Maria one day while waiting on set about her plans for Val's bachelorette party and the secret gift she had gotten.

He turned back into the penthouse and rushed into Val's bedroom, looking for Maria's suitcase. He saw it piled in the corner behind a modern-looking parlor chair. Pulling it out, he unzipped it and dug through some of her clothing until he saw the elaborately decorated box.

Putting everything back in place, he walked out and saw that Val had brought Jung-hyun to the couch. He was putting his arms out for her to hug him like a needy child.

Hwan Soo walked over to the lovebirds and held out the dark-pink package with a hot-pink ribbon. Val took it cautiously.

"Maria wanted to give this to you for your wedding night, but this is my way of saying thank you. Jung-hyun waits outside your apartment every time we leave you in the hopes that you will invite him up. He says it's just to make sure you get to your apartment safely, but I can see how much he doesn't want to be separated from you. And that's a good thing considering you're about to get married, but I can tell both of you want more. While I get you're trying to be 'traditional' about this, I can tell you guys both want to act on your desires. She bought that for you to enjoy. So, sober his ass up and enjoy." He grabbed her arm and pecked her on the cheek in thanks. Her eyes went wide.

"Sorry. Saw that in American shows and felt it fit." He shrugged.

She laughed, tears now falling from her eyes as she leaned in and gave him a peck on the cheek as well.

"It did. You're truly a great friend to Jung-hyun, and I would be lucky as hell to have you as my best friend's future whatever. So please go and prove how much you love her because I could tell how much she felt for you and if I am right about it, she loves you just as much."

They bowed to each other and he rushed out of the apartment, out of the building and down the block. He didn't have time to wait for a cab. With the address in hand, he simply continued to run. He needed to see her, and his feet would carry him a lot faster than a cab stuck in traffic.

Korean Vocabulary:

무슨 일이야? - moosun ileeya - what's up?

니가 뭔데? - neega mwondae - who are you?

장난하냐? - jangnanhanya? - are you kidding or is this a joke

이런 쌍년 - eeron ssyang nyeon- that bitch

Chapter 51 (쉰하나)

Hwan Soo arrived at the front of the luxury hotel, not surprised that Jung-hyun would be putting all the out-of-country guests up in such a nice spot. The marble floors, the modern blown-glass chandelier, the leather and crushed velvet couches, and chairs that easily cost more than some people's houses all made the atmosphere suffocating.

Is that what Maria had meant about feeling like a fish out of water? While he had been born into the privilege of being able to afford anything within that lobby, he chose a much less extravagant lifestyle. Yes, he could dine out at amazing places, and yes, he was forced to go to large gala events, but he loved being in his quaint home or on set doing the one thing he enjoyed doing. But he had to admit his lifestyle wasn't normal.

He understood Maria's need to be with Sul Bin. A normal guy who could take her to normal places and do normal things with her, without the worry of her face ending up on the front of a tabloid.

His train of thought ceased when a young woman appeared in front of him bowing politely and asking if she could help him. He bowed, muttering a greeting and tried to move past her, but she got in front of him again.

"I'm going to see someone. I don't need your help. Thank you," he explained.

"I'm not supposed to do this. It is highly unprofessional. But..." She trailed off, bowing again and handing him a piece of paper and a pen.

"싸인 해 주세요?" she whispered.

"네?" He looked down at the paper in shock.

"팬이예요." She looked up from bowing and smiled nervously.

"어. 감사합니다." He dipped his head and quickly signed the paper. She bowed again in gratitude as he walked to the elevator bank. Double-checking the room number Val texted him, he climbed into the elevator and went over everything he wanted and needed to say.

The bell rang, and the elevator halted. When the doors slid open, he stayed frozen in place, not sure he was ready to face her anymore. But as the doors started to close again, he jumped out and followed the signs directing him to the room he needed.

It was like the hall was never-ending. His nerves were catching up to him as the room numbers crept closer to hers. He hadn't had enough time to form a game plan of what he was going to say when she answered the door. He half expected her to slam it in his face, but he had to talk to her. He had to explain everything that happened, everything he was feeling for her. Mustering what bravery he could find to face her, he found himself standing before the right room.

Taking a few deep breaths, he knocked on the black-stained wood door gently. He could hear movement from beyond the threshold but the door stayed closed. When no one opened the door, he knocked again.

It opened slowly to reveal a slightly older version of Maria. Short dark-auburn hair framed a slightly more rounded face. But those same brown-green eyes had dark circles beneath them. Her lips were thinner, but he wasn't sure if that was just because they were pursed while she surveyed him.

"Can I help you?" she asked when he said nothing.

"어...네. Ah. I mean, yes. Hi. I'm—"

"I know who you are, Lee Hwan Soo. I'm asking if I can help you with something." She crossed her arms and tapped her foot. She truly was a future snapshot of Maria.

"I was wondering if I could speak to Maria?" He tried to get a better view into the room, but he could only see the narrow hallway.

"She isn't here." She spoke harshly, but Hwan Soo caught her glance to the side as she said it. He could also make out the sound of water running. Maria was there, but her mother was stopping him from seeing her.

Val must've been mistaken if she thought this woman was going to help Hwan Soo get Maria back.

"Oh. Umm...Val said she was staying with you. If she isn't with you, could you possibly tell me where she is? I really need to talk to her," he explained.

"I would say you sure do, young man." Maria's mother scanned him up and down with a judgmental glare very similar to one his mother would use when she was deciding the level of anger she should be feeling. "My daughter doesn't like to waste time on men. As her mother, I should know. I have set her up on countless dates that never went anywhere. I started to think she hated men in general and wanted to be a spinster." He wanted to tell her he knew exactly what she meant because his mother was the same, but thought better of interrupting.

"But my daughter spent a lot of time on you, Lee Hwan Soo. Not just time, but energy. Working as your assistant, learning your culture, including practicing Korean. I can't say I've seen her do so much for someone she didn't care about." Her eyes started to wonder.

He tried to take a deep breath, but it came in short, pained gasps as he held back his own tears. His hands fisted at his sides, his nails pressing so hard into his palms he was sure he was bleeding, but he didn't feel it. His heart was slowly breaking into pieces as Maria's mother spoke. The small bits of hope he had left were disappearing right before his eyes.

"You seem like a lovely man. You saved her from that scumbag who tried to harm her, and I thank you for that. However, you hurt her and I can't let that slide."

"Ma'am, I can explain everything. Please give me the chance to—" He heard the shower cut off. They both faced the source of the sound. Maria's mother tried to shut the door on him, but he slammed his hand on it to hold it open.

"I love your daughter. I am in love with her. It sounds like such a stupid line, but I never knew what love was until I met her. I thought I did, but I was so stupid and young and nothing compares to how I feel about her. I messed up. Massively. I know that, but I need to explain everything to her. The truth. From start to finish." He pulled away from the door, bringing his hands together in a praying manner, still desperate that he could crack the woman's defensive shell.

Her face pinched as she looked behind her, clearly trying to decide whether or not to let him speak to Maria.

"Please." He begged again, rubbing his hands together.

Before she could respond, there was the loud thunk of the bathroom door handle being pulled and light and steam streamed out.

"Mom, was that the room service we order—" Maria walked out of the bathroom, steam billowing around her bare legs. A towel was wrapped tightly around her body, her cleavage pressed against the towel, her collarbones shimmering with small beads of water, her hair wrapped up with a similar towel. But it was her wide eyes that had Hwan Soo riveted.

He had flashbacks to when he saw her in a similar situation after buying them 짜장면. But while that encounter produced rosy cheeks of embarrassment and wide eyes of surprise, now her eyes told a different story entirely. They were puffy like she had been crying, and her mouth was wide open as she glared at him. He saw the black and blue forming on her hand where he guessed the hospital IV must have been inserted, and his heart tore into millions of pieces.

"Maria," he breathed out her name, just relieved to see her standing in front of him. She said nothing, glancing up and down his body before turning away to stride farther into the room and out of sight.

"Maria! 부탁이야! Give me a chance to explain!" he shouted into the room, wanting to push his way in, but he was prevented by a rather strong mother holding him back.

"I think it's best you leave," her mother said.

"Yeah. You don't want to keep Hae So waiting!" Maria shouted.

"You've got it all wrong. Nothing happened between us! The paparazzi made those accusations, but we both denied them! I wouldn't do that to you, Maria." He heard no response.

"Give her some time," her mother cooed. "I am sure you have somewhere to be right now. You're in very high demand from what all the blogs say." Her mother smiled nervously, trying to shoo him away.

He couldn't leave without talking to her. Face to face, not shouting into a hotel room. So he did what he knew he had to do. He dropped to his knees and bowed his head to the floor.

"I am so sorry, Maria. You have no idea how sorry I am."

"Stand up." Her mother tried pulling him from the hotel hallway floor.

"This is my sincerest apology, Maria. I can't take back any of the dumb shit I did, but I'm happy it all happened. I got to meet you and be with you. That night in the van wasn't just some kiss. It was so much more. I was too afraid to tell you because I didn't know if you felt the same way. I still don't. From your anger, I have the smallest bit of hope that you do. I promise I will never pull any ridiculous stunts like I did before." Hwan Soo choked out his plea as he stayed on his knees, awaiting a response. His chest tightened, and his eyes could no longer hold back the tears. He was desperate, absolutely 110 percent desperate for the woman he loved to simply talk to him.

"Can you let me know when the food comes, Mom?" Maria asked callously.

"Hwan Soo, I really think you should go," her mother begged.

He bowed his head as he heard the click of the door being closed, but he knew he wouldn't be leaving until he was able to talk to Maria. He would wait as long as she needed. He would apologize to Maria no matter what it would take.

And so, he waited.

Korean Vocabulary:

싸인 해 주세요? - ssaeein hae joosayyo - Can I have your autograph?

팬이예요 - paneeyeyo - I'm your fan.

부탁이야 - butakeeya - I'm begging you

Chapter 52 (쉰둘)

Maria awoke to the smell of coffee and the sound of the shower running. She couldn't call what she did sleep. It was more just tossing and turning, trying to rack her brain for how she was going to face Val, Jung-hyun, and at some point before the wedding, Hwan Soo.

She didn't expect to see him at her mother's hotel door the night before. Especially since she had finally told her mother that she thought she might've been in love with him, and he broke her heart. She wasn't ready to face him for a few more days. She needed to resolve her issues with Val first.

Maria sprang up from the bed with a determination to face the day head-on. She would go to Val's apartment so they could talk out their problems like friends should and move on.

"Mom, I'm going to go to Val's for a bit so we can talk. I'll be back before lunch so I can show you around a bit, okay?" Maria shouted to the bathroom door as she tossed on an oversized hoodie and sweatpants. She could actually hear Hwan Soo scolding her for going out looking like that, which made her all the more happy to do it.

Throwing her phone and wallet in the hoodie's front pocket, she pulled open the door and found a figure on his knees, head drooped in slumber at the door.

"깜짝이야." She jumped back into the hotel room, frightened that some drunk idiot had fallen asleep in front of the wrong hotel room.

"야, 비켜줘요." She spoke loud enough for the person to hopefully come to, but when they looked up, she realized the man was no stranger.

"Hwan Soo-아?" She hadn't meant to use his name informally, but seeing him caught her off guard.

His eyes were bloodshot and puffy, lips hung slightly open and chapped.

"Maria?" He stared at her like she was a hallucination. A figment of his imagination.

"What the hell are you doing here? When did you come back?" She scanned the hallway to make sure no one was there to nab another photo of them together before she pulled him into the room.

"I never left." His voice was hoarse, straining to talk as he stretched his legs slowly she could hear his knees crack.

She grabbed one of the bottles of water sitting on the coffee table and handed it to him. He bowed sluggishly, and twisted off the cap before nearly finishing the entire bottle in one go.

While she wanted to avoid him, her heartbeat skipped seeing him again. And while she cursed herself for having that reaction to his presence, she still felt an urge to take care of him and make sure he was going to be okay. Even after everything he told her he did.

But remembering what he'd done sent a fresh stab of betrayal through her chest. Not only had he used her, but he had also manipulated another relationship she could've had for his own selfish gain.

"You've been out there all night?" she asked, watching his Adam's apple bob up and down as he chugged.

He nodded, his cheeks puffed full of water.

"For what reason?" She crossed her arms.

"I need to talk to you. To apologize and tell you how much I—"

"Lee Hwan Soo-씨, you've said what you have to say. And right now, you're not my main concern. What is and what should've been since the day I got here is Val and her happily ever after." Maria hadn't expected to see him so soon, but she needed to be blunt and dissolve her feelings for him quickly.

"I got distracted," she continued. "Your world was new and different. I shouldn't have even met Sul Bin or Hae So, or even Gi Young. Go on with your life as you normally would, and I will finish what I need to here before going back to my own." Her chest felt that undeniable cracking pain as she kept her cool outwardly, but internally she was falling apart. She walked past him—his woodsy scent still strong after sitting in the hallway all night—back to the door pulling it open for him to leave.

"Maria this isn't what I want for us. Please, if you would let me just explain everything..." He grabbed her hand, its warmth still able to send waves of delight through her body.

She pulled away, scowling at him and letting the door close.

"For 'us'? There isn't an us. There never was and never will be. I don't want your explanation. I've been in situations like this more times than I care to admit. 잘 들어. We are going to walk out of here, separately, and I am going to go to Val, you to Jung-hyun. We are going to do our duties as the maid of honor and the best man, and that is the end of this. I don't want to see you again unless it is absolutely necessary." Maria again pulled open the door and tried to push him out just as she heard the shower turn off.

"Honey, were you talking to me? I could swear I heard you saying something," her mother shouted from behind the closed bathroom door.

"She was talking to me, ma'am. Hwan Soo," he answered instead, and Maria glared at him as she pictured cutting his head off.

The door flung open and Maria's mother was wrapped up in the hotel's luxurious bathrobe, her hair hanging and dripping onto the plush cotton.

"Hwan Soo? You came back?" Her mother's eyes lit up like it was a Valentine's Day miracle.

"He never left," Maria grumbled, pushing him toward the door. "But he is leaving now. I will see you later, Mom."

As she pushed him out the door, she was also gently nudged out by her mother. The door then closed on both of them, and she could've sworn there was a glint of amusement in her mother's eye.

"I will take you to Val's," he said coldly. Clearly, he had chosen to heed her words.

"It's okay. I can walk." She started to walk away from him and toward the elevator.

"I never said I was driving. And I also need to go that way to pick up Jung-hyun." He smirked, and she glared at him. Something was up, and her curiosity was getting the best of her.

"His house is in a different direction."

"I have a feeling they're probably together." His smirk turned to a full-on grin, causing her to get suspicious.

"What did you do?" A ding sounded, and a set of the elevator doors slid open.

He walked in, leaned against the back wall, and she was overcome with a sense of déjà vu of their first moments alone together. She could remember the moment he had pinned her against the wall of the elevator trying to prove he was not gay, egging her on to make a move. It infuriated her and now she had a similar distaste for him. Unfortunately, under her anger, her heart still yearned for him.

He pressed the lobby button, the doors closed, and they started their descent. The silence was painful. She wasn't ready to see him so soon. She needed time to heal, even if it was the smallest amount. Being in a confined space where she could feel his eyes constantly flitting over to her, and having to hold her resolve to not do the same to him, was stressful.

"We should probably take a taxi," he said as elevator stopped on the lobby floor.

"Like I said, I would rather walk. I need the fresh air." She scurried out of the elevator the second the doors opened enough for her to squeeze through.

"Maria!" he shouted after her.

But she'd already stopped. Because ahead of her, filling several of the lobby couches and chairs, were men and women with still and video cameras as well as microphones, clearly looking for the one and only Hwan Soo.

"Mar—" She covered his mouth and pushed him back into the elevator. She slammed the "door close" button and they rode back up to give her time to think of what they could do.

He pulled her hand away from his mouth. "What are you doing?"

"There were a bunch of paparazzi out in the lobby. If you yelled at me any more, they would've seen you and come running. No need to ruin your new popularity and relationship. Hae So would be crushed." She spat the last sentence out to emphasize her distaste.

"We are not a thing, if you would let me explain," he countered.

"We don't have time for you to lie to me some more. We need to find a way to get out of here without you being seen." She started to pull at her hoodie strings, picking at the plastic aglet at the end.

"Give me your hoodie," he commanded.

"뭐?" she snapped, covering her chest.

"I can wear it to cover my face since the hood is so large. I can walk out without them even noticing. And whoever told them I was here also knows what I was wearing when I came, but now I'll be wearing something different, so they won't suspect me," he explained. "And I'll give you my shirt and jacket to wear."

While it was a smart plan, there was only one problem.

"I'm not wearing anything under my hoodie," she confessed.

"I've seen you in a towel before. And in your bra and underwear. It isn't anything I haven't seen before." He shrugged.

"I mean nothing, Lee Hwan Soo-씨." Her cheeks heated up, and he blushed to the tips of his ears.

He turned away from her and shrugged his long jacket off. He pulled off his crew neck sweater and handed them both to her with his back still facing her. The soft cotton of his t-shirt stretched across his broad shoulder blades, the muscles of his arms tensed, and the veins bulged on his forearm and hand.

She pulled her eyes away from ogling his body and saw the elevator still had time to climb. She pulled her hoodie off, tossed it onto his head and tugged his sweater on. If she thought being near his woodsy scent was a problem, having it envelop her in his clothing was a nuclear meltdown. Before he turned back toward her, she took a small sniff, enjoying how good it smelled.

"고마워." He turned around as he pulled the hood over his hair.

"I didn't really have another option. I'll get off when the elevator stops on the twentieth floor. You take it back down, and I will catch the next elevator." She threw his jacket over her shoulder as the door dinged their arrival.

She walked out but before the doors closed, she fished out the mask she had in her sweatpants pocket.

"You're probably gonna need this more than me." She tossed the black mask to him, and as he caught it with an appreciative smile, the doors closed.

She leaned on the wall to catch her breath. She had survived her first extended period with Hwan Soo after the fallout, and she didn't cry. Sure, she was on the verge of tears when the elevator doors closed, but she took several deep breaths, collected herself and soon made her own exit from the building. The paparazzi still sat on the couches showing no sense of urgency, letting her know Hwan Soo had made it out unnoticed.

Maria opened the front door of Val's apartment to see a pair of male shoes. Not surprising since Jung-hyun would come by to pick Val up for whatever wedding plans they had that day. What was surprising was there was no scent of breakfast being made in the kitchen, no sounds of chatting in the living room.

She walked into the apartment, and the place was overturned.

The stools at the kitchen counter were all pushed around, most of the appliances that were on top of the counter were either toppled over or on the floor. As she made her way toward the living room, her breathing grew erratic and her stomach dropped.

The living room was in shambles. Pillows and blankets were tossed all over the floor, the coffee table had been knocked over, and all the books and remotes were in a messy pile on the floor.

Could someone have broken in?

Oh no! The closet! The amount of designer clothes in there would make a robber scream that they hit the jackpot.

Maria quickly walked over to the bedroom door, where she heard some odd shuffling and moving around.

Oh shit! They're still in the apartment.

She surveyed the area for some sort of weapon, grabbing the closest thing to her, a large vase. Psyching herself up, ready to destroy whoever was trying to steal her best friends' stuff, she ripped open the door.

"Ahhhhh!" she screamed, trying to scare them, but what she beheld was not a burglar. Rather her friend and her friend's fiancé were naked, in some rather wild position on the side of the bed.

"Ahhhhh!" all three of them shrieked before Maria closed her eyes and felt her way out of the room.

The three of them sat awkwardly on the couch unsure of how to start the conversation. Val's hair was untamed, and Jung-hyun's was in a similar state of shambles. Maria couldn't stop herself from laughing at the sight. She was happy Val had decided to take that step in their relationship and not follow everything his family wanted.

Soon all three of them were laughing at the hilarity of getting caught doing the nasty by Val's best friend and then trying to skirt the subject.

"We have you and Hwan Soo-아 to thank for...eh-hem...this," Val laughed as she looked around the torn apart penthouse.

"How?" Maria asked.

"Well, you bought the lingerie set. Hwan Soo said you were waiting to give it to me for my bachelorette party gift but since I had helped him find you, he would help me. I don't know what came over me, but the second I saw what you bought, I put it on and showed it off to Jung-hyun and we've been—"

"I see what you've been up to." Maria stopped her friend politely. She already had the image of them going at it like rabbits forever imprinted in her head.

"Right." Val chuckled before continuing, "How did it go with Hwan Soo?"

"What do you mean?" Maria didn't want to talk about him at the moment. She wanted to apologize to Val about how she reacted in the hospital.

"Well, he came to see you last night, didn't he? What did he say? Are you guys, I don't know, good now?" Val shrugged as she tried to put her hair back into some kind of order.

"He did show up at the hotel room last night, but I had nothing to say to him." Maria leaned back on the couch, frustrated she had to have this conversation.

"Is that why you're wearing his sweater and his jacket is in the foyer?" Jung-hyun interjected.

Val's eyes went wide as she inspected her friend.

"He came to the hotel room. I ignored him, and he proceeded to kneel in front of my mother's door the whole night," Maria explained. "When I started leaving the room to come here, he was still there. Paparazzi found out he was in the hotel so we switched clothing so he could leave without causing a scene. I'm not about to be caught in another ridiculous scandal."

"And throughout that entire thing, he didn't tell you anything important?" Val was probing for an answer she wasn't going to get.

"We barely spoke. I'm not interested in what excuses he makes for his actions. And besides that, whatever happened between us is done and over. I came here for you and your wedding to the man you love. I shouldn't be getting mixed up in my own dumb crap. I am here for you, and I'm sorry for getting mad when all you were trying to do was be a good friend." Maria sat back up as she apologize.

"I'm sorry too, Mari. I never should've gone behind your back to set you up with Hwan Soo. You should've found out for yourself what an amazing guy he is. And that he's totally hooked on you and wants to give you the world." Val's backhanded apology made Maria roll her eyes.

"But I'm also sorry for not telling you exactly what was going on between Jung-hyun and me in the beginning," Val continued. "I was embarrassed when it all started. How could I tell you that I was getting paid to be his girlfriend? I felt horrible for doing it, but because I needed the money for my future, I was willing to. Luckily, we fell in love on the way." Val moved from her seat on the couch to sit beside Maria.

"I'm sorry you felt like you couldn't tell me. I never want you to feel like that. So please, in the future, if your soon-to-be husband tries to pay you off again, let me know," Maria joked as she pulled her friend into a tight hug. Val squeezed tightly, and they held each other for a little while longer.

"I'm glad you guys were able to work this all out. You're amazing friends," Jung-hyun chimed in from cleaning up the sex mess they'd made in the kitchen.

"Me too," Val whispered into Maria's ear.

"Damn straight. Also, once he is gone, you better give me details on why this apartment looked like it had been ransacked because you guys were doing the freaky deaky," Maria whispered back, and they both chuckled in their embrace.

∾

Hwan Soo had seen everything in the elevator. He hadn't meant to but when he turned around to give her privacy, he saw her reflection in a mirror in the top corner. Before he could say anything, Maria had pulled her hoodie over her head, and he couldn't take his eyes off her. He saw the soft skin he had remembered stroking in his van, and he imagined feeling her body again. His palms started to get clammy, his heart pumped blood to his lower extremity, which would only cause more problems for him if she were to notice.

He was happy the oversized hoodie she tossed him was large enough to cover just below his belt to keep his excitement out of view.

He knew it was wrong to look, to think what he was thinking at such a time, but he knew what was going to happen once they left that elevator, and he worried that he couldn't fix what he had broken, so he indulged himself. When he caught her taking in a small whiff from his sweater collar, he held out hope he could fix their relationship.

After she threw the mask to him and the doors closed, he felt like he could breathe easier. Only because he wasn't having to hold everything in.

When the elevator doors opened on the lobby floor, he walked out, casually passing the paparazzi who were paying more attention to their phones than to what was around them. He held in a chuckle when he saw his picture being zoomed in on by one of the reporters who hadn't even noticed him pass by.

Once outside, he strolled down the block with no destination in mind. As much as he wanted to, he wouldn't go to Val's. Maria was not going to want to see him again until necessary and maybe if he gave her that space, he could finally tell her everything. Even if it would lead to nothing more than an accepted apology.

He had watched her as the doors closed on the elevator. Her eyes filled with pain he had caused, her hands pulling at the cuffs of his sweater uncomfortably. And her sigh of relief when they were finally apart. He hated himself more after seeing her in such a state.

With his own deep resigned sigh he concluded he was going to give up on love for good. He had said that after Hae So, but he realized that had never been love. It was naivety and lust.

Maria was love. And he was going to have to give her up. He had hurt her, like other men had done before. He had no intention of doing so, but in the end, he was no better than the rest.

한잔 하고 싶어.

He looked for the closest bar and as luck would have it, the building he had been walking toward was advertising its "magnificent" rooftop bar.

The day of the wedding was fast approaching. Only four days left until Hwan Soo's most trusted confidant got wifed-up. Jung-hyun and Val had made all sorts of plans to keep Hwan Soo and Maria separated for the time being. He could tell it was at Maria's request, and he accepted it.

Of course, every night after they wrapped up shooting, he would hit the closest bar, get drunk enough to try and drunk text her, but inevitably his phone would be taken away by his manager. Gi Young had made it impossible for Hwan Soo to unlock his phone if drunk after the third time he had been called to pick up Hwan Soo from a bar by the servers.

Luckily, there was an excuse to get drunk on one special day leading up to the wedding: the bachelor party.

Hwan Soo had called on a few of Jung-hyun's friends. Since they all had social standing, Hwan Soo chose to start the night off at a small hole-in-the-wall barbecue spot where they wouldn't be recognized. As they drank, one of the friends mentioned a local "members only" club that he happened to be a part of and said he could get them all in.

Hwan Soo didn't like the sound of the club. It didn't sit right with him that a lot of the other men grinned devilishly when the club was mentioned, but Jung-hyun seemed naive to what could possibly be in store. To Hwan Soo, it sounded like trouble.

When they arrived, Hwan Soo's worries were confirmed. It wasn't the kind of "members only" club where one sat in an upscale bar with expensive furnishings, lavish decorations, and high-end liquors brought to the table by the bottle. It was the kind of club where women would not just serve drinks, but also offer their company—for a price, of course.

They were brought to a soundproof room with gaudy gold and crimson wallpaper, dimly lit crystal chandeliers, a table filled with bottles of every kind of booze one could want, and a leather U-shaped booth—Hwan Soo didn't want to think about what had been done on it. Rounding out the aesthetic was a large TV on one wall with microphones set up on the floor near it to better play off this farce of a boys' karaoke night. Normally Hwan Soo wouldn't be bothered by the fact that the second the pretty young lady shut the door to their private room, creating dead silence in the room, but knowing what happens in these rooms made a disgusted shiver run down his spine.

"얘들아!" Jung-hyun's "friend" who had the idea to come to such a place called for their attention. He had that arrogant, rich, dipshit vibe Hwan Soo had seen in dramas but had always avoided in real life. How he was one of Jung-hyun's friends confused Hwan Soo. He couldn't even remember a time Jung-hyun had brought him up in a conversation.

"To one of the last nights our little Jung-hyun-이 is a single man. Let's make sure he doesn't forget it!" The guy grabbed one of the bottles of champagne off the table and ripped the cork out with a loud pop. The whole party cheered except for Hwan Soo and Jung-hyun, who exchanged nervous smiles.

The drinks flowed, shot after shot, beer after beer. The men all took turns on the karaoke machine, and Hwan Soo thought he might've mistaken their intentions about why they had been brought to the club.

That was until Hwan Soo caught the piece of shit pressing a

button on the intercom by the door. Within minutes, a harem of women walked in, scantily dressed with devious eyes hunting for their prey.

"형, I really don't think this is a good idea," Hwan Soo whispered to Jung-hyun, whose face bored a similar discomfort to his own.

"I agree, but how the hell do we get out of here?" he asked, sounding slightly panicked.

"Let me think. Let me think." Hwan Soo looked at all the other men becoming easily distracted by the women pouring them drinks, either into a glass or straight into their mouths.

These men are disgusting.

"Remind me never to do business with these men again," Jung-hyun spat.

"Business? These aren't your friends from America?" Hwan Soo's head snapped to his friend, toward whom a very friendly woman was now inching closer and closer.

"안돼! You are my only friend. But since you insisted on throwing me a party and these guys had come into town early for the wedding —my mother's demand, not mine—I chose to invite them. Clearly that was not the right call." Jung-hyun explained as he repeatedly pushed the woman's roaming hands off of him.

"Oh, the future husband is a little shy!" One of the men, who had become even more intoxicated, stumbled toward Jung-hyun.

"Come on! Let the girl give you a drink." He plopped hard into the small space between Hwan Soo and Jung-hyun.

"I'm really not interested in—"

"한잔 더! 한잔 더! 한잔 더!" Soon all the men in the group were chanting for Jung-hyun to take a shot from the woman at his side.

Hwan Soo rose from his seat, ready to tell them all to shut up, but before he could say a word, loud cheers erupted from the group. He turned to see the woman pouring a drink directly into Jung-hyun's mouth, her chest pressed against his arm so hard, her breasts engulfed it.

Jung-hyun bowed his head in thanks to the young woman, but

she took it as the go-ahead to feed him more. Hwan Soo took a step toward them, but one of the young ladies stepped in front of him.

She was in a tight purple dress that hugged her curves while forcing her breasts to spill out the top. Her heels were tall stilettos on which she teetered like a man on a tightrope. He was about to push her away when she pressed her body against his.

"I know you," she whispered as she played with the collar of his button-up shirt, her fingers skimming his neck.

"Great. If you'll excuse me..." He grabbed her hand, angered she had laid a finger on him. Not because of her profession, but because he didn't want any woman but Maria to ever touch him in that way.

"I can help you get your friend out of here," she said, piquing his interest. "Follow my lead." She winked as she grabbed his hand.

"All right, boys," she said, drawing everyone's attention to her, "your friend over here asked for me to give the future husband some special treatment."

She swayed over to Jung-hyun, whose eyes had glazed over from the drinks the woman, still pressed against him, was funneling down his throat. The men started cheering, and one even came over to pat Hwan Soo on the back for his "great gift".

The young woman pulled on Jung-hyun's hand while the other girl stood to follow. Hwan Soo stepped in, separating her from his friend and took the shot she offered.

As they tried to exit the room, one of the men stopped Hwan Soo. "Why are you going along?"

Before he could answer, the young woman stepped between them, her chest pressed against Hwan Soo. She turned her head as she said over her shoulder, "Two men are better than one."

She winked, and the men became even more rowdy at her proposition. Hwan Soo wanted to punch each and every one of them in the face for how vile they all were.

Once out of the room, he felt a small amount of relief. Jung-hyun kept mumbling that he wanted one more drink, even though he couldn't keep his eyes open, and Hwan Soo and the girl had to hold him upright.

"많이 취했네. 더 이상 마시지마," Hwan Soo said.

She brought them to the elevator bank, continuing to help Hwan Soo support Jung-hyun. Leaning against the cool metal on the back of the elevator, Jung-hyun's head fell onto Hwan Soo's shoulder and he let out a slight snore.

"어떡하지?" he asked, trying to keep his breathing steady and hide how exhausted he was from pulling his buddy along. Meanwhile, she hadn't even broken a sweat.

"I can walk you guys out the front door. That's as far as I can go," she explained.

"I appreciate this. Truly," he responded.

"I saw how uncomfortable you two were. Most of the men who come here don't look like that. I also recognized you from a drama I watched," she said, blushing. "I've seen other actors here, but your face is the only sincere one I've encountered. I will definitely support you." She laughed, but behind the laugh he could tell she had trauma. She was a beautiful woman and clearly clever enough to get out of sticky situations.

The elevator came to a stop, the doors opened, and she helped steady Jung-hyun to get them out of the building. Once out onto the street, Hwan Soo inhaled the city air and felt the relief fill his body. She released Jung-hyun and stood upright, fixing the straps of her dress.

"감사합니다." He bowed his head to thank her. "I wish there was more I could do to thank you." He smiled warmly at her.

"같이 자 자구." She reached out to grab his collar like she had in the club.

He tried to step away, but holding his drunk, sleepy friend made it hard for him. Instead, he brushed her hand off him, and she laughed.

"I just wanted to see if you really were the nice guy I thought."

She pouted, looking disappointed that he didn't take her up on her offer. She reached up again to pick a loose thread off his shirt.

She leaned up to peck him on the cheek and walked back into the club. He smiled at her, wondering how such a nice woman could end up in such a rough kind of job.

"자기야," Jung-hyun mumbled out.

"I'm Hwan Soo, not your fiancée." Hwan Soo chuckled at his drunk friend as he became more like dead weight.

"여보!" a female voice shouted nearby. Normally Hwan Soo would ignore it. The area was known for drunk people being belligerent. However, the voice was familiar. Looking around, his eyes landed on the culprit.

"Val?"

Korean Vocabulary:

깜짝이야 -kamjakeeya - you scared me

비켜줘요 -peeyojwoyo - move

한잔 하고 싶어 - I need a drink

얘들아 - yaydula - everyone

한잔 더 - hanjan do - one more drink

많이 취했네. 더 이상 마시지마 -manhi chwihaessnae. do eesab masheechi ma - you drank a lot. you don't need anymore

같이 자 자구 - gatchi ja jagu - let's sleep together

Chapter 53 (쉰셋)

Maria hoped her eyes were playing tricks on her. She wanted to blame the alcohol, but she had barely drunk so she could keep an eye on Val, who had established a habit of running off drunk where no one could find her.

"Is that Jung-hyun and Hwan Soo?" Tina asked, Val's old boss and current aid to keeping Val standing as they walked down the street.

"Looks like it," Maria grumbled as Tina, who had one of Val's arms wrapped around her neck, tried to pull them toward the men Maria desperately wanted to avoid.

Hwan Soo was dressed in a loose button-up, one piece of the front half tucked into his dark jeans while the other hung freely billowing in the night breeze. His collarbones one of Maria's favorite places to look on his chest, protruded from the opened shirt collar.

"Ugh, if I were just a few years younger...I would climb Hwan Soo like a tree. I mean, his brother is sexy as well, but there is something about Hwan Soo. Maybe it's his lips," Tina fantasized while Maria internally screamed for her to shut up.

Tina was the dream most younger women had when they

thought of aging gracefully. Long, slender legs, an hourglass figure, and a face that was as youthful as a twenty-something, Tina probably could land a man like Hwan Soo without even trying.

"Funny meeting you here." Tina bowed as they neared the guys, causing Val and Maria, who had Val's other arm around her neck, to bow as well.

Hwan Soo returned a similar bow with his drunken compatriot.

When Tina glanced up to the building the men had exited, her eyebrow rose inquisitively.

"What were you men doing in a place like this?" Tina probed, and Hwan Soo's increasingly widening eyes scanned the vicinity.

Maria surveyed the storefront and thought it looked rather boring. The entrance was discreet with the name in vinyl on the door indicating it was some sort of club. Maria couldn't make anything of the floors above the entrance. Looking up to the several floors it encompassed, she couldn't see much of anything. The windows were blacked out and signage for other businesses in the building covered the exterior.

"It wasn't by choice, I can tell you that." Hwan Soo smirked at Tina, laying on the charm.

"What kind of place is this exactly?" Maria questioned.

"You don't want to know." Hwan Soo's voice was calm, but there was a sense of pleading not to further the line of questioning.

She wanted to continue, like when they first started hanging around each other, but Tina interjected.

"Well since we've all met up, how about we get some food in these lovebirds' stomachs to help them sober up a bit? I know I could use some 닭꼬치 and every type of 튀김 a stall has to offer. 콜?"

Even in their drunken states, Val and Jung-hyun lifted their heads with dazed smiles and shouted, "콜!"

The five of them sat at one of the metal-top tables, on short, hard plastic chairs, with a stack of different types of 튀김 and 닭꼬치. Maria nervously picked up one of the sticks, where a long battered and deep fried item was hanging at the end.

"It's 고추 튀김," Hwan Soo leaned over and whispered, his lips accidently skimming the shell of her ear.

She worked to suppress a shiver as his breath traipsed down her neck, but her heart took control of her reactions and she moved involuntarily.

"You'll like it, I promise," he whispered. Again, his lips brushed her ear.

Finally getting hold of herself, Maria shuffled her little plastic stool away from him a bit and examined him with a hint of annoyance.

"I don't need your opinion of whether I will like it or not. Maybe look after Jung-hyun, who is about to face plant into the table." She gestured to their drunk friend, whose head was dropping slowly to the table.

Hwan Soo immediately caught Jung-hyun, who awoke with a bright smile on his face.

"Aww," his half-lidded eyes swung between Maria and Hwan Soo, "you two are talking again! Finally!"

"형, shhh," Hwan Soo said.

"They're the cutest!" Val's head sprang up from its slumped position on Tina's shoulder.

"They should get married next!" Jung-hyun grabbed one of the skewers from the center of the table and brandished it like a sword. Val grabbed a skewer as well, meeting his in the middle of the table.

"They're not wrong," Tina giggled. "You two would make a very cute couple. That's coming from the woman who saw the potential in Val and Jung-hyun when they started dating."

Hwan Soo grabbed Jung-hyun's arm while Maria grabbed Val's, bringing the skewers back down to the table. Maria could cut the tension that had built with a knife. She peeked over at Hwan Soo and in the bright lights of the tent, she saw something on his cheek that made her stomach churn, her blood boil, and her brain run wild. She imagined shoving his face into the tray of boiling 떡볶이 sauce.

"You got some lipstick on your cheek," she said coldly.

"Huh?" He rubbed at one of his cheeks.

"Other one, Hwan Soo." Tina pointed to the other cheek with a devious smile. She crossed her arms and leaned forward onto the table. "Are you sure I had the wrong idea about what you boys were up to?"

"Yes, Tina. I can assure you that nothing happened." He began to rub his other cheek. "One of the women helped Jung-hyun and me escape. I didn't even plan to go there. His 'friend' forced us to go. Sick 'friends,'" Hwan Soo spat.

"What was that place?" Maria asked again.

"A place where men go to spend some time with female company." Tina smirked.

Hwan Soo's eyes bulged as he stared at Tina before turning to explain to Maria, who quickly dipped her head down to focus on her food.

"Maria, I swear it was not my idea to go there." His hands came into her view and encompassed hers. Her heart clenched at the warmth of his fingers engulfing hers. A few days ago, she would be over the moon that he was holding her hands so gently.

"You said that already." She pulled her hand out from his and lifted her head to see all eyes, including two pairs of half-lidded drunken ones watching them.

"Honestly, Maria, neither of us wanted to be there," Jung-hyun explained. "The guys we went with are scummy. I only invited them because they were business partners and my mother insisted." He was surprisingly eloquent for an inebriated person.

"Ugh. Your mother?" Val rolled her eyes dramatically. "Of course she would invite those douchey dudes from San Fran."

"Right? I mean, I knew they weren't my type of people outside of work, but after what I saw tonight, I will no longer be doing business with them either." Jung-hyun started to eat a lot more of the food that was sprawled on the table. Val happily reached over the table to feed him.

"많이 먹어." Tina pushed more food toward the couple feeding one another while Maria and Hwan Soo sat in silence.

The parties finally parted ways at almost three o'clock in the morning, and Maria heaved a sigh of relief when the three women walked through the door of Val's penthouse apartment. Her feet ached from walking in heels; her body was physically exhausted from carrying Val and she was mentally exhausted from picturing Hwan Soo with a "lady of the night".

Once Val was tucked into bed, Tina and Maria walked to the living room to destress and scanned the large panoramic windows overlooking the Seoul skyline.

"You and Hwan Soo, huh?" Tina asked as she settled into the couch.

"Excuse me?" Maria exclaimed.

"Don't play dumb, Maria. It's unbecoming," Tina scolded, sounding eerily similar to her mother.

"We weren't anything, really." Maria stared at her hands, fingers picking at her cuticles.

"But there was something there," Tina pushed. "I could tell by the way you both watched each other. He hurt you." She scooted closer to Maria on the couch.

Taking an unsteady breath, Maria nodded as tears filled her eyes.

"He's sorry for whatever happened. I could see he is just as heart-broken as you are." Tina said softly. "But he's hurt because he hurt you and is desperate to make it up to you. You should give him that chance."

"I thought you were an interior designer, not a therapist." Maria tried to lighten the tension while swiftly wiping away the tears before they fell. Tina sighed, clearly not having Maria's obvious attempt at trying to change the subject.

"It's not worth it," Maria said hopelessly. "I leave in less than a week. After Val and Jung-hyun are married, I board a plane and leave this whole place behind. That includes Hwan Soo." She sank farther into the couch, wishing it could just swallow her whole.

"And that's a reason not to accept his apology?" Tina asked. "Your best friend and his are about to be tied together forever, doesn't that mean you will be too?"

She had a point. Maria might be leaving after the wedding, but that didn't mean she was never going to visit Val. Which meant getting together with Jung-hyun and his friends.

"All I'm saying is, that boy is hurting too, and I think the best thing for both of you is to talk and lay everything out," Tina explained.

"You want me to tell him I'm in love with hi—" Maria stopped short when Tina's eyes widened and her jaw dropped open.

But Tina's eyes weren't on Maria.

Maria turned to find Val leaning unsteadily on the couch with the widest smile on her face.

"I knew it!" Val cried. "You love him. And he loves you. Hwan Soo may not have told me, but he told your mother. She texted me the night he came to her hotel room. He professed his love for you and said he wanted to fix what he did." Val walked around to take a seat on the couch. "And to be honest, if you can forgive me for all the dumb shit I've done, why can't you forgive him for what he's done?" Val put her arm around Maria.

Maria glanced between the two women who were trying to help her solve her relationship problem. She gave a resigned sigh and grabbed her phone. The wild smile on Val's lips and Tina's knowing smirk pushed Maria to make a move she hadn't expected to make.

The two women leaned over Maria's shoulders as she typed.

Maria: 애기 좀 하자. 잠깐이면 돼.

"Ohhh. 한국말 잘하신다," Tina praised.

"What are you gonna say to him?" Val asked.

"I'll know when I see him." Maria nervously stared at the phone waiting for a response. The three dots popped up, dancing in the bubble as he typed a response. But the bubble disappeared.

The three of them grumbled, losing hope. But as Maria was about to toss her phone on the coffee table and pretend nothing happened, it began to ring loudly.

The women huddled together to see the name lighting up the screen.

HWAN SOO

Taking a deep breath, Maria swiped to answer. Before she could speak, she heard the voice of someone unexpected.

"Hey Maria, it's Hae So. DON'T HANG UP! Hwan Soo's manager asked me to help him bring Hwan Soo home. Apparently, he got really drunk and all he's been doing since we got him home is ask for you. Can you get over here? He's your problem, not mine. Honestly, why did Gi Young ask me to come and not you? 짜증나." Hae So sounded frustrated.

"We just saw him a little while ago, and he was sober," Maria said.

"Well since you haven't been on set this last week, I'd at least think Gi Young would've told you," Hae So groaned, sounding annoyed that she had to explain. "Hwan Soo has been getting pretty drunk almost every night after filming. Gi Young has had to follow him around and take his phone most nights. Now that I think about it, it started when you stopped coming to the set."

"야! Whatever you did, get over here and fix this!" Hae So shrieked, making Maria pull the phone away from her ear.

The line went dead, and she glanced at the women, who were anxiously waiting to hear what happened.

"I need to talk to him, right?" She needed a small pep talk before making her final decision.

They both eagerly nodded.

"Well then." She got up from the couch and headed toward the bedroom, neither woman saying anything. She popped her head out from the doorway to see them whispering to each other.

"You guys gonna help me pick an outfit that says 'We need to talk', but also 'I'm not trying hard for you to notice me but notice me?'" she asked.

The women smiled, jumping from the couch to help Maria.

~

Maria stood at Hwan Soo's gate, surprised there was no paparazzi camping out like they were only a week ago. She called his phone again, and Gi Young answered.

"Maria? 괜찮아요?" His voice was filled with worry. She had missed him the last few days. They had bonded during their van rides, breaks in filming, and generally running around together ensuring Hwan Soo had everything he needed.

"네. I'm actually outside Hwan Soo's right now," she whispered in case any crazy fan or photographer was hiding in the vicinity. "Do you think you could let me in?"

"You're what?" She could hear him holler from inside Hwan Soo's house.

There was a loud buzz, and she pulled open the metal gate within the fence. Once on the property, she watched Gi Young rip open the front door, his face awash with disbelief and hope. His shoulders dropped with a massive exhale as he took large steps toward her.

"You're really here." Before she could say anything, he wrapped her in a strong hug that crushed the air from her lungs.

"네. 왔어," she strained out with what little air she had left.

He released her from his death-grip hug, and she saw he had tears in his eyes.

"울지마." She laughed at his dramatics.

"I'm just really happy you're here. Why exactly are you here?" he asked.

"I wanted to talk to Hwan Soo. I texted him, and Hae So called, telling me to come over and take care of him because it wasn't her job." Maria laughed at the ridiculousness of the situation. "Which begs me to ask, is he really that drunk? We literally only parted ways a couple of hours ago."

"That's all it takes for him now. In fact, it usually only takes about an hour for him to get belligerent. I've had to make his phone impossible to unlock so he doesn't try to call you all the time." Gi Young sounded so deflated. And when Maria took a good look at his face, the dark bags under his eyes and scratching at what looked like a stress rash on his neck showed his concern not only for his client but his friend.

"You go home and rest, Gi Young, I will take it from here." She patted his shoulder and was instantly wrapped in another strong hug.

"고마워!" he exclaimed once letting her go. "He has a shoot tomorrow. His last one before the wedding, so he needs to be there. I will be here around noon to pick him up. Please, please, please make sure he is sober and functioning. I have faith in you." Gi Young gave her a hard pat on the back and ran down the walkway and out of the property.

Taking a deep breath, she entered the very house she had been actively avoiding. The smell of alcohol slapped her in the face the second she opened the door, and she could hear loud moans coming from the living room. She kicked her shoes off and made her way quickly to the pained noises.

Every liquor imaginable littered the coffee table and kitchen counter. Most were empty and collecting dust, but as Maria crossed the room one was snatched from the coffee table by the hands of none other than Hwan Soo.

"No, no, no, no, no more alcohol for you." She ripped the bottle out of his hand.

"야!" he shouted. When his head lifted and his glassy eyes met hers, his furrowed brows rose with surprise.

"What are you doing here? You shouldn't be here. You hate me."

He let out small hiccups in between several of his slurred words, but she got the picture.

"I don't hate you." Maria started to pick up all the bottles around him so that he wouldn't get any more ideas to drink.

"You do." He let out a girly giggle. "You really do. I deserve it though. 미안해. You should go home. I'll be alright." He bowed his head but fell right onto the cushion of the couch.

"I am not leaving you," Maria huffed. "I'm here because everyone else is stressed and annoyed having to babysit you after your benders." She started to fill a trash bag with all the empty liquor bottles.

When she came back to his slumped body on the couch, she crouched down and saw he was still awake, staring at nothing. But when his eyes refocused on her, a soft smile spread across his face.

He struggled to pull his arm out from under him and sit up, but once free, he cupped her cheek. She froze as his warm hand caressed her face. Her eyes met his, and she watched a tear fall from his eye and roll over the bridge of his nose before dropping onto the couch cushion.

"I really fucked up, losing a girl like you," he mumbled dejectedly, his thumb rubbing her cheekbone.

"Hwan Soo-씨..."

"Please," he begged. "Please call me Hwan Soo-아."

More tears welled in his eyes, and Maria could feel eyes doing the same. She couldn't deny his request. He was drunk and most likely wouldn't remember this when he woke up anyway.

"Hwan Soo-아," she whispered, her voice gravelly with unshed tears. His eyes lit from within and his hand on her cheek pressed more firmly against her skin.

"Hwan Soo-아, you need to stop all this drinking," she gently reprimanded "Everyone is worried about you. How did you get like this? I saw you a little while ago."

"And you saw that stupid lipstick," he grumbled. "I swear nothing happened. I hated her touching me. All I could think about was how

I only want you to touch me. And I went and fucked that up." She noticed that his language always turned foul when he had too much to drink. It made him seem so human.

His hand started to fall from her face, but Maria couldn't bear to lose the warmth it had brought. She grabbed his hand to keep it against her cheek. Unshed tears clogged her throat as she stared at his pained face. She tried to take a full unwavering breath before she spoke.

"Hwan Soo-아, we should talk about this when you're sober. When you'll remember what you're saying. You're drunk right now, and I have a lot I want to say and I want to make sure you remember—"

"사랑해."

She lost her balance for a second as her breath caught in the back of her throat. She could've been hearing him wrong. But he was drunk. He could just be telling her what he thought she wanted to hear. And oh man, did she want to hear him say that. Hell, she felt the same way. But he could've just been saying it to try to make amends, and he would most likely forget they had this conversation.

"I really do, Maria. That night...the night that ruined everything, I was coming to see you and tell you how I felt. How that kiss in the van changed everything for me. I had fallen for you before that but..." He trailed off and gently tried to pull her closer with his hand that she was holding on her cheek. She could feel his breath on her face, the scent of alcohol tickling her nose just before the tip of his nose brushed hers, sending a well-known shiver of pleasure down her spine.

She felt herself yield.

"사랑해, Maria." He said it again before his eyes slid closed, and he fell asleep.

She watched him slump onto the couch, his lips hung open, his breathing steadily evening out into a snore. His hair fell into his face, and his nose crinkled adorably from the strand tickling him. She smiled, remembering when he had drunkenly passed out in her lap at the barbecue place and refused to let anyone else touch her.

She brought the hand she had been holding to her cheek back down to rest on the couch and reached over to brush the hair out of his face. As her finger skimmed his forehead, he lazily opened his eyes to meet hers. She swallowed hard and turned away, glancing everywhere around the room to avoid his stare, but his hand on her wrist brought her attention right to him.

He sat up, rather steadily for someone who was barely able to keep himself upright only a few minutes ago, and stood, pulling her up with him. He wobbled for a second, but once he got his bearings, he led them toward his room.

"Hwan Soo-아." She pulled her hand from his, attempting to hold him back from what he was trying to do.

"We need a good night's sleep if I'm going to be able to work." He didn't turn back to face her, but he didn't take another step toward the door, waiting for her response.

She took a step forward, easing the tension from him holding her wrist, and he continued into the hall.

Maria had slept in the same bed as several men before, but Hwan Soo was vastly different from them. Her heart raced every time she saw him, his touch sent an electric current through her body, and when they got to know each other she realized how in love with him she was. She wanted to tell him. She would've if he hadn't been so inebriated when she got to his house.

He pushed open the door, the warm dim light from his bedside lamp and the scent of his cologne had her mind racing. He released her hand to walk around to one side of the bed and climb under the covers. She went to the opposite side and climbed in as well, trying to calm herself from feeling the warmth of his body radiating next to her. She forced her hands to hold each other to keep her urge to touch him in check. Like a movie montage, her mind replayed him saying that he loved her over everything they had been through. And more intimately she heard him saying 사랑해 over the memory of his lips

434

on her neck as their hands explored each other during their one interlude.

"You were right about this blanket. It is like sleeping on a cloud." He turned his head to study her with a sweet but sad smile.

She ran her hand along the comforter and smiled.

"Oh yeah. This comforter is amazing." She laughed, snuggling in more comfortably and smiling back at him.

"키스해도 돼?" he whispered nervously.

She gaped at him, her cheeks flushing red at the thought of them kissing again. Her plan in the beginning was to sit and talk everything out with him. Lay her feelings out on the table with the hopes that maybe they could come to some kind of understanding. Instead, she got a drunk who professed his love and had just asked if he could kiss her. And while her heart was screaming to let him...

"I don't think that's a smart idea, Hwan Soo-아."

"Right, right. You're right. That was dumb of me to ask." He turned away from her and flicked his bedside table lamp off, plummeting them into darkness.

Her eyes adjusted and his garden window allowed in just enough light from the city outside for her to see his breathing was even. He had fallen asleep immediately.

"If you asked me when you were sober, I would've said yes," she whispered to herself with a hope that maybe he would hear it and remember the next morning.

Korean Vocabulary:

고추 튀김 - gochu twigum - fried hot pepper

많이 먹어 - mahni mogo - eat well

얘기 좀 하자. 잠깐이면 돼 - yaygi chom haja. jamkaneemyun dwae - I need to talk to you. It'll be quick.

한국말 잘하신다 - hangukmal jalhashinda - you speak korean well

울지마 - ooljima - don't cry

키스해도 돼 - kisseuhaedu dwae - can I kiss you?

Chapter 54 (쉰넷)

Hwan Soo knew exactly who was in his arms when he woke up. The scent of roses from her hair, the warmth of her curves fitting against him like puzzle pieces. He was, however, baffled how Maria ended up there. All he could remember was being mortified and defeated by her seeing the lipstick on his cheek, dropping everyone off and coming home to drink his weight in 소주, 막걸리, and 맥주.

He could also vaguely remember Gi Young stopping by and the face of the dazzling woman he loved so much crouching down in front of him making sure he was okay.

"*사랑해.*"

He'd told Maria he loved her. He one hundred percent told her he loved her.

Had she responded? She must've. *Why can't I remember what happened after that?*

Hwan Soo opened his eyes to gauge the situation, forcing himself to jog his memory. He gazed down at Maria's head in the crook of his shoulder, her hair strewn across the pillow, her hand resting against

437

his chest. He remembered the times he had made snotty remarks about the way she slept, but when he looked at her in that moment, all he could think was how he wished to wake up with her in his arms for the rest of his life.

His exhaled sigh of relief caused her hand to slide down his pec and closer to his abs. That's when he noticed he was shirtless. He panicked for a second before realizing she was completely clothed.

Thank God. If I slept with her and didn't remember, I would've thrown myself into the 한강.

"Ma-Ma-Maria," he stuttered, worried he would wake himself up from what had to be a dream.

She stirred, rubbing her face against the side of his torso. Her hair tickled Hwan Soo's pec, and he held back a laugh that quickly turned to a moan fueled by the innate desire to flip them over and pin her beneath him, finally fulfilling the thoughts he had been having since he first met her.

Her eyes fluttered open, a soft smile on her lips. Until she saw what she had been rubbing her face against. She halted and slowly tilted her head until her frightened eyes met his joyous ones. She tried to shift out of his hold, but his arm that she had been lying on tightened, keeping her warm curvaceous body against him.

"Hwan Soo-야..." Her morning voice was low and nervous. His nipples—and something below his belt—grew hard as her breath washed across his chest. But what had him almost throw caution to the wind was what she had uttered so softly.

She called him Hwan Soo-야! If his head wasn't already spinning from the aftereffects of alcohol and the feel of Maria in his arms, it would've exploded at her uttering his name informally.

"네, 나야." He hoped his smile conveyed his joy at hearing her say his name.

"You need to get up." She pushed his chest harder and sat up. Hwan Soo hated the loss of her warmth from his side. He had thoughts of wrapping his arms around her waist to bring her back to his chest, burying his face in her neck begging her not to leave so they could spend the whole day in bed together.

"I've got time, it's only—" He turned to see the clock on his bedside table and leaped up, shocked at how late it was. "Oh shit."

Storming off to his closet, Hwan Soo grabbed a clean hoodie and fresh pair of jeans. Glancing in the mirror, he saw how disheveled his hair was, the bags under his eyes darker than the night sky, and the small amount of bloat from eating all the unhealthy food the previous night. The makeup team was going to scold him...again.

When he came back to the bedroom, he found Maria still perched on the bed, arms wrapped around her legs as her head lolled between the slopes of her knees. She was so cute and beautiful at the same time, he once again imagined sauntering over to her, plucking her out from under the sheets and kissing her endlessly. But her voice yanked him out of his daydream.

"You threw up a couple hours ago. You were shockingly quick enough to get to the bathroom, but sadly you still got some vomit on your clothes." She gestured to a pile on a chair in the corner. "I thought it would just be smart to take them off and get you into something else, but by the time I came back to the bed to help you dress, you were already fast asleep."

"I'm so sorry about last night. I didn't mean to call you." He tried to cover his tracks. "Usually, Gi Young would've stopped me...not that I call you that often. I mean—"

"You didn't call me."

"어?" he asked, surprised. Gi Young would scold him constantly about his almost nightly attempts to drunkenly call her. He thought this one time Gi Young had failed.

"I actually texted you," she explained. "Gi Young-오빠 had Hae So help bring you home. I had texted you, and she called me to come over since it wasn't her job to take care of you. And to everyone on set, it is mine."

He crossed the room to her and sat down on the edge of the bed, causing her to lurch forward slightly. Closer to him. His eyes couldn't leave her face, his insides felt like they were competing in the Olympics. His stomach was doing backflips while his heart felt like it was performing rhythmic gymnastics from being so close to her again.

"You texted me?" he questioned, desperate to know why. "And I swear Hae So is nothing but a coworker. She means nothing to me. I don't know why Gi Young would think she would be—"

"아라." She smirked playfully, which surprised him.

"So why did you text me?" he asked, his nerves tingling awaiting an answer.

"Oh yeah." She cleared her throat, her golden-brown, green eyes twinkled as they met his. "I thought it was time for us, well mainly me, to apologize."

"I don't think that's nece—"

"미안해. You were trying to help me and keep me out of some sketchy situations. I was just mad to have been fooled again. As for Hae So..." She took a deep, unsteady breath and he waited for her to continue.

"I was quick to assume. I should've realized with your feelings toward her that the paparazzi were just looking for a story." Her twinkling eyes had become red and tear-filled.

He instinctively reached out to wipe away her tears, and he had a flashback to doing something similar the night before. Just like he remembered, she pressed her cheek into his hand for comfort.

This was it. This was his moment to make his move, lay everything out and hope she reciprocated his feelings.

"Maria I—"

"Thank God she got you up in time!" Gi Young's voice cut in as he pushed open the bedroom door.

"형," Hwan Soo groaned.

"오빠!" Maria said in surprise, her heated cheek still in Hwan Soo's hand. He knew he should stop, but jealousy got the best of him.

He really did not like her calling Gi Young 오빠. He wished Gi Young had never made the friendly suggestion. In all honesty, that's all it was. Friendly. But his blood boiled when he heard Maria say it to another man.

"We have to leave now, otherwise I'm going to get more than a verbal assault from my boss for you showing up late to set this time." Gi Young walked over and grabbed Hwan Soo's arm, ignoring the fact they were in the middle of something pretty freaking important.

As they walked out of the room, or rather, Hwan Soo was forcibly removed, they halted and turned back to Maria.

"You coming?" they asked in perfect unison.

What made Hwan Soo's heart feel as though he had a chance at fixing their relationship was how her smile grew wide, her eyes glimmered, and her cheeks grew flush as she sat up from the bed and quickly walked to catch up to them.

"친구!" a very happy Hae So called as Hwan Soo arrived on set. A rather genuine smile spread across her face, and she waved.

"친구?" Maria asked, clearly perplexed. Her eyebrows crept toward her hairline as the woman who had been evil up until a week ago happily skipped toward them.

"Uh..." Hwan Soo pondered how he could explain what had changed between him and his costar. "That night where...well...she actually came to talk about what happened at the party, and I told her about us. She actually ended up saving all of us from a major scandal. Since then, she's been a better person. I sometimes think she has an ulterior motive, but I haven't been able to figure out if that's true or not."

"Surprising, but she was also rather normal on the phone last night when she asked me to come and help. Well, as normal as I think she can be." Maria laughed, a smirk playing on the corner of her mouth.

"It's a good thing you guys are getting along better though. It will help with your chemistry on screen," Maria nervously rambled. "I will make sure to take a bunch of photos for Gi Young 오빠 to post on your socials."

"About that. You have been posting photos on my SNS pages?" he asked.

"No. I just take the photos, play around with them on some silly phone editing app and send them off." She shrugged nonchalantly. "They liked my photos and since your photographer friend threw my name out to your management company, they wanted to see the photos I've taken since being here. They asked for me to continue taking them. I told them sure, until I leave in a few days, that is. So I'm trying to get as many shots as I can so they can have stuff to work with for a little bit before they're on their own."

Hwan Soo stopped halfway to the makeup trailer as quickly as his heart stopped, realizing soon she wouldn't be in Korea. He thought he finally had a chance to express exactly how he felt about her, but she was about to walk out of his life. He wouldn't be able to see her, talk to her, touch her.

She spun around to face him, their eyes met, his sad gaze meeting her confused one.

"You better hurry. They need you on set soon." She gestured with her head in the direction of the makeup trailer.

What if I just put it all on the table now?

"Maria I—"

"Lee Hwan Soo-씨! Let's go! We need to get your makeup done to start shooting." One of the artists had poked her head out of the trailer to shout across the milling crowd.

Why is the world doing this to me?!

"Coming!" Maria shouted back, her pointed stare making it obvious Hwan Soo needed to get a move on. He shook it off, deciding he would be able to get her alone and tell her everything after work.

" Annnnnnd 끝!" the director called on the last take for the evening. Many on set clapped and bowed their thanks as others started to pack up the lighting and sound equipment. The actors went back to their staff to move on to their next engagements.

Maria grabbed her phone from the handy little fanny pack Gi Young had given her to aid in her "managerial duties" for Hwan Soo. She saw it was almost two in the morning, and her mother had called at least four times in the last thirty minutes and texted close to twenty.

"아이씨," she grumbled, quickly dialing her mother back before the Seoul police descended on the set looking for her.

Before the second ring ended, her mother answered.

"Maria! Do you have any idea what time it is?" Maria pulled the phone away from her ear as her mother shouted. "You were supposed to be here at nine for dinner. It is two in the freaking morning. I called Val, and she didn't know where you were! Where the hell are you? Are you okay?"

"Hey, Maria!" Hwan Soo shouted from behind her.

"Who was that? That sounded like Hwan Soo. Are you with him?" Her mother's tone instantly perked up. "Did you guys make up?"

"엄마, I'll call you back." Maria quickly hung up, nervous Hwan Soo would think she was talking to Sul Bin again, and tossed her phone back into the pack at her hip.

"네, Hwan Soo-씨." She gave a small bow in an effort to seem as professional as possible. But as he strode toward her, her thoughts were anything but.

His hair was still styled so his wavy and almost cloud-like bangs were parted on the side. His eyes were bright and the wide smile that spread across his face bunched his cheeks, making her heart flutter. Even as he lightly jogged to catch up to her, the swagger barely contained in his tailored gray pinstripe suit was devastating.

"No one is around. Hwan Soo-아 is fine." He rubbed his hand on the back of his head and rested it on his neck. She watched his mouth

443

open and close a few times as if attempting to say something, but the tension between them built as the silence stretched.

"Did you need something, Hwan Soo-아?" she asked. His eyes lit up at her using the informality, and it made her already pounding heart swell with warmth.

"어?어..." He trailed off before taking a deep breath. Whatever he had to say seemed to be important.

"Do you have any plans tonight?" he asked.

Huh?

She scrunched up her nose, her eyebrows pressed together, and her lips pursed. That's all he wanted to say?

"Actually, I did have plans. I wasn't supposed to be here today and was supposed to meet my mom for dinner five hours ago." She laughed, scratching the top of her head and kicking loose dirt and rocks by her feet.

"Oh crap. 미안해, Maria. I had no idea. You could've left if you needed—"

"괜찮아," she laughed. "I had to say goodbye to all the crew. It's the last day I'll be here. I'm gonna miss it." She glanced behind him at the staff who were packing up the cameras, lights, and other film equipment. "I don't think I will ever have an experience like this again. I owe it to you. I don't think I'll ever be able to say I worked for a celebrity again. 고마워," she giggled, remembering all the ups and down she had experienced throughout her entire trip.

"Don't forget you have a job here in Seoul if you choose to take it." He smiled, taking a small step closer to her. His broad shoulders blocked a breeze she hadn't noticed until he towered over her.

She rolled her eyes and gently pushed his chest with a laugh. "You and I both know he was just being nice."

"No one is that nice in this business. Not unless they see talent." He took another step toward her, his eyes scanning her face. But she nervously retreated a step. "And I'm pretty sure we established you have talent. Not only a famous photographer saw it, but my agency saw it. You thought your dream wouldn't make you a living and you've shown you can in fact be successful while following your dream and not just live for a paycheck at a dead-end job you hate."

He took another step toward her, getting dangerously close. She could smell his cologne. It was a new scent. Teak and a type of flower she couldn't place—a combination that made her dizzy.

"I...uh...I should get going, Hwan Soo-아. My mom called me a million times and was worried sick. I probably should go and see her." She looked to the street behind them wondering if there would be any taxis available so late into the night.

"Let me take you to her hotel." He grabbed her wrist, drawing her attention back to him. And yet again, he was closer. She leaned back, lifting her head so their eyes met.

His held much more meaning than simply being courteous and driving her to her mother's hotel. They held a question. A question she desperately wanted to know and more so wanted to answer.

But he didn't speak. Instead Gi Young interrupted them, breaking the moment.

~

For the entire ride, Maria could feel that Hwan Soo wanted to say something. She would glance over to find him staring at her, and at some point during the drive, he had given up trying to hide it.

When they pulled up to the hotel, he unbuckled himself, jumped out of the van and helped Maria climb out of the car. She wondered if he had started to remember what he said the previous night.

She sure hadn't forgotten. Him whispering 사랑해 played on repeat in her head. His polite request for permission to kiss her was living rent free. And while she wanted to bring it up, she knew it was not the time or place. He had work to focus on, they both had the wedding to think about, and she would be leaving in a few days.

Maybe it was for the best that they didn't discuss their feelings. Unrequited love. What good could come out of her professing her love for him when she would only leave? And with his line of work, if they were to follow their feelings, they would have more to deal with than just his disapproving family, they'd also have overprotective fans and a prying agency. He could lose a lot just by saying he liked her in a public forum. Yes. Unrequited it shall be.

"Lost in thought again?" he asked, scaring the living hell out of her. She hadn't noticed he was walking beside her up to the entrance of the hotel.

"Are you walking me to the door?" she asked.

"Oh, I'm not." He shook his head in denial but an adorable half smile played upon his lips. "I'm going to say hello to your mother. It would be rude of me to just throw you out of the car. Seeing you make it to her safely will hopefully keep her from wanting to rip my head off for having you out so late."

While he laughed in amusement, she laughed with nerves. It was obvious that her mother had already taken a liking to Hwan Soo, which wasn't a bad thing. But if Maria continued to ignore Hwan Soo's drunken profession of love, it wouldn't look good to her mother that she chose to go back to her dead-end job back home.

"How very chivalrous of you." She tried to match the light, fun energy he was giving off. Even though everything he said made her question if he had remembered the night before. She had replayed it countless times, and every single instance she felt he meant what he had said.

"And maybe because..." After rubbing the back of his head, he shoved his hands into the pockets of the tailored pants. "너랑 더 있고 싶어."

She wished she could understand what he said. It seemed important. She begged the heavens to be fluent in Korean at that moment, but she stared blankly. Nervous that if she asked what he meant, she could possibly not like the answer. The time couldn't have been more perfect that they got to the door of the hotel. He opened it, allowing her to enter first.

She laughed. "Wow. Holding doors? Who are you?"

"I embraced that aspect of Western culture." He smiled as they made their way to the elevator.

There was a loud ding, the doors peeled open and they went in. As they ascended to her mother's hotel room floor, her mind replayed what he had said as they had entered the hotel. 너랑... she knew that meant something along the lines of "with you". Maybe he had said something about being with her? Or doing something with her? Maybe it was another confession—a sober one, at that—and she couldn't understand it.

The doors opened, and they turned toward her mother's door. By some unspoken agreement, they kept their steps slow and small her to spend a few more seconds with him, which she hoped might've been his reasoning as well. As they approached the door, she glanced over at him. His jaw was tense, and his hands were balled into fists in his pockets, stretching the fabric.

"We're here." She looked at the large door.

"That we are." He rocked back and forth from the heels to the balls of his feet.

Since when did going to see her mother turn into the awkward end of a date? Neither party wanting to leave, but neither one admitting it.

"Maria, I—"

"I thought I heard voices out here!" Her mother flung open the door, cutting off whatever Hwan Soo was about to say.

"Oh Hwan Soo, did you drive Maria here? You didn't need to do that." Her mother's sickly-sweet voice was giving Maria cavities.

"네 어머님." He bowed to her. "I am sorry to keep your daughter out so late. We were filming, and your hotel is on the way to my house so it was no trouble." His eyes sparkled, and his smile was a blend of nerves and happiness.

But what he said was a total lie. His house was almost the complete opposite direction of where he had to drive to drop her off. Maria nudged his arm to try to get his attention, but he continued to butter up her mother with compliments and kindness.

"I should probably get going. I have to wrap up some stuff before the wedding. Only two days until our friends are married," he said cheerily.

"It's crazy." Maria's excitement grew at the thought as well.

"Oh, how I love happily ever afters," her mother gushed. But then she looked between Maria and Hwan Soo with those sneaky eyes Maria knew all too well.

Maria began pushing her mother into the room before she could say anything else embarrassing, and she faced Hwan Soo.

"I'll see you in a couple days?" Maria asked. Why she needed him to confirm that was baffling to her, but she needed it.

"Of course." His smile was sweet, his eyes softly tracing over her face. "I wouldn't miss it for the world."

With a final wave, he started to the elevator bank. She was about to close the door but something made her peek out through the narrow opening. As if he felt her eyes on him, he glanced back at her. Another small wave had her cheeks flushing and tingles spreading throughout her body.

Maria really had fallen hard. She was going to miss him. More than she would ever admit to her mother. Even though she knew she was in love with him, letting her mom have any hope they had a future as a couple wouldn't be fair to either of them.

Her mother had settled on the bed, watching TV. When Maria drew nearer, she saw she was engrossed in a drama. Laughing, Maria climbed under the covers and snuggled up with her mother to watch the show.

"These shows are really good! I could see how you got hooked." Her mother wrapped her arms around her, squeezing her in a big hug as she kissed the top of Maria's forehead. There was comfort in her hug and kiss. It told Maria that her mother knew exactly what Maria was feeling, but wasn't going to press the matter.

"Yeah, they're great," Maria choked out. Her eyes started watering as she accepted the comfort and let her emotions come to a head.

"Shhh...it's okay, dear. It's all gonna be okay," her mother cooed, which only made her cry harder.

Korean Vocabulary:

나야 - naya - it's me

너랑 더 있고 싶어 - neorang deo issgo sip-eo - I want to be with you more

어머님 - ohmonim - mother (formal)

Chapter 55 (쉰다섯)

T he day had finally arrived. Hwan Soo's best friend was going to embark on the wild ride that is marriage. The boy who swore love between people didn't exist, citing his parents as his reason on countless occasions, and who said the only love he would ever have was running his family's business. The boy who didn't kiss a girl until he was in college; of course, he was a sixteen-year-old prodigy in college, and the girl was a daughter of a professor trying to get her father's attention. But Hwan Soo knew the obstacles, the giant walls built around his friend's heart that Val had to overcome to win Jung-hyun, and Hwan Soo was thrilled Jung-hyun had found someone who could change his mind about love.

Pulling up to the wedding hall, Hwan Soo was surprised. He knew Val had an eye for design, but what welcomed him and Jung-hyun was stunning. A uniformed doorman greeted them with bows, pulled open the black iron-framed glass door and led them to their wedding's designated area.

Hwan Soo admired the high-vaulted ceilings with wood arches reaching toward several crystal chandeliers that were so colossal, one could take up Hwan Soo's entire living room. Narrow dark wood tables adorned with bouquets of different colors filled vases of varying heights and flanked the larger-than-life door frames. The natural beauty of the varying woods was offset with large, ornate iron-work-framed windows letting in the daylight. Beyond the windows but within view lay the venue's extensive back garden, boasting many fountains that created intricate displays of water propulsion and light reflection.

The venue brilliantly mixed natural elements with those of a bustling city skyscraper. It was nothing less than spectacular and exactly the type of place Hwan Soo pictured for the soon-to-be-married couple.

When they arrived at their groomsmen's room, they were greeted with a table overflowing with booze and snacks. Their tuxes were hung on the wall, still zipped neatly in their garment bags, and one of the many photographers stood ready to start shooting for the day.

Despite all the joy and anticipation of Jung-hyun's impending nuptials, Hwan Soo's mind was in a fog as he went through the motions of changing into his tuxedo. He wanted his mind to stay focused on celebrating with his friend, but it chose its own path. And that path always led back to Maria.

Even after the men had a few drinks to ease their nerves before the main event, Hwan Soo questioned whether even with Maria's forgiveness and their relationship heading in a good direction, would he be able to make her stay in Seoul? And not just stay in Seoul but build a life with him? They adjusted their bow ties in the mirror while the loud clicks from the camera came from behind them, capturing even the simplest moments in the wedding day.

"You ready?" Hwan Soo shook himself from his thoughts and looked to the friend he had grown up with. He could plainly see the nerves on Jung-hyun's face and the anticipation in his stance. While he was standing tall, he fidgeted with every little detail of his tux. Picking at small fibers on his sleeves, adjusting his cufflinks for the tenth time, brushing invisible lint from his pant legs.

"괜찮아 보이냐?" Jung-hyun asked, his breathing uneven as he paced in front of the mirror.

"형, you look like 십억 원." Hwan Soo hyped up his friend.

"거짓말." Jung-hyun turned to the mirror once again, ensuring every hair was in place, and the little bit of makeup he wore to stay blemish free for all the photos was still doing its job.

"거짓말 아니야!" Hwan Soo grabbed his friend's shoulders so they could face each other fully. "형, I have never seen you so in love. You found the girl of your dreams. And guess what? She loves you too and is probably just as nervous and excited as you are right now. So take a few deep breaths and find relief in the knowledge you've found your person. You two are the lucky ones."

He gave Jung-hyun's shoulder a strong pat, doing his best to keep him hype and not on the verge of passing out.

"She loves me, and I love her." Jung-hyun spoke his new mantra.

"Yes. She loves you, and you love her." Hwan Soo repeated, biting his cheek to keep from smiling.

Jung-hyun started bobbing his head repeatedly, pacing, and Hwan Soo could hear the whisper of his new chant.

A knock sounded on the door behind them, and a petite young woman stuck her head in to tell them the ceremony was ready to begin. Hwan Soo bowed to her and turned back to Jung-hyun to give the final primp.

All the anxiousness was back. Jung-hyun was desperately trying to take deep breaths while struggling to find a good place to put his hands, finally settling on fists in the tux pants pockets.

"형 I got the rings." Hwan Soo patted his chest plate feeling the outline of the rings against his peck. "Now let's go get you married."

They stood behind a pair of goliath closed doors, hearing the murmuring of the guests and the music beginning just beyond. The same young woman who had announced the ceremony manned one of the large doors, while another employee manned the other. Jung-hyun gave them a curt nod, and she spoke into her walkie before the doors were pulled open.

Hundreds of guests—mostly business acquaintances and deal makers, but scattered throughout were family and friends of the bride and groom—turned in unison. Hwan Soo noticed Val's family and friends' smiles were all the biggest and brightest.

The room itself was even more ornate and jaw dropping than the lobby, clearly bearing the design touches of Val and Tina. Flowers Hwan Soo had never even seen before lined the large aisle in hues of blush pinks and purples, intermixed with white, and grey fuzzy looking greenery. Twinkling lights hung at all different heights above the entire room, like stars in the sky. The aisle met the altar before a monolith of flowers, similar to the ones lining the aisle, but some brighter shades of pinks and purples formed two letters: J and V.

As they started their walk down the aisle, one face Hwan Soo recognized immediately was Maria's mother, who already had tears in her eyes. Their gazes met, and she waved politely to him as he bowed to her.

At the end of the aisle, Jung-hyun and Hwan Soo greeted the officiant and took their places to the side of the altar. The doors they had walked through only a minute ago were closed once again.

While Jung-hyun continued to subtly fidget, trying to shake out the nerves, Hwan Soo had a sudden rush of anxiety swell in his chest. Not because he was worried about the wedding. It would go off without a hitch. He was worried how he was going to react to seeing Maria walk down the aisle. His mind went back to the wedding dress Val had convinced Maria to wear and sneakily took photos of her in. His heart raced and his palms began to sweat. Just as his anxiety reached fever pitch, the towering doors opened wide and a blinding white light washed over them.

Squinting until his eyes adjusted to the light, he saw a vision in white. Val was truly breathtaking in a ballgown as wide as the aisle, beading on her bodice that shimmered in the spotlight. The dress modestly flaunted her clavicle, and the see-through peasant sleeves flowed from gathered shoulder to delicate wrist. The gossamer veil covering her face rippled from the breeze of the opening doors. She was a beauty.

But as every eye followed Val down the aisle, his eyes were behind her, focused on her bridesmaid.

Her hair was elegantly simple, falling in soft curls across her bare shoulders. Thin straps arched over delicate collar bones and off-the-shoulder sleeves hugged the gentle curve of her upper arms. He loved when she showed skin. It made his mouth water. The color of the dress matched the soft purple of the flowers throughout the room, and the lace on the figure-hugging gown shimmered slightly as she walked down the aisle behind her friend.

The love of his life was walking down the aisle. His Maria.

Tonight, I tell her how I feel. Nothing will stop me this time. I need to tell her I love her.

Maria's emotions were in a tangle, to say the least. She and Val had arrived at the venue before the sun came up and from the second they entered, there were a multitude of things that needed to be done. Hair, makeup, even nails, and before Maria knew it, several hours had passed. She was now dressed in her bridesmaid dress waiting excitedly outside the dressing room for Val's final reveal. When the assistant pushed open the curtain, Val walked out of the dressing room, her smile so wide it looked like it could almost stretch off her face. Her eyes glittered not only from the shimmering eyeshadow, but brimming with tears.

Seeing her best friend's face glowing with excitement, in love and eager to be marrying the man of her dreams, Maria's heart filled with love and joy. These feelings had solidified in herself her desire for all those things as well. All at once, she was overwhelmed with emotion. She wanted to stay in Seoul, work a job she dreamed of being her life's work, and be with the man she loved and who she hoped loved her back.

Hwan Soo hadn't left her mind since the night he dropped her off in her mother's hotel room. He had been so on edge the whole day, like he wanted to say something to her but lost every opportunity. She had held out some hope that her feelings were mutual when he had turned back before getting on the elevator, but once he left, she didn't hear a word from him. He said he was going to be busy wrapping up some things. She had been busy herself running around for last-minute bridal emergencies and late-night editing photos for Hwan Soo's team to use for his SNS pages.

Seeing him standing by Jung-hyun at the altar would be the first time she'd have seen him in two days, though it felt like longer, and her heart was doing cartwheels down to her stomach.

"어때?" Val asked, her voice wavering as she lifted the dress and shuffled toward the mirrors to get a view of herself.

"Val...Valerie." Maria knew that Jung-hyun was the only one who regularly called her Valerie, but she wanted to make her point. "You have always been and will always be the most beautiful person I know. Not just how breathtakingly stunning you are, but because of the person you are. And I know Jung-hyun is going to bawl his damn eyes out the second he sees you enter the room. Every eye in that room is going to be on you. But Jung-hyun is who matters." She choked out the last few sentences, emotions clogging her throat.

"울지마. If you start crying, then I am gonna start and we both just had our makeup done." Val tried to laugh but her emotions got the best of her as well and soon the tears started flowing.

"어머! 어머! 어머!" Jisoo, the makeup artist, shouted and rushed over, grabbing face cushions and tissues to touch up anything they ruined. When Maria had met Jisoo, she found it odd how informal she was with Val. But Val explained that Jung-hyun had introduced her to Jisoo in San Francisco when they had to attend events where perfect hair and makeup were required. They had formed a friendship from all the times they had seen each other.

"Jisoo, 미안." Val laughed through her tears. She was pretty badass-looking in Maria's eyes. While Jisoo was petite, she had a multitude of piercings around her ears, and her one arm was covered in gorgeous ink that looked like it could be hung in high-end art galleries.

"Luckily most of the makeup is waterproof, but I need to make sure you look flawless walking down the aisle. No need to get Jung-hyun's mom on me and never hire me again," Jisoo joked, but from what Val had told Maria about his mother, Jisoo wasn't kidding.

There was a knock at the door of the suite, and a young woman popped her head in. "준비됐어요?"

Val contemplated for a second before nodding. Maria grabbed the bouquet of white and pink peonies, white bells of Lily of the Valley, and the fuzzy leaves of dusty millers. The fragrance tickled her nose pleasantly as she handed it to her best friend, the glowing bride.

They followed the woman down the grandiose hall to a set of tall doors that Maria guessed led to the wedding hall. Once in front of the doors, Maria adjusted the train of the dress and veil, bringing the blusher veil in front of Val's face.

"Let's get you married." Maria smiled and took her place behind Val who was bobbing gently, her dress bunching and unbunching, her breaths loud and short, working out her last bit of nerves before giving a small bow to the two door handlers.

Maria composed herself, prepared to see the face of the man she had been longing to have a few more moments with before she left, and the doors were pulled open.

Blinding white spotlights blared down, leaving spots in Maria's eyes as the music began playing. It wasn't the standard processional music. Val went for the unconventional, and it was a song Maria wouldn't have recognized until she started binging dramas a few weeks ago. It was from Val's favorite drama. It was one of the first dramas Val had introduced to Maria because it was the one Jung-hyun and she had first watched together.

"You would," Maria whispered, catching Val's shoulders rise and fall with a small chuckle.

When Maria's eyes finally adjusted to the light, she took in the enormity of the room. The flower arrangements lining the aisle, the hundreds of guests standing to look at the bride, so many happy smiles, and several people's eyes filled with tears, including Val's parents, Maria's mother, and even Jung-hyun's mother.

Val took her first steps into the room, and Maria waited for Val to get onto the elevated aisle before following slowly after, ensuring the veil and train were still perfectly situated for photos as Val walked towards her almost-husband.

That's when Maria's eyes found the altar. For a moment, she saw Jung-hyun. Like she had guessed, tears shimmered in his eyes upon seeing Val in her stunning dress. But Maria's gaze quickly jumped to the man standing beside the groom.

Hwan Soo's black tuxedo seemed to make him standing even taller, as if he wasn't already a head above any crowd. The simplicity of the tux brought attention to every sharp contour of his face that Maria loved. His jawline, his lips, the long bridge of his nose, and finally his eyes. Eyes that were looking intently right at her. Not faltering. She sharply inhaled, her mind running through the last month of her life like a movie leading up to that very moment, walking down the aisle toward Hwan Soo.

A small smirk came to his lips, his cheeks rosy as his eyes never left hers. She smiled back, and a blush rose across her chest and cheeks as she got closer to the altar.

Reaching the dais, Jung-hyun extended a hand to Val, drawing her gently closer to him and the officiant. He whispered something to her, and she responded just as hushed, making both smile widely with joy. Maria fixed Val's train and veil before grabbing the bouquet and moving off to the side for the ceremony to begin.

She tried to understand what the man was saying, but he was speaking so fast. She had a moment of internal panic about how people would react to her speech later in the night. Instinctively, she tried to calm her mind and heart by looking at Hwan Soo, who must've felt her eyes on him. He drew his gaze from the couple and met hers. He smiled and took a deep breath as a direction for her to follow. Which she did, taking one after another, deep inhale and exhale, settling her mind.

They didn't need words to speak. There was no language barrier with their actions, and Maria loved that. She gave Hwan Soo a small smirk and he reciprocated with a wink, causing heat to build below her stomach. They both silently laughed before refocusing on their friends getting married.

The wedding was picturesque and perfect, just like Maria knew it would be. After Jung-hyun professed his love to his wife three times by waving his hands in the air and screaming 사랑합니다, they were officially husband and wife. The happy couple walked down the aisle as husband and wife to the cheers of family, friends, and the acquaintances they were forced to invite due to Jung-hyun's standing in society, a place that now included Val as well.

While Val and Jung-hyun were off taking their couple photos and photos with their families during cocktail hour, Maria stood alone on the side of the reception hall. She sipped on her glass of champagne as she replayed the moment Hwan Soo held his arm out for her to grab and follow the bride and groom out of the wedding hall. He had rested his hand on hers with a smile that eased all the tension in her body.

"Oh honey, you looked so beautiful up there, but you look even more stunning close up!" her mother gushed as she gave Maria a hug, bringing her back to the present. "Hold on, Hwan Soo said '연예인 같으세요'. Does that mean you look gorgeous?"

Maria laughed. "와 대박 엄마! You've learned quickly! I guess I know where I get it from. But to clarify, he said you look like a celebrity." She smiled as her mother flushed like a schoolgirl, twisting a small bit of her hair between two fingers and biting her bottom lip.

"I like him, Maria." Her mother cupped Maria's free hand between hers. "He seems like such a good guy. He made mistakes, but you did too. I saw how he looked at you, how he still looks at you. He loves you just as much as you love him."

"Mom, I don't want to talk about this right no—"

"Maria?" Hwan Soo's voice cut into a conversation Maria desperately wanted to avoid. Had he heard what her mother said?

Panicked, she grasped one of her mother's hands that had been holding hers.

"네?" She smiled kindly as her eyes drank him in once again. He stood tall, his shoulders broad as he extended a hand toward her.

"We need to go take photos with the bride and groom before their entrance to the reception." His smile exuded calm, and his eyes glittered with delight.

Too nervous to speak, she handed her champagne flute to her mother, who gently pulled her hand out of Maria's death grip and passed it to Hwan Soo. His fingers slid between hers and at once fit perfectly. He gave a soft squeeze as he led her out of the room, and she tightened her hold to enjoy the sweetness as long as she could.

As the doors closed behind them, it became deadly silent.

"아름다워," he said confidently.

She snapped her attention up, her eyes meeting his.

"I wanted to tell you before, but I got dragged all different ways once the ceremony was over. I'm sorry you were left alone." He dipped his head in apology, his hand squeezing hers again.

"Don't apologize for being who you are." She squeezed his hand back. "You have a presence. I am shocked you only just got a lead role. But I know you're gonna have more in the future. I'm going to brag to everyone I know about you." She laughed even though her heart cracked slightly. "I'll get all my friends to watch your shows. You'll be an international sensation in no time." She had to force a smile as she talked about leaving.

"So you really aren't going to take the job here?" His voice held a heat that hung in the air, nearly suffocating her. Could her mother be right about his feelings? She could hear his whisper of '사랑해' in her head.

"Hwan Soo we should tal—"

"어왔오?" Jung-hyun popped out from a large door and walked up to them, his eyes slightly puffy from crying. Maria internally giggled imagining what the photos of him were going to look like as he saw his bride walking down the aisle.

"축하해!" Maria exclaimed. She had no time to bow before Jung-hyun wrapped his arms around her in a cheerful hug. She was about to wrap hers around him to reciprocate the joyful expression when she felt her hand that Hwan Soo still held get tugged and a throat to her side being cleared.

Jung-hyun removed his arms from around her and looked to his best friend, whose jaw, Maria saw, was clenched almost as tightly as his hand held hers.

"친구, we want to get some photos of the four of us and then a few shots of the two of you. Is that okay with both of you?" Jung-hyun asked, his dazzling smile unable to leave his face.

"그럼요," Maria and Hwan Soo said in unison.

"Wow…" Jung-hyun laughed lightly, patting his friend on the shoulder.

The three of them walked into the room where a large ornately upholstered white couch sat in the center with flowers from the ceremony on pedestals of various height; flowers also hung from the white organza backdrop. Val sat in the middle of the couch, bouquet in her lap, her blinding white smile matching her husband's as she saw them enter the room.

When their eyes met, more happy tears formed. Maria couldn't put into words how joyful she was for her best friend. Neither of their love lives up until that point were that of fairytales or romance novels. They had their first kisses, their potential partners, their failed relationships, their heartbreaks. And when Maria had first heard Val talk about Jung-hyun, she could tell something was different. She had hoped it was. All she wanted was for her best friend to be the happiest she could—she deserved the world.

And as best friends do...they didn't need words.

A breath skimmed Maria's ear and her favorite deep voice whispered against her ear, "가."

Hwan Soo dropped his hand to the small of her back and gently guided her forward. His breath had already caused her blood to pump alarmingly fast, but his hand on her back ignited every nerve throughout her body.

Maria instinctively followed his simple direction and took long strides to her friend. They wrapped their arms around each other and just cried. These were happy, nervous tears. How would their friendship change? Would married life be everything she wanted?

"Jisoo is gonna kill us," Val finally laughed out through the tears.

"Yes, I am," Jisoo joked from behind the cameraman, who was currently snapping away while they sobbed in each other's arms.

"Alright, let's get these photos done so we can go and eat. I am starving," Val said, releasing Maria and waving for the men to join the group.

Jung-hyun sat next to his beautiful weepy bride and Maria and Hwan Soo were directed to stand behind them. Hwan Soo slipped beside her, naturally placing his hand around her waist and tugging her close.

She gazed up into his face, unable to help herself. His eyes were staring straight at the camera, his drama-like smile wide and bright, posing along with the happy couple. Trying to ignore the growing need to have him hold her like that forever, she turned her head to face the camera and put on her best smile.

"There better be no tears like this at the ceremony in a few days," Jisoo grumbled.

"Ceremony? In a few days?" Maria asked, unaware of any wedding activities after that night.

"어. It's the traditional Korean wedding. With 한복 and everything," Hwan Soo explained, trying to keep his smile from faltering. "It's only for the bride and groom and their immediate family."

"한복?" Maria asked, but then thought of the drama she and her mother had watched. She remembered the historical high-waisted dresses in vibrant colors, some with intricate patterns.

"It's—"

"I saw it in a drama I've been watching," she said, cutting Hwan Soo off. "They are very ornate. I love the hairpieces the women wear."

His hand gripped her waist tighter, pulling her to stand slightly in front of him.

"You would look gorgeous in a queen's 한복." His voice was commanding even in its whisper. Had it gotten deeper? It sounded like he was holding something back. Maybe weddings got to him. She had heard her friends say that weddings and funerals were like aphrodisiacs to some people.

"오케이." The photographer clapped his hands and began shuffling people around, pulling Maria and Hwan Soo to a corner of the room for their singular shots.

"Why they want shots of just the two of us is..." She trailed off, not sure what the right word was.

"이상해..." As he finished the sentence for her, Hwan Soo's breath trickled down her neck sweetly. It hadn't gone unnoticed that Hwan Soo kept a hold of her in one way or another through the whole photography process. Whether holding her hand, her waist, or at the small of her back. His warmth radiated through Maria's body and made her feel that his profession of love—however drunk he had been—might've been genuine.

She heard the sound of the shutter, not realizing she had been staring at Hwan Soo, and turned to the camera to put on her best smile. The man was pushing his hands together indicating that they should stand closer, but she didn't know how much closer they could be without being on top of each other.

Hwan Soo tugged her closer to his hip, her bottom grazing his pelvis. His hand on her waist gripped her tighter, and she had to hold back a squeak of arousal.

The photographer's rapid instructions made Maria smile awkwardly, unsure of how he wanted her to pose.

"He wants me to whisper something in your ear to get a funny reaction from both of us," Hwan Soo whispered. His lips grazed the shell of her ear, making her shiver and lean back against him involuntarily. She was thanking her lucky stars she was able to hold back a moan that had caught in her throat.

"Okay," she managed to say.

The photographer smiled with a nod for them to do what he had asked.

"키스해도 돼?" Hwan Soo whispered, and her gaze snapped up to his.

She gasped at his words, but when she saw his eyes were hungrily focused on her lips, her breath escaped in short, panicked pants. His small smile gave away that he knew she understood exactly what he had said to her.

The clarity of Hwan Soo's drunken actions had started to come back to him in bits and pieces in the days leading up to the wedding. He knew it was because when he tried to sleep, his mind always went back to the woman who had been snuggled so closely to him and had stolen his heart in the process.

He remembered she hadn't responded to his confession of love with words, but with her eyes. Her gorgeous green-brown eyes had looked at him wide in surprise and then quickly turned away from him with hurt that his declaration had been a drunken one—one she most likely didn't take seriously. And when he had asked to kiss her, she had explained that it wouldn't be a smart idea.

But what finally gave him the courage to tell her exactly how he felt before she left was the memory of hearing her whisper that if he had asked her when sober, she would've said yes.

And this was his moment. He had spoken to Jung-hyun after the ceremony about making his move during the photography session with the four of them and asked for some photos with just Hwan Soo and Maria. Jung-hyun was more than willing, and when Val heard the plan, she was even more on board.

He kept her near him. Feeling her heat on the palm of his hand had his mind running wild with thoughts of caressing her bare skin. And when she pressed her butt against his pelvis as he pulled her closer for the group pictures, he had visions of them in the throws of passion. Keeping his cool was getting harder with every passing minute.

And the moment had arrived. His opportunity to begin his confession. Seeing her face when he asked "키스해도 돼?" gave him all the confidence he needed to continue.

"What did you just say?" she whispered, the smell of champagne on her breath.

"I believe you said that if I asked when sober—"

"You heard that?" she said, cutting him off, a lovely blush stealing across not only her cheeks, but the tips of her ears and across her chest.

He nodded, words failing as the urge to kiss her grew with every second that passed. She hadn't given an answer, but she hadn't moved away from him and that made him hopeful. He made another bold move, bringing his hand to her rosy cheek that was velvety, warm, and a perfect fit for his palm. His thumb brushed her cheek, his heart soared to new heights when her eyes closed and she pressed her cheek into his palm.

He leaned down, his nose brushing hers and her eyes flew open.

"Hwan Soo-아..." Putting her hand to his chest, Maria gently pushed him to create some distance. He could see in her eyes that she was at odds with herself, which continued to give him hope that his feelings weren't one-sided.

"We should talk later," she whispered. She grabbed his hand from her cheek to break their connection, but his other hand was still on her waist and he kept her pressed against his chest.

"You promise?" he said, smiling, eyes filled with hope as his entire body begged for him to pin her to the wall and kiss her so thoroughly words wouldn't be needed.

"약속해," she responded.

His eyes roamed what he could see of her body, while his body drew a mental map of how well the rest of her fit perfectly against him. A throat cleared and the reality of their surroundings came rushing back.

Hwan Soo eased his hold on Maria's waist, feeling her exhale deeply, and the staff ushered them from the room for the big entrance into the reception hall to continue the evening's festivities.

"You really made your move in there," Jung-hyun joked as he surveyed the banquet room packed with people.

Hwan Soo had hoped to be seated beside Maria so they could talk like she had promised, but after the bride and groom's first dance as a married couple, the four of them were escorted to a long table filled with flowers, candelabras of varying heights, and expensive china sets, where Jung-hyun and Val sat in the middle with each of their friends to their side.

"I'm sorry about that," Hwan Soo apologized. "It's just that when

I'm around her, I forget where I am and everything else seems to disappear."

"That's how I feel around Valerie." Jung-hyun grabbed his bride's hand and brought it to his lips. She turned to face him, eyes half lidded, lips upturned in a happily dazed smile. She appeared lost in her own world when she looked at Jung-hyun as well.

When Hwan Soo glanced past the two lovebirds, he saw Maria's elbow resting on the table, her chin resting in the palm of her hand, with a glossy look in her eyes as she gazed around the room. He wondered what she could be thinking about. Was she having similar thoughts to those that plagued his mind? When she said they needed to talk, he didn't get a bad feeling. It was more so a hopeful one that led him to believe that if he told her how he felt, there could be a happily ever after for them.

He excused himself from the couple who had already forgotten he was there and made his move toward Maria. Pulled from her daydreaming, she lifted her head from its resting spot in her hand.

"Are you ready for your speech?" he asked, feeling his own nerves getting the best of him.

"As ready as I'll ever be." She huffed out a nervous breath. "They can't really fault me for my pronunciation. I am clearly not native."

"야...네이티브야!" He put his hand on her shoulder with a reassuring smile. The skin-to-skin contact distracted him from his pep talk. "Your Korean is great, Maria. Don't doubt yourself. And if all else fails, just thank everyone and toast the happy couple."

"Thanks, Hwan Soo. I'm sure your speech is going to be amazing as well." Maria gave him a comforting grin while she tried to keep her breathing steady. His large, warm hand on her shoulder had been doing a number on her pulse.

As if the MC had heard their conversation, he appeared at the edge of their table to tell them it was time for the speeches to begin.

Maria gave a quick nod and reached into her clutch for the small bit of paper she had scribbled her speech on. Her hands shook to the point that she fumbled the paper several times before it ultimately fell to the ground.

Hwan Soo dipped down to scoop it off the floor. Handing it back, he took Maria's hand in his. He squeezed it, his warmth again causing her pulse to rise.

"천천히," he whispered and mimicked taking deep breaths. She followed his instructions and took slow, steady breaths, feeling her body return to a somewhat less panicked state.

"There you go." His smile lit up as he brought her hand to his lips. She couldn't take her eyes off his full lips pressed to her nervously clammy skin.

"할 수있어," he said before giving her hand one final kiss and striding to the middle of the dance floor for his speech.

천천히... 할 수있어...천천히... 할 수있어, she repeated in her head. But Maria's insides melted like butter when Hwan Soo grabbed the microphone and turned toward the happy couple, tears already welling in his eyes and a warm smile on his face.

Then his eyes landed on her, and Maria's mind started repeating a new mantra.

사랑해 Hwan Soo, *사랑해* Hwan Soo, *사랑해* Hwan Soo.

Korean Vocabulary:

괜찮아 보이냐 - gwenchana bueenya - Do I look ok?

거짓말 - kojitmal - you're lying

거짓말 아니야 - kojitmal aniya – I'm not lying

울지마 - uljima - don't cry

연예인 같으세요 - yonyaein katoosatyo - you look like a celebrity

와 대박 엄마 - wah daebak omma - wow awesome mom

아름다워 -arumdawoah - beautiful

어왔오 - oh wasso - oh youre here

축하해 - chukahae - congrats

그럼요 - kromyo - of course

한복 - hanbok - hanbok is traditonal korean dress

오케이 - okaeee - okay
약속해 - yasokhae - promise
네이티브야 - naetibooya - native (you sound native)
천천히 - chochonhee - go slowly, take it slow
할 수있어 - halsuisso - you can do it

Chapter 56 (쉰여섯)

Maria's heart fluttered as Hwan Soo stared at her. Her mind repeated her love for him again and again. He cleared his throat and began his speech. She tried to keep up with what he was saying, but since it was his native tongue, he was much faster than anything she could ever remotely grasp after only a month of learning.

What she could pick up was him mentioning the love Jung-hyun had for Val and how happy he was to see his friend happy. At one point he looked to Maria, as did the rest of the guests and the bride and groom as he said something, his eyes full of kindness and affection. Maria's heart swelled and pumped blood vigorously throughout her body, putting every nerve ending on high alert and causing her cheeks to flush.

Seemingly oblivious to the riot going on in her body, Hwan Soo simply raised his glass with the rest of the room and toasted the bride and groom. He walked over, handed Maria the microphone, and nodded his head, whispering another supportive phrase before taking his seat beside Jung-hyun.

The microphone slipped out of her clammy hands, making a thud that echoed through the room. Dipping to pick it up off the table, her grip on the microphone tightened so she wouldn't make the same mistake twice. There was some awkward applause, and she looked around to see her mother clapping softly, trying to help her calm her nerves.

Maria rose from her seat and stared at the sea of people awkwardly waiting for her to start speaking.

"안녕하세요 저는 Valerie의 친구, Maria 입니다. Val과 저는 어린 시절부터 베프 였어요. 처음 Val이 결혼한다고 했을때 진심으로 기쁘고 또 행복했지만 동시에 결혼하는 상대가 누구일지 걱정스러웠어요. 모두 아시다시피 베프란 항상 친구에 대해 관심을 가지고 지켜봐야 하죠. 정현을 만나 Val을 사랑스럽게 바라보는 그의 눈, 감정을 절대 숨기지 않는 모습, 그리고 Val을 공주처럼 대하는걸 보았어요. 정현이 바로 Val의 그 사람이라는 걸 알 수 있었죠."

The crowd was silent as Maria finished, making her worry she had said something wrong, but the tears she saw in Val's eyes as well as Jung-hyun's appreciative smile told her that her speech was going well. Taking a deep breath and grabbing her champagne flute, she raised the glass for the final toast.

"You and Jung-hyun have shown me what true love looks like. It can start in the most peculiar ways and blossom into something so magnificent and uniquely your own. This is only the beginning of your love story, and I wish you forever happiness. Love you, girl. To Valerie and Jung-hyun." Maria turned to clink her glass with the married couple while everyone toasted, clinking their glasses at their tables as slow jazz music began playing.

She leaned over to Val, whose tears made Maria's heart full. Her best friend's strong arms wrapped around her neck, yanking her forward into a loving death grip.

"Thank you, Maria. I love you, girlie," Val whispered.

"I love you too." Maria gripped her friend tightly.

"We should probably make the rounds to all the tables," Jung-hyun interrupted.

"Of course you should." Maria gently pulled out of her friend's hold to let them greet their guests.

Suddenly alone, Maria felt like she needed a shoulder to cry on. Her eyes landed on her mother, who was waving her over. She sauntered to her mother's table, taking the empty seat available and her mom wrapped her in a big hug.

"Oh honey, that was such a beautiful speech." her mother gushed. "I'm sure the Korean part was just as wonderful."

"I have no clue, honestly. I hope I made sense," Maria laughed.

"Well Val and Jung-hyun seemed to appreciate it." Her mother grabbed her hands and with a sneaky smirk added, "And Hwan Soo didn't take his eyes off you for a second."

"Mom..." She rolled her eyes.

Not wasting a second, her mother asked, "Have you talked to him?"

"Not yet but—"

She was cut off by the clearing of a throat beside her. Maria turned slowly to see the man they had just been discussing staring down at her, his hand held out toward her.

"Can I have this dance?" Hwan Soo's outstretched hand was like a siren's call. She didn't need to look at her mother to know she was jumping in her seat for Maria to accept.

Without a word, she slipped her hand in his. His hold was tight, as if making sure she wouldn't leave his side. But she wasn't going anywhere. She wanted to stay in his arms for as long as she could.

They walked onto the dance floor, and he gave her a spin before pulling her against his chest, one hand on the small of her back, the other still gripping her hand. The warmth emanating from him pooled deep in her stomach, and she unconsciously leaned closer.

"Your speech was really good," he praised.

"Oh please. You're just saying that," she laughed.

"I'm serious," he chuckled. "You put your heart in it. I could tell. And I could see Val and Jung-hyun did as well. They are really the only ones who matter."

They lapsed into silence, Maria unable to find a way to accept his praise. But as they gently twirled, her mind also danced around what he had said when their pictures were being taken, and she had already made up her mind about telling him exactly how she felt.

"Hwan Soo-야," She turned her head upward to find him already watching her. "About what you said in the suite..."

"And when we were in bed together. That's really the first time I said it," he added.

"You remember saying that?" she asked again.

"네. I guess I should say I started to remember," he explained as his fingers tapped at her skin. "It started coming to me in bits and pieces over the last couple of days. At first, I thought it was a dream, but slowly I started to realize they were memories." He paused. "I also remember you turning me down. Then saying something about if I asked you when I was sober—"

"You heard that?" Mortified, Maria tried to step out of his hold but the fingers that had been tapping nervously suddenly gripped her waist, keeping her pressed against his chest.

"Maria." Hwan Soo took a deep breath before speaking again. "I have now asked. Fully sober. I want to...아니...I need to know your answer now."

More people began to join them on the dance floor, and she knew she needed to give him the truthful answer. It was now or never.

"네." It was short and very much to the point. And with that simple word, a wave of relief crashed over her. It was out in the open. She had put herself out there for him to either accept or deny.

"네?" he asked with a hopeful grin that gave her the feeling he loved her answer.

Laughing, she repeated, "네."

The DJ switched the tempo from slow jazz to upbeat pop music that had many of the guests rush to the dance floor. From the corner of her eye, she could see rather bizarre dance moves around the two of them, who were still swaying back and forth in each other's arms.

Maria wanted to be alone with him. She needed to savor every last moment. And now that she had laid some of her cards on the table, she took his hand and made a getaway for some fresh air. She gathered her dress high enough to give her legs a better stride as they pushed through the large doors of the reception hall, down a small corridor to a glass door that opened to the back gardens of the venue.

With a gentle night breeze, the fountains sprayed a light mist through the air, cooling her flushed cheeks as she took a deep breath. The aroma of roses, peonies, and lavender filled her mind with romantic professions of love like she had started to dream about after all the dramas she had watched.

"Did you think you would be able to get away from what we were talking about?" Hwan Soo's voice broke through the white noise of the fountain's constant streaming water.

"I just needed some fresh air." She fanned herself with her hand.

And as fate always seemed to have it, the sounds of more people getting fresh air broke into their private getaway.

Hwan Soo grabbed her hand and pulled her into one of the small rose bush mazes, shrouding them in darkness. The only light was from a streetlamp just outside the hall's boundary wall and wisps of moonlight peeking through the clouds.

"Maria," he whispered. "Please tell me you understand what you said—"

"네." She knew it was now or never.

"Good." He tugged her hand to pull her closer, his free arm wrapping around her waist so she was flush against his chest. He pressed his lips against hers.

It took her less than a second to react. Her arms snaked around his neck, making sure he knew she didn't want the kiss to end anytime soon. His lips moved hungrily against hers, his tongue swiping along her bottom lip as one hand gripped the fabric at her waist and the other cradled her neck, his thumb brushing along her jawline.

She leaned her body against his even more to feel every inch of him behind the shirt that hid his lean but fit six-pack. His belt buckle caught on the front of her dress but she was more focused on what was just below his belt.

She had felt it against her when they had their steamy make-out session in his van and she was surprised at how perfect a fit it felt for her. Standing there, pressed against him once again, knowing he was the man she loved, had her imagining all kinds of X-rated things they could do in the cloak of the rosebush maze.

Boy, did she want to, but there was still more she needed to say to him, so she moved her mouth away from his. He leaned in farther trying to reclaim her lips, but she turned, causing his lips to land on her cheek.

"I have something else I need to say," she laughed.

His lips moved from her cheek, kissing down to her jaw and neck. The tip of his tongue then traced a line back up to her ear where he gently bit the lobe.

"Go ahead." His breath hit the skin of her ear with a warming effect and a pleasurable shiver ran down her spin. She wanted to say "screw it" and continue to make out with him, but she also needed to make her feelings one hundred percent understood.

"I know you lied about what 사랑해 meant when I first asked you a few weeks ago," she started but was distracted by his tongue back on her throat.

He paused his exploration and let out a low laugh; she felt his grin on her shoulder.

"I figured you would learn it sooner or later with the amount of dramas you've been binging. Plus, considering how many times it was said today, you'd pick it up from context." He pulled his lips away from her skin, his eyes meeting hers. "Are you looking for me to apologize for that?"

"No." She shook her head. "But you said you started to remember the night you had asked to kiss me..." She trailed off, assuming that he had remembered everything else he had said that night.

When she saw his eyes go wide, she knew she was correct in her assumption. He cleared his throat, and even with the dim lighting she could see a deep blush covered not only his cheeks but ran all the way up to the tips of his ears.

"Maria, when I said that—"

"Did you mean it?" she said, cutting him off.

"네?"

"Did you mean what you said that night? That you...love me." Her heart felt it was sinking into her stomach as he stared at her, slack-jawed.

She hoped his answer would be quick, a fast proclamation of his love, but instead all she could hear was the rustling of the bushes from the breeze. She wanted to bury herself in a hole. How could she think he really meant those drunken words?

She tried to back out of his embrace, but his hand gripped her waist firmly, keeping her in place against the warmth of his body. His eyes scanned her face but kept returning to her lips, causing her to nervously bite down, hoping he would say something. Anything.

"사-사-사랑해," he whispered.

"네?" She heard what he said but she needed to hear it again. In fact, she wanted it on repeat.

He cupped her cheek, his eyes sparkling as they reflected the moon, his lips spreading into a smile.

"사랑해," he said strongly, his thumb brushing her cheek.

"Hwan Soo—"

"사랑해, Maria. I have been in love with you since...actually, I don't know the exact moment. But the second I saw you walk into the bar to meet me for the first time, I knew you would change my life somehow." He reached down to grab her hand and brought it to his lips before holding it against his chest.

She felt the hard pounding of his heart, the beat as fast as hers.

"I love you so much that the thought of you leaving has been killing me. I love seeing you every day. Waking up to you, working with you, eating side by side, and going home together," he confessed. "I like that you shared your secret of wanting to be a photographer with me, and how your mother is just like mine, setting us up on useless blind dates. They were so useless because in actuality the world was just waiting for our paths to cross. Val and Jung-hyun knew it before we did. Hell, they laid out schemes to get us to spend as much time as possible together."

It seemed as if once he started, he couldn't stop. His words caused tears to well in her eyes.

"저도 사랑해," she confessed.

"뭐?" He was blinking rapidly, studying her face, gripping her hand against his chest harder, his eyes staying on her lips as they formed the same words he had just professed. It made her smile and she repeated them slowly.

"저...도...사...랑—" She was cut off once again by his lips crashing onto hers.

Hwan Soo couldn't stop himself. He knew what he had heard and while he wanted her to repeat it, he also wanted to make up for lost time. The time they spent bickering, nipping, and misunderstanding each other, he needed to make up for it all. Between peppering kisses all along her face, her giggles making him never want to let her go, he whispered how much he loved her and she responded happily.

"어떤히지?" he finally said.

"I already suspect Val and Jung-hyun know, but we should tell them. I will tell my mom when we—" He cut her off with another kiss, wanting to scream from the top of a mountain top how in love with her he was.

"I agree we need to tell our friends and families, but I meant with the distance and being together." His heart soared, but he knew there was the reality of the fact that she lived in America and he in South Korea.

"Oh..." She smiled embarrassedly and turned her head away. The little bit of light in their secluded spot of the rose maze allowed him to see her flushed cheeks, lips swollen from their kisses, which he hoped to continue, and her eyes wide and brimming with tears.

"I..." She sounded nervous her eyes looking everywhere but him as she took a deep breath and blurted out, "I quit my job back home and I called the photographer and asked to join his company as an apprentice. I am going to have to fill out a lot of papers, visa stuff, legal documents and such but I hope to be moving here in a few months."

"네..." He wasn't sure what to say. And so he didn't say anything. He grabbed her chin between his fingers, gently navigating her eyes back to him. And taking his time, dipped his head, gently kissing her lips.

It was to show her how happy, excited, and proud of her he was. She melted against him, her arms wrapping around his neck once again, her one hand sliding up into his hair. A pleasurable moan escaped his lips.

His hand moved up from her waist to skim her skin, playing up and down her spine, her body growing warmer to the touch, and he felt her shudder against him which sent his gentle kiss into dangerous territory.

Her teeth nipped at his bottom lip, making him want to go feral. He pulled his lips from hers.

"Maria, we're outside right now." He tried to keep his voice calm, but it wavered, almost becoming a growl. "And what I have thought about doing, at least the first time, should be done properly, not out where we might get caught."

Her eyes went wide, her breath catching, causing his eyes to roam down to her chest, his hunger growing.

She gently pulled on the back of his neck to bring him down to her level. Her lips went to his ear and whispered, "How much longer do you think is socially acceptable to stay at our best friends' wedding before we can make a break for it?"

It was his turn to shudder at her implication. His patience had disappeared the second his lips met hers. He looked at his watch, seeing it was already rather late and the reception would be wrapping up soon.

He laughed, her eyebrows raised in surprise, and he bent down, picking her up and gently throwing her over his shoulder.

She squealed and slapped his back, but unlike the first time he had tossed her over his shoulder to get her to shower and she shouted in protest, this time she laughed and her slapping was playful. He walked back to the reception hall entrance, where he stopped dead in his tracks.

Jung-hyun had Val pressed against the exterior wall of the building, his hands roaming what he could access beyond her gown, his head dipped into Val's neck.

"Why'd you stop?" Maria's voice made Jung-hyun jump away from Val as if they were the same sides of a magnet, his eyes meeting Hwan Soo's with shock. But upon realizing who his friend had tossed over his shoulder, he smirked and scoffed.

Instead of telling her, he spun around for her to get her own view of her friend and now husband, disheveled and panting. Two things he hoped were in their immediate future as well.

"어?" she expressed lightly. "At least you're clothed this time. 그럼..."

"네? Clothed? 무슨-?"

"I'll explain later. I think we should leave the happy couple to it." She laughed, patting his back as a signal that they should leave.

He spun back to his friend, whose smile was wide. Val's eyes were bright with gleeful excitement as she and Jung-hyun looked approvingly at Hwan Soo and Maria. He bowed his head and strode into the building; the few remaining people watched them, some pulling out their phones.

"If they take pictures—" she whispered, and he could feel her body tense against him.

"Let them." He cut her off in a low tone. "I'll deal with the repercussions later. Right now all I care about is getting you home. Our home."

"우리 집? You sure move fast once you profess your love, don't you?" He couldn't see, but he knew her cheeks were rosy red, and all he could think about was seeing how much skin that blush really covered.

"Not fast enough."

Six Months Later...

Hwan Soo missed Maria like crazy. Every day she wasn't in his arms was like torture. FaceTime calls at all hours of the night and early mornings couldn't soothe his need to be near her. He had made plans to visit her once the filming of his latest drama was finished because even the smallest amount of time near her would help until she was in Korea permanently.

After 나랑 같이있어, he became one of the hottest new rising stars in Korea. His face was in magazines, billboards, commercials, he even saw some small shops had photocard sets, like playing cards, of his face. Fansites popped up and barricades had to be consistently put up when he arrived to shows and events.

Hae So had even begun to praise him publicly about how well he had been able to handle his sudden burst into fame. Funny enough, after they hashed through everything that had gone on between them and she profusely apologized for her scheming and manipulation, she turned out to be a person he could trust—within reason. Their friendship even made headlines. While some people started to ship them together, they both made it very clear that wouldn't happen.

Hwan Soo wasn't able to share the fact that he was in a relationship just yet. The people Maria had been worried would post photos from the wedding did in fact do so. However, he was happy to see her face was covered by a cute sticker or blurred. Tabloids and fans made their assumptions though. They had known he was at his high-profile friend's wedding. They knew she not only was Val's best friend but also had been seen with Hwan Soo on set as an assistant. His team covered it up, saying she was drunk and he was simply getting her home.

He did get her home, and they didn't leave the house until she had to board a plane back to the States.

Maria had been understanding of his situation, which made him feel guilty about having to keep her hidden for the time being. But since she was still in America sorting out her paperwork and everything else she had to do, it made the secret thing fairly easy.

"You ready?" one of the production assistants asked, pulling Hwan Soo from his thoughts of Maria.

He was going to need to call her the second he finished filming. He nodded and followed the assistant to the set. In his head he practiced his lines over and over again, imagining the feelings, and readying himself for the scene.

The PA stopped abruptly, causing Hwan Soo to bump into the young man, apologizing.

"오랜만이야." A voice he had just been thinking about hit his eardrums.

When he looked up, his eyes were fixed on the woman. The love of his life. Maria. There she stood in the middle of his set like she was meant to be there, black stiletto heels, a long blush skirt that covered to just above her ankle, a loose black blouse with a dainty necklace against her collarbones, and when he got to her face his heart stopped.

She looked just as beautiful as the day he first saw her. Green-brown eyes sparkled in the set lights, her smile bright and full of hope, a dusting of red on her cheeks.

"Maria," he breathed out, unsure he could form much more than that.

"I travel all this way and that's the welcome I get," she laughed, taking one step toward him.

Before her foot could hit the ground, he ran up and swooped her into his arms. She let out a laugh, and feeling her warmth against him, he knew she was real. She had finally come back.

"Ho...wha...how—" He couldn't figure out what words to use as he held her in his arms.

When he finally put her down, her arms stayed wrapped around his neck, his around her waist.

"Hae So and Sul Bin helped," Maria chuckled.

"야! That was supposed to be a secret!" Hae So's voice came from behind one of the cameramen, everyone turning to see her throwing a small fit.

"She isn't so bad, once you get past all the drama. And Sul Bin sends his regards from NYC. I heard you pulled a few strings to help him out." Maria smiled, sending Hwan Soo's heart pounding like a drum, every nerve ending tingling with the pleasure of Maria being there, against his chest, with the most cheerful smile.

"Does this mean you're here for good?" He cupped her cheek, and her soft skin under his touch turned an even brighter rose color reminding him of everywhere else he remembered her blush covering.

"I'm staying with Val and Jung-hyun for bit before—"

"Ridiculous." He cut her off, pulling her even closer. "You can come stay with me. Preferably forever."

"Hwan Soo." She shook her head, dropping it to his chest.

"We can look for a new place. A place to call ours." He picked her chin up between his fingers, so their eyes met. "I have been apart from you for six months. That's long enough, in my opinion."

"But what about the press? Won't your agency get mad if you suddenly start living with someone? Not just someone, a woman?" She picked at the fuzz on his sweater.

He grabbed her hands, bringing them to his lips, knowing he was about to make one of the biggest leaps in his life.

"I don't care what they say. Or do. I've learned to do it now and ask for forgiveness later." He smiled before lowering his lips to hers.

A smattering of gasps, cheers, and phone cameras snapping images were heard all around, but he was set on making sure Maria knew he was all hers and the world would know as well.

When he pulled his lips away, he felt her trying to lean in to maintain the connection, which made him smile. She kept her eyes closed as if trying to keep the memory alive.

"사랑해," she whispered as she fluttered her eyes open to meet his.

After being heartbroken and swearing he would never find real love, Maria walked into his life with her feistiness, sweet heart, desire, humility, and had him fall head over heels. Their souls found each other when neither thought they had been searching for passion, friendship, and adoration.

"영원히 자기야." He smiled, cupping her cheek to bring her lips back to his and more gasps and cheers surrounded them as he put their love out there for the world to see.

The End 끝

Korean Vocabulary:
안녕하세요 저는 Valerie의 친구, Maria 입니다. Val과 저는 어린 시절부터 베프 였어요.- annyeonghaseyo jeoneun Valerie-ui chingu, Maria ibnida. Valgwa jeoneun eolin sijeolbuteo bepeu yeoss-eoyo. - Hello, I'm Maria, Valerie's friend. Val and I have been best friends since childhood.

처음 Val이 결혼한다고 했을때 진심으로 기쁘고 또 행복했지만 동시에 결혼하는 상대가 누구일지 걱정스러웠어요. - cheoeum Val-i gyeolhonhandago haess-eulttae jinsim-eulo gippeugo tto haeng-boghaessjiman dongsie gyeolhonhaneun sangdaega nugu-ilji geog-jeongseuleowoss-eoyo. - When Val first announced that she was getting married, I was really happy and excited, but at the same time, I was worried about who she would marry.

모두 아시다시피 베프란 항상 친구에 대해 관심을 가지고 지켜봐야 하죠. - modu asidasipi bepeulan hangsang chingue daehae gwan-sim-eul gajigo jikyeobwaya hajyo. - As we all know, a best friend always needs to watch over her friend.

정현을 만나 Val을 사랑스럽게 바라보는 그의 눈, 감정을 절대 숨

기지 않는 모습, 그리고 Val을 공주처럼 대하는걸 보았어요. 정현이 바로 Val의 그 사람이라는 걸 알 수 있었죠. - jeonghyeon-eul manna Val-eul salangseuleobge balaboneun geuui nun, gamjeong-eul jeoldae sumgiji anhneun moseub, geuligo Val-eul gongjucheoleom daehane-ungeol boass-eoyo. jeonghyeon-i balo Val-ui geu salam-ilaneun geol al su iss-eossjyo - I met Jung-hyun and saw his loving eyes on Val, the way he never hides his emotions, and how he treats Val like a princess. I could tell that Jung-hyun was that person for Val.

어떤히지 - ohddonheejee - what do we do now?

우리 집 - uri chi - our house

영원히 자기야 - yongwanhee jagiya - forever baby

Epilogue

Nerves were getting the best of Maria. She had followed all the traditional 폐백 ceremony rules. She and Hwan Soo entered bowing to the family, they served tea and wine to their parents, and they listened to words of advice from both of parents. But when it came time to throwing the nuts, Maria began to panic.

Hwan Soo noticed and asked if they could take a small break because he was feeling a bit lightheaded from all the pins in his hair keeping his headpiece in place. She loved how he could always tell when she needed a breather, and he would always help however he could.

They were granted five minutes. Maria saw his mother's dissatisfied expression as she walked out and knew he was going to get an earful about how it was uncouth for them to break from tradition. The woman still hadn't fully warmed up to Maria being the one he chose to spend his life with.

As all the negative thoughts flew around her head, she stood up and began to pace back and forth in front of the large table covered with food and white envelopes filled with money.

"Baby, sit." Hwan Soo grabbed Maria's arm, gently pulling her into his lap, bumping the table in front of them. The wooden ducks he had presented to her parents as a symbol of his commitment to Maria almost fell off.

"How can I? This is such a traditional process." She huffed. "What if I mess up this last part and your mother hates me even more? And then our moms might start to hate each other again."

Sitting in his lap did calm her nerves a small amount, but his hand rubbing her back was the real stress reliever. He always had a way of soothing her without having to say a word.

When they moved in together, she would come home stressed from a shoot where she thought she did a terrible job and he would plop her into his lap and cradle her against his chest, just rubbing her back like he was doing in that very moment.

"You and I have rehearsed this several times. Jung-hyun and Val helped. You got through the hard parts. These final two bits are really the easiest." He brought his hand to her cheek, trying not to hit the little pink sticker dots, a tradition she had to giggle at since it was supposed to represent virginity and youth. Hwan Soo even cracked a joke about her not wearing them and his mother's head almost spun off.

"Our parents are going to walk in, and they are going to celebrate this joyous occasion, throw some dates and walnuts at us, and then I am going to carry you out of here as both our families watch because they are happy this day has finally come. Especially our mothers," he joked.

Their parents had met several times before. The first few meetings between the mothers were slightly hostile. Her mother unhappy with how his mother had treated Maria the first time they'd met, and his mother unhappy he was choosing to marry non-traditionally, to put it kindly.

But when the topic of blind dates came up, both women perked up and began talking about all the ways in which they had tried to set up their children who were now madly in love. Maria even joked to

Hwan Soo that their mothers should start a matchmaking service, to which he responded it would fail considering they never did find either of them the perfect match.

He gently nuzzled her neck trying to keep her out of her own head, but his headpiece bumped into her chin and they both grumbled.

"I cannot wait to get out of this." He adjusted the pins in his hair. And when he looked back up at her he had a devilish smirk. He grabbed the knot at the top of her dress as he added, "And I can't wait to get you out of this 한복 either."

He leaned up, his lips meeting hers gently.

There was a knock at the door letting them know the five minutes was up and the families had come back. She moved to take her seat beside him, fixing her skirt and adjusting her headpiece.

"I was right, by the way," he mused.

"About what?"

"A year and some change ago, at Jung-hyun and Val's wedding, I said that you would look good in 한복. I was right." He reached over to grab her hand, giving it a gentle squeeze before the doors opened and their families entered to finish making them husband and wife.

Matching Set Preview

There was a knock on Val's office door which pulled her out of her productive train of thought. She expected to look up from her drawings to find her boss Tina, but was shocked to see 박지애. One of the most powerful women in San Francisco, Tina's highest paying client, and Val's fake boyfriend's mother.

"박지애씨? Did you need to see Tina? She is on site right now-" Val stood from her chair and walked around her drawing table to bow politely getting a good gander at the red on the heel breast of the woman's shoes.

"I'm not here to see her. It's you I need to talk to." 박지애put her YSL clutch down on the desk to take a step closer to Val inspecting every inch of her frame.

God, what did I get myself into?

"저요?" Val pointed to herself surprised such an affluent woman would come to the office to talk to the smallest fish in the pond.

"You're 종현's girlfriend are you not?" The woman raised a well-shaped inquisitive brow.

Shit. Of course, she came to size me up.

"맞습니다." Val concurred bowing again.

"So, it's true you are seeing my son?" She walked circles around Val, making Val stand back up straight, her posture the best it had ever been.

"예." Val responded with a curt nod.

"And what is it that you like about my son? His money? His influence?" She probed coming to a halt meeting Val's eye.

The woman showed no concern when she asked the demeaning questions. Like it had nothing to do with her son's heart potentially being broken. It was her protecting her business and its success. To her, Val was just a money hungry, power thirsty trollop who was using her son to gain affluence.

What bothered Val more than the judgment of her character, was that his mother didn't believe a woman could love her own son because of who he was and not what he had.

"With all due respect ma'am your assumptions of me are insulting." Val watched the woman's eyes widen quickly from her bold statement but retrained back into the disparaging mother. But Val knew she had struck a nerve. "I met your son while working together for his apartment redesign. We clicked instantly. Your son is kind-hearted, sweet, a little naïve when it comes to dating, which makes him cute."

None of what she said was a lie. They did get along instantly, it might not have been a love at first sight kind of thing, but Val found him endearing for being such a powerful man who brought companies to their knees. He treated her as his equal not as someone who simply worked for him. And she had to admit when he used her full name there was always a small shiver that tingled down her spine and a blush that rose on her warm terra-cotta skin.

"He's intelligent, strong, can command a room but also shows compassion and enthusiasm for those he works alongside. Maybe that's why I was first attracted to him." She smiled thinking of just how well he had handled himself during their few interactions thus far.

"Cut the dreamy eyes child." His mother waved her hand in

annoyance, her nose crinkling in disgust. "I don't know what my son thinks he sees in you, but I want you to end whatever it is you think you have with him."

"네?" Val was so perplexed she couldn't be formal.

"He needs a woman who has something else to offer other than her body. You seem nice enough, but you have zero connections that are remotely useful to building our portfolio." 박지애 gave a final distasteful once over of Val.

"I believe you should be having this conversation with him since you're so concerned with his choice in women." Val had tried to be civil as the woman continued to judge her with no knowledge of her but she drew the line at basically being called a tramp. "I can call him and let him know you stopped by or that you plan to stop by his office. I'm sure he would appreciate me telling him so you don't just show up unannounced while he's working."

Another wide-eyed surprise hidden within a second. Val took pride in being able to make this woman waver, even if it was only for less than a second. 박지애 chose not to respond making Val make another bold move.

"Was there any other reason you came here? Or was it simply to insult me to see if I would crack under your scrutiny?" Val turned back to her desk making sure his mother couldn't see the fear in her face as she dared talk to 박지애 like that. "If you're done, I have work to finish before I meet your son for our date tonight."

She heard two steps closer to her, and she saw the expensive leather YSL bag disappear from her desk, and more clacks of heels on the floor the sound dissipating out of her office.

Falling back into her seat, Val grabbed her phone, hands shaking as she found 종현'snumber and texted him.

Val: Your mother just came to visit me at my office.

종현: 당장 거기서 나오세요!

Val: 괜찮아요. 그녀는 떠났다. But I think we are really going to have to do some serious work for her to believe we are couple. She came to tell me I should leave you.

종현: She's ridiculous! I'm headed to a meeting right now otherwise I would call and see how you are. Let's discuss this tonight at dinner. I will have my driver pick you up.

종현: Better yet, I'll pick you up. Be outside your office at 7.

Her heart raced at the thought of him coming to her office. Dressed in his tailored suit hugging all the right places, the large expensive timepiece on his wrist showing off the strong veins in his hands, and his hair parted on the side but pushed back making his jawline even more pronounced.

I'm in so much trouble.

Korean Vocabulary:

박지애씨 – Park Ji Ae ssi – Mrs. Park Ji Ae

저요? – joyo? – me?

맞습니다 – majsoobnida – correct

예 – yeae -yes (formal)

네 – nae – literally means yes but can be used in many ways. This way is in a "what?" or "huh?" kind of way.

당장 거기서 나오세요 – dangjang kogiso nausaeyo - get out of there now.

그녀는 떠났다 – kunyeonoon ddonassda – she left.

괜찮아요 – gwaenchanhayo – it's fine.

Acknowledgments

Wow. There are so many people I want to/ need to thank for Seoul Searching being what it has become. I obviously need to start with my amazing husband. The man who I constantly sprinkle into the male leads as he is the male lead in my life. My parents for always supporting me. My dad, while not understanding my obsession with K-pop and K-dramas but still sending me any latest news articles he finds. And my mom, who not only gave me the writing gene, but always pushes me to not be afraid to put myself and my work out there.

Joan McDonald. The woman who let me ramble on and on about my website and book idea and when I finally made myself shut up mentioned she worked for Forbes and told me she loved the idea. And I ended up being interviewed for an article. She made me believe that what I had created was not only a passion project but one that people would get behind and could bring people together.

Elisa and 승혜 for helping me grow in my Korean education and making sure I brought authenticity to what I've written. Aleda, the friend who offered to help edit mid me writing and posting this story online. She saved me a lot of energy before it went to the amazing editors at Proof Positive. Teri, who out of the kindness of her heart asked if she could use Seoul Searching as a practice for her narration and now will be narrating the actual freakin' book! KC the amazing artist who took my horrible attempt at a cover and made something so beautiful I want it hanging on my wall like an art piece. Liddell, the man who worked tirelessly to help create the promo stickers.

Lindsay, Roselyn, Melissa, Alyssa, Bridgette, Jess Freakin' P, Jess F., Garnet, Valerie, Kat, Kaina, KC (Different one), Brisbane, Dafne, Alegna, and so many more people that will just have to wait until the next book to be thanked personally. Haha.

From the bottom of my heart, 고마워.

More Playlists

For more playlists : https://open.spotify.com/
user/zkv0r49bhw5x9n93j4ngxkjmf

Follow Me:

Website: koreanfromcontext.com
TikTok: @koreanfromcontext
Instagram: @koreanfromcontext
Twitter: @koreanfrmcntxt

Helpful sites/apps to continue your Korean Learning:

Teuida
Papago
Viki (Learn mode ON)
Netflix (Language Reactor plug-in)

Printed in Great Britain
by Amazon

33143610R00285